# TALES OF ORC *Sworn*

OFFERED BY THE ORC
TRYGGRED BY THE ORC
YULED BY THE ORCS

FINLEY FENN

# CONTENTS

**Tales of Orc Sworn**
Cover artwork of Stella and Silfast by Elaine Ho
Cover design by Sylvia at The Book Brander

~


Edited by Eris Adderly
Supported by the generous members of the Orc Sworn Patreon


Edited by Eris Adderly
Supported by the generous members of the Orc Sworn Patreon

~



~

## ALSO BY FINLEY FENN

**ORC SWORN**

The Lady and the Orc

The Heiress and the Orc

The Librarian and the Orc

The Duchess and the Orc

The Midwife and the Orc

The Maid and the Orcs

The Governess and the Orc

The Beauty and the Orcs

The Widow and the Orcs

Offered by the Orc

Tryggred by the Orc

Yuled by the Orcs

**ORC FORGED**

The Sins of the Orc

The Fall of the Orc

**THE MAGES**

The Mage's Maid

The Mage's Match

The Mage's Master

The Mage's Groom

# Offered by the Orc

A MONSTER FANTASY ROMANCE TALE

FINLEY FENN

# OFFERED BY THE ORC

*The monster needs a sacrifice. And she's on the altar...*

When Stella wanders the forest alone one fateful night, she only seeks peace, relief, escape. A few stolen moments on a secret, ancient altar, at one with the moon above.

Until she's accosted by a hulking, hideous, bloodthirsty orc. An orc who demands a sacrifice—not by his sword, but by Stella's complete surrender. To his claws, his sharp teeth, his huge muscled body. His every humiliating, thrilling command...

But Stella would never offer herself up to be used and sacrificed by a monster—would she? Even if her surrender just might grant her the moon's favour—and open her heart to a whole new fate?

# AUTHOR'S NOTE

Greetings, dear reader! Thank you so much for reading my very first Orc Sworn novella!

This story is about 14,000 words (or seven chapters) long, and it's a super-steamy single encounter between our heroine and a VERY dominant orc who's determined to get his way. If you'd like more details on what to expect, please visit this book's page on my website at finleyfenn.com.

In terms of a timeline, this story happens a few months after *The Lady and the Orc* (the first book in my Orc Sworn series) but it also reads as a total stand-alone.

I hope you enjoy it... and that you're ready for some heat! ;) Thanks again for reading!

# 1

Surely, Stella was going mad.

There was no other possible explanation, she thought grimly, as she strode through the tall tree-trunks, illuminated only by the dappled light of the full moon high above. She was losing her mind.

Even so, she didn't close the filmy linen shawl she'd casually slung over her bare shoulder, and if anything, she let it fall further open as she raised her face to the moonlight, and breathed in deep. Showing her naked, pale body to the silent, watching forest all around.

But of course, no one was looking. No one was there. No one cared.

It was a certainty that had only grown over the past year, as Stella had watched Lothar leave the house again, and again, and again. He worked as a merchant's guard, so of course he needed to travel regularly—but Stella's visions of exploring the realm at her strapping new husband's side had been very quickly dashed, in favour of the harsh, bitter truth. Lothar had wanted someone to leave behind. Someone to hold and maintain his beloved ancestral home in the countryside, while he drank and fought and wenched his way across the continent.

Stella squeezed her eyes shut, and drew in a long, bracing breath. No. She would not think of Lothar here. This forest was her own place, the one solace in her tedious, isolated life. By day she would be all that a dutiful wife should be, toiling away at the house and its land—but at nights, she would walk bare and silent through the nearby trees, and drink up their strength and their bravery like a fine, rich wine.

It was madness. And Stella knew it.

But all the same, nearly every night these past months, she'd done it. She'd walked these trees, clad only in the flimsiest of clothing, sometimes carrying a lantern, sometimes not. Tonight not, because the moon was so white and glimmering, casting its cool magic onto Stella's dark head and now-bare shoulders with silent, intoxicating ease.

She raised her head again, breathing deep, and let the shawl fall away entirely, pooling onto the path below. No one was looking. No one cared. So why should she not lie with the moon this night? Why should she not embrace the madness, and take her pleasure with it?

She felt her steps quickening, her bare feet almost silent on the path below, as she approached the small clearing. It was a near-perfect circle, surrounded by tall trees, and in the middle of it was a huge, round-edged stone, not unlike a massive grist-wheel, lying on its side. It was most certainly unnatural, and when Stella had asked Lothar about it, he'd dismissed it with an uncaring wave of his hand.

"It's an ancient elf altar, or some such shit," he'd said. "Or maybe orcs. I can't remember."

"Um, an *orc altar*?" Stella had echoed, blinking wide-eyed at Lothar's handsome face. "*Here*? A stone's-throw from the house I live in, *alone*?"

Again, Lothar had dismissed said concerns with a vague wave of his hand. "You don't live alone, I live here too," he'd said, a rather rich statement, considering that at that point, he'd stayed there for perhaps a dozen nights in their half-year marriage. "And stop worrying. There haven't been orcs in those woods for centuries."

That hadn't been reassuring, especially given that just a few short months before, four of the realm's southern provinces had apparently come to some kind of deal with the orcs. One that allowed the brutal, bloodthirsty beasts to roam freely through those lands, pillaging and kidnapping and ravaging hapless women along the way.

"Are you *sure* it's safe?" Stella had asked, her voice wavering. "Perhaps I shouldn't be here by myself?"

"Oh, you're fine," Lothar had said, with a shrug. "Just don't go in the woods alone. And"—he'd shot her an odd, lingering look—"make sure you're properly dressed, when you're outside. Every time. That's an order, Stella."

And that, perhaps, was where this madness had begun. Stella was to be dressed, and out of the woods, even if orcs were supposedly nothing to worry about. So here she was, naked and alone in the trees, and coming to stand before an orc altar in the moonlight.

The altar was about waist height, impressively flat and smooth, and entirely covered with a carpet of soft green moss. It was a lovely place to sit and think, and to lie down upon, and it had been on a similar night to this, months before, when Stella had first lain back on the soft moss, spread her legs wide, and brought herself to ecstasy under the cool, silent light of the moon.

The moss was just as soft tonight, just as easy on her hands and knees as it always was. Almost as though inviting one to lie naked upon it, to feel that softness brush against one's bare skin. And as Stella lay back, tilting her face to the moonlight, she could already feel the wetness pooling between her parted thighs, dripping onto the moss below. She'd gone mad, but she didn't care. She would make love to the moon this night.

She already had her hand between her spread thighs, delving slightly inside, when she heard it. A noise. A noise that didn't belong. And it was close.

Stella's head snapped up, fear suddenly sparking ice-cold under her skin, and she fought to breathe, to calm her suddenly galloping heartbeat. Surely it was nothing, surely just a deer, a hare, something...

But there, *there*, across the clearing—and coming rapidly closer—was a shape. Dark, and huge, like a man, but not... not... because...

It was an *orc*.

# 2

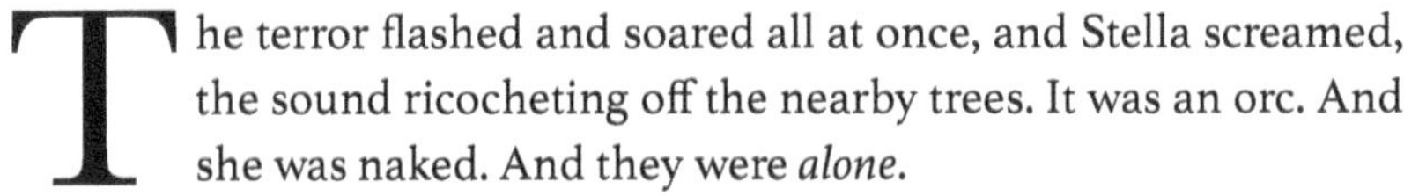

The terror flashed and soared all at once, and Stella screamed, the sound ricocheting off the nearby trees. It was an orc. And she was naked. And they were *alone*.

It felt like her body was made of mud, suddenly, moving far too slowly toward the altar's edge—and already it was too late, because that was the distinct, terrifying feeling of a big, powerful hand, clamping around her ankle, and holding her still. Holding her there. Trapped.

Stella kicked and flailed, fighting desperately to shove herself off the opposite side of the altar, but somehow the orc caught her other ankle, too. Clutching it in a strong, powerful grip that circled all the way around, and Stella screamed again at the feel of multiple sharp points—its *claws?!*—piercing against her skin.

"Silence," ordered a voice, so deep that it seemed to resonate into Stella's very bones. "I shall not kill you."

I shall not kill you. Stella's scream had faded, becoming something more like a wail, and she felt herself trembling all over, her eyes finally focusing on the sight looming between her legs.

And it was—monstrous. It was shaped like a man, but far larger, with a bushy black head, a thick neck, and powerful corded shoulders. Its torso was broad and bare, covered over with a mass of black hair and deadly-looking scars, and its skin was coloured a mottled grey, or maybe even green, in the pale, unforgiving moonlight.

And its *face*. It was a face of nightmares, harsh and scarred, with a mashed nose, and heavy black brows over glittering black eyes. And its mouth was a thin grey slash, hard and leering, pulling back to show a row of pointed white teeth, not unlike those of a wolf.

"Better," that voice said, deep and powerful. "It is no use fighting me."

His hands clenched again on Stella's ankles, as if to prove that point beyond all doubt, and a frantic glance toward those hands showed them indeed boasting claws, long and black and sharp. An orc, here, in the forest, holding Stella's *ankles*, and far too late she snapped one shaking hand over her breasts, and the other over the sight between her spread legs. And had the orc *seen* that, of course he'd seen that, and those terrifying black eyes only seemed to confirm it, following Stella's hand downwards with something not unlike mockery.

"Foolish woman," he said. "You shall not hide from me. Nor shall you escape me."

The fear only spiked up again, strong enough to make Stella's teeth chatter, and the orc's amusement seemed to fade, his bushy black head tilting. "I have said, I shall not kill you," his voice rumbled. "You should not fear."

That wasn't helpful, this was a total and unmitigated *catastrophe*, and Stella dragged in air through her still-chattering teeth. "W-w-why should I not," she heard herself say. "Y-you're an—an *orc*."

"I am," he replied, now with a twinge of impatience in his voice. "And I have said, I shall not kill you. You should thank me for my mercy."

Stella shuddered again, yanking her legs uselessly against the powerful grip of his hands. "Th-this," she managed, "is mercy?"

"Yes," the orc replied, his black eyebrows furrowing. "When a woman prostrates herself on the altar of the Goddess of Bautul, it is the orc's right to choose her sacrifice. And I choose"—his gaze softened slightly—"to accept what you have shown me. I choose to cleanse you and spill your juices upon this altar, rather than your blood."

Cleanse her? Her *juices*? Stella opened her trembling mouth, about to ask what the *hell* he was talking about—but then the orc's black eyes had dropped briefly to her breasts, still covered by her arm, and then further down. Lingering without shame on the place between her spread-apart thighs, which was, mercifully, still shielded by Stella's other hand.

"You are a strong, ripe woman," he said approvingly. "Your teats are large enough to fill my hands, and your womb is wet and open. It shall please me to handle you and carry out this offering."

What? *What*? "I—I offered," Stella stammered, at that hideous face, "n-nothing. To you, or a goddess, or *anyone*."

Said hideous face gave a deep scowl, his lip curling up to show a sharp white fang. "Foolish woman," he said. "Did you not walk the forest bare and alone, under the full moon, and choose to come to this altar? Did you not lie upon it, and spread your thighs, and anoint it with the first of your juices? This is what the goddess asks of a sacrifice, and all this you have done."

The words seemed to worm deep into Stella's still-shouting thoughts, and she blinked at the orc's huge form, his harsh face, his massive hands still gripping her ankles. Because—she *had* done all that. Hadn't she?

Madness, her thoughts whispered, unpleasantly, and she sucked back more air, and shot a furtive glance toward the full moon above. "I—I've never even *heard* of this goddess of battle," she countered. "How could I offer myself to a deity I don't even *know*?"

"She is Goddess of *Bautul*," the orc corrected her. "My clan is named thus also, after her. She is the goddess of the moon. You obeyed her command, and you look to her even now. Thus, you know her."

Stella stared back at the orc, from where she'd been indeed looking at the moon, in all its pale shining beauty. Surely all this was just the madness speaking, it was just pure coincidence that this altar apparently belonged to the moon goddess, right?

Right?

"At times of change," the orc's deep voice continued, "the Goddess of Bautul calls for sacrifice. I felt this call also, and that is why I have come here, so far from my home. And here, on this night, I have found you."

His voice seemed to go softer and lower, vibrating oddly under

Stella's bare skin, and she felt her chest heaving against her still-covering arm. "That's impossible," she said, but the words came out thin. "It's got to be just—a random, ridiculous coincidence. That's *all*."

"No," the orc countered. "It is the goddess at work. We must obey her command. Do you not feel this, woman?"

There was a strange, nagging whisper rising in Stella's thoughts—*did* she feel this?—and too late she gathered her courage, and gave a furious, desperate shake of her head. He was an orc. He was trying to *force* her. And she'd let herself be drawn in by Lothar, she'd ignored her instincts to her doom, surely she could find her voice against an *orc*...

"I feel nothing," she choked out. "I see only a hideous, foul *beast*, who seeks a convenient excuse to take what he wants without recourse. I see a *savage*."

The orc's nostrils flared, and he gave a guttural, terrifying growl. "Do not claim false to me, woman," he hissed. "I have journeyed long, I have only this night to please my goddess, and I do not suffer fools. Do you wish me to spill your blood for this sacrifice instead?"

As he spoke, he abruptly let go of one of her ankles, and reached a quick, graceful hand toward what looked to be a thick leather belt around his waist. And there was a shirr of metal, a flash of light—and the orc was holding a huge steel scimitar, wickedly sharp and deadly.

"What is your wish," he demanded. "You will speak now, or feed this altar with your blood."

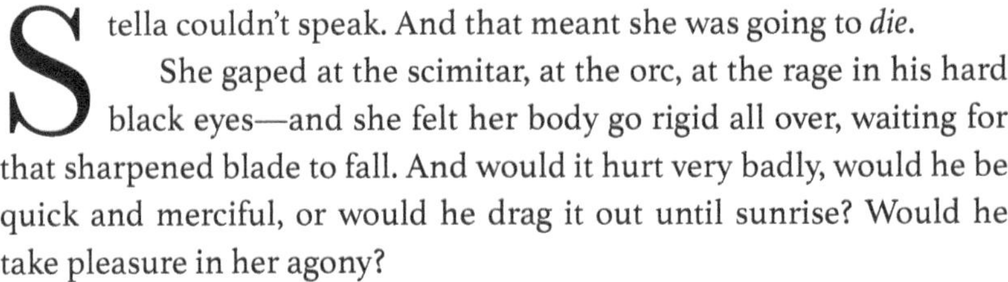

# 3

Stella couldn't speak. And that meant she was going to *die*.

She gaped at the scimitar, at the orc, at the rage in his hard black eyes—and she felt her body go rigid all over, waiting for that sharpened blade to fall. And would it hurt very badly, would he be quick and merciful, or would he drag it out until sunrise? Would he take pleasure in her agony?

And worse, once it was done, would anyone even notice, or care? Stella had no family left, and Lothar wouldn't be back for weeks, if not longer. And even if he were sad at first, he would eventually only shrug, and go find himself someone new to keep his house, and forget all about her.

It was that certainty, ridiculously enough, that finally set Stella weeping. Abandoning her modesty altogether, in favour of curling up on the altar, covering her face, and gasping out harsh, broken sobs. No one cared. No one had ever cared, not since her dear mother had passed, so many years before. And now Stella would die at the hand of a merciless bloodthirsty orc, and perhaps it was for the best, in the end. Maybe death was preferable to the helplessness, the misery, the constant, gnawing loneliness.

So she waited, weeping, her hands pressed to her face, her body trembling and tense as she braced for the sharp steel's impact—but it still hadn't come. Only a taut stricken silence, waiting and waiting and waiting. And after another endless moment, Stella finally dared to spread her fingers apart, risking a furtive glance upwards, terrified at what she might find.

But to her vague surprise, the huge orc no longer held the scimitar. He no longer touched her, either, and in fact wasn't even looking at her. Instead, his hard face was turned up toward the moon, and his eyes were closed, his lashes thick and black against his grey skin.

Stella blinked at the sight, and felt her sobs finally choke off, her body's tension wrenching odd and sideways. Surely if he was going to kill her, he would have done so already? Or was he just waiting for a better moment? Perhaps a clean strike to her neck against the rock?

But the orc still wasn't looking at her—in fact, it almost seemed as though he'd forgotten she was there. As though he was instead lost in the moon, in his goddess, in his worship.

And as Stella stared, she could see his throat bobbing, his big chest rising and falling. His hands were in clawed fists at his sides, his bare arms thick and wrapped with muscle, and for the first time Stella caught a glimpse of his powerful thighs under tight trousers, the tall leather boots laced up over strong calves. Hideous still, yes, but with a kind of… wildness. Coldness. Fierceness. But all held in his goddess' thrall, in service to her command, honour bound to make her sacrifice…

It was madness.

"The goddess does not wish," the orc said finally, quiet, toward the moon, "that I should kill you, woman."

The relief was an almost visceral thing, shuddering at Stella's bones, and she let out a slow, shaky breath. "Oh really?" she made herself say, her voice wavering. "So you just get to force me instead? Isn't that what you really wanted anyway?"

The orc's frown immediately returned, transforming his face back into utter ugliness again. "I do not *force*," he snapped, as though the very word were distasteful. "I fulfill your sacrifice to the goddess. She wishes for your pleasure this night. Not your pain."

Well. Stella couldn't seem to muster a response to that, and the orc sighed, and turned his face back toward the moon. "You have long walked under the goddess' eye," he said. "You have bravely bared your suffering before her. There is strength in this."

Stella felt her throat convulse—how could an orc possibly know such things?—and her gaze followed his toward the moon, and its cool silvery light. Shining steady and silent, almost as though it were indeed watching them, waiting. Seeking to enlighten, to illuminate, to fulfill.

"I ought not to have threatened to kill you," the orc continued, softer now. "Not after I made this choice under the goddess' eye. I frightened you and caused you pain. I am sorry, woman."

Stella kept her eyes on the moon, but after an instant's silence, she felt herself give a tight little nod. Which was patently ridiculous, because you didn't accept apologies from a *beast*, especially one who'd just tried to murder you in cold blood, right?

But the goddess—the moon, rather—was watching. And Stella felt her eyes flutter closed, her breath coming out slow. A sacrifice. Pleasure.

Was *that* what she wanted? What she'd longed for when she'd stepped into the forest this night? Truly?

"I, too, have endured much under the goddess' eye," the orc said, his words slow and careful. "I too crave reprieve and relief. I should be honoured to seek this together with you."

His voice had turned into something liquid and low, rumbling deep into Stella's skin, and she felt her head tilting. Waiting. Wanting, perhaps, for him to speak more.

"Mayhap we shall please the goddess together," the orc continued, even softer. "Mayhap we shall find a new fate upon this altar tonight. Mayhap we shall find—peace."

A new fate. Peace.

And it was madness, it was sheer and utter insanity, there was surely no peace to be found in this—but Stella could almost feel herself uncoiling, the tension easing away. Pleasure. *Peace*.

And he was an orc, a beast, he couldn't be trusted, Stella couldn't possibly be contemplating such a thing—but on that hideous face, in those foreign black eyes, there was something almost—familiar. Something bared that was supposed to be secret, something like fear, and like... hope. Peace.

"And you won't harm me?" Stella whispered, to those eyes. "You promise?"

His answering nod was slow, intent, true. "I swear this," he whispered back. "Under the goddess' eye. Should I harm you now, she shall strike me to my death."

And somehow, for some inexplicable reason, it was enough. Enough for Stella to take a thick, fortifying breath, and then lower her naked body slowly, carefully back against the moss. Feeling its softness stroke against her bare skin, smooth and quiet and approving, like it had been waiting for just this moment.

And as the orc's glittering eyes watched—madness, it was utter *madness*—Stella spread her legs wide, and turned her face to the watching moon.

# 4

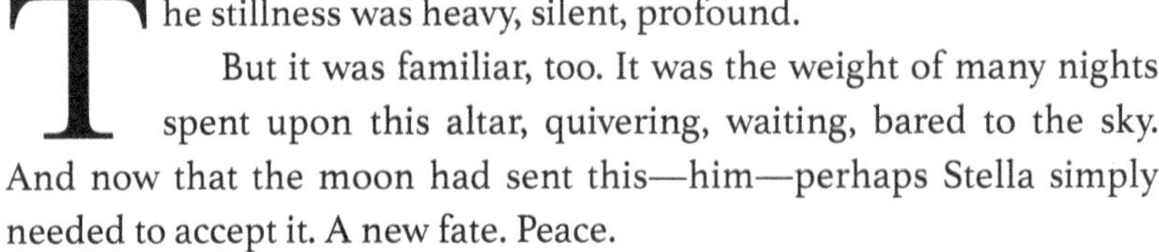

The stillness was heavy, silent, profound.

But it was familiar, too. It was the weight of many nights spent upon this altar, quivering, waiting, bared to the sky. And now that the moon had sent this—him—perhaps Stella simply needed to accept it. A new fate. Peace.

So she waited. Keeping her eyes closed, her face tilted toward the moon, her legs spread wide. Baring her most vulnerable parts for it, for him, for this. A sacrifice. An offering.

She couldn't hear the orc moving, or breathing, and there was an instant's hurtling fear that perhaps he'd leave, or worse, make a mockery of her—but suddenly there was a touch, warm and gentle, to her ankle. Pulling it slightly to the side, spreading her further apart, but Stella didn't resist, didn't even twitch.

"If you indeed wish me to fulfill your sacrifice, woman," the orc's deep voice said, "I must now handle you. I must cleanse and prepare you for your offering."

Stella's eyes fluttered open, and suddenly she could feel her heartbeat, thudding against her chest. Because the orc was kneeling on the altar between her legs, and looking at her naked body with greedy, glittering eyes. And he was so appalling, so breathtakingly hideous, surely this wasn't what the goddess would wish, surely this was madness—

But then—Stella froze all over—he touched her. Not between her legs, where she'd perhaps expected it, but again on her ankles. His hands big, warm, powerful, and sliding slowly, inexorably upwards. Over her calves, her knees, her thighs. Skirting away from her groin, for now, in favour of curving over her hips, her sides, her shoulders.

And then, inexplicably, those warm hands came to her face. Cradling it between big callused palms, his fingers spreading wide, his thumbs stroking gently against her cheeks. And the scent of him was rising in the air now, warm and surprisingly sweet, and Stella couldn't stop blinking at it, at him, all furious hair and black-lashed eyes, and the world seemed to stutter, caught, frozen—

"Your obedience pleases the goddess, woman," he said, his voice a rumbling caress of its own. "This is as it should be."

Stella could only keep blinking up at him, snared in whatever this was, as those hands went up to her long brown hair. Carding it swiftly and efficiently out of the loose braid it had been in, in favour of spreading it out wide around her head upon the altar, almost as though it were a halo, or a crown.

He nodded his approval, his eyes lingering on the sight with a disconcerting intensity—and finally those gentle hands slid downward again. Over Stella's neck and collarbones, first, and then coming to curve close around her breasts. They indeed filled his big hands—which were somehow now without claws—and she could feel him squeezing slightly, could see her pale skin bulging out between his large grey fingers.

It was a disconcerting sight, a disconcerting thought, and Stella belatedly shut her eyes away from it, and instead just felt it, and breathed. Big hands rubbing and caressing her breasts, coaxing her nipples to hardness, and then slipping downwards again, over her soft belly. And then to either side of her groin, caressing her hips again, before slowly coming to her thighs, and spreading them further apart.

And then—Stella felt her body arch, her mouth gasping—he touched her, *there*. Sliding over it, at first, so lightly that his hand only traced at her coarse dark hair—but then with more intent, more pressure. Allowing his fingers to delve slightly, parting her around them, and Stella shuddered and keened, her body clenching against warm, gentle fingers.

They only stroked and petted at first, soft and surprisingly tender, while Stella writhed and twitched against them—and when one finger finally broke from the rest, and slid slowly inside, she actually moaned, the sound far too loud in the open clearing. And in reply the orc huffed out a deep, head-swarming chuckle, snapping Stella's gaze toward him as he nudged a second finger slowly inside.

"You are already dripping wet, woman," his deep voice murmured, and though that should have perhaps been insulting, Stella could only seem to gasp, her body clenching hard and frantic around those invading fingers. "It pleases the goddess to see this, and hear your hungry cries."

Stella belatedly tried for a frown at the orc, but his black eyes were gleaming, his mouth twitched up to show a sharp, pointed fang. "You shall take more," he said. "You must be cleansed, and thus prove yourself worthy."

Stella nodded, without at all meaning to, and the orc's smile widened into something smug and dangerous as he pressed a third finger inside her. Not quite so gentle this time, but more powerful and demanding, and Stella cried out again as she felt herself opening wider for him, taking him deep, while her greedy clenching body seemed to only demand more, more, more. She was so close she could taste it, and she felt her thighs spreading, her swollen wetness fighting him, gripping at him, trying to swallow him up—

But it was then, when her release was dangerously tilting, that the confounded orc yanked his hand away. Leaving her wide open and clenching at nothing, the bastard, even as he again gave that smug smile, and slowly, purposefully trailed his wet fingers up her bare body, until they came to nudge against her already-parted lips.

"Suckle me clean," he ordered, sliding those fingers deep into her mouth, and to Stella's distant amazement, she immediately obeyed. Sucking frantic and sloppy around his fingers' invading heft, tasting her own sharp saltiness, until he snatched them away again, and dropped both hands back to her breasts. Not gently caressing, now, but plucking and squeezing at her hard pink nipples, rolling them between familiar, audacious fingers.

"Your fat teats beg to be pinched and prodded," he said, with clear satisfaction, as he gave one an experimental little slap, and watched it bounce and jiggle in response. "They wish to be handled and cleansed before your goddess."

Stella replied with a humiliating groan, staring downward as the orc proceeded to alternately pinch and slap at her increasingly tender breasts, watching their reddened weight bounce and sway before his approving eyes. And it was appalling that he was doing such a thing, and appalling that she was responding like this, her chest heaving, her cheeks flushed and hot, her groin clenching again and again at emptiness.

"And now," the orc murmured, with one last purposeful, almost painful, pinch at Stella's breast, "your wet, greedy womb must have this also."

Stella had already let out another helpless, dragging moan, earning yet another insolent smile from that orc's mouth, at disconcerting odds with the tenderness of his hand, once again sliding down to cup between her legs. And then—Stella shouted aloud—there was a light but purposeful slap, right there, against her still-clenching wetness.

"My strong handling pleases you," he said, his voice slightly breathless, as he did it again, and then again. "It pleases the goddess, also. You may yet be a brave woman, in spite of your weeping at the sight of my sword."

Stella blinked at him—weeping, she'd wept, had that only been moments ago?—and some distant, surging, incomprehensible part of her managed to reach down and grasp his now-slick hand, holding it still.

"I didn't weep at the sight of your sword," she said, her hazy eyes fighting to focus on his, even as she twitched at the surprising conviction in her voice. "I wept because—because I realized no one would care. When I died."

The orc's head tilted, studying her, until his hand gently pulled away from hers, and went back between her legs. Not slapping this time, but stroking gently again, as though this would be reassuring, and perhaps, for some ridiculous reason, it was.

"The goddess would have cared when you died," he said finally. "I would have cared."

Stella shook her head, and suddenly there was a hot prickling behind her eyes, threatening to escape. "No," she countered, and was she truly still trying to argue with an *orc*? "You would have *killed* me."

"Yes, if the goddess had commanded it," came the orc's blunt reply. "And yet, I would have mourned this. One does not take joy in killing weak unarmed little humans, let alone one so lovely and ripe as you."

Stella heard herself snort, though it came out dangerously close to a sob. "I'm not little or lovely," she said. "I'm not lithe or slim, and my nose is crooked, and my face is plain. And the one man who I thought *did* love me actually just wanted a live-in housekeeper, so he could gallivant around the realm and fuck whoever the hell he wanted. *Not* me."

Her voice broke at the last, her eyes blinking hard, away from the orc's watching face. Because all of that was true, something she'd never before dared to speak aloud, and what if this orc *agreed* with it, what if he mocked her for it, or what if he stood up and walked away too, and left her miserable and alone.

"My face is frightful to men and orcs alike," he said finally. "Why should I place worth on yours? I place worth on strength, and forbearance, and piety. There is worth in one who endures, and who is loyal to one's kin, and one's goddess. And there is worth"—his big hand grasped Stella's chin, and tilted it back toward him—"in one who eagerly welcomes strong handling, to better please the goddess, and give her a worthy sacrifice."

His other hand had continued petting between Stella's legs as he spoke, but now gave a hard, jolting, thrilling slap with the flat of his hand. "There is yet more you must do to prepare," he said firmly. "Are you ready for what comes next?"

And it was yet madness, surely. It was all that was wrong with Stella, weak and gullible and hungry and needy, sprawled here naked upon this altar, with an orc's hand lingering between her legs. But she'd spoken, he'd listened and stayed, he was here with her in it...

And she *was* ready. Wasn't she?

"Yes," she whispered. "I am."

# 5

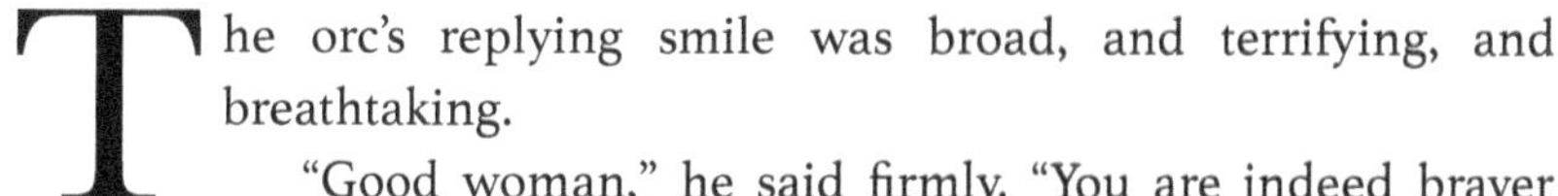

The orc's replying smile was broad, and terrifying, and breathtaking.

"Good woman," he said firmly. "You are indeed braver than I thought."

With that, he swiftly leaned backwards, rising up onto one knee, and bringing his other foot up onto the altar. It was yet clad in one of those mud-stained leather boots, and Stella blinked as that boot came closer, nudging powerfully against her bare thigh.

"Next you shall undress me," he ordered. "Remove my boots, woman."

Stella blinked again—gods, his foot was so *big*—but after a moment's hurtling, breathless staring, she obediently pulled herself up, and began picking at the laces of his boot. They were wrapped up his calf in a criss-cross pattern, digging into the soft leather, and once she'd mostly loosened one boot, he kicked it off behind him, and unceremoniously offered the other one.

"Mark the pattern," he said, "as you shall lace them for me again, after I am done with you."

The words should have felt ominous, but instead seemed to send yet another powerful wave of heat deep into Stella's groin. And her fingers felt almost eager, suddenly, as they tugged at the boot's laces, her fingers sliding against the surprisingly smooth leather.

"Good," he said firmly, once she'd finished, and he kicked off that boot, too. Revealing cropped trousers, a muscled, hairy calf, and then a disturbingly large foot, complete with sharp black claws—but rather than recoiling, as she surely should have done, Stella felt her tongue come to her lips, her breath coming out harsh. He was an orc. Dear goddess, he was an *orc*...

It was only the feel of the orc's hand on her face that brought her gaze back up, the smell of him twirling oddly sweet through her nostrils. "Now," he said, "you must finish undressing me."

Stella could only seem to give a silent nod, and she watched as her inexplicably deft hands obediently dropped to his leather belt, unfastening the simple buckle before thrusting it away. And then she pushed the trousers downward, so that—her breath choked all at once in her throat—that distinct male part of him could shove its way out, jutting straight and huge toward her.

*Gods.* Stella had perhaps been ignoring this particular point, trying with reasonable success to shove it away beneath all the rest, but now that it was here, in front of her face, it was shocking that she could have thought of anything else.

Because she'd heard the hushed tales about orcs. Hadn't she? Those tales of massive cocks, forced pleasure, biting and drinking blood, filling hapless women with their wicked seed, and their large, powerful sons. And surely even the goddess wouldn't expect a woman to risk such things, surely this was where Stella had to be rational, resist the madness, remember Lothar...

But the orc's hand was once again touching her, gripping strong at her chin, tilting it up so he could look at her. And his hideous face now wore a terrifying frown, his black eyes sharp, speculative, crackling.

"You fear my prick," he said flatly. "Why? You are strong and hale, you are not a maiden, and your womb is open and dripping wet. You shall take my ploughing with ease."

Stella's breath choked again, and she had to close her eyes, feel for the cool touch of the moon on her skin. "I was just thinking," she whispered, "of the—the *sons*."

There was an instant's stillness, in which those fingers clenched slightly on her face. "You do not wish for this?" he said. "You should reject a child sired under the blessing of the goddess?"

Stella gulped for air, and felt her head shaking, saying no. *No*?!

"I shouldn't reject a child," she said finally, a truly appalling statement that she couldn't seem to take back. "But bearing orc sons is dangerous for women. It could *kill* me. And even if didn't, what should I do, where would I go, I have a husband who would never tolerate such a thing. People would reject me and ignore me even more than they already do, I need to survive, I need to *eat*, this is my *life*—"

She risked a glance up at the orc's face as she spoke—surely she'd confessed too much, surely now he would leave—but he only looked almost confused, his heavy brow furrowed. "You must not fear this," he said, as his other hand came up, and stroked gently against her hair. "I should never abandon the mother of my son. I should protect you, and care for you. And there are those among my brothers with the gifts of healing, who should help you bring my son forth in safety. And if ever death were to befall me, my brothers should also care for you in my place. Our mountain is safe now for women and sons."

He said the last part with satisfied finality, as though he were personally responsible for that, and as though the matter were entirely settled. As though Stella would pack up her entire life and move to a dangerous, faraway orc mountain if she conceived an orc son, and place herself under this orc's protection and care, when he'd just threatened to *kill* her a half-hour past?

"We—we don't even *know* each other," she said faintly, and that was the wrong point, wasn't it? "Surely you wouldn't wish to *live* with me at your home?"

"We are coming to know one another," the orc said, without hesitation. "My strength and my touch please you, and your piety and obedience please me. Your ripe womb and your fat teats please me also. And once you have been fully cleansed and purified before the goddess, and we have made your sacrifice, we shall know all we need."

It didn't make even the slightest sense, or did it, but all the same, Stella felt her traitorous body relaxing, her mouth curving into a slight, relieved smile. Drawing the orc's thumb up to brush against it, again unfurling that oddly sweet scent of him deep into Stella's nostrils.

"Your eager meekness greatly pleases me also," he said softly, "but there is yet more cleansing to come. Next, I shall have your mouth, and you shall suck me."

He again spoke like it was a foregone conclusion, and again, perhaps it was. Because Stella's eyes had dropped downwards, toward that swollen bare cock, and she felt herself swallow hard, her tongue licking against her dry lips. He was so *huge*, long and grey and thick, with a blunted round end, and a smooth, deep slit. And as Stella watched, his big hand came to circle around the heft of it, giving a strong pump upwards, and bringing out a growing, glistening string of white.

"I said, you shall suck me," his voice repeated, though it came out even softer than before. "Obey me, woman."

Stella felt her eyes flutter, but she gave a shaky nod, and leaned forward. And she wasn't doing this, she couldn't truly be doing this—but then the world seemed to spin and resettle all at once, because—she *was*. Touching her lips to that blunt thick head, feeling its surprising smoothness, and then brushing a careful tongue up against the deep cleft of him, tasting him. Tasting an *orc*.

And it was the madness again, it had to be, because he tasted—*good*. Better than good, in fact, better than almost anything Stella had tasted in her life, and when she gave an experimental little suck there was more of that rich liquid, oh *gods*, pumping easy and smooth onto her tongue.

She let out a short, unwilling moan, earning in reply a low chuckle from the orc above her, and a flick of his clawed finger against her cheek. Making her blink up at where he was looking down at her, his mouth twitched up, that white fang sharp against his lip.

"You will look at me when you suck me," he said, all sheer insolent arrogance. "The goddess would wish for you to match the bitter sight of my face with the sweet taste of my seed. This shall make my face easier for you to look upon, in time."

In time? Stella felt herself frowning at him, a difficult task when one's mouth was filled with an orc's prick, and without warning his big hand came back up, and gave a light, gentle slap against her cheek.

"You must be cleansed," he said sharply, his voice at odds with his now-caressing hand—at least, until it pulled back and slapped her again, sharper this time. "I must needs do this. Now suck me deeper."

It was madness, it was a shameful and desperately wicked compulsion, because once again, Stella willingly obeyed. Sucking his huge, invading orc-prick even deeper into her mouth, as deep as it could go, until she nearly gagged on it, her throat convulsing against its smooth delving head.

But the orc didn't pull away, and instead only slowly, gently brought his strong hands to her head, sinking his clawed fingers tight and commanding through her loose dark hair. And then he drew her closer, gentle but inexorable, sinking his twitching, leaking heft even deeper into her throat. While those hard glittering eyes just kept watching, smiling, almost as though taking satisfaction in her discomfort.

"Your soft mouth pleases the goddess," he purred. "But you must suck harder, if you wish to be cleansed."

That seemed impossible, truly, when Stella was already busy fighting the urge to choke—but she gave it her best effort anyway, fighting to suck harder, to welcome his invasion even deeper. Bringing an unmistakable groan to his mouth, surprisingly thrilling in the madness, and even more so when he drew himself out slightly, and sank slowly back inside.

"Better," he said, sounding almost breathless. "Now I shall use your throat. And you must keep sucking with strength, until I have filled your empty belly with my good seed."

Stella only moaned again, blinking frantically toward those glinting eyes—and then the sight blurred into the night, because there was a huge orc-prick slamming in and out of her mouth, again and again and again. And there was no way to keep the suction, no way to control or counter this, only feeling tasting drinking, the hard grey heft slipping and sliding, the thick liquid dripping from him, dripping from her mouth down her chin. Her eyes watering, her lips trembling her jaw aching, his deep voice speaking words she couldn't even begin to follow, in the chaos.

Another slap struck against her cheek, with the flat of his hand this time, and when she desperately fought to regain the suction there was a caress, approval. And that was good, it was *all* so good, and she distantly realized her own wetness was dripping down her thighs, cleansing her anew for the goddess—

The hot succulent liquid surged into her mouth all at once, without warning or recourse, and her first instinct to spit was swiftly crushed by the desperate need to taste, to swallow, to drink. Gulping noisily and messily on the heft of him, even as that wetness kept pulsing out, slipping out thick and hot between her lips.

When he finally pulled away, sudden and forceful, it left Stella swaying in place, blinking dazed and dizzy toward the watching orc. The orc whose hand had again come to her face, not wiping her off, but instead smearing his sticky mess wide against her cheeks. And then—Stella couldn't help a shaky cry—his other hand slapped her cheek, gently, but still speaking of his displeasure. He was *displeased* with her, after quite possibly the most powerful moment of Stella's entire life, and she couldn't stop blinking, feeling the wetness suddenly prickling again behind her eyes.

"I do not wish to punish one whose mouth is so eager," the orc said. "But it is the goddess' wish for you to be cleansed, and you are not cleansed when you disobey under the goddess' eye. I told you to suck me with strength, and you did not."

Stella's heart seemed to plummet, and she blinked desperately up toward his watching eyes. "But I tried," she whispered. "I really did."

"Yes," came his curt answer. "You did, and this pleased me. Yet you still must be cleansed, else your sacrifice shall not please the goddess."

Stella kept blinking, but felt herself give a shaky nod, and in reply the orc tilted his head, brushing a soft hand against her swollen lips. "Good," he said. "Now turn over to your hands and knees, and bare yourself to me for your punishment."

What? Stella seemed caught, suddenly, trapped in the sheer shocking vision of that, and that hand kept stroking her, running soft against her cheek. "I shall have your obedience, woman," he said, almost regretfully. "You must be cleansed."

Stella could feel the conviction behind his words, reverberating taut between them, and she drank them in, strong enough to shove the madness back, away. And then, with a deep breath, she turned over onto her hands and knees on the soft moss, and raised her messy, sticky face to the moon.

She would obey. She would be cleansed. She would earn the goddess' favour, and give a just sacrifice, worthy and bare and whole.

"I am ready, orc," she whispered. "Punish me."

# 6

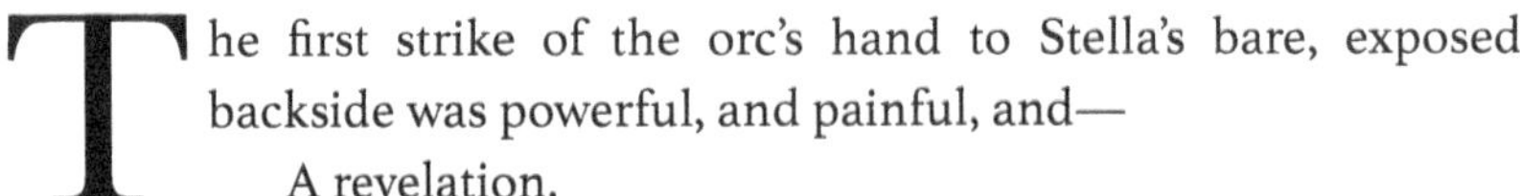

The first strike of the orc's hand to Stella's bare, exposed backside was powerful, and painful, and—

A revelation.

She'd cried out at the shock and the strength of it, her body shuddering on her hands and knees, but by the second strike, the noise from her mouth was already more of a moan. Because there was something primal and fundamentally powerful about this, about kneeling on an ancient altar in the moonlight, her face used and smeared, her breasts flushed and swollen, her groin streaming wetness down her parted legs—while her orc, her handler, paid his singleminded devotion to her bared, stinging arse.

And it felt like devotion, this punishment. Not painful beyond endurance, but surely enough to make marks, to inflame that part of her as much as the rest. To wash away the shame and the fear and the madness altogether, and replace it with hunger, and craving, and an inexplicable, astonishing relief.

And when Stella arched into the orc's punishment, exposing even more of her inflamed body to his purposeful striking hand, she could hear his guttural moan, despite his best effort to choke it back. He was trying to stay impartial and powerful, trying to show the goddess the strength of his supplication—and suddenly, surging to life in Stella's thoughts, there was something dangerously close to warmth, or perhaps even affection.

"Thank you," she gasped, even as she twitched all over at yet another hard strike of his hand against her stinging arse-cheek. "For handling me. For helping to cleanse me."

She braced for the next strike, but there was only stillness, unfurling wide around them. And then—Stella very nearly sobbed aloud—there was the feel of warm fingers, sliding soft and gentle against her exposed, dripping-wet heat.

"By speaking thus," his quiet voice said, "you have bravely fulfilled your punishment, and made amends for your disobedience. This pleases the goddess, woman."

A sparkling thrill shot down Stella's back at the praise, and then again at the feel of those gentle fingers, slipping deeper against her swollen wetness. And her body was clenching greedily against those fingers in return, silently begging for more, and her handler knew it, judging by the husky, satisfied chuckle behind her.

"You are almost ready to be bared for the goddess," he said. "But first, there is one more place I must cleanse."

Stella turned her head to look at him, finding those glittering black eyes in the moonlight. And as that thin mouth twitched up, showing that sharp white fang, his big grey hand slowly, deliberately lifted, and came down to clamp hard against Stella's hot, smarting arse-cheek.

Stella wasn't following—at least, not until the other hand came to the other side, and pulled her powerfully apart. Showing him absolutely *everything*, all her most shameful parts stretched wide open for those smug, insolent, commanding eyes.

"This too must be opened and cleansed," he said. "It has been tainted by that man I smell upon you."

That man. It was the first time he'd made any reference to her husband—Lothar, Stella's sluggish brain supplied—and more than that, the orc could *smell* that? He *knew* she and Lothar had done that?

And it was desperately shameful for Stella to have agreed to it, she well knew, but between Lothar's whispered promises and his eager touch, it had been worth it, in that moment, and again in those afterwards. And there had been pleasure in it, far beyond what Stella had expected, but not—she yelped aloud—at all the same as watching, and feeling, a huge, blunted, slippery orc-prick, coming to press hard and powerful against it.

"You shall bravely take this," he said, voice and eyes commanding as he bore down, as Stella clenched back compulsively against him. "You shall draw me deep inside you. And then, when you have swallowed all my prick, you again"—his black eyelashes fluttered—"shall thank me."

That strange, hurtling affection surged again, beyond all rational sense, and again Stella nodded. "Yes," she whispered. "I shall try."

He gave a silent, twitchy nod back—and then, against Stella's quivering, too-sensitive opening, there was pressure. The feel of that blunt, slick head pushing, seeking, demanding a way in—but it had been *months* since Stella had done this last, and she'd had no preparation, and he was huge, he was an *orc*—

"You must soften yourself for me, woman," came his low, heated voice, and with it was another light, thrilling slap of his hand. "You must open yourself to be cleansed. I shall have your obedience."

Stella desperately fought for air, and tried for another nod, earning an approving grip of that warm hand against her arse. And when that slick hardness pushed again, she somehow managed to relax enough to open to it, to allow that blunt head to ram its way inside.

And already it felt like too much, like she was being pinned to its heft, split apart from the inside out. Far worse than with Lothar, eons worse—and also so much better, slick and careful and gentle, sliding so slowly it was almost like he wasn't moving at all.

But he was, the orc was sinking deeper and deeper inside her with agonizing deliberation, with every ragged breath from Stella's gasping mouth. And his breath was coming ragged too, harsh enough that Stella could feel it against her back, and a furtive glance over her shoulder showed him looking down at the sight of them, of him, his huge prick disappearing deep into Stella's clenching, quivering heat.

With one last, guttural breath he was all the way there, his groin pressed flat against Stella's tender arse-cheeks, and she could only seem to moan, and press herself back against him. She'd never taken anything so huge there before, she'd never felt *anything* like this before, her very insides conquered and subdued, stretched and pushed to their very limits, cleansed and bared and whole before the goddess.

The orc behind her had gone still and silent, but for those harsh breaths against her skin, and Stella pressed back again, felt herself grip even tighter around the heft of his invasion. "Thank you," she whispered. "For cleansing me."

The pleasure in his replying moan was unmistakable, thick and dark and honeyed with heat, and Stella sank into the truth of that, into all the hard hungry power of his body inside hers. Not moving, just remaining still, and a distant part of her knew it was a mercy, what with how tight she was stretched, how little it would take to snap.

"And thank you," she continued, breathless, "for your gentleness, in this."

There was another guttural, liquid growl behind her, a light squeeze of his big hands against her flaming arse-cheeks. "I must not be too gentle," he rasped, as he slowly, deliberately began to draw himself out again. "I am charged with handling you, and cleansing you. But"—he drew out further, further, until Stella's clenching body released him with a humiliating sound—"you have shown yourself brave in this, woman. You have pleased the goddess."

His hands were still touching her, gently stroking against both her still-stretched arse, and her thick, dripping-wet heat below. The part of her that felt almost painfully swollen now, clutching frantically at even the slightest touch, silently begging him, pleading him, for more.

"Do I," she heard her wavering voice say, "please *you*?"

He was quiet for an instant, long enough that Stella once again craned her head to look at him. But he wasn't looking at her face, and instead his eyes were carefully downward, on where his hand was now sliding wide on her reddened, smarting arse-cheek.

"Yes," he said finally, the word a lone quiet caress. "You please me like no other woman before you. There is great worth in your obedience and forbearance, and in the purity of your hunger. It is joy to handle a woman such as this. It is joy to break you to my command."

The words sent warmth swarming across Stella's skin, but the words caught at something else, too. "So you've had other women, too?" she whispered. "Here, before the goddess?"

And she couldn't explain why, but it felt almost a betrayal, somehow, to think that he might have done this here before, with someone else—but he fixed her with a sudden frown, and gave a hard shake of his bushy head.

"I have had other women, but no orc comes to the altar more than once," he said firmly. "This night here shall be my first, and my last."

Oh. The warmth swirled again, deeper this time, and Stella felt her mouth twitch into a slow, relieved smile. "I'm glad," she heard her audacious voice whisper. "Is my cleansing now complete, for you? Or do I yet need more?"

Even the thought brought heat to her cheeks, but the orc's gaze on her was intent, quiet, speculative. "Turn over," he said, "and lie on your back."

Stella immediately obeyed, wincing a little as her smarting, reddened arse made contact with the soft moss, but now the orc was here, kneeling on the altar between her legs, leaning over her. Looking suddenly huge and brutal and powerful as his clawed hands once again grasped her ankles, and pulled them apart.

"I must now survey my work, and complete your preparation," he said, as his hands folded her ankles back, close toward her thighs, exposing everything in between. "I must be sure you are utterly cleansed and marked and open, and bared for the goddess' eyes. Only then shall I begin your sacrifice."

Stella nodded numbly, and blinked as those hands came up, now with their sharp black claws clearly visible, and carefully cupped her face between them. Stroking her still-sticky cheeks first, and then her mouth, slipping two swift, searching clawed fingers between her lips. And when Stella sucked and licked at them, curling her tongue around them, he gave a satisfied nod—and then, without warning, a hard, stinging slap against her cheek.

Stella felt herself moan aloud, her eyelashes fluttering—and the orc again nodded his approval, as his hand lingered gently, almost reverently, against her smarting cheek. While his other fingers slid out of her mouth, curving wet over her other cheek—until they, too, drew backwards, and gave her a swift, stinging slap. But this time with just a trace of those sharp, deadly claws, scraping strong and shocking against her skin.

But Stella could only seem to gasp and moan and stare at him, her breath and body desperately heaving, while those dark eyes stared back. While his big clawed hand, now just slightly trembling, came back to her cheek where he'd struck it, tracing slow and reverent against the new marks he'd made on her skin.

"Brave woman," he whispered, his eyes blinking, his head briefly bowing—but now his hands were moving again, this time back up to her hair. Again spreading it out around her head, his hands smooth and tender against the dark waves as he again made her halo, for him, for the goddess.

Once he was finished he pulled back slightly, his head tilted, almost as though assessing his work—but then his clawed hand came back to Stella's mouth, his finger slipping again between her lips, tugging them apart. "This," he ordered, quiet, "must be open, for the sacrifice."

Stella again nodded her agreement, and after a curt nod in return, the orc's hands began moving downwards again. Lingering first against her neck, and then sliding wide and thorough over her shoulders and upper arms. And then—Stella gasped—they went back to her still-flushed breasts, stroking and kneading them at first, and then rising to full-on pinches and slaps, again scraping those sharp claws against her skin. But the brief flares of pain only seemed to fuse the pleasure higher, making Stella writhe and moan beneath him, her hips bucking up, her hungry heat liberally dripping onto the moss below.

"Good," the orc murmured, as those clawed hands briefly paused, moving to catch at Stella's wrists. And then bringing her hands up to her stinging, scraped, reddened breasts—not to cover them, Stella's twirling thoughts noted, but instead to curve her fingers close around the base of them. Squeezing slightly, bulging them up and out, as if displaying them, wanton and brazen, to the goddess' watching eye.

The orc had leaned back to watch too, his eyes flaring with clear approval, his two clawed hands again coming up to palm at each bulging breast, and then giving a hard, painful, thoroughly thrilling pinch at each swollen, jutting nipple. Bringing even more desperate groans to Stella's still-open mouth, more shouting, craving hunger to her dripping-wet groin.

"Good," the orc murmured again, his voice hoarse. "Your teats must stay thus, for your sacrifice."

Stella could only frantically nod, staring at where the orc's gaze had now dropped back to his hands, now curving over her waist, and then down to her hips, her thighs. And when he slowly shoved her thighs open wide, as wide as they could possibly go, there wasn't even a thought of resisting, only watching, waiting, with bated breath.

He began with light slaps again, on both her arse-cheeks and her swollen dripping core, and as they grew in intensity, harder and faster, Stella heard her cries rising to match, her whole body arching, while the sparks seemed to pulse wider across her skin at every stinging, glorious touch. Her own orc, her handler, appointed by the goddess to cleanse her—

"Oh goddess," she choked out, without thought, when the orc rubbed a gentle finger against her still-stretched arse, and then slid it slowly, surely inside. Setting her clenching desperate and frantic around it, but he only circled his finger wider, and then slipped another finger inside. And then another, oh merciful goddess, again circling those fingers further, invading even deeper, her tight opening stretched and stinging and shouting for more.

"This, too, must stay thus," ordered the orc's heated voice, as he slowly, deliberately slid his fingers out again, leaving that tightness stretched, loose, gaping open wide. "You must keep it open, for your sacrifice."

Stella's replying nod was frantic, tortured, desperate—and then even more so when that orc's broad palm gave it a slow, firm slap. Testing her, she knew, but she didn't flinch or clench or resist, not even when he did it again, and again, and again.

"Good," he said, as he softly slipped an approving finger inside, and back out again. "You are almost ready, woman, but for this."

This. He meant the swollen, dripping core of her, frantically and desperately clenching for his touch—and finally, *finally*, his other hand was there, sliding smooth and easy against her slick, dripping heat.

"I shall open this," he whispered, promised, "while you look to the goddess, and show her your cleansed form, and bare all your secret parts open to her eyes. You must draw her favour, and ask for her blessing."

There was no possible argument, no resistance. Only flaring jolting hunger, a shout from Stella's open mouth, her entire body arching and begging and baring itself wide. While that orc's thick fingers gently, deliberately spread her swollen lips apart, and began to press slow and sure inside...

"Please, Goddess of Bautul," she gasped, writhed, choked. "Please, please, grant me your favour. Grant me your blessing. *Take me.*"

# 7

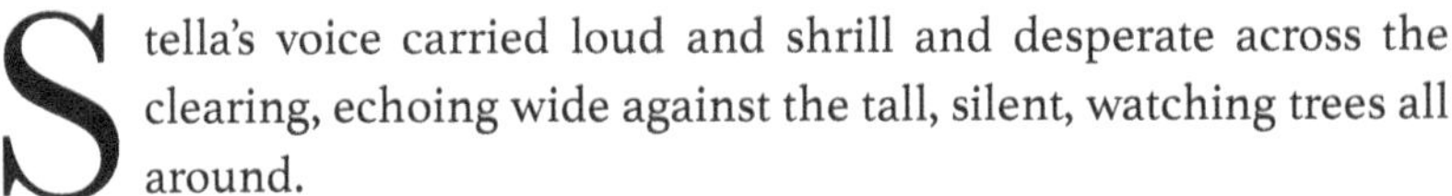

Stella's voice carried loud and shrill and desperate across the clearing, echoing wide against the tall, silent, watching trees all around.

But there was only silence in return, pooling calm and quiet and close around them. And somehow, suddenly, it seemed wrong to ask further, or to beg. Stella needed to show, her handler had said. To bare.

And she *was* bare, her body flushed and sparking and cleansed, carefully prepared upon this ancient orc altar by one of the goddess' own favoured servants. Her hair spread wide, her lips parted, her mouth reddened and swollen, her throat bruised, her tongue still tasting of rich thick orc-seed.

And her cheeks were red and sticky, marked with her handler's claws, and stained with his seed. And her breasts, bulging full out of her still-gripping fingers, were scraped and reddened too, obscenely on display, her pink nipples hard and brazen and jutting to the sky.

And then, of course, her spread-wide thighs. Her arse-cheeks, stinging and red and marked with claws. And between them, gaping wide open, that most secret place, used and stretched and exposed by not only an orc's hands, but also his massive orc-prick.

And there, kneeling between her legs, was the orc himself. With his dark head bowed, almost as if in worship, while those two invading fingers kept sliding slow into Stella's dripping-wet heat, splitting her wet lips, slowly but surely opening her wide apart.

The feeling, the moment, was almost shockingly powerful, and suddenly it felt like Stella's entire body was blazing, flaring, sparks crawling alive under her skin. And all she could do was gasp and writhe and welcome it, show her body bare and cleansed and pure for his eyes, for the goddess' eyes. Squeeze her breasts, open her mouth, spread her legs wider, drink him in, take everything—

He was sliding in a third finger now, drawing her swollen wetness tighter around him, but the hunger only kept shouting, screaming, wheeling wide and close. Stella needed this, needed more and more and more of this—and when she felt his fourth finger, delving huge and painful and impossible inside, she only spread her legs wider, brandish her breasts show the goddess more, she was bared and stretched beyond imagining, beyond her limits, she needed him so desperately she would tear herself apart—

When suddenly, around them, the world went still. Utterly caught and silent, its only movement Stella's trembling, sparking, writhing body upon the altar, with the orc between her knees, his huge hand clamped halfway up inside her.

But he'd gone still too, but for his own heaving chest—and as Stella whimpered and trembled and stared, his free hand clenched to a clawed powerful fist, and came to cross over his chest. His wild head bowing toward the moon, his shoulders shuddering, the white light dancing against his thick black hair.

"Goddess of Bautul," he said, the words quiet, reverent, entirely fitting with the watching, shining, whispering world all around. "Your servants await your blessing."

There was only more quivering silence, the cool light rippling light and shadow against her handler's pearly grey skin, almost as though he were part of the night itself. And it occurred to Stella, crazed and distant but certain, that this was how this orc was meant to be seen, where he was meant to live and walk and breathe. In the forest under the moonlight, kneeling upon an ancient altar with his fist over his heart, a sacrifice bared wide and trembling at his knees, with his strong hand deep inside her, holding her safe. Waiting, with the utmost faith and certainty, until—

The blast of wind charged all at once, whirling through the trees, breaking the stillness with deafening force. Whipping the orc's black hair around his face, setting it even wilder in the moonlight, and for an instant, Stella's frantic, writhing body had somehow gone languid and quiet and still. Her eyes watching with a hushed, stilted awe as he slowly raised his face toward the moon, his harsh features lit with the bare honesty of his devotion.

"Thank you," he whispered, the words almost inaudible to Stella's ears. "We are honoured to obey."

There was another moment's silence, deep and reverent—and then, with an almost compelling slowness, the orc turned his head, and looked toward Stella.

And in that hurtling instant, in the silvery light of the goddess' benediction, he was—beautiful. Wild and untamed, strength and chaos, fierce and unstoppable. Her orc, her handler, her rescuer, holding her, invading her, gazing at her with an intensity so powerful it nearly made her want to weep.

"Please," Stella heard herself whisper to those eyes, her trembly hand coming up to brush against his muscled arm—and with the touch, it was like a spell had broken. Flooding her with the strength of his sudden movement, his fingers swiftly drawing out of her, leaving her stretched and dripping and open all over, fully, finally ready for her sacrifice. And then the heady sweet rush of his scent, the sound of his growl rising, and the hurtling, entirely fitting sight of him rearing up and howling toward the moon—

And when it all settled again, he was there. Huge and close and warm above Stella on the altar, his upper body propped up on his elbows, his hips hot and heavy between her spread legs. And then—Stella cried out, her hands clutching frantic against his broad back—there was the thrilling, breathtaking feel of that hard, huge prick, finally nudging gently against her dripping, grasping, wide-open heat.

"Oh goddess," she moaned, arching up against him, spreading herself wider against the tantalizing threat of his invasion—and in another blazing, shocking movement, he slammed himself inside. Splitting her apart in one single, deadly, exquisitely painful stroke, impaling her deep upon him, so much larger than his fingers had been—and Stella heard herself scream, the shrill sound piercing through the trees.

But her handler didn't relent, didn't weaken in his resolve. Only kept pressing in deeper against her, spearing her whole upon the brute force of his strength, as her body kicked and flailed and surged, entirely helpless against his solid, unrelenting weight.

"With this, I begin your true sacrifice, woman," came his whisper, hot and breathless against her ear. "I break you open before the goddess. You must now accept the full force of my conquering, if you wish to complete your offering. You must yield."

The urge to agree was there, rushing deep and immediate through Stella's thoughts—but her invaded, impaled, bared body seemed to have gained a strange, powerful will of its own. Twitching and writhing beneath her conqueror, pierced painfully on the heft of his huge, hot prick, and in reply that prick seemed to swell and surge even deeper against her resistance, dragging another scream from her raw, ragged throat.

"Be brave, woman," he ordered, close and urgent. "Accept this."

But Stella couldn't, suddenly, it was impossible, it was an invasion far beyond flesh and blood, and into her very soul. Dragging another hoarse, unbidden scream from her throat—until it was broken by the sudden, jarring feel of one of those huge hands, circling gentle but close around her neck.

"You bared yourself for my cleansing, woman," he hissed. "Now you shall yield to my breaking. You shall be sacrificed."

Stella couldn't speak, couldn't do anything but squirm and gasp and flail—and in reply her handler's lips pulled back, baring his sharp white teeth. And that hand on her throat had yanked sideways, tilting her head with it, exposing her neck to his eyes—and with another surging, world-swirling movement, his face was in her neck, sharp teeth catching against her skin, terror and pleasure wheeling wide apart—

The bite of his teeth was another flash of sheer pain, white-hot inside Stella's skull—but it was gone just as quickly, chased by warm lips and a strong tongue, licking against torn, tender skin. And her handler's throat was swallowing, he was *drinking* her, even as that hard heft between her legs began circling, grinding, gouging himself even deeper.

It was madness, her handler was driving and hurling himself at the madness, battering mighty and unrelenting against all Stella's resistance. Drinking her pounding her owning her, stabbing and breaching her, fierce vicious power flaying her alive on their goddess' altar, trammelling her thoughts, crushing everything—

But in return, Stella's body only fought harder. Desperately drowning all conscious thought deep below, and instead thrashing and weeping and shouting and clawing, lost and trapped and clinging. Wanting to yield but grasping at nothing, he'd said peace but there was only fear, loneliness, anger, Lothar, misery, death—

Her handler's invasion only seemed to grow in power and strength, punching deep between Stella's legs, whirling up even more of the furious wailing misery. She'd worked so hard, fought so hard just to survive, hungry and lonely and hopeless, and then Lothar had come with his smiles and his easy promises. And it had been so easy to ignore her instincts, to ignore the hints and the uncertainties, and in return the pain had only struck deeper when he'd walked away, again and again and again—

There was a light slap to Stella's face, barely noticeable in the chaos, her eyes squeezed shut, her head wildly shaking back and forth—but there it was again, harder this time, the sting echoing wide through her thoughts.

"Woman," his voice ordered. "Look at me."

Stella somehow blinked up toward it, and found her handler's hideous face looking down at her. His black eyes glinting wild, his hair a spiky mess, his mouth dripping with liquid red.

"You shall be brave," he said slowly, the words ringing deep and powerful into the scattered frenzy of her thoughts. "You shall accept this. You shall yield, and be open and bare, and offer *all* to the goddess. Not only your blood and your tears and your juices, but also your past. Your regrets. That man. *All.*"

All. And in that moment, staring at terrifying black eyes and a face dripping with her own life's blood, somehow, Stella suddenly—impossibly—understood. She needed to—accept.

The next slap of her handler's palm against her cheek made her twitch, but she was here again, he was here. And she felt herself give a trembly nod at that face, earning a soft caress of those fingers against her skin, wiping away the streaks of her tears.

"Brave woman," he whispered—and then he leaned down, and kissed her.

It was like the world exploded again all at once, fuelled by the scent and the colour and the warmth of him, his hot slick tongue invading her mouth, tasting of iron and salt and sweetness. Twitching again at the madness—Stella was drinking her own *blood* from an orc's tongue, while his huge prick pummelled her again and again—but then, somehow, she thrust the madness back again, and faced herself in its truth.

She was being taken by an orc under the moon. She was being brutally fucked, drank, kissed beyond anything she'd known before in her life. She was betraying Lothar, she was breaking her wedding-vows, she was wreaking her own revenge on a year—gods, half a *lifetime*—of utter hell.

And more than that, she was embracing a new rite, a new faith. She was following her own instincts, facing the truth of her own desires. She'd been fully opened and bared and cleansed, found pleasing to her goddess' sight. And now she was enduring—no, she was welcoming—her handler's rough treatment, his aggression and his power, because she so desperately craved this forceful single-mindedness, this determined hurling away of all the rest. Guiding her, cleansing her, showing her the way to—peace.

And when Stella finally began kissing her handler back, twining her tongue hard against his, she could almost feel his relief, the way his big body sagged slightly against hers. And when her hands carded into the wildness of his hair, it brought the rightness even deeper, his big body moving now more with hers than against it, and when her legs came up to wrap tight around his hips he moaned aloud into her mouth, the sound melting honey on her tongue.

"Yes," he whispered, against her lips, as that thick strength below rocked inside again, again, again. "Accept this. Offer all to this."

Stella could see it now, could feel it, and she nodded against him, drawing another groan of pleasure from his mouth. "Yes, woman," he said. "Speak."

Speak. And while words would have been impossible, only a few short moments ago, somehow they seemed to come easy now, flowing out of Stella's mouth. "I accept this," she heard herself say. "I offer myself to the goddess. I offer myself"—her voice broke, her hands fluttering to her orc's face—"to you."

Those black eyes briefly stilled, that hard strength inside her making one shocking final gouge, locking in deep—and then it erupted. Surging out thick and powerful into her, pulsing again and again with the pure essence of him, force and life inside her.

Stella's voice was shouting again, her hands clinging frantic and desperate against him—and all at once her own release broke and crashed. Wringing herself out around him, all glorious grasping trammelling heat, while his own howl rose to match hers. Their bodies and souls locked, clamped together, bared and flayed open, flaring as one, pouring out their hard-won relief before the goddess' eyes.

When Stella finally sank back against the altar again, it was with a sated, swirling, strangely contented exhaustion. Almost as though she'd fought her way through a vicious, brutal battle, and had come out wounded but victorious on the other side.

The orc above her almost seemed the same, his big body heavy and sticky above hers, his breath exhaling slow and powerful against her cheek. But his eyes on hers were still alert, watchful, and Stella felt his big hand trail down her throat, coming to brush against the still-stinging bite-marks he'd left upon her skin.

"Brave woman," he said, and there was a new, tenuous carefulness in his voice. "You have offered up all upon this altar this night, and made a pure and worthy sacrifice. You have pleased the Goddess of Bautul, and earned her blessing."

The words were like a rich, soothing balm, quieting away the last dregs of the whispering madness. And Stella felt herself let out a slow breath, while her fingers played against the thick strands of his hair, surprisingly smooth despite the mess.

"How do you know?" she finally asked, her voice just as tenuous as his. "That the goddess is pleased?"

His big hand was back to stroking her face, his thumb brushing away the lingering wetness beside her eyes. “I can feel this,” he said. “Can you not feel this also?”

Stella’s eyes glanced belatedly up toward the goddess’ moon, glowing so still and quiet and silvery above them. Watching them both with its pure gentle light, illuminating their sated entwined bodies with its cool, undeniable truth.

Stella had bared all, opened all, offered all. And the goddess had watched, and approved, and accepted it.

And not only that, but the orc had accepted it, too. Hadn't he?

The truth of that set Stella’s still-tender cheeks oddly flushing, her gaze snapping back to the safety of his messy hair. “Yes,” she said. “I can feel it.”

There was a slow exhale from his weight above her, a spreading of that hand against her cheek. “Good,” he said. “I am deeply moved by your devotion and your obedience, woman. The goddess has brought me a rare gift this night.”

Stella risked a glance at those eyes, her cheeks still strangely hot, and found him studying her with that same alert, careful intensity. “You will keep this vow, will you not?” he asked, his voice very quiet. “When you offered yourself to me?”

So he hadn’t missed that, then, and Stella swallowed hard, felt her fingers tighten in the chaotic silk of his hair. “I—” she began, and then took another breath, let it out. “I’m not sure I know exactly what that means.”

“It means you shall be my mate,” he replied, without hesitation. “You shall come away with me, and live with me and my kin in our mountain. You shall bear my sons and raise them with me, and in return I shall keep you well tended, and fed, and safe.”

He spoke the words so easily, but they seemed suddenly impossible, like a preposterous vision that couldn’t conceivably be real, and Stella groped for words, for some way to find truth beneath them. “And I—I’d have to wait on you, and serve you?” she ventured. “And you’d leave me behind alone and trapped there, whenever you travel?”

The orc’s thick eyebrows drew together in clear disapproval. “I should not leave you behind, unless the danger is dire,” he said flatly.

"A meek, hungry woman such as you must be handled and tended often. I could not leave you to languish."

A deep flare of longing seemed to unfurl through Stella's gut, but there had to be a catch, there had to be. "But," she began, "you still barely *know* me. And I barely know you."

The orc's scowl deepened, his lip curling up to show that sharp fang. "I know much of you now," he said firmly. "You are brave, and pious, and obedient. You are eager for strong handling, you endure much without complaint, and you meekly accept punishment when it is due. And"—his voice lowered slightly—"you please me with your wet womb, and your fat teats, and your sweet suckling mouth. And the next time I handle you, you shall please me even more, since I have now taught you what I shall expect of you, and"—his mouth twitched up, his smile almost shockingly wolfish—"cleansed away that foolish man's weak scent, and covered it with my own."

There was another deep thrill in Stella's belly, so strong that she barely managed to muster a frown at him. "Wait," she said. "All your high talk of cleansing me—you were just getting rid of Lothar's *smell*?"

That smile curved up even more, sending yet another thrill down Stella's entire form, even to where—she couldn't help a strangled gasp—that hard prick was still filling her, swelling just slightly inside.

"Not only this," he purred. "A sacrifice must be carefully handled and prepared, until she is dripping wet and begging for her handler's taking. But if this cleansing washes away a weak man's scent from all the woman's bounty, this is all the better. Especially when the handler wishes to keep the woman for his own, once the sacrifice is complete."

Stella's eyelashes were fluttering, her breath coming short, but she needed to keep to the point, damn him. "But," she managed, "you don't even know my *name*."

The orc's head tilted slightly, like that thought hadn't once occurred to him, and he gave another smile, perhaps almost affectionate this time. "Then speak it, woman."

The odd heat was flushing Stella's cheeks again, but she drew in a breath, and nodded. "Stella."

There was an instant's silence, but then the orc nodded too, his hand again stroking against her cheek. "Stella," he repeated, as though he were testing out the word on his tongue. "I am Silfast, of clan Bautul."

Silfast. A strange name, perhaps, but one that suited him, and Stella felt her mouth twitch a smile toward his watching eyes. "Right then," she whispered. "And what do you do with your days, Silfast of clan Bautul? Beyond wandering the countryside and accosting unsuspecting women on ancient altars?"

The orc—Silfast—tilted his head again, showing just a hint of a sharp-fanged smile. "I have long served as a battle-captain among my brothers," he replied. "But this is a time of change. Mayhap I shall need to learn new roles, or find new ways to spend my days."

Stella considered that, her eyes searching his harsh face, and weighing it against his words. Of course this orc would be a battle-captain, of course he would command and conquer and kill. And while she likely should have been alarmed by that—it would have been *humans* he was fighting against, all that time—there was instead a quiet, curious understanding. An acceptance.

"And how does a battle-captain treat his mate, in their daily life?" she asked. "What if she disobeys him, or disagrees with him, or reproaches him? What if she doesn't yield to his command?"

She was watching him very carefully, now, and she could see her own wariness reflected in those black eyes. "Ach. You think because I am exacting in this"—his hand gave a vague gesture toward their entwined bodies—"I shall be a tyrant in all things."

Stella couldn't help a relieved nod—it was astonishing, really, that this orc could already follow her thoughts so easily—and he kept studying her with those watchful, careful eyes. "I should never betray or harm my bonded mate, should she displease me, or disobey me," he said slowly. "But I also shall not accept lies or mockery or contempt. I am an orc of strong will and high standing, and I shall expect truth, and bravery, and honour where I am due."

The words felt right, settling slow and orderly into Stella's thoughts, but now the orc's throat was convulsing, his eyes flicking slightly away from hers. "And when my mate is bare before me," he said, quieter, "as you are now, I shall always expect meekness, and obedience. You shall seek to eagerly please me, and obey, lest you face my punishment."

A choked, betraying gasp had escaped from Stella's throat, drawing his eyes back to hers. But they were still searching, cautious, and she could feel the odd tension in him, vibrating close above her. "If this is not what you wish, woman," he said, "then you may withdraw your pledge to me, and return to your home. I shall not"—that throat bobbed again—"seek to stop you."

The fondness seemed to flare all at once, so strong that it felt like Stella's heart might crack in two. "Thank you, Silfast," she whispered, tracing a slow finger down his harsh, scarred cheek. "But I'd far rather come away with you. I should be glad to yield to your command in this, and welcome your punishment when it is due."

His black eyes blinked at her, once—but then she could feel the relief, shuddering hard and long through his big body above her. His eyes closing briefly, his head bowing, his clawed hand clutching close against her hair.

"Good," he breathed. "We shall leave for the mountain tonight. But, for your sake, woman"—those eyes blinked open, studying her—"mayhap we shall wait to speak our vows, until the next full moon. This shall give you time to return here, if you find I am not what you wish."

There was only more affection, swarming through Stella's entire being with inexplicable intensity, and she found herself blinking back at him, her mouth curving up into a slow, genuine smile. And he was looking back at her with eyes that were oddly bright, his hand again coming to cradle her cheek as though it were something secret, precious, beyond price.

"You say you are not lovely," he murmured, "when in truth, you are the fairest sight to ever greet my eyes. You shall keep me roused at all hours of the day and night, woman. You may never escape my prick again."

Stella couldn't help a choked laugh, even as her body again clenched close around that still-invading hardness, and the hunger swirled deep through her groin. "Is that an order?" she whispered, giving an experimental wriggle beneath him. "Or just a possibility? Because I'm sure I could escape, if I really—"

Her words were cut off by a rising, menacing growl, betrayed only by the teasing hint of fang against his crooked mouth. "You dare test me already, woman?" he demanded. "Do you yet need another deep cleansing upon this altar, under the goddess' gaze?"

And looking up at his heated, sparkling eyes, there was no fear, no shame, no madness. Only that easy, quiet acceptance, the strength of his weight above her. A new fate. Peace.

"Yes, my worthy Silfast," she whispered. "I am at your mercy. Cleanse me."

THE END

AN MM MONSTER ROMANCE TALE

FINLEY FENN

## TRYGGRED BY THE ORC

***He's supposed to run... but he wants to be caught.***

In a world of orcs and men, Eben of Clan Ka-esh is shy, awkward, and desperately lonely. No one notices the sickroom's quietest scholar, not even when he's saving lives, or offering up decadent pleasures in Orc Mountain's darkest depths.

Until Tryggr, of Clan Skai. A tall, shameless, laughing orc warrior, who can have anyone he wants...

And Tryggr keeps looking at Eben. *Seeing* Eben.

But Skai are risky, reckless, dangerous—and all his life, Eben's been taught to run from them. To hide safe and quiet and alone. Or else he'll be forever crushed and conquered beneath a deadly Skai's claws and teeth...

But maybe Eben *wants* to be conquered.

And maybe Tryggr is just the conqueror he needs...

*Written for my generous supporters and friends on Patreon. Thank you.*

# AUTHOR'S NOTE

Thank you so much for reading this MM Orc Sworn novella!

This book was first written for the generous members of my Orc Sworn Patreon, who wanted to learn how a swaggering Skai like Tryggr first fell for a shy sweetheart like Eben. Therefore, this book happens at the same time as *The Maid and the Orcs* (the sixth full-length book in my Orc Sworn series).

But this time, we'll get to see the other side of the story, and find out what really went on behind the scenes! This means you will get multiple spoilers for *The Maid and the Orcs*—and while this story can still be read as a stand-alone, I think you'll appreciate it more if you've already read *The Maid and the Orcs.*

Also, this story does include some dark themes and situations, unhealthy dynamics, and very intense scenes. If you'd like full details on what to expect, please visit this book's page on my website at finleyfenn.com.

I really hope you have fun with *Tryggred by the Orc*! Hugs from Orc Mountain!

# 1

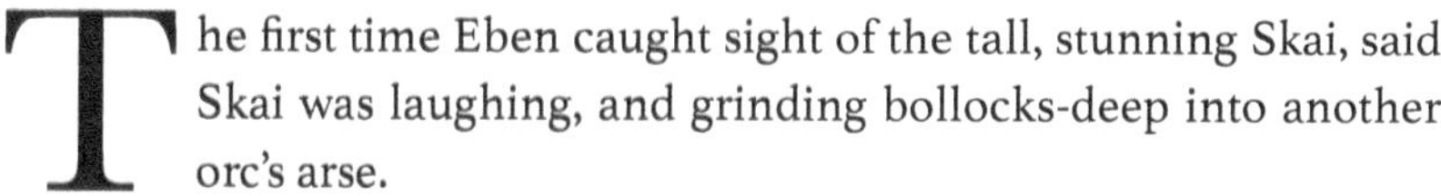

The first time Eben caught sight of the tall, stunning Skai, said Skai was laughing, and grinding bollocks-deep into another orc's arse.

"Ach, you like that?" the Skai said, his voice hungry and low. "Wish for more?"

The bent-over orc—another Skai, by the scent of it—groaned and nodded, his claws dragging against the wall. And behind him, the tall orc laughed again as he drew himself out, slowly revealing a long, slick, heavily scarred prick. A prick that looked just as dangerous as the rest of him, what with his tall, muscled grey body, his long black claws, and his messy black topknot, with a gleaming steel *dagger* casually stabbed through it.

But he was still smiling down at the groaning orc, his dark eyes warm and approving, his claws slowly dragging down the orc's sides—and in a sharp snap of hips, he slammed back inside. Burying himself deep in one swift, stabbing stroke, while the orc yelped and shuddered upon him.

Eben shivered too, and his grip on the bottle of tonic in his hand had slackened, enough that it nearly dropped to the floor. But he fumbled and caught it just in time, gripping it with shaky fingers, clutching it close to his wildly thudding heartbeat.

Foolish. Foolish, to notice such things. Foolish to care. He could have a good hard ploughing anytime he wished, and many of the orcs who frequented the Ka-esh *dýflissa* were just as commanding, just as handsome. And like most of the Ka-esh, this Skai was keeping to his own clan for his pleasures, for it was easier that way. Safer. Most of all when it came to Clan Skai.

*Never trust a Skai*, Eben's father had warned him again and again, all through the years of his youth. *Never let one touch you or find you alone. Instead you run as deep as you can, until you find a tunnel you can collapse behind you.*

Eben had studiously heeded the warning, and all the dark tales that had whispered and festered beneath it. Skai were greedy. Lawless. Reckless. Dangerous. And even now, so many summers after his father's passing, Eben still kept a careful distance—to the point where his boss Efterar, the mountain's Chief Healer, had needed to prod him to bring up this tonic to Dvergr, whose room was deep in the Skai wing.

*You'll be perfectly safe*, Efterar had said in his usual matter-of-fact way, giving a firm clasp of his hand to Eben's shoulder. *No Skai's going to look twice at you.*

Eben had nodded and obeyed, though the unease had kept twisting, tangling with something damnably like fear, as he'd quietly crept through the Skai wing, sniffing out Dvergr's distant scent. *Perfectly safe. No Skai's going to look twice at you.*

But now—Eben's breath caught as the tall, lean Skai laughed again, and ground in deeper—maybe Eben *wanted* a Skai to look at him. Wanted *this* Skai to look at him, with that easy, greedy grin, those warm, approving eyes. But those eyes were still fixed on the bent-over orc, and one of those clawed hands was digging into the orc's trembling flank, while the other hand gave a ringing little slap to his arse.

"More, sweet thing," the tall Skai ordered, husky but firm. "Know you can milk me harder than this, ach?"

The orc choked and nodded, his face contorting with palpable effort, and behind him the tall orc rasped out a low groan, his head tilting back. "Ach, that's good," he breathed, his hands stroking with obvious approval. "Don't stop."

The scent of his pleasure was now unfurling through the air, simmering sweet and heavy in Eben's nostrils. Strong enough to set his own prick stirring, the hunger coiling deep in his belly—and he flinched at the feel of it, jerked a hard shake of his head.

No. No. *Foolish.* The orc was Skai, reckless, dangerous, and openly fucking in the corridors was against the rules now, not that any Skai had ever seemed to notice. And—a sharp pang caught and twisted in Eben's chest as he watched the orc's stroking hands—maybe these orcs were... mated. Maybe the tall Skai was bound to the bent-over one. For as long as Eben could remember, Skai had refused to take other orcs as mates, or even offer them fidelity—until a few moons before, when the Skai had finally come together to alter their customs and recognize such bonds. And this tall, stunning Skai could have his choice of mates, could he not? Could pick from any number of eager worshippers, willing to bend and kneel, and offer him the fealty he deserved...

Foolish, *foolish*, and Eben squeezed his eyes shut, and forced himself to move again. To step that way, over there, toward Dvergr's distant scent, away...

"Looking for something, Ka-esh?" cut in a voice, and Eben gasped and startled, whipped around to where the tall Skai was—looking at him. Looking at him, oh, his brow creasing, even as he kept grinding into the other orc's upraised rump. "Not lost, are you?"

Eben nearly dropped the tonic again, but he clutched it closer against his chest, and desperately fought to find his voice. "I am seeking—Dvergr," he said, in a cracked, croaking whisper. "Wish to give him—tonic. Medicine. From the sickroom."

He winced even as he spoke, shaking his head, because curse him, from where else could the tonic have come—but the tall orc's mouth drew into a smile again, quick and easy and approving. "Ach, I see," he replied, with a sideways jerk of his dagger-adorned head. "Good of you to bring it. An' he's just down that way, ach? Keep turning left, you can't miss him."

Right. Eben rapidly nodded, too hard and urgent, but his feet seemed frozen in place, his eyes fixed on the orc's face. On that warm, genial smile, so stunning, so approving. And not fading even a little as Eben kept standing there staring, his face flooding with heat and shame and longing...

"Just come back if you get lost," the orc's voice continued, as his clawed hands spread wider against the orc's hips, his own hips moving more leisurely now, his fat, scarred, dripping length slipping in and out with brazen, astonishing ease. "I can show you the way, ach?"

Oh. Oh, fuck. And the orc even winked at Eben—*winked*, at him!—as he kept sliding in and out of the other orc's rump. As if he wanted Eben to look, as if he liked him looking, liked making him hot and flustered and—

And miserable. Miserable, or even despairing, because there was no way. No way something like this would ever end well. No way this Skai wouldn't crush Eben underfoot, and leave him ruined and empty.

*Never trust a Skai. Never let one touch you, or get you alone...*

And with a jolt, a flinch, a frantic gulp from his throat, Eben spun around, and fled.

# 2

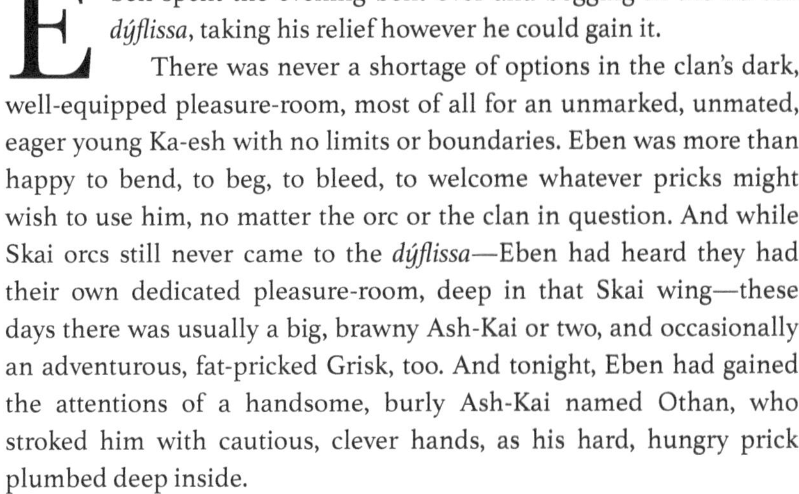

Eben spent the evening bent over and begging in the Ka-esh *dýflissa*, taking his relief however he could gain it.

There was never a shortage of options in the clan's dark, well-equipped pleasure-room, most of all for an unmarked, unmated, eager young Ka-esh with no limits or boundaries. Eben was more than happy to bend, to beg, to bleed, to welcome whatever pricks might wish to use him, no matter the orc or the clan in question. And while Skai orcs still never came to the *dýflissa*—Eben had heard they had their own dedicated pleasure-room, deep in that Skai wing—these days there was usually a big, brawny Ash-Kai or two, and occasionally an adventurous, fat-pricked Grisk, too. And tonight, Eben had gained the attentions of a handsome, burly Ash-Kai named Othan, who stroked him with cautious, clever hands, as his hard, hungry prick plumbed deep inside.

"Ach, sweet Ka-esh," Othan grunted, falling free of Eben's spasming body with a squelch, before plunging back inside, seating himself deep in a single unbroken stroke. "Can you always take it this easy and deep? Ach, I ken I have reached your"—he gasped, as Eben purposefully clutched him—"your *heart*."

It betrayed a shocking lack of anatomical awareness, or even basic education, but in this moment, Eben didn't care. Not with this much hard prick buried inside him, taking pleasure with him, pumping its seed deep. Not as deep as that Skai would have gone, no, and Othan's prick didn't boast a single scar, either. But Othan was fucking Eben, now, and Eben belatedly, fervently nodded, clamping tighter against that thick pulsing prick.

"You can go harder, too, if you like," he breathed over his shoulder, his usual hesitations blessedly buried beneath the pleasure and the frenzy, the stark desperate craving. "Use your claws and teeth, or a switch, or a whip. Whatever you please."

But behind him, Othan's chuckle was hoarse and disbelieving, his big hands carefully caressing Eben's shivering flanks. "Couldn't harm you, sweet Ka-esh," he gasped. "Wish for your joy, ach?"

Eben had to choke down the surge of dark, bitter frustration, but he appeased himself with driving back deeper onto Othan's prick, sinking into the sensation of it, the challenge of gripping it as hard as he could, locking it into place. And that was enough to make Othan wrench all over, crying out shocked and shrill—and yes, yes, there was his seed, flooding fast and abundant into Eben, filling his empty places from the bottom up, until he felt almost full, almost, *almost* content.

Afterwards, Othan wanted to kiss and cuddle him, but Eben suddenly couldn't bear his touch, the longing in his eyes—and his desperate glance around the room thankfully settled on Gareth, who'd just finished with the excessively beautiful Julian, his first fuck of the evening. And Gareth was a good friend, a generous Ka-esh clanmate, because upon seeing the look on Eben's face, he instantly came over toward them. Not sparing a single glance for Othan as he smiled at Eben, and reached to slide a slow, suggestive hand against his arse.

"Ready for more, brother?" Gareth asked, and yes, he was already turning Eben around, guiding him away from Othan. "Wish for some steel in your rump, this time?"

Eben furiously nodded, and shot what he hoped was an apologetic smile toward Othan's rather crestfallen face. And when Gareth shoved Eben double, he gratefully arched and opened for Gareth's familiar prick, hissing with the sweet, stunning pain of it slamming inside.

The pain was due to Gareth's multiple solid steel piercings, which were embedded not only in his cleft, but all the way down his shaft. They'd sent more than one orc to the sickroom, Eben knew, but he usually had enough control to handle it, to make himself open when he needed to, and not to let that steel-studded head anywhere near the delicate tissues deeper within. But today, his control seemed frayed, lost somewhere else, and he choked aloud at the sudden scrape of pain, the distinct scent of blood as Gareth drew out again.

"All right, brother?" Gareth asked behind him, his voice sharp with genuine concern, and Eben had to draw in a shaky breath, squeezing his eyes shut. No. Foolish. He would not weep over being asked a stupid single question, and he knew Gareth didn't care, not like that. As thoughtful and considerate as Gareth usually was, Eben knew how deeply he longed for someone who would fight him over the pain, who would greet his grating invading steel with vengeance and teeth. But Eben was not that kind of orc, had never been that kind of orc, Eben wanted... he wanted...

"Ach, I am well," Eben belatedly replied, and then he twitched and gasped at the sweet, surprising sensation of Gareth's breath, his slick seeking tongue, delving into his open, dripping crease, licking at his fresh wound. A gift, truly, and Eben fought to keep Othan's seed inside, away from Gareth's lovely licking mouth. "Th-thank you."

He could already feel the pain prickling, fading beneath the wondrous analgesic of orc saliva, and when Gareth stood tall behind him again, perhaps hesitating, Eben blatantly arched and opened himself, as wide as he could. Shuddering at the feel of Othan's hot seed escaping, streaking liberally down his trembling thighs, but he knew Gareth didn't care about other orcs' seed on his prick, and oh, he was already leaning forward and nudging in again, more gently this time.

"You are sure?" Gareth asked, pushing in with a little more certainty, until Eben stopped it, clamped him tightly in place. "Naught is amiss? I thought"—his voice dropped as he drew out again—"you should have welcomed an orc such as Othan ploughing you thus, and wishing to tend you and fuss over you, after."

Eben couldn't hide his wince, or his shameful, foolish reply, not with the beautiful strength of Gareth's steel dragging deep inside him. "Ach, I should have welcomed this," he gasped, squeezing his eyes shut. "But today, I was in the—Skai wing, and I—"

His voice failed him there, his thoughts blooming with the vision of the tall Skai's fat, scarred, dripping prick, his quick, approving smile.

While behind him, Gareth's thrusts slowed, and Eben could feel his focus now, could taste the surprise in his scent. "You did not—mate with a Skai, did you?" he asked. "I cannot scent this upon you...?"

He left the question dangling, and Eben shook his head, shoved back a little harder onto that scraping steel. "No," he said, too insistent, too betraying. "But I—"

He... what? He could have done it? He'd wanted to do it? He'd wanted to wander aimlessly about the Skai wing, and then turn around, and find that tall, smiling orc again. And in another realm, one where Eben was calm and confident and desirable, he might have smiled and said, *It turns out I am lost after all, good sir. Would you show me the way?*

*Foolish*, his distant thoughts chanted, and he again shook his head, focused on staying soft for that sweet sliding steel. "It was foolish," he croaked. "There was just one who was—kind. Helped me. Not like—I thought."

He winced again, shaking his head, because a moment's kindness in a corridor had nothing to do with an entire clan's sins, with the path of Ka-esh grief and devastation the Skai had left in their wake for the past half-century. And it made no sense for Eben to even notice that Skai, or care, let alone to have him ruin a perfectly good evening of perfectly good ploughing pricks.

"You ken we cannot judge a whole clan upon the actions of some, many years past," came Gareth's slow, thoughtful voice behind Eben, in strong contrast to how his steel-studded prick was sinking in faster now, scattering out jolts of pain and pleasure around it. "You ken the Skai have new leaders now, and they are seeking these new ways, ach? And seeking to make amends for their past sins."

Eben nodded, shifting his upper body heavier against the wall, feeling the welcome scrape of rough stone against his sweaty skin. "But they still aren't even following the rules," he gasped, because it was the only safe statement he could grasp at, in the whirling mess now clouding his thoughts. "They were openly fucking in the corridor!"

His voice came out sounding inordinately irate, and he fully deserved Gareth's amused chuckle behind him, the sharper thrust of his hips. "I had you outside the forge just last week, did I not?" he said wryly. "What is the harm, if there are only orcs of age within scenting distance? We all know what is afoot, whether it is before our eyes, or no."

But there *was* a harm, Eben's aggravated thoughts pointed out. A harm of some clumsy, unsuspecting fool Ka-esh walking past, and not being able to look away. Not being able to stop thinking of that tall, stunning Skai, and his beautiful scarred prick. A prick that would be a true joy to milk and squeeze, to welcome deep inside, into one's most tender places...

And it would be a joy to drink from, too. For those scars, those teeth-marks, laddered up the Skai's prick, meant that he often offered the gift of his fresh blood and seed together—and there was no other taste like it in all the realm. Eben's own extensive research had suggested that there was no other nourishment like it, either, nothing else that would better fatten a sick or weakened or weary orc.

And even the thought of it, of that stunning smiling Skai offering it, was drawing up Eben's bollocks, coiling the longing tight and close. But he suddenly couldn't bear to empty himself on the vision of this, the too-powerful memory of this, and therefore welcome even more of that Skai's destruction, his devastation, without even a touch—

"Could you use—the switch," he gasped over his shoulder. "Or the whip. Please."

Gareth's breath huffed against Eben's sweaty back, but he accordingly reached up to the well-stocked wall beside them, and pulled down a short, coiled whip. But even as he unfurled it, giving an experimental little snap into the air, his other hand stroked at Eben's flank, perhaps felt the heavy dragging of his gasping breaths.

"There's naught wrong with broadening your view of others, as you grow older and wiser," Gareth's low voice said, even as the whip's fall gently teased at Eben's back. "And naught wrong with desiring a Skai, either."

Eben knew that, of course he knew that—broadening views along with desires was embedded deep in the Ka-esh clan's very soul, was it not? And he rapidly, fervently nodded, but the lash still didn't strike, just kept taunting and trailing like that, making him pay attention, making him listen.

"I ken you only need to learn more," Gareth continued, slower. "To mayhap watch them for a spell, and see what they do, and how they live. How they treat their kin and those they care for. What they long for, in their kin, and their mates. And then, after this"—a very gentle, teasing swat of the lash—"you can choose what to do with this. Whether you should welcome a Skai into your life, or your bed."

It was sound advice, Eben could admit, and far more generous than he likely deserved. And far more presumptuous, too, because Eben wasn't nearly interesting or compelling enough for any Skai to want in his bed, most of all a Skai like that—but even so, he couldn't help his swift, grateful smile over his shoulder, his eyes warm on Gareth's flushed face. Feeling how Gareth's cock had swelled larger, too, scraping his walls with that sweet sharp steel, while the whip raised high, quivering in the air...

And with a hiss and a splatter, Eben was breaking beneath the lash, the Skai finally, blissfully forgotten amidst the pain and the screams.

# 3

For the next few weeks, Eben followed Gareth's good guidance, and just... observed.

It was his natural state, borne of many years of shyness, self-consciousness, and solitary, scholarly pursuits. And though he only caught a few brief glimpses of the tall, smiling orc from the corridor, he instead focused his attention on the Skai orcs he did encounter, most of whom had ended up in the sickroom with various illnesses or injuries.

And the more Eben observed, the more he found himself... surprised. Many of the Skai bore harsh faces and curt, dismissive demeanours, which—together with all the tales and warnings—had always been enough to keep him at a safe, careful distance. But upon further inspection, even when a wounded Skai snapped sharply at the sickroom staff, or glowered viciously toward any other patients who came too close, he would frequently soften when offered any kind of unexpected generosity, or when loved ones came to visit. A huge, horribly injured orc named Ulfarr had nearly wept when his friend Killik had shown up with a basket of snacks, and Simon, the massive and terrifying Enforcer of Orc Mountain, had fully ignored his painful cracked femur in favour of doting upon his mate and son from his bed.

And when Eben had gathered his courage one afternoon, and

collected some sweet treats from the kitchen to distribute to a handful of wounded Skai, they'd been surprised, and grateful, and even *kind*—at least, until one big, blood-covered warrior had blatantly looked Eben up and down, and invited him into his bed. An invitation that had instantly sent Eben fleeing back for the safety of his workbench, while Efterar had snapped a sharp reprimand across the room. And in return, the orc—much to Eben's surprise—had blushed, and winced, and *apologized*.

But the most enlightening situation of all happened perhaps a half-moon later, with the unexpected arrival of a new patient—a blonde, grievously injured human woman named Alma. Her pale, weakened body had been covered with contusions and lacerations, and she'd inhaled smoke and particulates at length, before almost drowning in a river. She had only survived thanks to a daring rescue by a prominent Grisk orc named Baldr, who served as the Left Hand to Orc Mountain's captain—but during the rescue, Alma and Baldr had formed a deep, irrevocable scent-bond. Which wasn't surprising, perhaps, given the high emotions and close physical proximity inherent in such an event—except for the fact that Baldr was already mated to the mountain's Right Hand, a tall, glowering Skai named Drafli.

Eben had always found Drafli highly alarming, for he seemed the epitome of the cold, vicious, dangerous Skai. He prowled instead of walked, he reeked of human blood and death, and he only spoke with sharp, furious gestures, due to having had his throat cut by humans, whom he had then gone and killed with his bare hands. Drafli was widely acclaimed as the best, most terrifying fighter in the mountain, and Eben had often heard hushed, awed whispers of his many exploits in the Skai arena—along with his many conquests in pleasure, none of whom he had ever appeared to notice, let alone favour.

But at some point the year before, Drafli had strongly endorsed that change to the Skai mating customs, and had immediately sworn vows to this Baldr. Drafli had been the first Skai in living history to take an orc mate... and now, not even a full year later, his new mate had turned about and formed a permanent, unbreakable scent-bond with a human woman.

It was a situation that would have been highly trying for any orc, especially a Skai as notorious as Drafli—but to Eben's genuine astonishment, Drafli hadn't shown even the slightest hint of anger toward his wayward mate. Each night, once most of the sickroom's inhabitants were asleep, Drafli and Baldr would come and sit beside the unconscious Alma's bed, and Drafli would firmly caress Baldr, and kiss his hair. And even across the room, Eben could easily trace their fresh strong scents upon one another, untainted by any others. Meaning that Drafli had continued to bed his mate, and favour him, despite the betrayal of the scent-bond with the woman.

"You should leave me, Draf," Eben heard Baldr whisper into Drafli's neck, on the third night of this. "Go find someone else. Someone stronger. Better."

There were no other orcs awake in the room to hear this—Efterar and his ever-present mate Kesst had gone out together on a call—and Eben held his breath as he listened, his body quiet and unmoving behind his workbench. Waiting, watching, as Drafli wordlessly hissed back at his mate, his clawed hands snapping out movements between them—speaking something in the Skai clan's sign language, something Baldr answered with a choked sob, and a shake of his head.

But Drafli said it again, and again—and when Baldr kept weeping, Drafli whirled up, grasped him by the neck, and... *attacked.* Shoving Baldr down hard to the bed, so he could straddle over him, and... *kiss* him.

Oh. Ohhhh. Eben startled, his breath choking in his throat—but if they'd noticed him, neither of them seemed to care. Instead, Baldr's eyes had fluttered with palpable longing, his body pressing into the scrape of Drafli's claws, the deep, dragging bite of his kiss. And when Drafli drew away, and then shoved Baldr over onto his front, Baldr only moaned and arched for him, even when Drafli's clawed hand yanked down his trousers, exposing Baldr's muscled, trembling arse to the room.

For a breath, Drafli only gazed down at that bared arse with hooded eyes, his hand curving slow and proprietary over its smooth green skin—and then he shoved at his own trousers, too. Releasing his own long, bobbing, leaking prick, with vivid scars laddered all the way up its grey length.

Eben shivered all over, his vision briefly blurring, and suddenly it was as though he was back in the corridor, watching that tall, laughing Skai. Because Drafli's prick looked far too much the same, jutting hard and hungry from above sagging trousers, seeking its way between quivering arse-cheeks... and then slamming deep with a sharp slap of skin, while his helpless lover gasped and writhed beneath it.

Fuck. And though a distant part of Eben pointed out that this was certainly against the rules—what with all the sleeping patients in the room—he couldn't seem to move, let alone speak, caught in the vision before his eyes. Baldr flinching and writhing and moaning beneath his Skai mate's onslaught, the look on his face pulling low and familiar in Eben's belly, whispering of that perfect mingled pleasure and pain...

Drafli even kept speaking in their sign language as he drove inside, one hand swiftly moving before Baldr's fluttering eyes, while his mouth kissed and scraped at Baldr's shoulder. As his hips kept snapping him in deeper, faster, flooding all his mate's senses at once—and Eben nearly staggered beneath the scent of Baldr's lurching, shattering release, sweeping across the room, while Drafli's thrusts slowed into sweet, steady circles, his lips gently kissing at his trembling mate's neck.

It was a dazzling display of skill and force and tenderness, the kind of attention that would have had Eben blatantly spreading and begging in the *dýflissa*. And before he could compromise himself any further, he belatedly rushed for the sickroom's back latrine, yanked down his trousers, and took his own straining prick in hand. And as he stroked, the visions swarming his scattering thoughts were again all that tall, laughing Skai in the corridor, touching his own bent-over lover with that same heady blend of skill, tenderness, and command. Sliding his fat, scarred length in and out, again and again, while the orc moaned and shuddered beneath his sharp claws, that firm slap of his hand...

Eben gasped as his release sprayed out, shooting down the latrine in furious arcs of spurting seed and sweet, shattering pleasure. *You like that? More, sweet thing. I can show you the way...*

But once it was done, Eben's body felt shaky and weak, his heartbeat pounding far too loud against his ribs, his skull. And he sank heavily back to the nearest wall, gulping down deep breaths, and rubbing at his eyes.

Fuck, what had come over him? He was only meant to be observing, learning, not drowning in lust over a random Skai in the corridor. And not longing for what he'd just witnessed, either, aching all over at the thought of a deadly, capable mate who would offer such loyalty, such unflinching care and kindness, even amidst his own loss and pain...

It took far too long for Eben to collect himself, to walk on shaky legs back out toward the sickroom. Where he instantly caught sight of Baldr, now sprawled in the bed with his eyes closed, his scent speaking of quiet, steady sleep. While Drafli was... he was...

Drafli was standing tall and silent over the sleeping woman's bed, and holding a sharpened dagger over her throat.

# 4

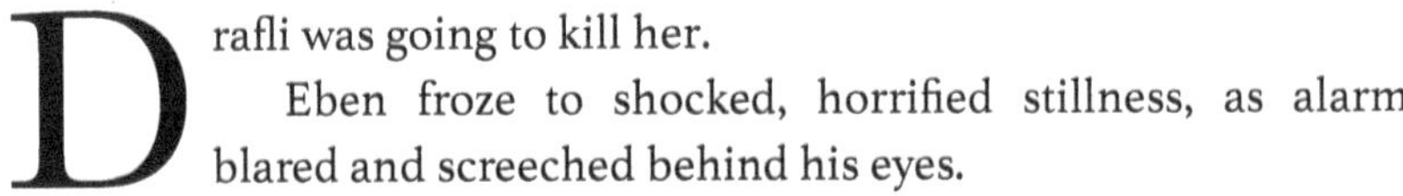

Drafli was going to kill her.

Eben froze to shocked, horrified stillness, as alarm blared and screeched behind his eyes.

*Never trust a Skai, never trust a Skai...*

Drafli's head whipped around toward Eben with sudden, deadly purpose, his eyes snapped to narrow slits, his lip curled to show all his sharp teeth. As if he would kill Eben, too, without hesitation or regret—and Eben needed to run, to hide, to collapse the nearest tunnel behind him. Or maybe dash back into the latrine and cower in a corner, wait for the sweet scent of human blood to filter through the air...

But no. No. He couldn't. He *couldn't*. The woman was a patient, she was defenseless, she was Eben's responsibility. And that certainty was enough to make Eben draw in a shaky, shallow breath, to focus his hazy eyes on the vicious, murderous Skai with the dagger. The Skai who looked so, so different from how he'd looked only a short time ago, when he'd tended to his distraught mate with such intent, ardent care.

And that was something, something, and Eben drew in more breath, desperately gathered his courage. "It will n-not—work," he croaked, into the empty, crackling silence. "To break the s-scent-bond. You will only—h-hurt your mate."

Drafli's flashing eyes darted back toward Baldr's sleeping body in the bed, and Eben clutched for the doorframe at his side, and hauled down another breath. "Y-you would not wish him b-bonded to a corpse in a crypt," he gulped. "And you would not wish him to—know, with every scent, that this was—your doing. This should—p-poison you, and him, and this—this deep trust you have, between you. This—gift."

He was fully trembling by the end of it, his claws clattering against the stone of the doorframe. And for an instant, staring at Drafli's coiled body, Eben was certain he would still do it. He would slit the woman's throat, and then hurl the dagger straight at Eben, too...

But then, Drafli—closed his eyes. Tilted his head back, as if in a brief, desperate prayer. And then he spun and stalked for the door, his shoulders rigid, his gleaming dagger still clasped tightly in his fist. And that might have been a faint, visceral shudder, quivering up his bare back, as he spun into the corridor, and vanished from sight.

Fuck. Eben didn't know how long he stood there, clinging to the wall, staring at the empty doorway, while his heart hammered sick and dizzying in his throat. *Never trust a Skai.*

He only vaguely noticed Efterar and Kesst finally returning to the sickroom, both their scents reeking of exhaustion. And though neither of them spared Eben a glance before falling into their own bed together, it was enough that Eben could somehow move again, could pry his numb fingers from the doorframe, and then stagger toward the door. Toward the Ka-esh wing. Toward—the *dýflissa.*

As always, it offered distraction and relief and pain, and as many dominant, powerful orcs as Eben could ask for. Some of them seeking his pleasure, some of them only his screams—but no matter how much Eben begged for more, none of it was strong enough to fully clear the chaotic mess clouding his thoughts. And finally he dragged his sore, sweaty, bloody body back through the long corridors to his cold, empty bedroom.

*Foolish*, he told himself, as he lay there alone in his hard bunk, the pain pulsing through his torn back, his still-slack arse. *Foolish.* He'd done his job tonight, he'd helped protect his patient, and that was all. And in truth, he'd faced far worse throughout the course of his career as a medic, hadn't he? He'd witnessed horrifying grief and pain and regret, he'd wept as he'd heard dying orcs' last words, he'd saved and lost too many lives to count. So why did he even care so much about these damned Skai? Why was he still thinking about that laughing orc from the corridor, all these weeks later? Why was he still caught on this, trapped in this, when he had his own life, his own work, and as many willing Ka-esh lovers as he could ever ask for?

*You never focus on what is important*, Eben could still hear his father saying, with his typical frustration and disappointment leaching bitterly through his scent. *You waste your talent and your time. You do a deep disservice to all your Ka-esh kin. You show yourself foolish and weak.*

Eben sighed and shoved over in the bed, yanking the blanket off his sore back, but the ache was still there, scraping across his skin, wrenching deep in his belly. He'd tried, with his father. He'd tried so hard to please him, to study mathematics and geology, to become a master Ka-esh engineer. Just as his father had been, and his father before him.

But it had been such dull, dreary work, dragging at Eben's energy and his motivation. And his spare time spent with human anatomy books and medical research had been so much more intriguing, with so many more unexplored possibilities. There was just so much about orc biology that was yet fully unknown—from their inherent healing abilities, to the many properties of seed and saliva and blood, to the mysteries and devastating dangers of orc-human reproduction.

Eben's own mother had died during his birth, which he knew had happened in wartime, in highly unsanitary conditions deep underground. And thanks to his studies, he'd also learned that his own relatively small size was due at least in part to the fact that his mother would have seen little sun during her pregnancy, if at all—and she'd likely been lacking in the crucial nutrients humans needed from fruit, grains, and cooked meat.

And perhaps it was Eben's guilt and grief over his mother's death that had kept driving him back to those human textbooks again and again. Seeking out the answers that could help prevent such unnecessary deaths in the future, and maybe even help rebuild their species. And eventually Eben had progressed to making his own notes, too, keeping his own journals, and hiding it all from his increasingly enraged father.

*You told them you wish to specialize in medicine, like a human?* his father had demanded after a particularly trying day, during which a teenage Eben's distraction on a tunnel dig had led to the loss of three entire days' work. *You told them you wish to never dig a tunnel again?!*

Eben certainly hadn't meant to admit such things, let alone to fellow students who had become increasingly contemptuous toward him and his intelligence. But the grating endless tedium had been so strong, so utterly overwhelming, that he'd finally confessed it all to his father between gulping, gasping sobs. *I want to study medicine. I care about it, and I'm good at it. I want to learn, and help people. I want to help save our kin.*

His father had listened in stony silence, his scent hardening with every breath, and when Eben had finally finished, his father had raised himself tall, and pointed at the door. *Get out,* he'd said. *And do not return here or speak to me again, until you come to your senses.*

So Eben had left their familiar *hellir*, embedded deep with the scents of his ancestors, and with many scents of his own far happier childhood. And he'd gone as far away as he could, to the very edge of the Ka-esh wing, and found a small, dry room to sleep in. And he'd been here ever since, summer after summer, changing his path whenever he scented his father nearby, and averting his eyes whenever they met in a corridor. Until one morning he'd realized he hadn't scented his father in many days, and when he'd finally dared to return to the *hellir*, he'd found his father gravely ill and incoherent, scenting of whispering death.

So Eben had cared for his ill father with the full extent of his knowledge, easing the pain with the strongest herbs, bringing him fresh blood to drink, moving him regularly, even licking his bedsores to help him heal. And while it had without question made his father's final weeks more peaceful, it still hadn't saved his life—and Eben still didn't know if his father had even recognized him, let alone understood all that he'd done.

Eben was somehow weeping into his fur, the water streaking off his face in hot rivulets, the ache clutching again and again at his heaving chest. And here was the damned vision of the Skai again, smiling at him, so confident, so certain, so... pleased. So blithely, genuinely pleased by Eben's bringing his clanmate tonic, to the point where he'd offered his help. Maybe even his... pleasure.

*Ach, I see. Good of you to bring it. Just come back if you get lost. I can show you the way.*

It again heated in Eben's belly, so starkly, impossibly powerful, and tangling with it now were the clashing visions of Drafli, too. Cradling his lost mate so tenderly in his arms, drawing out his pleasure with such focused, single-minded purpose, as if he would never stop caring for him, would never hurt him or let him go...

And the way he'd stood over that sleeping woman, with pure hatred in his eyes, and his dagger flashing over her throat. Ready to kill a weakened, already-wounded patient, to snuff out her entire life, because she'd committed the unforgivable sin of being rescued by his mate, and succumbing to an orc-induced biological response she surely hadn't even known existed.

*Never trust a Skai. Never let one touch you, or get you alone...*

But Eben's sobs wouldn't stop coming, wracking through his aching body again and again and again. Until finally they drew him down with them, and locked him into lonely, empty sleep.

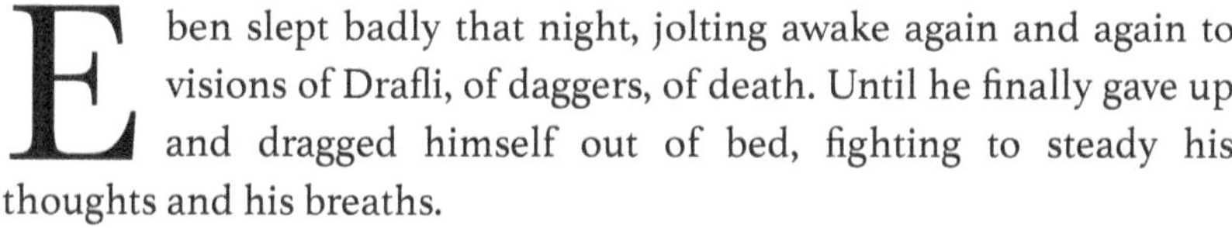

# 5

Eben slept badly that night, jolting awake again and again to visions of Drafli, of daggers, of death. Until he finally gave up and dragged himself out of bed, fighting to steady his thoughts and his breaths.

Perhaps last night had just been—a mistake, for Drafli. A moment of weakness. Perhaps he had learned his lesson, and would henceforth stay out of the sickroom, well away from the woman, where he could resist any murderous impulses he felt toward her. And perhaps if Baldr stayed away long enough, the scent-bond would eventually weaken, and this entire situation could be forgotten.

Eben's cautious optimism rose once he reached the sickroom, and found no sign or scent of Drafli or Baldr whatsoever. Alma's condition had also continued to improve overnight, to the point where Efterar had finally deemed her well enough to awaken—and she soon proved to be a shy, polite woman, who greeted the sickroom staff with quiet, earnest gratefulness.

"I—I'm truly sorry to have inconvenienced you, sir," she told Efterar, her voice thin and raspy through her still-compromised throat. "If you'd be so kind as to draw up the bill, I will—"

But Efterar firmly waved the matter away, as always, and began his usual patient briefing, while Eben pulled over Alma's chart and began adding notes. As usual, he and his fellow Ka-esh medic Salvi had been mixing daily tonics specifically tailored toward Efterar's ongoing assessments of her needs, and this would surely provide some helpful insights, and—

And then Baldr burst into the room, his eyes wide and panicked, his scent reeking of alarm. Suggesting, damn it, that the scent-bond was still exerting a considerable draw upon him, enough that he'd been able to sense Alma's awakening, from wherever he'd been. But wait, he'd likely been with *Drafli*—and yes, there, the scent faint but coming closer, was Drafli himself.

Eben's heart jolted in his chest, and his sweaty, shaky hand abruptly dropped his quill, smearing ink all over Alma's chart. Curse it, curse it—and though Eben frantically fought to mop it up, he didn't miss Alma's genuine-seeming pleasure upon seeing Baldr, or Baldr's ever-increasing scent of alarm as he also glanced toward the door. Toward where Drafli was now striding into the room, his head held high, his clawed hands hanging with dangerous casualness at his sides.

Eben only distantly noticed his own ink-stained hands clutching at the workbench, his heartbeat hammering louder in his ears. What would Drafli do now? Would he pull out a dagger, threaten Alma again, kill her before they'd even seen him move? Or, perhaps he would finally punish his mate for having succumbed to the call of the scent-bond, against whatever self-control he'd clearly found for the past day?

But in a jerky movement, Baldr spun and rushed straight toward Drafli, relief reeling through his scent. And rather than refusing, or pushing his mate away, Drafli instantly drew him closer. Sinking a possessive hand into Baldr's hair, guiding his head into his own shoulder, even as his eyes dangerously narrowed, glowering toward Alma in the bed.

Alma blanched, clutching her blanket to her chin, the scent of her fear sharpening in the air—and wait, wait, Drafli and Baldr were both moving *toward* her. Toward her, rather than away. And what the hell were they doing, was Baldr... making *introductions*?!

But no one in the room seemed to notice, or share Eben's rapidly rising panic. Efterar had already turned away to another patient, while beside Eben, Salvi was actually attempting to talk to him, speaking words Eben couldn't even slightly hear through the shrieking in his ears, and the scent of Drafli's ever-rising rage in his nostrils. A scent that was far too similar to the night before, to that moment when he'd held that dagger over Alma's throat—

Eben's body was already lurching, staggering over toward them, when suddenly Drafli spun around and stalked toward the door, his eyes blazing, his hands in fists. Leaving Baldr to trail unhappily after him, his scent reeking of misery and pain, while Alma had already curled up beneath her fur, and the sounds of her soft, sniffling sobs began scraping through the room.

"You all right, brother?" Salvi's distant voice cut in, as his elbow nudged into Eben's side. "Not feeling ill yourself, are you?"

Eben's breath exhaled in a harsh, shaky sigh, and he rapidly shook his head, and forced his focus back to his work. But it was a miserable way to spend a morning, breathing in the scents of a helpless human's anguish, while casting constant worried glances toward the door. And even when Alma fell asleep again, Eben could still scarcely concentrate, making multiple foolish errors mixing his tonics, until Salvi finally dragged him off for a meal with him and his Ka-esh mate Tristan. And while Eben considered them both good friends, and made a concerted attempt to chat and smile through his misery, he returned to work feeling even more bleary and exhausted than before.

But at least there had been no further sign of Drafli or Baldr, and Alma was awake again, sitting up in her bed, and even weakly smiling at Efterar's mate Kesst, who was clearly plying her with all his considerable charm. But Alma's eyes were still puffy and swollen, her scent laced with misery and unease that echoed Eben's own—especially when Kesst shot a sly, assessing glance across the room toward the workbench. Toward—Eben?

"Have you met any of our orcs yet?" Kesst asked Alma, his voice deceptively light. "If you're feeling up to it, maybe one of them could give you a tour? How about you, Eben?"

What? Wait, was Kesst implying that Eben—*liked* Alma? Like that? Enough to personally take her on a damned *tour*, where a murderous Drafli might emerge at any moment?! And curse it, Eben's hands were suddenly spasming again, sloshing his jar of blood thinner all over the workbench—to which Kesst triumphantly smirked, while Alma flushed, scenting of both flattery and chagrin. And beside Eben, Salvi cursed under his breath as he snatched Eben's priceless notebook to safety, and then tossed a rag into his hot face.

Eben wiped up the mess as well as he could, though his cheeks wouldn't stop burning, and he couldn't even hear the rest of their conversation through the ringing in his ears. But finally, it seemed that Kesst had offered to take Alma on the mountain tour himself, and soon they were leaving the room together, Alma's steps still slow and halting, while Kesst cheerfully chattered away beside her.

Eben helplessly watched them go, his miserable alarm jolting higher—surely even Drafli wouldn't attempt to kill Alma in the corridor, with multiple witnesses?—until Salvi bumped him with his shoulder, his familiar scent tasting of both amusement and exasperation. "What the hell's going on with you today, brother?" he asked under his breath. "You aren't actually interested in her, are you?"

In Eben's exhausted state, he couldn't stop his incredulous glare back, because Salvi should know better by now, shouldn't he? "*Ach*, no," he replied, too sharp. "I am only... tired, I ken."

He reflexively shifted on his feet as he spoke, wincing at the distant pain still nagging in his sore back and arse—and Salvi instantly followed the movement, comprehension flaring across his eyes. "Ach, now I follow," he said cheerfully. "Took things too far in the *dýflissa* again last night, then? Mayhap you should have Efterar take a look at it?"

He'd angled a meaningful glance across the room toward Efterar, who was blearily working over a sleeping Bautul patient, but Eben grimaced, shaking his head. "Ach, no," he said again. "It was foolish. I shall heal."

Salvi's sidelong glance was a little too knowing this time, but he shrugged, and dipped his quill in the ink. "I heard Othan was asking about you yesterday," he said, as he began writing in his notebook. "He's a decent fellow, ach? Would treat you like you're made of gold."

Eben grimaced again, frowning down at his own notebook, as yet more misery plunged in his belly. Because that wasn't at all what he wanted, was it? He didn't want some bigger, stronger orc doting upon him, condescending to him, as if Eben was some kind of weak, fragile, stupid little pet... right? Or did he, and the memories of the laughing Skai orc were surging again, with his cool commands, his dragging, petting claws. *I can show you the way...*

And curse it, what the hell was wrong with Eben? Why was he still so caught on this? He'd surely observed more than enough Skai behaviour by now, to the point where he'd nearly witnessed a Skai murdering an innocent victim. He needed to pull himself together, and distance himself from this entire situation, and...

And just then, Alma rushed back into the room. Her head ducked low, her hands over her mouth, the bitter scents of her terror and pain swarming sudden and sickening through the air. And Eben couldn't move, couldn't think, as he watched her stagger toward her bed on shaky legs, before hurling her weakened body beneath her fur, and bursting into sobs.

"That vile prick Drafli," Kesst snarled from where he'd stalked in behind her, his eyes flashing on Efterar's confused face. "He was openly fucking Baldr in the baths, when he *knew* we were going that way! And then Drafli *lost* it on her, flailing and growling and spitting at her, while Alma begged and wept and *apologized* to him! Promised him she'd leave the mountain forever, so he'd never have to look at her again!"

Damn it. *Damn* it. Eben's stomach twisted and plunged, the bile roiling in his throat—so it hadn't been murder, but perhaps it very nearly had been. Perhaps it soon still would be. And what was he supposed to do, he should have told someone, he should have found help, confessed it all to someone stronger and wiser, who would know how to keep her safe. *Never trust a Skai, never, never, never...*

It was too close, too certain, too strong to bear, and Eben croaked an incoherent excuse to Salvi, and then rushed for the door. Not looking as he dodged into the corridor, his head ducked low, his breaths gasping and shallow, so thin he didn't even scent the orc striding around the corner—

Until he crashed straight into him.

The impact sent Eben reeling backwards, almost colliding with the wall behind him, as shock and humiliation flooded through his chest. And he couldn't even make his prickling eyes focus on the orc, the orc whose strong hands were grasping his shoulders, holding him still...

"Ach, Ka-esh!" the orc exclaimed, in a smooth, alarmingly familiar voice. "Watch where you're headed, ach?"

No. No, no, no. But Eben's blinking, burning eyes were squinting hard now, fighting to see in the too-bright light of the nearby lamp. And finding a handsome, horribly familiar face...

It was him. The laughing orc from the corridor. The Skai.

# 6

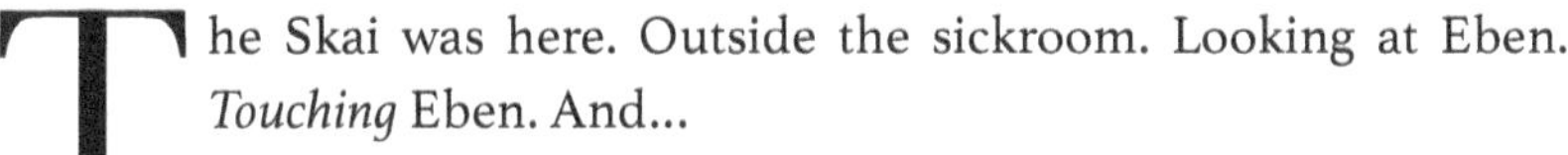

The Skai was here. Outside the sickroom. Looking at Eben. *Touching* Eben. And...

*Ach, Ka-esh! Watch where you're headed.*

And... chastising him. *Correcting* him.

The bitter, miserable humiliation swelled higher in Eben's chest, and he belatedly shook his head, squeezed his eyes shut. "I am—sorry," he gulped, without looking at the orc's face. "I only did not—"

But his voice broke there, because what? He hadn't looked? He hadn't scented? He was an orc, he was Ka-esh, he knew how to navigate without vision, had all his life, so why was he—why was he—

Why was he almost weeping, here in the damned corridor. What was wrong with him, what was happening to him, maybe he should march himself straight back to Efterar and—

"I am—sorry, sir," he gasped, pleading, blinking back up toward the orc's face. "It shall not—happen again."

He jerked backwards, twisting away, toward the distant safety of the Ka-esh wing—but nothing happened. Nothing moved. Because the orc's hands were still holding him here, his grip strong and firm against Eben's trembling shoulders.

"Ach, no need to apologize, Ka-esh!" the orc replied, a little rushed. "An' no need to scent thus, either! Didn't mean to vex you."

His voice had softened as he'd spoken, and Eben blinked blearily up at his handsome, too-close face, at the strange look in his eyes. At something almost like—concern?

"It is—quite all r-right," Eben stammered, his voice not even slightly his own. "I was—careless. Foolish."

The orc's brow creased, and one of his hands gave Eben's shoulder a little squeeze. "Ach, don't speak thus, Ka-esh," he said firmly. "No harm done, you ken?"

He squeezed Eben's shoulder again, his gaze searching but genial on Eben's face. On where Eben was blatantly staring back, curse it, and he swallowed hard, and attempted a nod. "Th-thank you," he croaked. "That is—very kind."

The orc flashed him a stunning, relieved smile, and gave a dismissive wave of his graceful, long-fingered hand. "No need to thank me, Ka-esh," he said. "Happy to help."

With that, he released Eben's arms, gave him a jaunty little wink, and then spun and strode toward... the sickroom. The sickroom? As if—he hadn't scented of illness, had he?

Eben wasn't moving, wasn't breathing, was now just straining to listen as the orc's voice carried out the sickroom door. "Just wanted to see how the new woman's faring," he was saying. "Can I bring her anything? Treats? A clean fur, mayhap?"

Eben blinked, because surely this orc had no association whatsoever with Alma... did he? Or perhaps—perhaps *he* was attempting to court her? Perhaps he carried that seemingly ubiquitous longing for women borne by so many of their kin?

Something cold had begun scraping up Eben's spine, and he was distantly gratified to hear Kesst's loud, derisive scoff. "What, have *you* developed a secret passion for Alma too, Tryggr?" he demanded. "Rest assured, she does not need any more Skai involvement in her life right now!"

Eben's body jolted all over, his heart skipping a beat in his chest. The orc's name was Tryggr. *Tryggr*. And Eben wanted to bless Kesst, curse Kesst, and what would this Tryggr say to being greeted like this, having his clan brought into this...

"Never spoken to the woman in my life," came Tryggr's voice, just a shade cooler than before. "An' haven't the slightest interest in her, either. But she's Boss's responsibility now, and since I'm working with Boss these days, I'm here to do my part."

Oh. Comprehension flared across Eben's thoughts, staggering him heavily against the nearby wall. This Tryggr worked with *Drafli*. And yes, Drafli did command his own small team of Skai scouts and fighters, didn't he? But... why would he send one of them to check on Alma? To help her? Because she was *Drafli's responsibility*?

Kesst seemed to share Eben's confusion, and another loud scoff filtered out through the doorway. "How is Alma Drafli's responsibility in any way whatsoever?" he demanded. "If you haven't heard, *he's* the one who just raged at her in the baths, and sent her running back here weeping!"

There was an instant's hanging silence, during which Eben fervently wished he could see this Tryggr's face—but when Tryggr spoke again, his voice was still smooth, almost deceptively easy. "Ach, I have heard of this, and wished to offer any help. But I'm glad you've got her looked after, and you'll keep a close eye on her, ach? Make sure she don't do anything rash?"

Kesst scoffed again, sounding highly affronted this time. "You can assure Drafli we have the situation well in hand," he drawled back. "And as if Alma's going to do anything rash in this state! Because of *him*!"

Another instant's stillness rang through the air, followed by a familiar low murmur—Efterar, no doubt seeking to settle his fractious mate. But there was no reply from this Tryggr, and suddenly he was—here. *Here*, striding out the sickroom door again, his head held high, his hands in fists—and no, Eben couldn't move in time, and Tryggr's shoulder knocked painfully into him, sending him reeling back against the wall.

Damn it, *damn* it, because Tryggr had already whirled around toward Eben, his eyes blazing. And Eben flinched, cringing backwards, bracing himself for this Tryggr's anger, or—or worse, his mockery. His inevitable realization that Eben had been shamefully lurking, eavesdropping on that entire conversation, and—

And then Tryggr's eyes... stilled. Softened. And that was a wry laugh, a shake of his head, as his hand came to Eben's shoulder, gave it a gentle squeeze.

"Sorry, Ka-esh," he said, hoarse. "Now I'm the one not seeing where I'm going! Some Skai I am, to not be able to walk down a hall without crashing."

He laughed again, but there was still a twinge of darkness in his eyes. And somehow Eben's commiseration was drowning out the alarm and shame, a wavering smile twitching at his mouth.

"N-no harm done," he managed, echoing Tryggr's own words from before. "Naught to apologize over."

The recognition shimmered across this Tryggr's eyes, and his smile flashed higher, warmer. "Ach, just so, Ka-esh," he replied. "Was just a bit worked up, I ken. That Ash-Kai is a real rabble-rouser, ain't he? No wonder you were in the same state last time we crashed. Must need a shocking amount of breaks, round here."

Oh. Eben couldn't help his own shaky laugh, or his deep, sudden surge of gratefulness toward this Tryggr. Because not only had Tryggr not judged him for lurking and eavesdropping in the corridor—but now he was identifying with him, and *sympathizing* with him, over *Kesst*. And while Eben personally found Kesst highly trying, he was also a very handsome, popular, charismatic orc, who was mated to the mountain's brilliant, universally respected Chief Healer—and thus, Eben had never heard anyone speak such blasphemy about him, not once. Or rather, not until now, until this Tryggr, and it felt warm and tenuous in his chest, almost about to burst. And Eben couldn't stop looking at Tryggr, smiling at Tryggr, even as his mouth opened on its own, about to say...

"But—why would Drafli send you to check on Alma?" his cursed voice asked, before he could stop it. "Or consider her—*his* responsibility? I thought..."

*I thought Drafli wanted to kill her*, he very nearly said, but he belatedly winced and clamped his fool mouth shut, and shook his head. What the hell was he saying, how had he become this much of a mess, he should still turn around and run, and...

"Ach, well, the woman's bonded to Boss's mate, ain't she?" Tryggr replied, and when Eben blinked at him, he was casually shrugging, his eyes easy and genial, as if there'd been nothing unusual whatsoever about Eben's question. "I ken it hasn't been an easy tangle to deal with, but Boss still won't want to see her come to harm. Wouldn't want to risk hurting his mate, you ken."

He spoke with such blithe confidence, without even a trace of guile in his voice—and Eben couldn't help frowning at him, the skepticism studding too strong in his own scent. "But how can you... be sure?" he asked thickly. "How can you know Drafli might not rather just... be rid of her?"

Tryggr blinked, but then shook his head. "He wouldn't," he said firmly. "Boss swore vows to his mate, swore to protect him with his life, and Skai don't take vows lightly, ach? An' besides"—he darted an irritable glance toward the sickroom door—"he specially asked me to come check in on her just now, ach? No doubt knew he'd be run off by that snippy Ash-Kai if he came himself—not that I fared much better, I ken."

He huffed a wry, regretful laugh, and gave another companionable squeeze to Eben's shoulder. Because wait, he was still touching Eben, had been touching Eben throughout all this—and perhaps it was that touch, that steady certainty, that seemed to inexplicably settle Eben's stiff shoulders, his breath slowly exhaling. And somehow, the tight knot of dread and misery that had been festering in his chest all these past days had finally seemed to... loosen, sinking into a strange, shaky relief. As if he almost... *believed* this orc. This *Skai*.

"Naught to fret over, Ka-esh," Tryggr said now, with a reassuring little shake to his shoulder. "Boss won't harm her. I ken he might not like her, or be glad she's here, and he's bound to lose his temper over it now and again. But he'll still want to make sure she's safe and looked after, so she can't bring any harm down on his mate. And if it makes you feel any better, we're all keeping an eye on him, too. Ach?"

The calm, confident certainty was still there, ringing in Tryggr's eyes and his voice and his scent, and for an instant, Eben's memory snapped backwards, to that moment with Drafli and the dagger. To how Drafli could have so easily have killed Alma, and Eben too—but he hadn't. He'd reconsidered it, and left. And despite his lapses in temper afterwards, he still hadn't made another actual murder attempt, had he? And did he really want Alma safe and looked after, could that be true, and maybe...

"Maybe I could—help you keep an eye on her," Eben blurted out, without at all meaning to. "On—on Alma, I mean. Let you know if aught is amiss."

Wait, was he saying that because he still didn't trust Drafli, or—curse him—because of this Tryggr. And Tryggr was blinking at him, something shifting in his eyes and his scent, something Eben couldn't at all read...

But then Tryggr jerked a curt nod, and his hand on Eben's shoulder gave him another firm little shake. "Y'know, that'd be good of you, Ka-esh," he said. "Real good. Thanks."

*Real good.* The praise flared and rippled up Eben's spine, pulled a small, shaky smile to his mouth. "Happy to help," he murmured, again echoing Tryggr's own words from before—and yes, yes, that was appreciation in Tryggr's eyes, in the new dimple quivering in his cheek. And oh, in the way he leaned in a little, his breath slowly inhaling, as if drawing in Eben's scent, lingering in it...

And fuck, Eben could scent him, too. Deep, and sweet, and rich. Strong enough that it watered in his mouth, stirred low in his groin...

"Then come to me whenever you need," Tryggr said now, leaning backwards again, giving Eben another quick smile, another bracing little shake. "I'll keep a nose out for your scent, ach?"

Right. *Right.* Tryggr had only been teaching himself Eben's scent, like any competent orc with a plan would do, and that was all. That was all, but it was still fizzling in Eben's belly, warming his eyes and his smile. He had a plan, with this Skai. With this... Tryggr.

And Tryggr was nodding again, and giving Eben one last companionable little shake before releasing his arm and striding down the corridor, away. His steps smooth and rolling, his soft black boots utterly silent on the stone floor, the dagger in his hair briefly gleaming in the lamplight. And Eben couldn't stop staring, drinking up the sight of him, of that lean strong back, that firm muscled arse in his trousers...

*Never trust a Skai,* his father's distant voice was droning, dragging up visions of Drafli with the dagger—but now another voice was rising, too. *No harm done. That'd be good of you, real good. Come to me whenever you need. I can show you the way...*

It seemed to keep shifting something, changing something deep and fundamental in Eben's thoughts. And he drew in a deep breath as he gazed down the empty corridor, tasted the remnants of Tryggr's sweet scent in the air.

Maybe he'd done enough observing. Maybe it was time... to act.

# 7

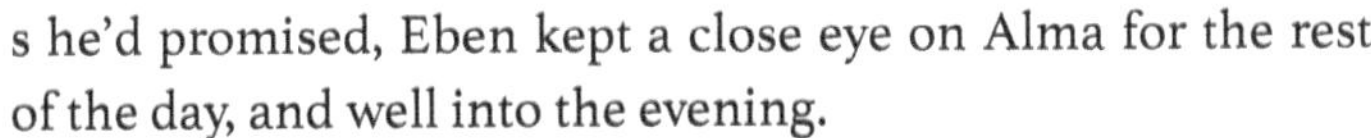

As he'd promised, Eben kept a close eye on Alma for the rest of the day, and well into the evening.

She'd mostly stayed huddled under her fur, either resting or sleeping, and she'd only stirred when spoken to, usually by Efterar, who had continued working over her throat. But she'd remained alive and unharmed, and Eben's breaths still came easier than before, his hands quick and efficient as he mixed tonics and medications for their patients.

He had a plan, with a Skai. With *Tryggr*.

He could almost still feel Tryggr's firm hands on his shoulders, could almost taste that sweet scent in the air—and he twitched all over when Tryggr himself strode back into the sickroom, early in the evening. His easy gaze catching on Eben at the workbench, and then darting down brief and curious to the tonic Eben was currently mixing. And though Eben's hands instantly began trembling, Tryggr didn't seem to notice, and he even gave Eben a quick, conspiratorial wink before striding across the room toward Efterar.

"How's the woman faring now, then?" Tryggr asked Efterar, who was still hovering his hand over Alma's sleeping body. "Any better?"

Efterar gave a distracted, noncommittal shrug, while across the room, Kesst loudly scoffed. "Here again, Tryggr?" he demanded.

"What, did you think we needed a helpful reminder of how Alma wouldn't even *be* in this state, if not for *your* so-called *Boss*?!"

Eben could see Tryggr stiffening, his hands clenching at his sides—but instead of retaliating in kind, he jerked a shrug, and strode back toward the door. His gaze briefly meeting Eben's on the way by, his expression shifting into something both aggrieved and amused as he gave an exaggerated roll of his eyes.

It sent even more warmth shivering up Eben's spine, and he willingly worked late into the night, only heading for bed once Efterar had firmly reassured him that he'd be staying with Alma until morning. And when Eben returned early the next day, Alma was indeed still sleeping safely in her bed, her scent noticeably brighter and clearer than it had been the night before.

"How's she doing now, then?" asked a cheerfully smiling Tryggr, when he strode back into the sickroom. "Scents better, don't she?"

Thankfully, Kesst was still asleep in a nearby bed, so Efterar was able to brief Tryggr without interruption. And when Tryggr left this time, he again winked at Eben, and—Eben startled—tossed him a shiny red apple before striding toward the door.

Eben scarcely managed to catch the apple, his face furiously burning, a foolish little smile pulling at his mouth. While beside him, Salvi—who Eben had nearly forgotten about—had abandoned his writing in favour of whirling around to stare at Eben, his scent surging with eager, gleeful curiosity.

"Who's the Skai?" he demanded. "And why's he bringing you *food*?"

Eben's mouth uselessly opened and closed, betraying far too much, damn it. And the gleefulness in Salvi's scent lurched even higher as his too-knowing gaze darted between Eben's hot face, the apple in his shaky hand, and the cursed obvious twitching in his trousers.

"Ach, it is naught," Eben began, too quickly. "He is only..."

But he couldn't finish, his face burning even hotter, because what *was* Tryggr, exactly? An acquaintance? A co-conspirator? The gorgeous, oblivious object of Eben's foolish, hopeless lust?

"Only your next bedmate, I ken," Salvi said, with a meaningful waggle of his eyebrows. "I ken you'll be reeking of Skai by the time we're back, ach?"

Salvi had been planning a fortnight-long trip north with Tristan,

Eben knew, visiting a library Tristan had long wanted to see—and for the first time since he'd heard of it, Eben didn't feel even the slightest twinge of envy. "Ach, no," he said thickly, shaking his head. "I am sure—Tryggr would not. And I..."

His voice hitched, broke, and beside him Salvi laughed, and companionably bumped him with his shoulder. "Ach, I can scent you, brother," he said lightly. "You'll see."

Eben waved it away, but it still fluttered and shimmered in his chest, warm and eager and almost... hopeful. And it made it even easier to keep working, keep watching over Alma, feeling genuine relief at her steady, continued improvement. He had a plan. He could try to trust a Skai...

But then, around noon, Alma received an unexpected visitor. It was Lady Jule, who was mated to the mountain's captain—and though Jule was smiling and bouncing her orcling son in her arms, she had a distinct scent of grim purpose about her, as if she had unpleasant news to share.

Eben's rising suspicions soon proved correct, because after a few moments' pleasant chatting with Kesst and a bleary-looking Alma, Jule regretfully gave Alma her news. Apparently, Alma's dreadful former employer now regretted running her off, and had begun publicly claiming she'd been kidnapped by orcs—in strong violation of the tenuous peace-treaty between orcs and men.

Alma's already-pale face went white as she listened, her scent jolting with alarm and dread—but then she pulled herself straight in her bed, and gave a resigned little nod. "Well, I've been meaning to head back anyway," she said, her voice impressively steady, despite the sheer terror now ringing through her scent. "And I'm feeling much better, so I can certainly leave at once."

Eben's alarm had begun simmering too, not only because of Alma's highly distressed state, but because her leaving the mountain was exactly what Tryggr—and perhaps Drafli—would want to prevent. Wasn't it?

But wait, Kesst was already barking a loud, disapproving scoff, and jabbing his sharp claw toward Alma's cringing body in the bed. "You aren't going *anywhere*, sweetheart," he snapped. "Not until you're well again, and especially not back to that scum, who's likely to take out all his thwarted pettiness on you. It is *not* safe for you there. Eft, please come tell her she can't leave?!"

Efterar—who had just returned from a room call—promptly strode over and reinforced Kesst's position, even as Eben could see his focus on Alma's throat. On where she clearly wasn't yet fully healed, despite how she was sitting up straight, and arguing her point with surprising intensity. "But—I still need to go," she protested, blinking between Kesst and Jule with pleading eyes. "I told Baldr and Drafli I would leave, at once. It would be best, for everyone, if I go. I *promised* them, and Drafli said—"

She'd stopped there, perhaps due to the sudden fearsome glowering from Kesst and Jule, both of whom then launched into another bout of passionate arguments. Including the surprising revelation that Alma had apparently committed to helping out with the mountain's housekeeping, particularly in the scullery.

"Have you seen that hole, Jules?" Kesst demanded, his voice half-teasing, half-irate. "It is vile. *Vile*!"

Again, Eben found himself in reluctant agreement with Kesst—the mountain's former Keeper had recently retired, and in his absence, the mountain's lone scullery had been sorely neglected, and was now in an appalling state of disarray. To the point where most Ka-esh had quietly taken on the tedious but necessary task of doing their own laundry, deep in the underground cisterns.

But Alma's scent had slightly brightened at the mention of the scullery, so Kesst and Jule kept on, even more enthusiastic than before. "And maybe we can bring over some orcs to keep you entertained," Kesst's cheerful voice said, in the tone of one making a convincing closing argument. "And you can see if any of *them* tickle your fancy?"

Alma didn't appear at all enthused by this proposal, and beside Kesst, Jule huffed a laugh, and rolled her eyes. "*Kesst*," she said. "Alma's not here to pick out an orc, like a new *pet*."

But at that, Kesst's gaze darted over his shoulder, across the room, toward—toward *Eben*. "Are you sure?" he said lightly. "I don't think Eben would mind being Alma's new pet, right, Eben? *Especially* if there was a collar and lead involved?"

Wait. What? *No*. The sudden, startling mortification jolted through Eben's entire body—Kesst truly hadn't just said that, out loud, to a human *patient*?!—and Eben's shaking hand somehow lost its grip on the empty flask he'd been holding, which fell to the workbench with a hard, ringing *thunk*. Ensuring that every awake eye in the room was now trained curiously upon him, witnessing his red face and trembling hands.

And though he instantly dropped his eyes, and fought to drag in deep breaths, he could still feel all those eyes judging him, chastising him, mocking him. Fully believing Kesst's preposterous claim that he wanted to be a human woman's *pet*, on a collar and lead. Even when the human woman was already thoroughly involved with two orcs, one of them a terrifying Skai who Eben had prevented from *killing* her.

Eben barely heard the rest of their conversation over the ringing in his ears, and the waves of hot and cold shuddering up and down his spine. And though he forced himself to keep working—he'd promised Tryggr he would keep an eye on Alma, he'd *promised*—it was slow and stumbling, with far too many thoughtless errors. And all the hopeful shimmering warmth from earlier had vanished too, sinking back into the dark, bitter misery.

*Foolish. Weak. You never focus on what is important...*

And in truth, what had Eben been thinking, to begin imagining that he and Tryggr were co-conspirators, somehow? After they'd met only one day before, and shared a single conversation in the corridor? And of course a capable, confident Skai like Tryggr wouldn't be interested in a weak, foolish orc like Eben, who his colleagues mocked and belittled as little better than a pet.

To make matters worse, Tryggr didn't return for the rest of the day, and Alma also seemed to become increasingly morose, reeking of grief and anguish as she slipped in and out of sleep beneath her blanket. Until Eben could scarcely breathe through the scent of it, let alone focus on his work—a state that again wasn't helped by Kesst, who had now begun irritably pacing back and forth across the sickroom, and casting pointed glances toward Eben and Salvi at the workbench.

"You know," Kesst announced, to no one in particular, "I'm sure Alma would be so much happier if she had some help cleaning up that vile scullery. If some helpful Ka-esh would arrange to fix its clogged drain, maybe."

Eben attempted to ignore it and keep working, emulating Salvi's blithe obliviousness beside him, but Kesst just kept pacing, casting narrow glances toward him, again and again. Until finally Eben huffed a harsh, frustrated sigh, snapped his book shut, and rushed over to the stinking, filthy scullery. Where he dealt with the foul clogged drain himself, mucking it out until his arms ached, and his thoughts screeched with panic and misery. He was supposed to be keeping an eye on Alma, what if Tryggr returned, what if he'd missed him...

He was nearly frantic by the time he'd washed up and raced back to the sickroom, but—he jolted to a halt in the doorway—Alma still was huddled sleeping in her bed, and there was no fresh scent of Tryggr anywhere. And from the workbench, Salvi was frowning at Eben, with a stubborn glint in his eyes—and before Eben could take another step, Salvi strode over, grasped his shoulders, and steered him back out the door.

"Good night," Salvi called behind them. "See you tomorrow!"

It took Eben's exhausted brain far too long to realize what was happening—they weren't *leaving*?—and he wrenched to a halt in the corridor, rubbing at his aching eyes. "I can't leave again!" he croaked at Salvi. "Not yet. I need to make sure—I promised—"

But Salvi only gripped Eben's shoulders tighter, letting his claws dig in as he steered him back down the corridor. "You've been in there all damned day, brother," he snapped. "And all day yesterday too. Your scent smells awful, ach? You need rest."

Eben again attempted to argue, but Salvi fully ignored him, and kept marching him toward the Ka-esh wing. "Also, you shouldn't let Kesst get to you like that," he said, quieter. "The scullery's not your job, and that pet comment was just a stupid joke. Not worth your time, ach?"

But Eben's misery lurched even darker at the reminder of Kesst's joke, because why had the joke needed to be about him? Why had it needed to strike at his softest, weakest places, before a laughing audience? Because no, Eben didn't want to be a human's pet in the slightest, but maybe—maybe it had hurt so much because part of him *did* want something like it. Maybe part of him wanted a confident, capable companion to show up, and take him firmly in hand, and say, *No harm done. No need to apologize. Come to me whenever you need...*

Eben didn't argue again, just kept his head down as Salvi steered him through the corridors, and finally into his chilly, lonely room, deep in the Ka-esh wing. "Sleep," Salvi said. "And I'll see you in a fortnight, ach?"

Right. Eben couldn't deny another dark flare of misery—what would it be like, to have a mate who cared enough to take you to visit a *library*—but he managed a nod, and some semblance of a farewell. And though it was a vague relief to finally collapse into his bed, the misery just kept marching, circling through his weary brain. And tangling together with a distant, rising unease, something he couldn't quite name.

*It would be—best, for everyone, if I go. I told Baldr and Drafli I would leave, I promised them, and Drafli said—*

Eben could almost still taste the panic in Alma's voice as she'd said it, just the same kind of panic he would have felt in her place. Alma had seemed a thoughtful, considerate human, who wanted to pay her debts, and stay well out of trouble... and what would Eben do, if he was in her place? If he'd acquired not only the wrath of Drafli, but of an enraged former employer, too?

Eben shoved up in bed, staring at nothing in the darkness, as his heartbeat thudded in his chest—and then he scrambled up, yanked on his clothes, and staggered toward the door. He just needed to check. Just needed to be sure. He'd promised Tryggr, he'd sworn to take action on this, to try to trust a Skai...

Eben rushed up through the corridors without looking, his eyes shut tight against the too-bright light of the lamps as his breaths dragged in, and his heartbeat thundered louder and louder through his ears. It was probably nothing. It had to be nothing. He'd get to the sickroom and find Efterar still working, and Alma still curled up under her fur...

But the instant Eben reached the corridor, he knew something was wrong. Something was off in the scent. The scent of Alma here, in the corridor, where it wasn't at all supposed to be, and...

And even as Eben skidded into the sickroom, searching it with frantic eyes, the certainty was already there, blaring through his pounding skull.

Alma was gone.

# 8

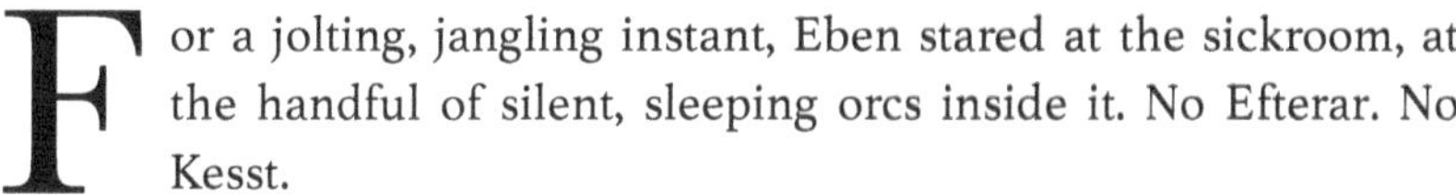

For a jolting, jangling instant, Eben stared at the sickroom, at the handful of silent, sleeping orcs inside it. No Efterar. No Kesst.

No Alma.

Maybe Kesst and Efterar had taken Alma somewhere, maybe they'd gone off together—but no, no, Eben could follow Kesst and Efterar's scents leading that way, up the mountain, toward the Skai wing. While Alma's scent went... down. Out. Away...

She'd gone. Just as she'd promised to do.

Eben spun around, and ran. Sprinting with all his strength toward the Skai wing, his eyes searching in the blessedly dim light. His breaths dragging in harsh and deep, desperately seeking that sweet, familiar scent. Seeking Tryggr.

And yes, yes, that was Tryggr's scent, shimmering amidst the others, leading into the Skai wing—and Eben sprinted faster, skidding around corners, chasing the scent to its source. Deeper and deeper into the Skai wing, into an area he'd never before dared to visit, the light fading further with every step, while a distinct, unnerving noise grew louder, and louder. The noise of orcs, multiple orcs, shouting and grunting and screeching, with victory, and—and with pain. With... *pleasure*.

Eben slid to a stop before the source of the noise, blinking blankly through the open doorway, toward the sight before him. Toward the... room. And in the room was a mass of—chaos. Utter rioting chaos, teeming with shouts and bodies and hot, sweaty, bloody scents, clashing in a frenzied, clamouring mess into Eben's lungs.

They were... fighting?

But yes, they were fighting, and—a distant part of Eben's whirling brain pointed out—this had to be the Skai arena. He'd only never imagined it like this, with so many orcs packed in at once, not only scenting of Skai, but also dozens of Bautul, and a few Ash-Kai, too. And wait, over there, a grim-looking Efterar was crouched over a copiously bleeding Bautul, while Kesst stood beside him with arms crossed, his lip curled with palpable contempt.

There was no sign of Alma, of course—she was probably well beyond the mountain by now—and Eben's frantically searching eyes couldn't seem to find Tryggr, either. But Tryggr's scent had led here, to this, and he had to be here, Eben had to find him, he'd promised, he'd *promised—*

So Eben edged into the room, his heart furiously thundering as he kept close to the wall, his eyes darting all around, his breaths still swarming with the mass of overwhelming scents. Pain, and triumph, and frustration, and—yes, pleasure, because that Skai had pinned another Skai down by the hair, and was grinding against his bare, sweaty arse. And that Skai there was being taken by a big burly Bautul, moaning as his hips slammed deep—and that Skai had another Bautul kneeling before him, his hand clamped around the Bautul's neck, his scarred Skai prick gouging down his throat.

Eben watched for an instant too long, his groin shamefully stirring—and he forced his eyes shut as he crept further against the wall, dragging in deep, searching breaths. Tryggr was here, he had to be here, and maybe that, that, over there...

Yes, yes, that scented familiar, scented right, and Eben kept his eyes closed as he edged closer, and closer. Keeping his body pressed flat against the stone wall, he was almost, almost there—

"Ach, pretty Ka-esh," interrupted a voice, and Eben's eyes snapped open, his heart surging into his throat. Because no, no, there was a strange Skai, *here*, huge and sweaty and dripping fresh blood—and he was leaning in far too close, his breaths heavy and sour in Eben's nostrils.

"What brings a sweet small Ka-esh like you to the Skai arena, this night?" the orc crooned, his eyes alight on Eben's face. "Seeking some pleasure, I ken?"

Eben's heart wheeled up harder, his stomach twisting in his gut, and he clutched his claws at the wall, and wildly shook his head. "N-no, naught of the sort," he croaked. "I am only here for a moment. Only—seeking someone."

But the orc only leaned closer, and his huge clawed hand settled to the wall beside Eben's head, blocking him from moving forward. "Ach, are you?" he drawled. "Seeking someone who can make you kneel and beg, mayhap? Just as a good little Ka-esh should?"

What? Eben stared at the orc for an instant too long, as the heat and the misery pounded through his cheeks, against his screaming skull. No. No. This could not be happening. He should have known better, he should never have come here—

"No," he gasped, pressing himself back further against the wall. "No. Please. I am only here for—for—Tryggr."

His voice was badly wavering, enough that Tryggr's name was scarcely audible—but wait, the orc's beady eyes had darted sideways. Sideways, perhaps only a dozen paces away, where—yes—there was Tryggr, on the floor amidst the mass of fighting orcs. And he was grappling with another lean, handsome Skai, both of them laughing and gasping and snapping their teeth—but Tryggr clearly had the upper hand, straddling the other orc like that, pinning his wrists to the floor...

And then—Eben's heart lurched—Tryggr roughly shoved the other Skai onto his belly, and yanked down the orc's trousers. Revealing a hard, muscled grey arse, oh—and Tryggr's clawed hand gave it a swift, ringing slap before yanking down his own trousers, releasing his own swollen, scarred, dripping prick. The same prick that had filled so many of Eben's thoughts these past weeks—and it was now sliding easy and hungry between the orc's bared, quivering arse-cheeks. Seeking its place, finding it, and then sinking inside slow and deep...

No. No. *No.* Eben didn't want to see it, couldn't bear to see it, but he couldn't look away from it, while the huge, horrifying orc before him—laughed. Laughed, because wait, he'd been letting Eben watch this, letting him see how his intended target was so obviously enamoured with someone else.

"Ach, Tryggr is busy, I ken," the orc drawled, as Eben's blinking, traitorous eyes watched Tryggr's hips start plunging, while the orc beneath him gasped and moaned. "Thus, mayhap you can find other pleasures also, ach?"

Curse this orc, curse this horrible overwhelming room, this horrible day, the horrible sick jealousy screeching in Eben's belly. This had been so foolish, so, so foolish, *never trust a Skai, never let one get you alone*, but Eben had promised, he had, and he needed to fulfill his promise, and then run as fast as he could, until he could collapse a tunnel behind him...

"Tryggr!" he shouted, through his hoarse throat. "*Tryggr*! Help!"

# 9

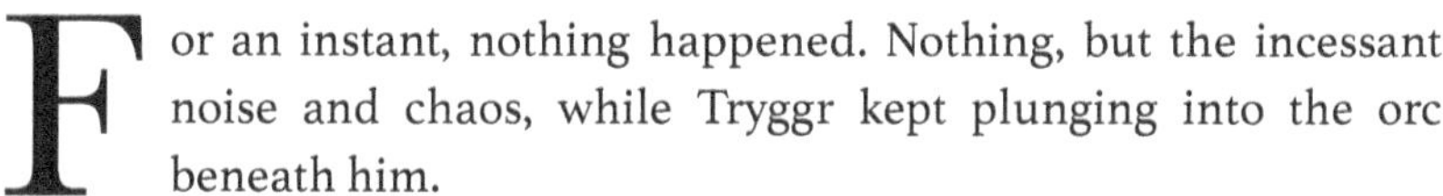

For an instant, nothing happened. Nothing, but the incessant noise and chaos, while Tryggr kept plunging into the orc beneath him.

And the huge orc saw it, and laughed. Laughed, loud and triumphant, as he pinned Eben closer against the wall, his breath hot and nauseating, his swollen groin grinding hard into Eben's belly.

Eben's panic was screaming white and wild, now, blinding his eyes, trembling his entire body against the orc's massive bulk. What could he do, surely someone would notice or help, maybe he could catch Efterar or Kesst's attention somehow—but the room was too full of noise and blood and mayhem, oh please, please—

"Help!" Eben gasped. "Help, please! Please! *Sir*!"

When—there. Tryggr's body jerked up, his head snapping sideways, toward—toward Eben. Toward where Eben was cringing and cowering against the wall, against the orc—and oh no, no, Eben could even feel water streaking down his cheeks, hot and shameful and humiliating. While Tryggr just kept blankly staring at him, as if not seeing, not following. Maybe not even—not even caring.

And oh, Eben didn't care, he didn't, *never trust a Skai*, never—but wait. Wait. Tryggr was leaping to his feet, yanking up his trousers. And then lurching over toward them with astonishing speed, vaulting over another pair of grappling orcs on the way.

"What the fuck, Skaap!" Tryggr snarled, as he drove his shoulder into the huge orc, and shoved him sideways. "Can't you scent how terrified he is? Skai-kesh above, he's *weeping*!"

And no, no, Eben wasn't weeping, why was he weeping, the water streaming down his face, his head hanging, his shoulders heaving. Betraying all his shame, his horrifying humiliation, for all these orcs to see, for this Skaap to see, for Tryggr to see—

"Ach, Ka-esh," came Tryggr's voice, rushed and urgent—and that was his hand on Eben's face, tilting it up toward him. "Ach, you're all right. I've got you. Naught to fear, ach?"

Oh. *Oh*. Eben sank against the wall behind him, his eyes fluttering closed, and that was an odd sound from Tryggr before him, much like a growl—but his hand kept cradling Eben's face, caressing against his wet cheek. "Ach, naught to fear, sweet Ka-esh. No need to scent thus. Skaap shall *never* come near you again."

His voice had deepened at the end, into something hard and almost dangerous—and when Eben blinked up again, Tryggr was baring his teeth, and glaring over his shoulder. Toward where a cold-eyed Skaap was rapidly backing away from them, sinking into the clamouring throng.

It was enough to sag Eben heavier against the wall, and perhaps he'd even managed a nod. And Tryggr's hand on his face gave another approving little caress, his eyes slowly softening, despite the grim tightness still on his mouth.

"You're all right, Ka-esh," he said, even gentler than before. "Now, is aught else amiss? You come here to find me? To speak to me?"

Eben twitched another nod, and suddenly the urgent surging panic was here again, stark and scraping in his belly. "It's—Alma," he gasped. "She's—gone. Run away."

Tryggr's eyes snapped wide, and then darted sideways, catching on—Drafli. Drafli, halfway across the room, his lean body whirling through the air, and hurling another orc onto the floor. But he'd almost seemed to sense Tryggr's gaze, somehow, because he twitched around, frowning—and then Tryggr's hand rapidly began moving in midair, speaking in their sign language.

Drafli instantly stiffened, his hand snatching sideways, toward—oh. Baldr, who'd been fighting close beside him. And at another sharp motion from Drafli's clawed hand, Baldr frowned and closed his eyes, inhaling deep—and then he stiffened all over, too. And without a word, or a single glance around them, they both sprinted for the door, dodging and leaping over other orcs as they went.

"I'd best round up a few brothers to help, just in case," Tryggr said now, turning back to Eben with unmistakable urgency in his scent. "Mayhap you oughta—"

He hesitated, grimacing and glancing around the still-chaotic room—but at least that terrifying Skaap orc was no longer in sight, and Eben drew in a thick, shaky breath. "I shall go," he replied, as steadily as he could. "I hope Alma shall soon—be found, and safe."

Tryggr twitched a nod, and that was distinct relief in his eyes. Wanting Eben well out of the way, clearly, and Eben fought to ignore the plunge in his belly as he took another breath, and shoved himself sideways. Lurching back along the wall toward the exit—which suddenly seemed very far away—and his panic was already rattling higher, his eyes darting around at the utter chaos of this horrible room. He could only push himself through it, hope no one else would notice him, and...

And then something grasped his hand, warm and firm—and when Eben startled to look, it was only Tryggr again, an apologetic smile on his mouth. "I'll walk you out, Ka-esh," he said. "Naught to fear, ach?"

Eben couldn't deny the sudden sinking relief, heavily dropping his shoulders, even as more bitter, shameful misery churned in his belly. Tryggr had seen his fear, and was now coddling him, condescending to him, as though Eben were some helpless, useless weakling, a *pet*, who couldn't cross a room unattended. And worst of all, it was true, and Eben desperately clung to that solid warm hand as Tryggr began striding toward the door, drawing Eben swiftly along behind him.

To Eben's relief, they reached the corridor without further incident, though the scent of Tryggr's urgency was now burning through the air—so Eben squared his shoulders, and withdrew his hand as quickly as he could. "Th-thank you," he said. "I wish you—all speed."

Tryggr nodded, and flashed Eben a brief, distracted smile—and then he spun around and away, disappearing back into the chaos of the room. While Eben just stood there outside the door, blinking hard, as his stomach twisted with more sinking, staggering misery. This had been so, so pathetic. So foolish. What had he been thinking, to have ever imagined he could—well. *Never trust a Skai. Never let one touch you, or get you alone...*

The sickening vision of Skaap was now churning with all the rest, the lingering scent of his breath still far too strong in Eben's nose, and he forced his shaky feet to move, away. Away, away, as far as he could go, as deep as he could go, where no Skai would ever find him again.

# 10

Eben ended up bloody and bent-over in the *dýflissa*, gasping and shivering and begging for more. Offering it up to any orc who wanted it, any orc who would fill him, flay him, force him to forget.

And though it was pain, and perhaps more humiliation, Eben couldn't stop. Couldn't bear to be empty, to lose that raw, reassuring certainty of a strong, hard prick plunged deep inside him. He was safe, like this. He was already full, already in pain. And despite how it looked, how it felt, there was still the awareness, low and fundamental, that he was still in control. If he wanted it to stop, it would, and every Ka-esh in the room would defend this, and hurl the offending orc out at once. Eben still held the power. The right to do this, to be this, to be a foolish, weeping orc who could take a half-dozen loads, and keep begging for more.

"Mayhap you ought to rest for a spell, Eben," a breathless Gareth finally said, once he'd emptied himself for the second time, and had begun gently licking at the fresh wounds on Eben's burning, aching back. "These are not healing as they should, ach?"

Eben's rebellion surged up before he could stop it, escaping in a low growl from his mouth—but Gareth just kept licking, kissing, even as his claws sank into Eben's hips. Knowing full well that Eben had never been able to refuse that heady, perfect blend of pain and tenderness, and Eben was already wilting beneath it, sagging weakly against the wall before him. And perhaps finally feeling the true extent of that pain, blaring across his back, and still coiling deep and despairing in his belly.

*Foolish. Never trust a Skai.*

"Come, then," came Gareth's low, soothing voice, as he nudged something soft—Eben's abandoned trousers—into his slack hand. "Rest for a spell, and come back tomorrow, if you yet need this relief."

Eben couldn't find the will to argue, and he suddenly felt so, so tired, worn and ragged and aching all over. And even putting on his trousers was far too difficult, and he was distantly, fervently grateful for Gareth's firm hand on his arm, holding him upright. And once Eben had finally managed it, Gareth pulled on his own trousers, passed Eben his tunic—which he would otherwise have fully forgotten—and guided him toward the door.

Eben went without looking, without scenting, with only more deep, dragging gratefulness toward Gareth, and a vague nattering dread of how much he would regret this tomorrow. And it wasn't until they were in the corridor that he suddenly scented—something. Something that didn't at all belong, and Eben's breath drew in, his bleary eyes snapping open, and finding—

Tryggr. Tryggr, standing here in the Ka-esh corridor, and staring at him.

Eben froze all over, alarm screeching through his chest—Skai never came here, he was supposed to be safe here. And curse him, he wasn't wearing his tunic, and even if Tryggr hadn't been able to scent the fresh blood and seed all over Eben's tired, trembling body, he now had a full-on view of it, his eyes narrowing as they rapidly ran up and down Eben's torso. And then shifting even darker as they darted toward Gareth, who was still holding Eben by the elbow.

"Who the hell are you?" Tryggr snapped at Gareth, his voice sharper than Eben had yet heard it. "An' where are you taking him?"

Eben blinked, as more confused alarm juddered through his exhausted body, but beside him, Gareth stayed solid and steady, without even a trace of fear in his scent. "I am Gareth—or oft, Gary," he replied mildly. "And I am only taking him to his room."

Tryggr's narrow gaze snapped back to Eben, as if wanting him to confirm the accuracy of this claim—and somehow, Eben nodded. Nodded, holding his wide eyes to Tryggr's, needing him to understand, to agree. And he was vaguely surprised to see Tryggr's eyes softening in return, his swallow bobbing in his throat.

"Ach, I see," he said thickly, as he ran a hand against his bound-back hair. "Didn't mean to interrupt. I'll leave you be, then, Ka-esh, and find you another time."

He was already backing away, about to leave, no, no—and Eben lurched forward, out of Gareth's grip. "Wait," he croaked, as a hazy awareness finally whirled in his brain, because Tryggr had to have news, right? "Is Alma well? Did they bring her back?"

Tryggr's gaze had again darted sideways, toward Gareth—who was already backing toward the *dýflissa*, his hands upraised. "Only call if you need me, brother," he said to Eben, a little too smoothly. "And sleep well, ach?"

Eben rapidly nodded, and couldn't help a grateful, genuine smile toward him, and a quick wave farewell. But once he turned back to Tryggr again, he found him still looking decidedly unsettled, and frowning darkly at where Gareth had gone.

"Is aught—amiss, then?" Eben croaked, into the stilted silence, as the alarm shuddered back through his chest. "Is Alma lost? Or harmed?"

Tryggr's lean body twitched, his gaze snapping back to Eben's face—and again, brief but unmistakable, down to his bare, sweaty, bloody chest. "No, they found her," he said, on a heavy exhale. "She's back in the sickroom now, and Boss is with her. He's gonna make her an offer, I ken, to make sure she stays put, where we can keep an eye on her. Not safe for her to be running about thus, ach?"

Eben couldn't even pretend to hide the surprise in his scent—Drafli was now going to make Alma an *offer*, to keep her here? To keep her safe, after all that? But there was again no trace of guile in Tryggr's scent, and it distantly occurred to Eben that if Drafli truly still wanted Alma dead, it would have been far easier to let her keep running, and then to stage some convenient accident afterwards... right?

*Never trust a Skai*, the voice was droning again, but Tryggr was still here, shifting on his feet, and thrusting something into Eben's arms. Something Eben hadn't even noticed him carrying, and when he blinked downwards, he found himself holding a small cloth sack, full of—fresh *fruit*?

"An' just—wanted to be sure you were—all good," Tryggr said, with a grimace. "Didn't feel right, leaving you how I did. 'Specially after you went outta your way to help, and find me, even after that scum Skaap—"

He broke off there, glowering beyond Eben up the corridor, his hands flexing at his sides. "Reported him to Boss and Simon, by the way, after a chat with my Pa," he said flatly. "The clan's gonna deal with him, ach?"

Something swerved in Eben's belly, because oh, Tryggr hadn't truly done that, for *him*? But wait, curse it, Eben didn't want to cause any trouble, either. Didn't want to be responsible for any kind of retaliation whatsoever, and what if this Skaap decided to take it out on Eben, or gain revenge, or—or—

But wait, Tryggr had lurched closer, and clasped his hand to Eben's shoulder. "Naught to fear, Ka-esh," he said, low and firm. "It's got naught now to do with you, and we just don't want it to happen again, ach? We can't have it being dangerous for someone to come bring us an urgent message, affecting our own kin. Boss never woulda forgiven himself if that woman had come to harm running alone out there, ach? Most of all if he'd known you were trying to get word to him, but couldn't, because you got attacked by a so-called brother instead."

His eyes on Eben's had darkened again, his hand tightening on his shoulder. "It was good of you, Ka-esh," he said, low. "Good of you, and brave as hell, too. You ever even walk in that arena before? Or witness a proper brawl?"

Eben shook his head, betraying a faint wince, because again, it was so weak, so foolish, he was supposed to be a medic, wasn't he? "N-not—thus," he confessed. "I mean—I have attended skirmishes and battlefields, afterwards, to offer care when it is needed. But I have never been sent into—the full midst of this."

And truly, it was a gift that the war with men had been over for most of Eben's time as a medic, because what would he have done, if he'd needed to go straight into a pitched battle? What would he have done if Efterar had even decided to send him into that arena, rather than going himself?

"Well, we're grateful, Ka-esh," Tryggr said, his eyes flinty on Eben's face. "You didn't need to do it, and you did it anyway, even when it couldn'a been easy for you. When it coulda *harmed* you."

An odd ripple snaked up Eben's spine, and he swallowed, attempted a smile. "I was glad to help," he said thickly. "And I am—quite all right, of course."

But Tryggr's eyes had again flicked down Eben's front, toward the sweat and scratches and blood. Almost as clear as if he'd spoken his doubt aloud, and Eben drew in breath, cleared his throat. "This was just—for pleasure," he said, with a vague, shaky wave toward the *dýflissa* up the corridor. "Ka-esh oft do this, for it is an easy way to clear one's thoughts, and forget—"

But wait, curse him, why was he saying this, betraying this, before this orc, of all orcs—but it was too late, and that was far too much awareness, shifting across Tryggr's watching eyes. "Seems like a lot to forget, though, if it takes what, eight orcs to do it?" he asked, his voice light. "An' what's this from, a lash?"

His claw had very lightly reached to touch Eben's chest, brushing against—Eben's wide eyes darted downwards—oh. Where the whip had very clearly curled around his torso, and drawn a vivid line against his skin, still seeping dark red blood. And wait, was Tryggr judging him, and had it really been eight orcs, and Tryggr could smell that, and—

The humiliation burned up into Eben's face, roiling hard and sick in his belly, and he needed to leave, needed to escape, run as deep as he could—but Tryggr's other hand was still clasping his shoulder, holding him here, where he could judge him, and mock him. And all that was left was for Eben to force his face up, to hold his blinking, miserable eyes to Tryggr's face.

"As if you have any right to judge me?" his thin voice demanded, harsh in his throat. "How many weakened orcs do you take in that arena, or mayhap in the corridors, once you have gained their defeat?"

He knew it was unfair even as he spoke it, but the sickness and exhaustion were still curdling in his belly, his vision flooded with images of Tryggr laughing with that Skai orc, pinning him down, driving his scarred swollen prick into him with such smooth, confident ease. And Eben wasn't jealous, he was *not*, and—

And wait, Tryggr was reeling backwards, away, his expression stunned, almost hurt. "This has naught to do with their defeat," he hissed back. "It's only what *Skai* oft do, when *we* wish for release. And I ken it's better than running a blood-soaked *rut* upon a weak small Ka-esh, and wielding a *lash* against him, when he's yet *reeking* of fear and despair!"

Oh. Oh, no. No, no, no. *A weak small Ka-esh. Reeking of fear and despair.* And the pain cracking through Eben's chest was far worse than his stinging back, or his aching, burning arse. He couldn't bear to let Tryggr see him weep, not again, please, please—

But Tryggr was seeing it, he was staring at Eben with more judgement in his eyes, and with something almost like—like contempt. Contempt toward Eben, for his size, his weakness, his fear, his despair...

*Never trust a Skai*, his father's grating voice shouted, *run as deep as you can*—and this time, Eben was listening. Listening, weeping, as he whirled away, covered his face, and ran.

# 11

Eben spent an endless, miserable night.

It took far too long to fall asleep, what with his leaking eyes, and the ever-increasing aches running through his weakened, exhausted body. Aches that eventually began to feel more like chills, and it belatedly occurred to his weary, overwhelmed brain that perhaps Gareth—and Tryggr—had been right. Perhaps he'd pushed it too far in the *dýflissa*. He'd had far too little sleep these past days, and beyond that apple Tryggr had thrown him, he couldn't recall if he'd eaten the day before, either—and curse him, he hadn't thought to drink even a bit of fresh seed in the *dýflissa*, either. Orc healing never worked as well when the orc was fatigued or under-nourished, or—Eben groaned into his fur—or under strain.

So he attempted to lie still, to rest, and eventually pulled over that sack of fruit Tryggr had given him, which he'd somehow carried all the way here. But he suddenly felt too weary to even eat it, and instead ended up sucking out a plum's juices as well as he could before collapsing again. His body still shivering with wave after wave of cold, though the fur beneath him was soaked with sweat, and his back felt like it was fully aflame, licking and crackling with agonizing heat.

Eventually he fell into a fitful, restless sleep, and when he awoke again, he was parched, the wet fur now frigid against his shivering skin. But he was too weak to get out of bed, and there was no water to be found, so he finally groped for another plum, and again sucked as much liquid from it as he could. And then sank his trembling body back onto the bed, fighting to ignore the distant shouting awareness that he was feverish, and that the whip-strikes had clearly become infected. *These are not healing as they should...*

Eben didn't know when he next awoke, but when he did, it was to the sound of a low, cursing voice. A familiar voice. And Eben had to be dreaming, dreaming that Tryggr was in his room, and yes, no, the scent was gone again—until it wasn't. And with it was another familiar scent, Gareth's scent, but hanging thick with metal and smoke, suggesting he'd just come from his work in the forge.

"How long's he been like this?" demanded Tryggr's voice. "An' why the fuck did none of you come check on him? Didn't you scent him, the other night, when you were tearing into him with a fucking *lash*, after he near got attacked and *forced* in the fucking Skai arena?!"

The sharp scent of Gareth's shock filtered through the air, and Eben could hear his low, hoarse exhale. "Ach, he spoke naught of this," he replied, his voice sounding odd to Eben's ears. "And he oft comes scenting thus, and begging for pain. And if I—or another friend—do not grant him this, he shall hurl himself toward any other who shall offer it. Oft those who shall not pay close heed to him, or his scents."

Oh. No. Gareth truly didn't think such things about Eben, he truly hadn't taken pleasure with Eben out of *pity*, or a sense of *responsibility*, all this time?! And it was surely a sign of Eben's miserable state that his sudden guilt and grief didn't even filter into his scent, at least not enough to reach Tryggr and Gareth beside him.

"And I only did not come to see him," continued Gareth's voice, still thick and unusually high-pitched, "because I thought—your scents—I thought he had gone with *you*."

There was an instant's silence, taut and heavy in the room, and a sound from Gareth that might have been a sniff. And then the sound of movement, of perhaps Tryggr pacing, his scent swaying unevenly into Eben's breath. "Then where are those pricks from the sickroom, those ones he works with!" Tryggr demanded. "Those Ash-Kai always got their noses poked in everyone else's business, and that mouthy one Kesst kept launching right into me for even *asking* about Boss's woman! Why ain't he down here gettin' his magic healer mate to deal with this!"

There was another moment's silence, broken by Gareth's heavy-sounding sigh. "Outside the *dýflissa*, he is not one to draw eyes to himself," his quiet voice said. "He is so meek and soft-spoken, I ken he is mayhap easy to... forget. Most of all in such a busy sickroom, ach?"

His words were followed by more uncomfortable silence, and a harsh, irritated growl from Tryggr. "So what's keeping you from running for Efterar now, then!" he snarled. "When *you're* part responsible for putting him in this state!"

There was a flare of bright alarm from Gareth, but then Eben could scent him rushing from the room, leaving only Tryggr's scent behind. And now something heavy was settling on the bed beside Eben, something warm and familiar touching his shoulder.

"Ach, you'll be all right, Ka-esh," came Tryggr's low voice. "You'll be all right real soon, ach? You've been real good to keep resting like this, real good."

Oh. Eben attempted to turn his head toward Tryggr, to blink his gritty eyes open, perhaps to speak—but nothing would come out. And despite that, Tryggr's warm hand had begun stroking his shoulder, slow and deeply reassuring, and Eben couldn't help curling a little closer into him, into his safe solid warmth.

"That's it, Ka-esh," Tryggr's soft voice continued. "You just relax and breathe, ach? That Efterar will be here real soon to help you, I ken."

Eben might have nodded, curling even closer, his head bumping something solid—something that was now shifting, slipping beneath his head, propping it up. And wait, wait, it was Tryggr's *thigh*, Eben's head was in Tryggr's *lap*—and Tryggr's warm hand was now stroking against his hair, against where it felt sticky and scraggly, surely half fallen out of its usual neat braid.

"Ach, just thus, Ka-esh," Tryggr said, even softer. "You get comfortable, and rest."

Eben somehow nodded, rubbing his hot cheek against the rough fabric of Tryggr's trousers, but oh, this was the best he'd felt in days, or maybe in weeks, or months. Just lying like this in a Skai's lap, while the Skai kept petting him, murmuring soft, sweet, wonderful words to him.

Eben didn't know how long he lay there, and he'd perhaps fallen back asleep—but he was jolted awake by Tryggr's voice again, now far louder and sharper than before. "Where the fuck have *you* been?" he demanded, and when Eben's scratchy eyes blinked open, he saw Efterar striding into the room, looking just as bleary and exhausted as Eben felt.

"I've been dealing with the fallout from that massive brawl of yours, Skai," Efterar snapped back, though Eben couldn't taste any actual ire in his scent. "Now help me turn him over, will you? *Gently.*"

Efterar was referring to Eben, he soon discovered, as careful hands shifted against his body, turning him around so his burning back faced out, toward Efterar. Which meant that Eben's face was now turned toward Tryggr, his nose nearly in Tryggr's groin, and he felt himself reflexively inhaling the rich sweet scent of it, as his aching body shuddered all over.

"Ach, that's a bad infection," said Efterar's voice, clipped and businesslike. "What did it, do you know?"

Tryggr's hand was again steadily stroking Eben's hair, seemingly not caring that it was nudging Eben's face closer into his groin. "A lash, he said," came Tryggr's flat reply. "An' a half-dozen fool greedy Ka-esh running a rut on him, too. Thought they were s'posed to be the geniuses round here."

Efterar didn't make any comment to this, though Eben could feel the unmistakable prickle of his powerful healing magic, shimmering into the aches on his skin. "He's badly dehydrated, too," said Efterar's matter-of-fact voice. "Lost a lot of blood. I don't suppose you thought to bring him any water, beyond this fruit?"

Tryggr's hand stilled, and Eben could feel his breath hissing out, hard enough to rustle his hair. "Ach, no, I didn't," he breathed. "Fuck. I shoulda thought of it. Didn't realize he didn't have any, the poor little pet."

Another hard shiver hurtled up Eben's back, and he could hear Efterar's low harrumph. "Well, fresh seed would be even better, if you'd want to give it," he said flatly. "No obligation whatsoever, of course, but it scents to me like you're both already halfway there."

Wait. Wait, what the hell had Efterar just said, and Eben couldn't stop shivering now, and somehow—somehow—twisting his head a little, and blinking up at Tryggr's face. At where Tryggr was blinking back down toward him, a stunned, strange look shifting across his eyes.

"Would that help, Ka-esh?" he asked, hoarse. "A bit of fresh seed? Just—for your health? Your healing?"

Right. Right, of course, just for that, and Eben couldn't deny his low, shaky moan, his tongue brushing his lips. And now he was even inhaling slow and deep, shamefully nuzzling his face into Tryggr's groin, into where—at some point—it had begun bulging far larger than before.

"Ach, then, Ka-esh," Tryggr breathed, and oh, *oh*, he was shifting his trousers, tugging them downwards, and releasing—that. That fat, scarred Skai prick, hovering huge and heavy over Eben's face. And this was not happening, this could not be happening, not with Efterar right there behind them—but Eben knew Efterar had witnessed such feedings hundreds of times, and he'd been the one to suggest it, and...

"Ach, Ka-esh?" Tryggr said, even as he shifted Eben a little on his lap, lowered that thick grey length toward Eben's mouth. "You're sure?"

But Eben's mouth was still watering, his head furtively nodding, his face seeking closer. His lips parting, opening, welcoming the gentle brush of that slick grey head, its seed brushing lightly across his tongue...

Fuck, it tasted good, different, richer and sweeter than any seed Eben had ever tasted in his life—and he moaned as he lurched closer, sucked it deeper into his mouth. While Tryggr gasped above him, and then huffed a husky laugh, his hand again stroking against Eben's hair, claws gently dragging against his scalp.

"Ach, there you are, Ka-esh," Tryggr murmured, as his cock in Eben's mouth shuddered and swelled larger, squeezing out a generous pulse of that rich sweetness onto Eben's tongue. "That's better, ain't it?"

Eben briefly, fervently nodded, earning another low laugh from Tryggr, another stroke of claws through his hair. "Good," he said softly. "Real good, Ka-esh. Drink as much as you like."

Oh, hell, and Eben moaned again, sucking harder, deeper—and that was a hiss from Tryggr this time. "Ach, that's it," he breathed, swelling even fuller in Eben's mouth, stretching it wider around him.

"Ach, you've got a tight, hot little mouth, don't you? You like having it filled with a good Skai prick?"

Eben's groan was hoarse, shameless, his mouth sucking even harder—and oh, it felt good, it tasted good, and perhaps it really was helping, too. Because Efterar's familiar healing prickle in his back was moving faster now, darting efficiently from laceration to laceration, and Eben's thoughts felt clearer, his body steadier. Enough that he remembered his tongue, flicking and teasing it at Tryggr's leaking slit, while Tryggr spasmed and sputtered into his mouth, thicker and smoother with every desperate gulp.

"Good, Ka-esh," Tryggr gasped, his clawed hand now gently curling around Eben's neck, his breaths heaving loud and harsh. "Ach, that's nice. Real nice. So good and tight and sweet, so pretty with a Skai in your mouth, opening you up, about to make you reek of—"

His voice faltered, broke into a hoarse, guttural cry—and yes, yes, there it was, the furious rush of sweet, stunning Skai seed, surging into Eben's mouth. And he was aware enough now to soften the suction, to open his throat, to just let the seed flow straight down, heating his esophagus, streaming into his empty waiting belly.

"Oh, *fuck*," Tryggr groaned, his hooded eyes bright and wild on Eben's face. "So *good*, Ka-esh. *Ach*."

Eben could have preened beneath the praise, beneath the sheer sweeping pleasure, the wondrous warm rightness of this powerful Skai so generously filling his mouth, flooding his belly. Offering him such great, stunning strength, and Eben held his worshipful eyes on Tryggr's flushed face as he kept his throat wide open, kept welcoming that sweet Skai seed inside him. Until he could feel the flow finally sputtering, slowing, and only then did he let his throat convulse against that hard invading flesh, even as his tongue stroked up its length. An action that instantly made Tryggr shudder and gasp, squeezing out another sustained spurt of seed—so Eben did it again, and again. Milking out more and more, squeezing again and again, until that slowly softening cock had fed him every last, succulent drop.

"Ach, Ka-esh," Tryggr breathed, or perhaps it was more a moan, as he bent over Eben's head, and inhaled slow and deep. "Ach, that was good. So tight. So *sweet*."

Eben softly drew away and smiled back up at him, his breath

slowly shuddering with his exhale, with his heavy, fluttering eyes. The peacefulness now settling quiet and boneless upon him, sinking him down into the warm safety of Tryggr's lap, his still-stroking hands. Liking him, approving of him, perhaps, perhaps...

"That better, Ka-esh?" breathed Tryggr's ragged voice. "Now mayhap you can sleep for me, ach?"

And yes, yes, Eben would, he would like nothing better than to please his lord, who had blessed him with such good seed, and such great kindness. So he kept smiling as he nodded, slow and grateful, and then closed his eyes, and slept.

# 12

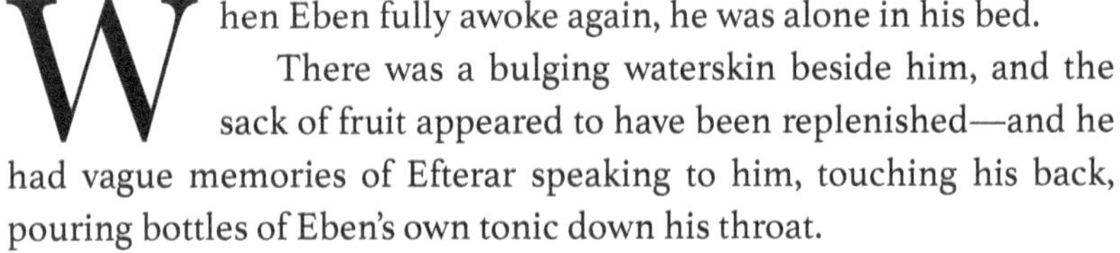

When Eben fully awoke again, he was alone in his bed.

There was a bulging waterskin beside him, and the sack of fruit appeared to have been replenished—and he had vague memories of Efterar speaking to him, touching his back, pouring bottles of Eben's own tonic down his throat.

*If you don't mind, I'd like to keep you here resting for a few days, Ka-esh*, Efterar's voice had said. *It feels like you haven't slept in a week, and you need the time to heal. You've done more than enough work lately.*

Eben had been too exhausted to argue, though he did recall searching for Tryggr, and finding a fresh trace of his scent, as if he'd recently been in the room. And it had been enough to lull Eben back to sleep again, sinking into the memories of it, the faint sweet taste of Tryggr on his tongue.

And even now, as Eben carefully shoved himself up in his bed, drawing in a slow breath, he could still *taste* Tryggr. Could still taste that distinct Skai sweetness not only on his lips, but in his own scent, in his flesh, embedded stark and powerful beneath his very skin.

He'd sucked off a Skai. A *Skai*.

Even the thought of it swarmed heat up Eben's spine, and deep into his already-swelling groin. *Good. Real good. Ach, you've got a tight, hot little mouth, don't you? You like having it filled with a good Skai prick?*

*Fuck.* It was as though Tryggr had struck straight to Eben's deepest, most fundamental cravings, without even the slightest effort. The easy commands. The praise. The claws in his hair, on his neck. The way Tryggr had looked, the way he'd gasped. As if, in that moment, he'd truly wanted Eben. As if he'd... cared.

But Tryggr wasn't here... now. He hadn't... stayed. But in truth, why would he? Because he'd only done that for Eben's health, right? There had been no other commitments, no agreements between them whatsoever—and even if Tryggr had found pleasure in it, that didn't mean anything, did it? That never meant anything, not among their kin, and especially not among the Skai. *Never trust a Skai.*

That thought hitched uncomfortably in Eben's chest, and he forced himself up and out of bed, staggering on shaky legs over to the nearby latrine. Where he washed up all over, brushing and braiding his hair, before dressing in a fresh tunic and trousers, and finally heading up to the sickroom.

His heartbeat pounded louder as he went, his traitorous breaths inhaling slow and deep. Seeking any hints of Tryggr's scent in the adjacent corridors or rooms, any suggestions he might have recently come this way—but there was no fresh trace of him, not in the Ka-esh wing, or the Grisk. Or—Eben couldn't deny the miserable plunge in his belly as he hesitated in the doorway—the sickroom.

Kesst and Alma weren't in the sickroom, either—or Salvi, due to his trip north. There was only Efterar, working on the other side of the room, and a variety of new Bautul and Skai patients, no doubt from that vicious brawl in the arena. Which now must have been multiple days ago, and Eben's scattering thoughts were fixed on the memory of Tryggr pinning that Skai orc down, sliding so easy inside him—

"Good to see you up again, Ka-esh," interrupted a familiar voice, and Eben blinked at where Efterar was now striding over, his eyes still red and heavy with exhaustion. "Feeling better, I hope?"

Eben nodded, and cleared his throat. "Yes, much better, thank you," he replied thickly. "It was good of you to come and see me."

Efterar waved it away, even as he reached around, and hovered his hand up and down over Eben's back. "Glad to help," he said. "Though you should still take it easy over the next week or two. Cut down your time working in here, and *rest.* Also"—he grimaced, as Eben felt a distinctive prickle in one of the mostly healed cuts—"I'm sorry I didn't catch your absence sooner. That Skai was very unimpressed with me."

There was an apologetic half-smile on his face, and Eben's heart pounded faster, a hot shudder streaking up his spine. "Have you—seen Tryggr?" he asked, before he could stop himself. "Or scented him, since then?"

Curse him, what was he saying, or betraying, but Efterar surely knew, Efterar had watched him desperately sucking Tryggr's prick, hadn't he? But thankfully, Efterar hadn't seemed to notice anything unusual about Eben's question, and he gave a distracted-looking shrug, his focus still fixed on Eben's back.

"Ach, he's been by a few times," he replied absently. "Recently tore a knee ligament, fighting in the arena."

Wait. Wait. Eben's body had suddenly turned to ice, his hands clenching, his eyes staring at nothing. Tryggr had already gone back to that arena. To do what Skai often did, he'd said, when they wished for release. To do, perhaps, what Eben had witnessed him doing the other day, laughing and snapping his teeth as he'd sunk deep inside...

But curse it, even if Tryggr had fucked a dozen orcs since then, what right did Eben have to care? He knew it hadn't meant anything. He *knew*. Tryggr was clearly a kind, considerate orc, who made a point of helping those in need. So when Eben had been in need, Tryggr had done what he could to help. And then he'd had every right to move on with his life, with his activities, and his pleasures.

And that was all. That had to be all. It hadn't meant anything. *Never trust a Skai.*

But it made for another long, lonely, empty day. And though Eben threw himself into work—briefing himself on all the new patients, updating their charts, refreshing bandages, prescribing and preparing and distributing tonic and herbs as needed—it didn't seem to help, or to keep his brain from wheeling back toward Tryggr again and again. It hadn't meant anything, it hadn't...

Eben worked late into the night again, his exhaustion growing heavier and heavier with every breath. And when a trace of a succulent, overpowering scent flared into his nostrils, he didn't even look up. Just kept crushing his herbs, squeezing his eyes shut, he was exhausted and imagining things, and that was all—

"Aren't you s'posed to be resting, Ka-esh?" asked a voice, low, familiar, far too close. And when Eben's eyes snapped open, it was—*Tryggr*. Tryggr, standing here beside his workbench, and looking at him.

Eben nearly dropped the pestle he'd been holding—Tryggr was *here*—but somehow he caught it again, and set it down with a clatter. "Oh," he croaked, and he couldn't help his inhale, dragging in the sweet, stunning scent swarming through the air. "I—I did rest. A lot."

Tryggr cocked a brow, as a wry smile pulled at his mouth. "Thing about resting, though," he said, "is that you gotta keep doing it, Ka-esh."

His voice was mild, but Eben could still feel the faint twinge of reprimand beneath it, and he couldn't suppress his reflexive wince, or his fervent, awkward nod. While Tryggr just kept looking at him, shifting on his feet, something moving in his eyes that Eben couldn't at all read.

"Healing all right, though?" Tryggr asked now, a little gruff. "An' you haven't gone back for any more ruts or lashings, have you?"

Eben winced again, and gripped his shaky, sweaty hands at the solid wood of the workbench. "N-no," he gulped. "N-not yet."

And wait, why had he said that, it sounded like he was *planning* to go back to the *dýflissa*—was he?—and he shook his head, opened his mouth. But nothing came out, and Tryggr's eyes shifted again, his arms smoothly folding over his chest.

"Well, take it easy in there next time, ach?" he said coolly. "Not much relief if it brings you real harm, is it? An' keeps you running back for more?"

Eben's wince felt like a flinch this time, and he couldn't help his reflexive glance downwards, toward Tryggr's legs. Because Efterar had said he'd torn a ligament fighting in the arena, hadn't he? And yes, yes, Tryggr was clearly favouring his left knee, betraying a faint hiss as he again shifted on his feet.

"M-mayhap I could say the—the same," Eben's hoarse voice stammered. "About the—the arena."

And curse him, *curse* him, because that was disbelief flaring across Tryggr's eyes, followed by a sudden, dark disapproval. "Not the same, Ka-esh," he snapped. "The arena's part of my *job*. We train to keep kin like you Ka-esh *safe*. To *help* you."

Oh. Part of his job, helping orcs like Eben. Weak orcs, Tryggr meant, foolish orcs, orcs who got themselves needlessly injured in the *dýflissa*, and therefore required impromptu feedings for their health. And of course it didn't mean anything, it had never meant anything, Eben had been dreaming, delirious, *never trust a Skai...*

"I know," he finally whispered, his voice cracking, his prickling eyes dropping to the workbench, to the mess of herbs he'd somehow made upon it. "I am s-sorry, sir."

There was a moment's brief, horrible silence, during which Eben's lip began badly quivering, betraying him, no, no, no. And he was about to abandon it all, to rush past Tryggr to the door, when something grasped his arm. Something—oh. Tryggr's hand.

Eben's fearful eyes darted up, blinking at where Tryggr was grimacing, and running his other hand against his hair. "No need to apologize, Ka-esh," he said, a little rushed. "Didn't mean to snap at you. It's just"—he grimaced again, shook his head—"I busted this knee in there the other day, and it's making me ornery, ach? Boss took me off duty scouting, and he's had me resting and doing rubbish jobs ever since. Says starting tomorrow, he's putting me to work helping his woman in the *scullery* instead. Doing *laundry* and shit."

Wait. Amidst all this, Eben had almost entirely forgotten about Alma and her plight—and she hadn't shown up in the sickroom all day, had she? Was that because—she'd gone to work in the scullery? And Drafli was now sending Tryggr to *help* her? Doing *laundry*?!

"Is Alma—well?" Eben asked, his voice a croak. "Well enough to be—doing laundry?"

Tryggr shot Eben a look he couldn't all read, and then abruptly released his grip on Eben's arm. "Guess so," he said, without enthusiasm. "Though I s'pose I'll be the one to keep an eye on her again to make sure, ach?"

Right. Because that was Tryggr's job, and that was all. Keeping weak kin safe. To the point where Drafli had ordered him to do it, and...

"And Drafli still truly wishes to... help Alma?" Eben asked, before he could stop it. "And have her... stay?"

His tired brain was belatedly dredging up the last he'd heard about this, when Tryggr had suggested that Drafli might make Alma an offer, to keep her close and safe. And Tryggr twitched a nod, though something sharp and strangely bitter flared through his scent, and his eyes shifted past Eben, narrowing on the wall behind his head.

"Ach, Boss made her the offer," Tryggr said flatly. "Got her a room of her own in the Grisk wing, gave her plenty of goods and credits—and then he took her to bed with him and his mate, too. Covered her all over with their scents, made sure she found joy in it."

Wait. Truly? Drafli had taken Alma to *bed*? With him, *and* Baldr? After he'd tried to *kill* her?

But Tryggr's face looked a little mulish, now, his nod decisive and firm. And blinking at him, Eben's longing was suddenly far too close, surging hard in his belly. Because what would it be like, to have a fierce, handsome Skai watching over you, giving you gifts, taking you to bed, making sure you found joy in it...

Tryggr was fully frowning now, his claws tapping at his biceps, his scent even sharper than before. And too late Eben realized he was just foolishly standing there staring, and reeking of hunger, or perhaps even jealousy.

"But," he croaked, before he even caught it, "Drafli still does not even... *like* Alma, ach? Or truly want her, in his bed, with his mate? Not after how she has come between him and Baldr, with the scent-bond?"

But Tryggr's frown only deepened, and he jerked a dismissive-looking shrug. "It hasn't been the best start, I ken," he said flatly. "But I'm told the woman's sweet and loyal, and a hard worker—and eager to please and obey in bed, too. All just as Skai like best, ach? So if she can keep it up, show Boss she's worth his time, I ken he'll come around."

Oh. *Oh*. Sweet, and loyal. A hard worker. Eager to please and obey in bed. *All just as Skai like best...*

Eben's heart was erratically pounding again, his eyes still frozen on Tryggr's face. On where Tryggr's frown twisted, tightened, as he jerked a swift, limping step backwards. "Well, glad you're feeling better, Kaesh," he said. "Best of luck with—not sleeping, I s'pose."

With that, he spun and strode for the door, his shoulders very straight, his steps lurching with his limp. And it wasn't until he'd vanished into the corridor that Eben realized it, recognized part of what had held him so caught, so transfixed, so foolish, that entire time.

Tryggr hadn't borne any other fresh scents. Not even after so many days, after he'd returned to the arena.

Tryggr had only scented of… *Eben*.

# 13

Tryggr had only scented of Eben.

The certainty shouted again and again through Eben's awareness as he finally dragged himself back to bed, and sank into a long, deep night's sleep. A sleep he'd unquestionably needed, and when he awoke, he felt far fresher, his thoughts far clearer than before.

Tryggr had been worried about him. Tryggr had wanted to make sure he was well. Tryggr had only scented of him. Of *him*.

But maybe—Eben's distant rational brain pointed out, as he washed and dressed—maybe it still meant nothing. Or even if it had, maybe he'd run Tryggr off entirely last night, with his exhaustion and his foolishness and his babbling. With how he'd implied he would soon return to the *dýflissa*.

And yes, that temptation still shimmered there, dark and low in Eben's belly—but the truth of Tryggr's scent was stronger. The truth of Tryggr's care, and his words. The way Tryggr had spoken of Alma, and of Drafli.

*The woman seems sweet. Loyal. A hard worker, eager to please in bed. All just as Skai like best. So if she can keep it up, show Boss she's worth his time, I ken he'll come around....*

Keep it up. Show him. *He'll come around.*

It meant something. It had to mean something. And Eben had to know. He had to try. He had to.

So instead of going straight to the sickroom, Eben first went for the scullery. Drawing in deep breaths as he strode through the corridors, through the Grisk wing, into the large, fragrant kitchen. Where he fought to ignore the odd glances from the silver-haired Ash-Kai and the frowning Skai working over the fire, and held his eyes on the open door of the small adjoining scullery up ahead.

Where—yes, yes—that was Tryggr's scent. Tryggr's scent, and another unfamiliar orc's, too. And when Eben halted in the scullery door, he found Tryggr kneeling over a washbasin, elbows-deep in soapy water, and blinking at him.

And Eben was blinking at Tryggr, too. At his wet-spattered bare chest, his strong, soapy forearms. The sheen of sweat across his forehead and high cheekbones, the long black strands of hair falling out of his topknot. All making him look more... vulnerable, somehow, more approachable, and perhaps even more appealing than before.

But most compelling of all was his scent. Hanging thick and heavy in the air, and still only tasting of... Eben.

"What is it, Ka-esh?" Tryggr finally said, into the dangling silence. "Looking for Alma? She's gone out for a spell, I ken."

Eben twitched and shook his head, and drew in a shaky breath. "I—" he began, tried again. "I only wished to ask if—if you might have any need for—help."

Tryggr's brows shot up, and then he glanced sideways, toward where—oh. Right. There was another orc, an older Skai, crawling out from where he'd apparently been under the counter. And as Eben blinked toward him, and then toward the counter—which held a towering pile of laundry—it occurred to him that the scullery still looked far cleaner than it had the last time he'd seen it, when he'd fixed that foul drain, and it had been overrun with ash and filth and vermin.

"Thanks, Ka-esh, but Duff's already helping with the laundry," Tryggr said, with a jerk of his head toward the older Skai, who was fully ignoring Eben, in favour of intently licking what scented like fresh blood from his fingers. "An' don't you already have work in the sickroom to do?"

Eben's stomach plummeted, his gaze dropping, and he gulped down a deep breath. A breath that filled his nostrils with more of Tryggr's scent, so unnaturally strong in this small stuffy room. A scent that still tasted of... Eben.

It was enough to raise Eben's eyes again, though his tooth bit hard at his wavering lip, and his clammy hands wiped at his trousers. "Ach, I do," he said, his voice hitching. "And I should never forego my work there, or our patients who need my help. But Efterar wished me to cut back my time there, and I only thought—if there was aught else a Ka-esh might help you with, such as—"

His eyes darted sideways, to where he could see the stone marking the nearest closed air-vent, and he edged toward it, and pulled it out with a shaky hand. Revealing the familiar cranking mechanism behind it, and after a few moments of squeaky turning, a rush of sweet fresh air poured through the vent and into the too-hot room.

"Wait, there's another vent?" Tryggr's sharp voice demanded, though it sounded distinctly relieved, too. "Thought there was only one, under the counter. How the hell'd you know that one was there?"

Eben shrugged, and gave a shaky wave of his hand. "They are marked the same in every room," he replied, slightly steadier than before. "There is another there"—he nodded toward the wall behind the Duff orc, and then up at the ceiling—"and there, I ken. Our fathers would not have built a scullery with only one vent, ach? This risks leaking tainted air into the kitchen, and spreading disease throughout all the mountain."

Tryggr was still staring at him, his arms immobile in the soapy water, while this Duff promptly turned around, and began poking at the vent Eben had pointed out behind him. But his hands were clearly arthritic, his frustration already jolting through the air, so Eben furtively went to join him, attempting a careful smile toward his wrinkled, reddening face.

"Ach, you near have it," he said softly. "Only twist, thus—ach, this is good. Once or twice more, I ken."

Duff obliged, turning the crank twice more—and he crowed aloud at the sudden blast of cool air in his face. But Eben winced, wrinkling his nose, because the scent behind also reeked of vermin—not only dung, but live mice too.

"Ach, it is infested," he told Duff. "It ought to be cleaned out, but—"

He cast an uneasy glance over his shoulder toward Tryggr, who hadn't wanted his help—but Tryggr was just watching, with a look Eben couldn't at all read in his eyes. While beside Eben, Duff was eagerly nodding, and waving him toward it. "Clean," he said flatly. "Get vermin *out*."

Eben couldn't argue with that—it was a genuine health hazard to have vermin living in a scullery—and he showed Duff how to release the vent's grate, and draw it out of the wall. And before Eben had even had a chance to look inside, Duff shot out a knobbly hand, grasped a live squirming mouse from inside the vent, and bit into its throat.

Eben blinked, but obligingly waited as Duff rapidly drained the mouse—cracking open its neck for good measure—before bending his silver head to peer longingly into the vent. "Other mice run off," he said mournfully. "Mayhap come back, if we put vent in again?"

Eben half-smiled and nodded, even as he glanced around, and went to collect a small shovel and a bucket. "Mayhap after we clean this out," he replied, with as much firmness as he could muster. "We should not wish to leave it there to fester for next time, ach?"

Thankfully, Duff didn't protest, and even helped Eben clean the vent with surprising enthusiasm. And while Tryggr had seemingly returned to his laundry-scrubbing behind them, Eben could almost feel him still listening, watching, his eyes prickling on Eben's back as he dumped the detritus down the scullery's ash chute, along with the drained mouse. Which, Duff sadly lamented, did not taste nearly as good as the rats.

"Ach?" Eben asked over his shoulder, as he scrubbed his hands in the sink, and then waved Duff toward it, too. "You ken, rats bear some properties that make them easier to digest, and thus may gain you more nutrients. Do you oft long for rats to eat?"

Duff fervently nodded as he washed his hands too, the scent of his hunger swirling into the air, and Eben considered that for another moment. "I ken you may need more of a specific nutrient, and this is why you crave this so strongly," he said thoughtfully. "I should be glad to bring you some of our tonics to try, should you wish? Most orcs like the taste very much, and some have fresh blood in them, also."

Duff looked cautiously intrigued by this, and behind them, Tryggr finally cleared his throat. "Can't see how it's not worth trying, Duff," he said firmly. "Thanks, Ka-esh."

Eben's face heated, but he smiled and waved it away. "I am happy to help," he said, and then twitched at the familiar words, at the way they caught and flared in Tryggr's eyes. And Tryggr wasn't washing again, was just kneeling there looking at Eben with something almost wolfish in his eyes, and Eben drew up to his full height, drew up his breath and his courage. He had to try.

*Keep it up. Show him. He'll come around...*

"I could help in—other ways, also," he said, too quickly. "I could"—his eyes darted downwards, toward the bloodstained tunic Tryggr was scrubbing—"bring some chalk powder, to help with stains. Or mayhap more lye, for soap. Or a solution to help keep the drain clean, and free of foul vapours that could harm you. Or harm Alma, who you are meant to watch over."

He was still speaking far too fast, his eyes wide and almost pleading on Tryggr's face. And oh, that was surely softness in Tryggr's eyes, in his rueful little half-smile, half-grimace.

"Ach, well, all right, then, Ka-esh," he said, husky. "We'll be glad to have you, I ken."

Eben couldn't help his sudden, relieved smile, beaming brightly down toward Tryggr's flushed face. And if he wasn't mistaken, Tryggr's hands fumbled the tunic in the water, his face gone slightly redder than before.

And it was something, it had to be something. And Eben's smile pulled even wider as he nodded, and drew in a deep breath of that sweet, succulent scent. Tasting of him. Only him.

"Thank you, sir," he said, to those watching, shifting eyes. "I shall do my best."

# 14

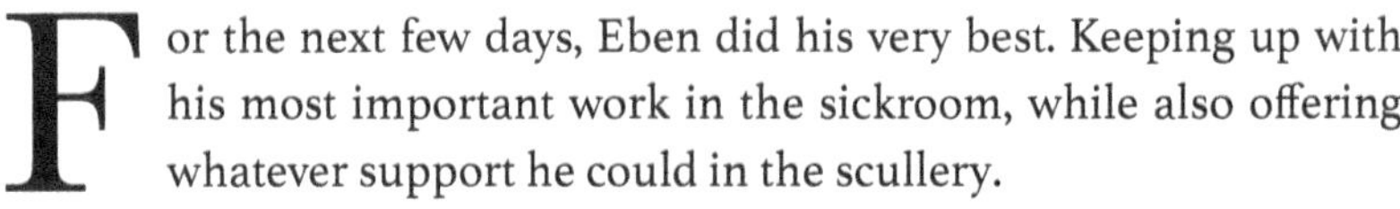

For the next few days, Eben did his very best. Keeping up with his most important work in the sickroom, while also offering whatever support he could in the scullery.

It made for more long, busy days, but somehow, they didn't seem nearly as exhausting as before. Perhaps because it meant Eben left the sickroom at a reasonable hour every afternoon, to ensure he could still catch Tryggr in the scullery—and more often than not, Tryggr would eventually send him away to supper, or to bed.

"Off with you, Ka-esh," he would say, with a militant glint in his eye. "You need rest, remember? Don't want you crashing like that again."

Eben hadn't once attempted to argue, and in truth, it was a strange, surprising relief to be told, to have all the doubts and obligations firmly snatched from his hands. And if he wasn't mistaken, Tryggr rather enjoyed having his orders obeyed, too—and he would watch intently as he waited for Eben's answer, his brows raised, his expression cool and assessing.

"Ach, I ken, sir," Eben would reply, reflexively putting his hand over his heart, in what he now knew was Skai sign language for *thank you*. "I shall return tomorrow."

He didn't think he imagined the satisfied hitch in Tryggr's scent—

especially at being called *sir*—and even if Eben continued to read in his bedroom after supper, he could still almost hear Tryggr's voice, close and hot in his ear. *You need rest. Keep it up. Show him. He'll come around...*

So Eben dutifully went to bed, though he often needed to stroke himself off before he could fall asleep, gasping and arching as visions of a hungry scarred prick and sharp Skai claws pulsed behind his eyes. He hadn't returned to the *dýflissa* since that night he'd been injured, and while he still longingly hesitated each time he passed it, he couldn't dare risk entering it again. Not now, not when Tryggr would instantly scent it upon him.

And Tryggr did scent for it, Eben was almost certain. Every day when Eben stepped into the scullery, Tryggr's frowning eyes would dart up, his nostrils flaring. And Eben couldn't deny scenting Tryggr, too, seeking out any changes, any new traces of other orcs—but there was still nothing. Still only *him*.

It made it too easy to beam at Tryggr's watching, wary eyes, and then even to shyly greet the scullery's other occupants. This almost always included Duff, but often an eager young Grisk named Timo, an indolent Bautul named Gaukr, and the Ash-Kai cook Gegnir—and, of course, Alma herself. And Eben had been pleased to see that Alma's condition had continued to steadily improve, to the point where she'd not only taken over the management of the scullery, but also the mountain's overall housekeeping efforts—essentially fulfilling the empty role of the mountain's former Keeper. A considerable and often thankless endeavour, to be sure, but Alma embraced the work with genuine-seeming enthusiasm, and treated her helpers with quiet, consistent kindness.

"Thank you so much," she would say to Eben, warm and earnest, whenever he brought in some lye, or drain cleaner, or even a long brush to scrub out the vents. "That will be a great help, I'm sure."

Eben always flushed and waved it away, though he often found himself glancing toward her afterwards, inhaling slow and deep. Not only scenting for any signs of further weakness or illness upon her, but also breathing in the distinct scents of Drafli and Baldr, now woven into her own, and deepening with every passing day. Suggesting, much to Eben's ongoing surprise and relief, that Drafli had indeed continued to honour the terms of that astonishing offer he'd made, welcoming Alma into his relationship, and his bed. Drafli had even made Alma kneel and suck his seed in the scullery, clearly marking both her and the room with his scent, as a true orc mate would—and according to Tryggr's gleeful retelling, Drafli had even done it while Tryggr and Duff had watched, signing her cool, casual orders that she'd instantly and eagerly obeyed.

Tryggr's admiring envy as he'd recounted the tale had been blatantly clear, prompting Eben to pay far closer attention to the Skai sign language, while also keeping an admittedly too-curious eye out for any sign of Drafli's return. And though he was disappointed in that regard, Eben also hadn't missed how several new buckets and cleaning implements had mysteriously appeared, bearing only Drafli's scent—and after hearing about the rodent infestation from Tryggr, Drafli had apparently even gone and brought Alma a *cat*.

*If she can keep it up, show Boss she's worth his time, I ken he'll come around...*

It was more relief in Eben's thoughts, more hope curling low in his belly. And as the days passed, it made it easier to laugh and chat—and even sign—with his new colleagues, and to keep offering whatever help he could. Which had so far included a thorough cleaning of the drain and vents, an expansion and repair of the ash chute, an ongoing supply of lye and chalk for soap and stains, and help with folding and delivering the laundry when needed. Eben had even begun a daily delivery of fresh tonic for Duff, formulated to include several of the proteins present in rat-meat. Which proved such a success that Tryggr showed up early one morning in the sickroom, and flashed Eben a sheepish smile from across the workbench.

"Duff's not feeling so good today," Tryggr said, "and he's been asking for the sweet Ka-esh's sweet drink. Would you mind making a batch early?"

Eben didn't mind at all, of course, and instantly set to work mixing it up, while Tryggr watched over the workbench. And though Eben's hands still shook as he worked, he managed not to spill anything, and smiled at Tryggr as he gave the bottle one final shake, and passed it over to him.

"I hope this helps," he said shyly. "I am glad he likes it."

Tryggr twitched a nod, his eyes lingering oddly on Eben's face. "Ach, he does," he replied. "An' I ken it does help him—he's always a bit more easy and alert afterwards. Enough to even keep making a fool of himself over that lazy arse Gaukr."

Eben couldn't help a laugh—Duff and Gaukr had begun a halting romance of sorts, these past days—but then he found that Tryggr was still hesitating, studying him over the workbench. His mouth pursed, his head tilted, his brow slowly furrowing.

"So... where'd you learn it all, anyway, Ka-esh?" he asked, his voice carefully light. "All this"—he gestured vaguely around at the sick-room—"and everything you know about the scullery, too? The vents, the drains, the chutes? The chalk for the bloodstains? How to make lye?"

More heat pooled into Eben's face, but he shrugged and gave a dismissive wave of his hand. "Most of it from reading and studying, I ken," he said, as steadily as he could. "The lye and chalk have oft been discussed in medical journals and treatises, for keeping clean is of great import in healing wounds, ach? And the engineering, I trained for many, many years upon this, for I was meant to be—"

His voice tripped, caught in his throat, but before him, Tryggr was still waiting, listening, his eyes curious and intent. So Eben forced himself to swallow, to draw in a deep breath of Tryggr's sweet scent. Still with only him, only him, upon it.

"I was meant to be our clan's Chief Structural Engineer," he said thickly. "Just as my father, and his father before him. But I wished—to learn medicine, instead. To seek answers to what ails our kin and our women, and offer the help they need."

Tryggr's eyes shifted, his head tilting a little further. "You have regrets, though?" he asked, careful now. "Wish you'd gone for the fancy title after all? Probably came with plenty of credits and acclaim, I ken?"

His voice sounded skeptical, almost suspicious, and curse it, Eben's scent must have betrayed something, must have hinted at all that old whispering darkness. And he had to draw in another deep, dragging breath, hold it in, only him, only him...

"I only regret—my father," he croaked out, his lip quivering hard enough that he bit down painfully against it. "He never forgave me for abandoning his great work, and he banished me from—our lives. Our home. Even upon his deathbed, he did not—"

He couldn't finish it, squeezing his eyes shut, shaking his head. And for an instant, there was silence before him, heavy and watchful—and then the feel of a warm, strong hand, gripping at his shoulder.

"Real sorry to hear that, Ka-esh," came Tryggr's low voice. "Your pa was a fool for not seeing how good you are at your work. An' how important it is, too."

Eben's shocked eyes blinked open, searching Tryggr's face, but there was no mockery in it, no trace of guile or sarcasm. Only a strange, serious stillness, something almost like… respect.

"It's good work, Ka-esh," Tryggr said, with a gentle squeeze to Eben's arm. "Real good, ach?"

What? Tryggr didn't… mean that. Did he? He thought Eben's work was good? Truly?

But yes, Tryggr was still looking at him like that, still holding Eben's shoulder, and now twitching a sad little smile. "You deserved better, Ka-esh," he said. "Not sure how I got two good fathers—between Pa and *Pabbi*—and you got dumped with yours. Don't seem fair, does it?"

Eben swallowed, his scrambling thoughts fighting to follow, to focus. Because yes, Tryggr had mentioned his father before, hadn't he? But he'd never brought up his *pabbi*—his adopted father—right?

"What—what are your fathers like?" Eben managed. "Are they both—good to you? Do they uphold—your goals? Your work?"

Tryggr's mouth twitched, his eyes flickering with warm, wry fondness. "Ach, always," he said. "Though it oft takes a bit of fussing to sort out, you ken. Pa first got it into his thick head that I oughta be a great Skai warrior, leading battles and such—but once I told him I'd rather work for Boss, he blustered for a day or two, and then went and set it all up for me. Told Boss he'd be a fool not to take me."

A small smile pulled at Eben's mouth—Tryggr's pa had to be a fearsome orc, to make demands of Drafli like that—and Tryggr's smile widened too, as he huffed a rueful little chuckle. "Don't mean Pa don't still try to poke his nose in wherever he can, though," he added lightly, with a roll of his eyes. "Thank Skai-kesh, *Pabbi* usually settles him down, and keeps him in line. Without him, I ken Pa would be sniffing about the scullery every damned day, asking after the sweet Ka-esh's scent. *Again.*"

Wait. Tryggr meant—his pa had been asking about… Eben? About Eben's scent? About Eben's scent on *Tryggr*, he surely meant, because of course Tryggr's family would smell it, and wonder at it. Wouldn't they?

And curse it, Eben's breath was coming too hard, the longing shivering fast and hungry into his scent. Strong enough that perhaps Tryggr had caught it too, his eyes gone blank as he twitched backwards, away—but then he hesitated, and raised the jar of milk toward Eben, as if in a little salute.

"Well, thanks again, Ka-esh," he said, husky. "An' see you later today?"

Eben fervently nodded and smiled, and again made the Skai sign for *thank you*, his hand over his heart. A movement that Tryggr looked at for an instant too long before he turned toward the door—but just before he left, he hesitated, and made a sign back, too. *My honour*, it said.

Eben couldn't stop smiling to himself for the rest of the day, as the happiness kept circling and skittering in his chest. Tryggr had come to see him. Tryggr had wanted his tonic. Tryggr had told him about his family. And most powerful of all, Tryggr had praised Eben's work.

*Your pa was a fool. It's good work. Real good.*

It was something no one else had ever said to Eben, not that he could ever recall. Among the Ka-esh, an engineer remained the highest possible calling, commanding praise and respect, while medicine was new, untested, unfamiliar. Something done mostly by the Ash-Kai clan, with their gifted healers like Efterar—or perhaps sometimes by the Grisk, with their care for kin and home. Until Eben, and then Salvi after him, it had never been a Ka-esh discipline, not in the slightest. And to be told—by a Skai!—of its worth felt deeply, fundamentally powerful. Like something Eben would forever treasure, for all his days.

That afternoon in the scullery, it was even easier to chat and laugh with Tryggr and Duff—who'd eagerly drunk the second bottle of tonic Eben had brought him—and with Alma, too. Alma still wasn't in the scullery as often as Tryggr and Duff, due to her ever-expanding work as the mountain's new Keeper, but today she was making more soap, while excitedly reviewing their plans to do a full floor-washing, all throughout the mountain.

It was an endeavour that required flooding the mountain from the top, and it had needed considerable amounts of Ka-esh input, including the involvement of multiple engineers. And Eben had willingly taken the lead on the Ka-esh side of the project, collecting and combining all the engineers' notes, reviewing and translating them into common-tongue, and adding his own annotations. And just the evening before, he'd finished a comprehensive summary of required processes and estimated timelines for Alma, so she could assign tasks to her helpers as needed, and create a proper schedule for the day.

"That document has just been so helpful," she said warmly over her shoulder, toward where Eben was currently hanging the clean wet laundry on the wall's rickety drying racks. "Thank you so much for pulling it together on such short notice. It must have been a shocking amount of work, on top of all your work in the sickroom."

Eben shrugged and waved it away, though he couldn't quite suppress his small, grateful smile toward her. To which Alma smiled back, a flush spreading across her pretty face—even as a dark, bitter scent filtered from Tryggr at the washbasin.

"So how're things going with Boss these days, woman?" Tryggr cut in, his voice sharp. "He still treating you properly, training you up, showing you off? Giving you lots of joy with his mate?"

Alma's face flushed even redder, and she mumbled something unintelligible toward the sink. But there was no mistaking the sudden surge of hunger and longing and pleasure in her scent, so strong it nearly swayed Eben on his feet, and flared a stab of envy deep into his belly. What must it be like, to have such a fearsome Skai treating you properly, training you up, showing you off? Giving you joy?

*He'll come around*, Tryggr had said. *If she can keep it up, show she's worth his time...*

Eben couldn't help a furtive look toward Tryggr at the basin, and found him frowning down at the water, his brow deeply furrowed. Looking so strangely troubled that Eben felt his own happiness—his own hopefulness—slightly faltering, skittering into his fingers. Into where he foolishly fumbled at a bar of the drying rack, and knocked half of it out of the damned wall entirely.

"Ach, Ka-esh!" Tryggr snapped, as he lurched over, and caught the bars before they tumbled to the floor. "Watch yourself!"

Oh. A cold shudder rippled up Eben's spine, his head instantly ducking, his eyes squeezing shut. "Sorry, sir," he croaked, thick in his throat. "It was a—a—"

*An accident*, he'd meant to say, but oh, he couldn't even speak, the sudden misery churning in his belly, flooding hot into his chest. Foolish. *Foolish*. And Tryggr was still frowning at him like that, like he was foolish, weak—and curse it, Eben wasn't about to start weeping, not here, not now, not where they all could see—

He mumbled a choked, halting excuse, and then spun around, and dodged for the door. Rushing out through the kitchen, into the corridor, as the vision of the distant Ka-esh wing bloomed behind his eyes. The vision of the *dýflissa*, yes, with its sweet promises of relief, of pain, of forgetting. It had been so long, the longest Eben could remember going without being touched in his entire adult life, and he just needed—he needed—

He crashed. Smashing straight into something warm and solid, sending him reeling backwards, staggering on his feet. Blinking, focusing, as more miserable panic shot through his chest, through his trembling, gulping mouth...

It was Drafli.

# 15

Drafli. The most terrifying orc in the mountain, *here*, looming over Eben in the dark empty corridor, and glowering at him with narrow, furious-looking eyes.

Fuck, how the hell did Eben keep doing this. Foolish, *foolish*, and visions of Drafli's dagger were already whirling into his thoughts, screaming behind his eyes. *Never let a Skai get you alone, run, run, run—*

But then Drafli—signed at him. Spoke to him, with the Skai sign language, slow and distinct enough that Eben could easily follow what it meant.

*Wait*, he signed. *Peace. Tryggr will come.*

What? No. No, he wouldn't, he wasn't, foolish, and Eben's darting glance up the corridor found only blackness, and more desperate panic in his chest. He was alone with Drafli. Drafli who had almost murdered Alma, and who now... scented of Alma. Scented of Alma, on his hands, his groin, his mouth, his... breath. And suddenly there was the jolting, utterly incongruous vision of Drafli with his face buried between Alma's legs, his cruel tongue licking her from the inside out, and he—he hadn't. Had he?

But it was still there on Drafli's scent, bright and clear, just as vivid as if Eben had seen it with his own eyes. And now that Eben was studying Drafli, breathing him in this close, he still scented only of

Alma and Baldr, too. Shouting that he'd still kept those vows. Kept to the terms of that offer he'd made. *Never trust a Skai...*

And wait, now Drafli was glancing purposefully up the corridor—and yes, oh, he'd somehow spoken truth in that, too. Because Tryggr was indeed jogging down the corridor toward them, his mouth grim, his eyes darting rapid and unreadable between Drafli and Eben.

*Good*, Drafli signed sharply at Tryggr, while running his piercing gaze up and down Eben's still-shivering body. *Now tend to him. You cannot allow your——to scent thus.*

Eben's blinking eyes hadn't at all caught what Drafli had called him, but Tryggr clearly understood, giving a shaky exhale, and a jerky nod. To which Drafli nodded too, and made to turn away—but then he stopped, and spun back to Tryggr again. *He is——*, he signed. *He helped me in a time of——, and spared me from a——wrong.*

Oh. Eben's racing heart skipped a beat, his eyes now darting between Drafli's hands and his face. Because Drafli hadn't just said that—whatever the full extent of it was—about him? But yes, yes, Drafli had given a curt nod between him and Tryggr, and then strode off up the corridor, not sparing a single look back.

It left Eben standing there blinking uneasily at Tryggr, who still looked distinctly uneasy, too. His face pale, his shoulders heaving, his swallow convulsing in his corded throat.

"Ach, Ka-esh," he said thickly. "You're all right, ach? No need to scent thus. Naught to fear."

Right. Eben couldn't hide his grimace, his eyes dropping, because of course Tryggr would only think he was afraid, and in need of comforting. Foolish, weak...

"An'—I'm sorry," Tryggr continued, faster. "Didn't mean to snap at you, or run you off like that, just now. I wasn't vexed with you, or tryna mock or shame you, ach? Could never be vexed with you, you ken. Was just"—he drew in a deep breath—"fussing over you, is all. Just means—I care."

Oh. *Oh*. Something warm and trembly shivered up Eben's spine, and his eyes snapped up, searching Tryggr's pale, watching face. He... meant that? He... cared?

"Oh," Eben whispered, without at all meaning to. "I—thank you, sir."

Tryggr's eyes briefly closed, his head tilting back in a way that looked almost despairing. "Ach, Ka-esh," he said, hoarse. "Don't need to thank me, either."

But Eben was searching him now, drinking in that undeniable truth of his own scent, and only his scent, on Tryggr's twitching, too-close body. Just like Drafli had only borne Baldr and Alma's scents... the same Drafli who had kept his word, and even praised Eben's efforts. His help.

Eben gathered his breath, gathered his courage, as his own trembling, tingling hand moved. Slipping up between them, slow, shaky—and then very lightly, very carefully, stroking up against Tryggr's warm bare chest.

"But you have been—so kind, sir," he ventured, very quiet. "It—pleases me, to thank you. To—honour you."

And oh, oh, what had he just said, what the hell was he doing—and he snatched his hand away, too late. But it still felt hot, trembly, alive with the feel of Tryggr's smooth warm skin, with the truth of his rich scent now lingering on Eben's fingers. And Tryggr's scent in the air had shifted too, flaring with something bright and sweet...

But Tryggr hadn't moved, or made any indication of responding in turn, and his face still looked pale, his jaw flexing in his cheek. "Ach, Ka-esh," he finally said. "Then—next time I speak thus to you, mayhap you'll just—ignore me. Or throw it back at me. But there's no need to run away, or scent as though I've just gone and kicked you in the heart, ach? 'Cause I'd *never*."

Oh. Well. Eben's relief exhaled heavy and harsh, and he could feel the slow smile pulling at his mouth, warming his eyes. "I am... glad," he murmured. "I... thank you, sir."

Tryggr half-laughed, half-groaned, his eyes glinting on Eben's face with frustration, and exasperation, and... something else. And for a breathless, dangling instant, Eben thought he might come closer, might even reach out and...

But then Tryggr cleared his throat, and took a purposeful step backwards. "You oughta get to bed, then, Ka-esh," he said firmly. "Big day tomorrow, ach?"

Right. Eben had of course committed to a full day of work supporting Alma's floor-cleaning project, and he jerked a nod, and fought to ignore the sharp little plunge in his belly. To which Tryggr let out another low, frustrated-sounding groan, as he lurched forward—and before Eben had even caught it, Tryggr bent over him, and pressed a soft, brief kiss to the top of his head.

"Sleep well, sweet Ka-esh," he said gruffly, as he backed away again, not meeting Eben's eyes. "See you tomorrow."

Eben couldn't even nod, let alone speak, and he stood frozen in place, tingling all over, watching Tryggr stride away up the corridor. His steps long and quick, his shoulders square, his hand rubbing at his face as he disappeared around the corner.

Tryggr had… kissed him. He'd *kissed* him.

It was a bright, jubilant awareness, firing warm and hopeful through Eben's chest. *Keep it up. Show him. He'll come around…*

Eben slept deep and contented that night, and the next morning he first stopped by the sickroom, checking with Efterar and preparing any urgent prescriptions, before heading to the scullery. Where he again threw himself into another full, intensive day of work, not only supporting Alma's project as best as he could, but dealing with the Ka-esh engineers—who made it clear they would rather be doing anything else—while also personally ensuring the sickroom got the deepest, most thorough cleaning possible. To the point where, late in the day, even Kesst looked satisfied, smiling gratefully at Eben as a faintly snoring Efterar slept soundly in a nearby bed.

"Looks and scents so much better, doesn't it?" Kesst said, without even a trace of mockery or sarcasm in his voice. "Such a damned relief. It was good of you Ka-esh to help Alma organize it all."

Eben smiled and waved it away—or at least, he attempted to, because suddenly a familiar scent had swarmed into the room, and snatched at his hand in midair. And even as Eben startled to look, he already knew—it was Tryggr. Tryggr, here, gripping his hand, and flashing Kesst a broad, if rather chilly, smile.

"It was good of *this* Ka-esh, you mean," he said to Kesst, as his hand gently squeezed Eben's. "You ken the rest of 'em woulda done near as much without him? He don't oft draw eyes to himself, but he's been working his pretty little arse off on this. Just like he does every day in here, too—not that any of *you* can be fussed to notice."

Eben froze to stunned stillness, his eyes aghast on Tryggr's face. He hadn't just said that... had he? To *Kesst*? One of the most popular, influential orcs in the mountain?!

But to Eben's ongoing astonishment, Kesst blinked between them, and then grimaced, and let out a heavy sigh. "Right," he said. "Sorry. I suppose it's—easy to overlook individual contributions in here, amidst all the filth and blood and exhaustion."

With that, he gave a wild-looking wave that seemed to encompass the entire room, before spinning and stalking off again. But beside Eben, Tryggr looked at least somewhat mollified, and more warmth was pooling and fizzing in Eben's belly. Tryggr had defended him. Tryggr had noticed his work. Tryggr had noticed his *pretty little arse*.

"Now c'mon, Ka-esh," Tryggr said firmly, with a gentle tug at where he was still holding Eben's hand. "You *reek* of weariness, and you're going to bed, ach?"

Eben meekly nodded, and willingly allowed Tryggr to lead him out the door, and down toward the Ka-esh wing. But instead of stopping and sending Eben onward, as Eben fully expected, Tryggr kept walking beside him, his grip on Eben's hand warm and firm, his eyes frowning on the corridor up ahead.

"It *was* real good of you, to do all that work today," Tryggr finally said, into the silence. "Heard you going at it with some of those Ka-esh earlier, spurring 'em on. I ken they'd have all stayed hunkered down here buried in their rocks and books, without you."

He wasn't wrong, and Eben huffed a short, wry little laugh. "Ach, well, we are not always naturally inclined to see beyond our own clan, I ken," he said. "Or beyond our books, either."

They'd reached the door of his room, and Eben shot a rueful glance at his own refreshed pile of books, stacked high on his small, rickety desk. With his enforced early bedtimes, he'd continued to expand his reading, and he was vaguely surprised to see Tryggr's mouth drop open, his eyes incredulous on Eben's face.

"Wait, Ka-esh," he snapped. "When I've been sending you to bed, you've been coming down here alone into this dank little hole, and *reading*, instead of sleeping?"

Eben blinked and bit his lip, the chagrin curdling sudden and sharp through his chest. "Um, I—" he began, between shaky breaths. "Just—a little? I just—*need* to read, sir."

He was cringing away, his eyes wide and fearful on Tryggr's face—but wait. Something was hitching in Tryggr's scent, something that called up a dark, ravenous hunger low in Eben's belly—and oh, Tryggr's hand was clasping tighter on Eben's, drawing him closer, as his other hand reached around, and gave a gentle slap to Eben's *arse*.

"I oughta thrash you for this, little Ka-esh," Tryggr breathed. "Oughta bend you over my knee, and teach you a fucking *lesson*."

Oh, *fuck*. Eben's gasp was almost a groan, dragging low and hungry out of his throat, shuddering his body all over, leaning closer into Tryggr's touch. Because oh, please, yes, would Tryggr really do that, please, *now*—

But curse him, maybe he'd betrayed too much, because Tryggr abruptly lurched backwards, rubbing his hand forcefully at his eyes. "Just joking!" he said, his voice far louder than before. "Just want you to sleep, Ka-esh! That's *all*."

He didn't wait for Eben's reply, and instead whirled around, and fled from the room. Leaving Eben standing there and breathing hard, his face hot, his cock rigid and straining helplessly in his trousers. What... what had that been about? Had Eben... truly displeased Tryggr, with the books? Upset him? Or was this just... not working, after all? Did Tryggr just... not care? Even with the truth of only Eben's scent upon him?

*Never trust a Skai*, his father's voice droned, and Eben squeezed his eyes shut, and shook his head. *Show him. He'll come around. I oughta bend you over my knee...*

Sleep was slow coming that night, amidst all the doubts and thwarted hunger now swirling Eben's thoughts, and he slept in far too late the next morning—but he gathered his determination as he washed and dressed, fetched a bucket of lye, and headed back up into the mountain. He had to keep trying. Tryggr would come around...

His heart pounded louder as he neared the scullery, his breaths short and shallow in his throat—but yes, yes, he could scent Tryggr, could see him just ahead, there. Alone in the scullery, bent over the washbasin, scrubbing at a stained tunic.

But for perhaps the first time since they'd begun this, Tryggr didn't acknowledge Eben's approach. Didn't even look up. Just kept frowning down at his scrubbing, his mouth set and thin, his scent strange in the air.

"Is aught—amiss, sir?" Eben asked, before he could help it. "Are you—feeling well?"

Tryggr huffed a laugh and shook his head, but kept his eyes on his scrubbing. "Ach, well enough," he said, aiming a brief glower over his shoulder toward the still-looming pile of laundry on the counter. "Just—weary of laundry, mayhap."

Of course. Tryggr had been washing clothes for multiple days on end now, and Eben felt a sudden jolt of sympathy, and perhaps regret, too. Despite all his efforts here, he'd so rarely thought about seeking ways to specifically help Tryggr—he always seemed so capable, so relaxed, so self-assured. But now, blinking at Tryggr's bowed head, it occurred to Eben that he did look weary, and a little sad, too. And for a Skai who was trained as a scout and a warrior, being ordered onto laundry duty for so long must have been a miserable—or even humiliating—experience, right? And how had Eben never considered that, never once considered how Tryggr might feel about all this?

"Well, I have been thinking," Eben said, too quickly, "that we ought to seek ways to make this washing more efficient. I have been meaning to speak to our engineers upon this, for I have read of machines in the north that can help, and make this faster."

His voice came out too eager, almost desperate, but Tryggr still didn't spare a look up. "Ach, mayhap," he said distractedly. "Thanks, Ka-esh."

Eben's belly dipped, his throat swallowing hard, but he jerked a nod, and made to stagger with the increasingly heavy bucket of lye toward the sink—a movement that finally snapped Tryggr's head up, his eyes flashing with sudden disbelief.

"Ach, Ka-esh!" he yelped, as he leapt to his feet. "Careful! Give me that!"

Right. Eben's belly plummeted again, but he managed another nod, and shoved the bucket toward Tryggr's waiting hands. And then attempted a smile up toward his face, as Tryggr's words from the corridor echoed through his thoughts. *Just fussing over you. Just means—I care.*

And surely Tryggr was thinking of it too, his eyes oddly intent on

Eben's face as he took the bucket, their fingers just brushing—but then Tryggr's gaze shifted purposefully beyond Eben. Toward where—oh. Alma. Scenting of uncertainty, and looking meaningfully toward Tryggr, as though she wished to speak with him.

Eben could take a hint, at least, so he rushed out the door, and headed back to the sickroom. Where he barely noticed Kesst's nod toward him as he entered—at least, until Kesst sighed, and came over to eye Eben over the workbench.

"Look, I just wanted to—apologize, again, for overlooking all your efforts, Eben," he said. "And for pushing you to help in the scullery, and teasing you like I did about Alma, too. I know it's not an excuse, but I've been a bit—out of sorts, lately."

Eben blinked, genuinely taken aback, but he attempted to smile, and wave it away. But perhaps it hadn't come out right, because Kesst sighed again, and gave Eben a look that was almost... sympathetic. "And I didn't even notice," he added, quieter, "that it's not Alma you've been pining over all this time, is it? It's that loudmouth Skai fuckboy *Tryggr*. Gods, you two even *scent* of each other."

Wait. No. Damn it. Eben couldn't move, couldn't breathe, could only stare aghast at Kesst's face, because now Kesst would tell Tryggr how Eben felt, Kesst would mock him and dismiss him and ruin everything—

"Gods, don't scent like that, I won't *tell* him," Kesst said, flapping a hand toward him. "I just thought maybe I owed you—a warning."

A warning. Eben still couldn't breathe, could only stand there and wait while his stomach pitched and churned in his gut, and Kesst sighed again. "You just—you know what Skai can be like, right?" he said thinly. "I mean, I know they're not all like that, I'm trying to examine my own biases here, but still, just"—he hesitated, his eyes almost sad on Eben's face—"just... be careful. You could end up—really hurt."

Oh. Eben's heart was erratically pinging in his chest, but he made himself nod, and mumble a thank-you. And long after Kesst had gone back to his own work, his words kept echoing through Eben's thoughts, again and again and again. *You know what Skai are like. Be careful. You could end up really hurt. Never trust a Skai...*

By the end of the workday, Eben was sweaty and jittery and half-panicked, rushing back to the scullery with shaky, frantic steps. But his heart dropped even before he entered, because he could already scent that Tryggr wasn't there—or Alma, either. Only Duff was still working, doggedly sloshing soapy water against a bloodstained pair of trousers.

"Young Tryg not here," he balefully informed Eben, without being asked. "In Skai arena, I ken."

Eben fought to quash his surging disappointment, and attempted to focus on helping with some washing instead. But Duff kept darting narrow glances toward him, and finally he bobbed his silver head toward the door. "You go," he said. "Fetch him yourself."

What? No. Eben couldn't possibly go to that terrifying arena, not alone, not again—but Duff jabbed a soapy, wizened finger at the door this time. "No Skai dare touch you," he said flatly, "now you bear young Tryg scent."

Oh. Truly? And Eben hadn't at all realized Duff knew about that, but of course he would have scented it, just like Kesst, just like Tryggr's fathers, just like they all had, perhaps. And it was enough to make Eben nod, to make him lurch for the door again. Not thinking, not thinking, as he staggered on shaky legs toward the Skai wing, his heartbeat thundering distantly through his chest. He was just walking, just seeking that sweet familiar scent, that was all, that was all...

And yes, yes, there it was, just a twinge of it, drawing Eben down this corridor, down that one. Winding deeper and deeper into the dim cozy Skai wing, and between the scent and the comforting darkness, it kept his steps moving, going, closer and closer and closer...

Until—this. This door. The arena. With far fewer scents flooding it this time, and Eben's eyes instantly caught on Tryggr. He was fighting against three other Skai orcs, his lean body writhing and snapping and kicking, his grunts and hisses filtering through the air. And for a startled, frozen instant, Eben could only stand there and stare at him, drink up the fierce fluid beauty of his strong, stunning body. Damn, he was gorgeous, he was everything, and there was nothing more Eben wanted than to...

But then, Tryggr froze. His head snapping up, his gaze darting toward—Eben. And for an instant, they only stared at each other, even as another orc landed what looked like a painful kick into Tryggr's side, setting him staggering on his feet, pitching sideways, toward...

Eben. Wait, wait, Tryggr was coming toward Eben, sprinting with astonishing speed, his eyes blazing. And before Eben could move, or catch it, or speak, Tryggr dragged him out into the corridor, shoved him up against the hard stone wall, and—pinned him there. Trapped him there.

Oh, this wasn't happening, it couldn't be happening—but it was, Tryggr's lean sweaty body was hot and shivery and far too close, his scent flooding all through Eben's breath. And oh, oh, his face was even nuzzling into Eben's neck, and inhaling slow and deep, while his hungry clawed hand slipped up Eben's chest, too. Moving slowly enough that Eben could easily knock it away, could run or refuse or escape—but instead he moaned and shivered all over as that hand found his neck, and circled certain and safe around it.

Fuck. Fuck, yes, this was what he wanted, what he needed, what he'd been craving all this time, and he arched up into it, offering his neck, offering anything Tryggr would take, anything he would give. And Tryggr would, he *was*, his teeth scraping against Eben's collarbone, seeking the best place to bite and drink, please, please...

But then—it was gone. Gone, gone, because Tryggr was staggering backwards, whipping his head back and forth, dragging his hands against his hair. And Eben was already following, desperate and instinctive, his hand reaching out, just needing it back, please, please—

"No, Ka-esh," Tryggr hissed, sharp and low, almost a bark. "I said, no!"

It was as though he'd struck Eben across the face, and Eben froze, stunned, mortified, as ice kicked and cracked in his belly. No? No?

"Look, I just—I can't, Ka-esh," Tryggr said, and he'd even spun away from Eben, his head tilting back, his hands rubbing at his face. "I know what you really want, and I just—can't, all right? I've seen it with Pa an' *Pabbi*, my whole fucking life, and I'm not gonna—ach. No. *No.*"

No. Eben couldn't breathe, couldn't think, could scarcely even follow Tryggr's words. He couldn't. He couldn't. He was saying no, no, *no*.

No.

"Look, I'm sorry," Tryggr said, too thick, still without looking at Eben. "But I just—just need some time away from you for a spell, ach?

Naught personal, it's not your fault, but you're just too—you just make me—I just—I *can't*, Ka-esh."

Oh. And even if Eben still couldn't follow the rest of it, he could follow this. Tryggr didn't want him. Tryggr wanted him to go away. After all that, after all Eben's foolish hopes and plans and longings, Tryggr was saying—no.

And it was as though something had broken, wretched and raw, deep in Eben's chest, in his heart. Something deeper than loss, or despair, so deep Eben couldn't bear to touch it, to look at it. Couldn't bear to even look at Tryggr, couldn't bear to scent him for another breath.

"Ach, then," he whispered, to the floor, go, go, go. "You shall not see me again."

And before he could buckle beneath it, he spun around, and staggered into the darkness.

# 16

Eben didn't know how he ended up in the Ka-esh wing, staring at the *dýflissa*.

The scents of pain and pleasure were so familiar, so sweet, the sounds of firm slaps and cracking whips thudding deep into his aching chest. But his prick stayed soft and slack in his trousers, and a distant part of Eben pointed out that he was so often soft, in the *dýflissa*. It wasn't like those moments with Tryggr, with all that desire and longing. It was... empty. Just as empty as he was.

"Eben?" asked a voice, Gareth's voice, and Eben blinked at where his familiar form was striding out of the *dýflissa*, his whip still in hand, his trousers sagging around his sweaty waist. "What is amiss? Are you hurt?"

Eben couldn't even speak, could only stare blankly at Gareth's face, at the slowly increasing concern in his eyes. "Is it that Skai?" Gareth demanded, sharper now. "What has he done to you?"

But it was enough to rouse some faint awareness in Eben's chest, and he shook his head. "He did naught," he said dully. "Naught at all."

Gareth kept studying him, the worry creasing his forehead. "Should you mayhap... wish for some relief, then?" he asked, tentative. "I should be glad to offer whatever you wish."

He'd even held up the whip, but still nothing stirred in Eben's trousers, and now he could hear Tryggr's voice again, echoing behind his blinking eyes. *Not much relief if it brings you real harm, is it? Keeps you running back for more?*

Eben's head seemed to shake on its own, and his sad little smile almost felt genuine. "Thank you, brother," he whispered, "but I ken it should be wiser to rest."

He was vaguely surprised at the strength of the disappointment in Gareth's scent, but he suddenly felt too weary to wonder at it. Too weary even to return to his own room, on the opposite side of the Ka-esh wing—and instead, his numb, staggering feet took him to a different room. A far larger room, just a corridor over, reeking of familiarity and pain.

His family's room. Their *hellir*.

Eben hadn't stepped foot in it since his father's death years before, but he was unsurprised to see that it hadn't been changed, or put to another use. It would still be considered his own *hellir* by the clan, even after all this time, and the furnishings were all still here, even his father's old clothes, now surely ruined by moths and mildew. And Eben blinked around at it for a dazed, stilted moment, before lurching over to sink onto his old stone bunk, burying his face in his hands.

*Never trust a Skai*, his father's voice shouted, so loud now. *You never focus on what is important. You waste your talent and your time. You do a deep disservice to all your Ka-esh kin. You show yourself foolish and weak.*

*Get out. Do not return here or speak to me again, until you come to your senses.*

Eben's mouth choked a sound like a laugh, or a sob, because he had never come to his senses, had he? He'd always been a disappointment, a failure, a waste for his kin and his clan. He'd always known it, his father had always known it, *never trust a Skai...*

Another sob tore from Eben's chest, heaving out of his trembling mouth. *Never trust a Skai*. A refrain, a mantra, a curse, that had spoken so strongly of his father's conviction, his clan's truth. And Eben had believed it, had believed it and feared it, just as he'd believed and feared all the rest of it, and maybe—

His head shook in his hands as more thick, ugly sobs barked from his throat. He'd believed it all for so, so long. And maybe—maybe

Tryggr had been—a hint of light, in the darkness. A rebellion. *I can show you the way.*

Because with Tryggr, Eben had fought against his father's words, even as he'd still feared them. For if a Skai could be trusted, after all, then maybe—maybe the rest of it might have been wrong, too.

*You never focus on what is important. You waste your talent and your time. You show yourself foolish and weak...*

But Tryggr—Tryggr had never treated Eben that way, not once. He'd never thought him or his efforts a waste. Even tonight, even amidst all that hurt and grief, Tryggr hadn't been harsh or cruel. *I'm sorry. Naught personal. Not your fault.*

The sobs kept choking from Eben's throat, his head shaking against his trembling fingers, but Tryggr's voice kept speaking now, steady and certain and so, so confident. *No need to apologize. Don't speak thus. I've got you. Naught to fear.*

*It was good of you, Ka-esh. Brave as hell. You didn't need to do it, and you did it anyway. We're grateful.*

And even stronger, sharper, those heady, impossible moments in Eben's room, with his head in Tryggr's lap. *Good. Real good, Ka-esh. Ach, you've got a tight, hot little mouth. Real nice. So good and tight and sweet, so pretty with a Skai in your mouth...*

But beyond that, even strongest of all, was still that day in the sick-room, when Tryggr had come to ask for Eben's tonic. For Eben's work. When he'd looked Eben in the eye, and spoken those impossible, unthinkable words, words Eben would never forget.

*It's good work, Ka-esh. Real good. Your pa was a fool for not seeing how good you are at your work. An' how important it is, too.*

*Your pa was a fool. It's good work. Real good.*

The words rang around and around in Eben's skull, behind his scratchy eyes, curling into his empty-feeling chest. *It's good work. Real good.*

And amidst his hollow, aching exhaustion, Eben could somehow, almost... agree. It *was* good work. It was. He'd seen how it had helped Duff. He'd seen how it had helped countless other patients, orcs, women, orclings. And that truth—that help—wasn't something his father could ever take from him.

His father had been... wrong.

*Never trust a Skai*, the grating voice chanted, but Eben shook his head, and drew in a deep, dragging breath. Because maybe... maybe his father had been wrong about that too, after all. Even if Tryggr hadn't wanted Eben, or hadn't even liked him—he'd still been so kind. So consistently generous. He'd looked out for Eben, he'd helped him, he'd praised him.

If nothing else, Tryggr had been... a friend. A real friend, who could be trusted, and relied upon.

And that, too, was something else Eben was sure about. Even if his own perceptions couldn't be trusted, Tryggr had still been a true friend to Alma. To Duff. Even to Drafli, doing all that miserable work in the scullery, seeking to support his boss in a time of great personal difficulty, and helping to make his new woman feel at home.

And yes, even Drafli had trusted Tryggr. The fiercest, most fearsome Skai in the mountain had trusted Tryggr alone with his woman, for days and days on end. And Tryggr had returned that trust with hard work, and with care, and with kindness.

*Never trust a...* began the voice, but Eben shook his head, and curled up on the bunk.

*Your pa was a fool. It's good work. Real good.*

He somehow slept like that, alone on the hard cold stone, breathing the scents of his father, his lost home. He even dreamt of his father, of his father speaking, speaking, speaking, hurling his conviction and his fear at his small, cowering child. A child who finally raised his wet, miserable face, and whispered, *It is good work, Father. It is.*

When Eben awoke again, his head still ached, his eyes puffy and gritty, his throat still raw from his weeping. But the emptiness in his chest had shifted, somehow, settled into a strange, unfamiliar certainty.

It was good work. It had been a good choice. He had worked hard, and done his best.

But then—he blinked, rubbed his face—a scent. A familiar scent. A scent he'd never expected to taste this close again, still whispering of... him.

"Tryggr?" he croaked, toward the door—and in a flash of

movement, Tryggr indeed lurched into view. Hovering in the doorway with an odd, jerky intensity, his forehead furrowed, his face pale.

"Sorry to bother you, Ka-esh," he said, his voice rough. "But there's been a bit of a mess up above, and I was wondering if you might be willing to—"

He broke off there, wincing, but Eben was already shoving himself up in bed, and nodding. Tryggr had been a friend. A gift. And Eben would never, ever forget that, as long as he lived.

"Ach, I am happy to help," he said, and he meant it. "Aught that you need. Always."

# 17

In all Eben's wildest fantasies about Tryggr, he had never once imagined the bizarre, surreal experience of sitting across from Tryggr in his family's *hellir*, and listening intently to his Skai tale of woe.

It turned out that Alma, Drafli, and Baldr had bitterly quarrelled, to the point where Alma was now convalescing in the sickroom, and Baldr had run off above ground, alone. This had put Drafli in the highly unenviable position of needing to choose between them, and he had finally taken off after Baldr, after leaving detailed instructions with his clanmates about Alma—who, apparently, was now also pregnant with their son.

"But now *she*'s planning to run off again too!" Tryggr continued, his voice more agitated than Eben had ever heard it. "An' all those meddling Ash-Kai are supporting it as some kinda grand scheme—'cause her old fool boss is still rattling his swords at us, saying we kidnapped her, so if she goes back to him, he can't blame us anymore! An' I ken I should follow her, keep an eye on her like I have been, but just before he left"—Tryggr dragged both hands against his hair—"Boss told me to stay stuck here on my arse, *again*, and fix up the scullery! Make it real nice and new for her, he said!"

It was taking Eben's full concentration to follow all this, a task made all the more difficult by the unsettling anxiety in Tryggr's scent, and the pleading, beseeching look in his eyes. As if expecting Eben to solve all this for him at once, and Eben had to close his own eyes, draw in more of that sweet, reassuring scent, with still only him in it.

"But would Drafli not have considered all this, before he left?" Eben asked, as steadily as he could. "He has seemed to... *come around* on Alma, as you said he would, ach? He cares for her, does he not? Mayhap even"—his thoughts flicked back to that scent on Drafli's mouth—"welcomed her? Longed for her?"

Tryggr gave a heavy exhale, and jerked a distracted nod. "Ach, sure he does," he said thickly. "How could he not? She's sweet, loyal, works hard, wishes to please. *You* ought to know this, ach?"

There was a strangely accusatory tone in his voice, his eyes suddenly dark on Eben's face, and Eben blinked, and again fought to think. "Well, it seems to me," he began carefully, "that Drafli would not have failed to consider all this—most of all if Alma is now pregnant with their son. Would he not have spoken to the Ash-Kai of this? And you said he gave orders to your other Skai kin also, ach? You have many strong scouts and warriors amongst you, do you not?"

Tryggr grimaced, frowning at the floor, and again Eben felt a sudden surge of commiseration, of understanding. Tryggr clearly wanted to win his Boss's approval, wanted to show himself a strong and capable Skai—and here he'd been left behind again, trapped in a scullery, doing dull, tedious work he didn't feel was important.

"I ken this work has not been easy for you," Eben continued, steadier now, his eyes intent on Tryggr's face. "But amidst it, you have again and again shown Drafli he can trust you. You have kept his woman safe, you have granted her much help, you have offered her laughter and relief. You have been a good, faithful Skai. You have done much good work, sir."

The *sir* had slipped out before Eben had caught it, and though he winced, he kept his gaze steady on Tryggr's unreadable face. "Drafli trusts you," he said firmly. "And if he again asked for your help in the scullery, I ken this means he trusts you in this, too. He knows you shall do this. He knows you shall do more good work with this."

There was an instant's silence from Tryggr, and then a slow, harsh exhale, his hand rubbing at his eyes. "But I still know fuck all about that curst scullery," he said heavily. "How the hell am I s'posed to fix it up for her, and show Boss I can pull it off, if I can't even..."

But his voice had slowly trailed off, his eyes narrowing toward Eben's face. And Eben twitched a shy, sheepish smile back, even as a distant, disbelieving part of him wondered if Drafli hadn't known how this would unfold. Surely the most fearsome orc in the mountain didn't pay that much heed to what went on in the scullery... did he?

"You can," Eben told Tryggr, the conviction quiet but sure in his voice. "For we shall fix the scullery, and help your Boss, and your kin. Together."

# 18

Eben wasted no time in hustling Tryggr up to the scullery, and setting to work.

Tryggr still seemed a bit dazed by it all, casting Eben frequent narrow, searching glances, but Eben fought to stay focused on the task at hand. On helping Tryggr, and being a friend.

"First of all, I ken we could polish the counters and floors, to make these smoother, and easier to clean," he said firmly, as he glanced around at the now-empty scullery. "We could also install new, stronger drying racks, for these ones are not safe, ach? Most of all for a pregnant woman, and soon an orcling. And"—he dropped his gaze to the old wooden washbasins—"we could forge new steel basins, mayhap. And I could seek to finish plans for this washing machine I spoke of, also."

Tryggr was fully staring at Eben now, his swallow visibly bobbing in his throat. "You actually… set to work, on that whole washing machine idea?" he asked. "Don't recall giving you much encouragement at the time, did I?"

Eben flushed and waved it away, though he couldn't quite meet Tryggr's eyes. "I wished to help you," he said, too quickly. "I ken this work has not always been easy for you. Most of all when you are such a fierce, fearsome warrior."

Tryggr blinked at him, and Eben was vaguely surprised to see a flush of red, creeping up his neck. "Uh, well, how long d'you think it'll all take, then?" he asked, with a curt wave between Eben and the room. "Forgot to tell you, Boss told me to spend whatever I need off his accounts, too."

Truly? Eben had already been uneasily recalling how much trouble his Ka-esh kin had given him over the floor-cleaning project, and he felt himself brightening, beaming at Tryggr's face. "That will be a great help," he replied. "And it is another sign of how much Drafli trusts you, is it not?"

The redness was spreading higher up Tryggr's neck, but he twitched a brief, grateful smile toward Eben, before lurching for the door. "Ach, then," he said, a little hoarse. "To the Ka-esh wing, then? But mayhap a stop by the sickroom first? See what's going on with Boss's woman?"

Eben nodded and warmly smiled back—he'd been about to suggest the same—and upon reaching the sickroom, they found it caught in a bustle of activity. It turned out that a morose but flinty-eyed Alma was indeed preparing to leave the mountain, and she had a variety of Ash-Kai and Grisk orcs hovering around her, all seemingly speaking at once. But lurking far more quietly near the door were two Skai orcs Eben now recognized, thanks to his previous observations—the lean scout Killik, and the huge, hulking warrior Ulfarr. Both of them obviously intending to accompany Alma on her journey, and Eben could feel Tryggr's shoulders sagging as he looked at them, and then signed something akin to, *You here for Boss? Watch over Alma?*

Killik's nod was curt and decisive, his hand signing back so swiftly that Eben couldn't fully follow it. But he could see Tryggr relaxing a little more at the sight of it, and then signing back slower, perhaps even so Eben could understand. *Thanks, brother. We'll have the scullery real nice for when you and Boss bring her back.*

Oh. So not only were these Skai joining Alma on her journey, but they were fully planning to return her in short order. And without at all meaning to, Eben reached and squeezed Tryggr's hand, and flashed him another swift, beaming smile.

Tryggr's glance toward Eben was grateful, his hand squeezing back, his claws gently prodding into Eben's skin. A sensation that had Eben twitching all over, heat pooling in his trousers—and it was enough to get him through a tearful goodbye with Alma, who seemed miserably unaware that she would very soon be returning.

"Thank you so much for all your help," she said, wiping at her eyes as she gave a weepy smile between Tryggr and Eben. "You've both been so wonderful."

The sight and scent of her sadness nearly had Eben weeping, too, and he was grateful when Tryggr managed most of the speaking, and then steered him out of the room. "Ach, naught to fret over, Ka-esh," Tryggr said firmly, with a little shake to his shoulder. "You were right that Boss has it all sorted out—Killik says he'll be boggled if she's away for more than a few days. So no need to scent thus, ach?"

Eben sniffed and nodded, aiming a grateful smile toward Tryggr's face—but Tryggr was frowning again, his eyes fixed to the corridor up ahead, his steps quickening on the stone floor. Perhaps just focused on how they apparently had a far shorter timeline than they'd anticipated, and Eben forced his attention back to the next tasks at hand. First collecting his own notes from his room, and then heading over to the engineers' *hellir*. Where, as expected, his former colleagues were initially highly reluctant to offer their support, but Eben countered their whining and demurring by offering shocking amounts of Drafli's coin, which soon sent several engineers scurrying for the scullery.

Next was a consultation with the construction and masonry teams, and after that was the forge, where Gareth instantly came out to meet them. His familiar genial face was flushed with heat from the ovens, his muscled arms and chest gleaming with sweat, and though he listened attentively to Eben's explanation, Eben didn't miss his frequent narrow glances toward Tryggr. Who, to Eben's vague surprise, was standing far closer to him than necessary, and frowning straight back toward Gareth, too.

"That fucking smith," Tryggr muttered afterwards, once Gareth had willingly agreed to work on the washbasins. "Skai-kesh above, I ken he'd do anything you asked, Ka-esh. An' then kneel and beg you for more."

What? Eben huffed a distracted, incredulous laugh, and shook his head. "Ach, no," he said, with a dismissive wave of his hand. "I am sure he would not. He wishes for someone who is a match for him. Someone... stronger."

His voice only slightly wavered as he spoke, angling a sheepish smile toward Tryggr's face, but Tryggr was studying him with sudden, surprising seriousness in his eyes. "You *are* strong, Ka-esh," he said flatly. "Strong, and brave, and true. One of the strongest orcs I've ever met."

What? The words struck Eben to stillness, right in the middle of the corridor, and Tryggr stopped too, flashing Eben a smile that didn't at all reach his eyes. "An' I bet you every one of my daggers, that smith misses you like hell right now," he continued, quieter, with a hollow little laugh. "Didn't realize how damn good he had it, ach?"

Eben couldn't seem to stop staring at Tryggr, breathing hard, while something knocked and swayed in his chest. Tryggr didn't... mean anything by that. Did he? He couldn't. He'd said he couldn't, he'd said he'd wanted a break from Eben. He'd said he'd seen it happen with his fathers, whatever *it* meant, but then... Tryggr had still come back, this morning. He was still here. As if...

"Gareth is only a friend," Eben finally replied, his voice a croak, his eyes holding to Tryggr's face. "Naught more. He is not... what I long for."

But wait, perhaps even that was too much, because something had darkened in Tryggr's eyes, and his scent suddenly tasted sharp, almost bitter. "Ach, I ken, Ka-esh," he said grimly. "I ken."

Well. Eben couldn't find a response to that, his stomach plummeting, his gaze dropping to the floor. Tryggr had made himself clear, yet again, and as much as it hurt, Eben had promised to help. To be a friend.

"Mayhap we ought to start cleaning the scullery next, then," he said, through his closed-off throat. "Ought to move out the laundry, before the masons begin sanding."

Tryggr didn't argue, and soon they'd rounded up a few more helpers, too—Duff, Gaukr, Timo, Gegnir, and even Alma's cat. And as they set to work cleaning, Eben did his best to keep smiling, being a friend, offering whatever support he could. Directing the Ka-esh masons when they arrived, liaising with Gareth and the engineers, and scrubbing laundry until his arms ached. Until finally Tryggr ordered him to bed, to which Eben blearily nodded, and then almost staggered straight into a wall.

"Ach, Ka-esh!" Tryggr yelped, and oh, that was his strong arm around Eben's shoulders, steering him toward the Ka-esh wing. And Eben willingly leaned into Tryggr's sweet-scented shoulder, his face shamefully tilting closer as Tryggr marched him down to his familiar room.

"D'you really *like* sleeping all the way down here in this hole?" Tryggr demanded, as he gently set Eben down on the bed, and then frowned around at the small room. "Not even close to the rest of your kin, is it? Or the library, if you need more books?"

Eben was far too weary to dissemble, and he shook his head. "I only came here because my father threw me out," he said, with a hollow laugh. "It was the furthest liveable room from our *hellir*, and I have been here ever since. But"—he shrugged, gave Tryggr a tired smile—"it is dark, at least, and quiet. I could not bear sleeping in a place like the sickroom or the Grisk wing, ach? Full of noise, and *lamps*."

He couldn't hide his shudder, followed by a regretful wince, because the lamps were important, they were there for the women who needed them—but to his vague surprise, Tryggr grimaced too, and nodded. "Couldn't bear it either," he said, as he nudged Eben's shoulder down toward the bed. "Glad Boss has kept some parts of the Skai wing dark for us."

Eben wistfully sighed and nodded—the Skai wing had been very cozy, and far more conveniently located, too—and curled up on his bed, as Tryggr draped a fur over him. And it was so easy to sink into sleep with Tryggr there, even if just for a moment...

The next day was full of even more intensive labour in the scullery, first cleaning up all the dust from the masons, and then helping to prepare the wall for the new drying racks, while continuing to work through the last of the laundry. Eben also made several stops by the sickroom, mixing up any necessary prescriptions as quickly as he could, until Tryggr again appeared, and marched him off to bed. But this time, instead of taking Eben down to the Ka-esh wing, Tryggr steered him... up. Up, into the far nearer Skai wing, down one of those cozy curling corridors, into a room that scented of... him.

It was small but clean, with a large fur-covered bed, several thick fur rugs, and multiple glinting weapons lining the walls. And Eben willingly sank onto the soft, sweet-scented bed, even as he blinked blankly at Tryggr's unreadable face.

"But this is—your room?" he asked, too tentative, because what was this, why had Tryggr brought him here—and Tryggr nudged him over on the bed, before dropping his own fully clothed body down beside Eben.

"You've been working your pretty little arse off on this project for me, Ka-esh," Tryggr said flatly. "Want you to at least get a good night's rest, away from that godsforsaken hole of yours."

Oh. Eben was again far too tired to argue, and he might have even leaned a little closer into Tryggr's warm body, inhaling the deep, rich sweetness of his scent. "Thank you, sir," he murmured, before he could stop it. "You have been so good to me."

Tryggr made a faint scoffing sound, but oh, that was his arm, nudging under Eben's head. Meaning that Eben could rest his head on Tryggr's shoulder, breathe in the beautiful scent of him for an entire night, and it made for sweet, wonderful dreams, full of home and safety and longing.

When Eben awoke again, it was to the feel of Tryggr shifting out of bed, and striding toward the door. Toward where the huge Skai Ulfarr was waiting, and darting a brief, narrow look at Eben in the bed. "Boss is headed back now, with both his mates," he told Tryggr, in a deep, flat voice. "Is this scullery ready for his woman? I ken he wishes it as part of his mating-gift to her."

Wait. Drafli had... taken Alma as his *mate*? As in, he'd sworn *vows* to her? And he'd meant the scullery project as part of his *mating-gift*?

Eben could feel the surprise flashing across Tryggr's scent, and then something almost like relief. Or even like pride, billowing brief and bright, because his Boss had trusted him with something as important as a mating-gift. And his nod toward Ulfarr was quick and jaunty, even as his eyes glanced back at Eben in the bed, lingering longer than Eben might have expected.

"Ach, we're almost done," he told Ulfarr. "You ken you can count on me, brother."

Ulfarr nodded in return, and even gave a brief little bow toward

Tryggr before turning away again. Making it clear that he—and surely by extension, Drafli, and the Skai—did know they could count on Tryggr. That in taking on this project, Tryggr had again proven he could be trusted. And maybe—maybe Eben had proven he could be a friend, too.

Eben couldn't help a shy, genuine smile toward Tryggr, and then—foolish—a little bow of his own, too, his hand over his heart. And why was Tryggr still looking at him like that, slowly prowling back across the room toward the bed, his hand reaching out, his claws tickling at Eben's neck...

The room suddenly felt very hot, Tryggr's scent far too strong and rich in the air—and oh, hell, that was a distinct swell at the front of Tryggr's trousers, too. Suggesting, hinting, offering, and Eben's mouth was watering, his tongue brushing his lips, his eyes rising hungry and beseeching to Tryggr's unreadable face...

But no, wait, *no*, Tryggr had said he didn't want that from Eben. He'd been very, very clear, and a true friend would respect that, and honour that. So Eben gritted his teeth, forced his eyes downwards, fought to draw in breath. "We do not have much time, then," he croaked. "I ought to go see about the basins, mayhap."

There was an instant's stillness, too thick in the choked air—and then Tryggr's hand dropped from Eben's neck, his body spinning away, his hands running against where his hair had half-fallen out of its topknot. "Ach," he said flatly. "I must go—wash. Meet you in the scullery?"

Eben jerked a nod that Tryggr didn't see, because he'd already dodged out the door. Leaving Eben sitting there alone, breathing hard, his hands in fists, his cock helplessly straining in his trousers. He was being a friend. A friend. That was all.

But he had to drag himself out of that lovely, sweet-scented room, and on to the day's work. First was to the sickroom, where he quickly washed up and consulted with Efterar before mixing the day's prescriptions. And next was down to the Ka-esh forge, where Gareth had begun assembling and testing the two new washing machines. "Ach, they shall be ready this afternoon, brother," Gareth firmly told him. "Naught to fear."

The reassurance didn't seem to have nearly the same effect as it did when Tryggr gave it, and Eben twitched a distracted nod, and rushed back up to the scullery. To where a team of Ka-esh builders were now installing the new drying racks, while Tryggr mopped the newly polished floor, Timo and Gegnir scrubbed the walls and counters, and Duff and Gaukr addressed the day's new laundry.

But by noon, Duff and Gaukr—whose romance had continued apace—had begun darting lingering glances at each other, the scents of their hunger spiking powerfully through the air. Until finally Tryggr threw up his hands, and ordered them off into Alma's back office, leaving Tryggr and Eben to finish the laundry together, alone. Both of them purposefully not looking at one another until what must have been late afternoon, when a sweaty Killik appeared at the scullery door, signed something at Tryggr, and left again.

"Ach, Boss and his mates are almost back!" Tryggr exclaimed, breathless. "Are we almost done? Where's the washing machines?"

His voice sounded unnaturally shrill, his eyes almost panicked, and Eben couldn't help a reflexive squeeze at his arm, and his most hopeful, reassuring smile. "I shall fetch them," he said. "Whilst you take the others, and greet your Boss and his mates. Show them how well you have done, and how right they were to trust you."

Tryggr's breath exhaled heavy and slow, his head nodding, his eyes intent and grateful on Eben's face. "Thanks, Ka-esh," he said gruffly. "Couldn'a done it without you. You've been—brilliant. The best."

Oh. Well. And again, Eben felt himself smiling, slow and genuine, as the contentment settled deep in his belly. He'd done it. He'd been a friend. He'd done—good work.

He could trust a Skai, and he could also trust... himself.

"Thank you, sir," he said to Tryggr, without dropping his eyes, without even a hitch in his voice. "I was happy to help."

# 19

Washing machines, Eben soon discovered, were far heavier than they had any right to be.

He found help carrying the first one up to the scullery, thanks to a kind Bautul—a former patient—who had taken pity on his plight. But the second one felt almost twice as heavy as the first, and by the time Eben reached the scullery, he was sweaty and staggering on his feet, and cursing himself for not thinking to have procured a cart.

"Ach, Ka-esh!" Tryggr exclaimed, upon catching sight of Eben at the scullery door—and he instantly rushed over, snatching the washer from Eben's twitching arms, and setting it onto one of the steel basins. "Watch yourself, Ka-esh. Or call for help when you need it, ach?"

There was true alarm in his scent, studding deep into Eben's belly, but this time it felt almost easy to smile back, despite the heat surging into his cheeks. "Sorry, sir," he replied, wincing even as it came out of his mouth—friends, *friends*—and he forced his gaze back up, away, toward the other scents in the room. And yes, here was Duff, and Gegnir, and Alma herself. Alma's pretty face was flushed and eager, her scent bright with delighted happiness—suggesting, surely, that she was pleased with their work on the scullery. She also reeked of both

Drafli and Baldr's fresh scents, even stronger and deeper than before. Proving that they had indeed settled matters between them, and brought her home again, for good.

*If she can keep it up, show Boss she's worth his time, I ken he'll come around.*

"And welcome back, Keeper," Eben shyly told her, as that familiar envious longing caught low in his belly. "We are glad you are home again."

Alma beamed back at him, while beside her, Tryggr loudly cleared his throat, and kicked at the new washbasin. "Well, don't keep her in suspense, Ka-esh," he said flatly. "Show her how it works, will you?"

Right. Eben's face flushed even hotter, but he quickly nodded and bent over the basin. "This is a washing machine," he explained, as his trembling hand found the handle, and gave it a careful turn. "We had heard of them being used in the north, and it is a simple concept, so we made our own, ach? You turn the handle, and the paddle beneath shall wash your clothes for you."

He turned it again, demonstrating how the large paddle swung through the basin below. A sight that sparked genuine awe in Alma's eyes and scent, so Eben waved her forward, and smiled as she gave it a tentative turn, too.

"It's brilliant," she fervently said, with a bright, grateful smile over her shoulder toward him. "And so well crafted, too. This will save us so much time. Thank you."

Eben waved it away, but the envious longing had slightly faded again, sinking into a deep, genuine contentment. He'd been a friend. He'd done good work. He had.

"Ach, I was happy to help," he said, and he meant it. "We all wish you to feel welcome, and stay."

There was an instant's tense, awkward silence, during which Alma blushed, and something dark and almost angry flashed through Tryggr's scent. Something that felt depressingly familiar at this point, because Eben had scented it on him so many times before—and as he blinked at Tryggr's frowning face, it distantly occurred to him that it had so often happened around... Alma. Except for that awful moment outside the Skai arena, perhaps, when Tryggr had scented just like this, and said, *I know what you really want. I just... can't. I've seen Pa and Pabbi go through it, my whole fucking life, and I'm not gonna...*

A strange, sudden suspicion had begun flaring in Eben's chest, while Tryggr's stiff body shifted, his eyes narrow on Eben's, his jaw flexing tight in his cheek. His breath drawing in, his shoulders pulling up, as if he was about to say...

"Maybe you haven't noticed, Ka-esh," Tryggr said, his voice hard. "But this woman's spoken for. Permanently."

Oh. Wait. *Wait.* Tryggr thought Eben was... what? That Eben was trying to... with *Alma*?!

Eben blinked, stared at Tryggr's grim, flinty eyes, tasted the bitter darkness in his scent—and suddenly it was as though time had frozen, halted, flashing wild shocked disbelief up Eben's spine, while memories marched behind his eyes. Memories of every time he'd spoken about Alma to Tryggr, spoken to Alma around Tryggr—and how Eben's own damned envy and longing had also been there, thick and choking in his scent. Telling Tryggr... *I want this. I long for this. I long for... her.*

Tryggr had scented Eben's envy, and he'd thought it meant Eben wanted Alma. A *woman.*

And now Tryggr's words—his distress—from outside the arena seemed to snap into a new light, too. *I just can't,* he'd said, *I've seen Pa and Pabbi go through it*—just as Eben had witnessed it with so many orcs, too. Becoming attached to an orc who truly wanted a woman was a path straight to misery, and no wonder Tryggr hadn't wanted that, Eben certainly didn't want it either, but had—had Tryggr really thought that, all this time?

But yes, yes, that scent was still there on Tryggr, deepening by the breath—and now that Eben was breathing it, looking at it, it did scent so much like... envy. Like jealousy. Like the same hopeless, helpless longing he knew far, far too well.

And curse it, Alma and Duff and Gegnir were still all standing here watching, listening, and Eben had to try. Had to say something, something that wouldn't insult Alma, something that wasn't *Of course I don't want her, I barely noticed her, I want you, you, you...*

But no, wait, maybe Eben was still wrong on this, too. Maybe he was still seeing what he wanted to see, from someone who he'd sworn to treat as a friend. And he needed to give Tryggr a way out, too, needed to offer a way for him to say no, to pretend none of this had ever happened—and curse it, what even had Tryggr said? *Maybe you haven't noticed, Ka-esh, but this woman's spoken for. Permanently.*

"Ach, I—I ken," Eben finally stammered, into the taut, waiting silence. "She has gained the most fearsome Skai in our mountain as her lord. Through not her beauty or her strength, but through"—he drew in a shaky breath—"her hard work. Her kindness."

And maybe it had still been foolish, or insulting, or betraying too much—but Eben trusted Tryggr, he did. They were still—friends. And that wasn't confusion or mockery flashing through Tryggr's eyes, lighting up his scent. No, no, it was...

Shock. Relief. Longing. And a slow, stunning smile, curling dark and delighted on his lips.

A smile that said, *I see. I see you. I can show you the way.*

"Is that so, pretty Ka-esh?" Tryggr said, his voice far lower, huskier, as the dizzying scent of his hunger blazed raw and reckless through the air. "You like the idea of catching a hungry Skai's eye, do you?"

Oh. Oh. Eben's breath escaped in a noiseless little whimper, his eyes wide and arrested on Tryggr's face. And he could taste his own yearning, tangled up with that same envy and greed, as his prick swelled to instant hardness in his trousers. A sight Tryggr certainly hadn't missed, his bright eyes darting downward, as his scent burned with gleeful satisfaction. With... *triumph.*

Eben only vaguely noticed Duff and Gegnir leaving the room, because Tryggr had already begun to prowl closer toward him, his steps slow and silent on the stone floor, his claws jutting sharp from his fingers. "Then why don't you bend over, little Ka-esh, and show us this again," he said, kicking his boot at the washbasin. "Give us a better look this time, ach?"

Oh, hell. He didn't mean it, he didn't, he couldn't—but the command was ringing in his eyes, in his heated hungry scent. *I see you. I can show you the way.*

*Bend over.*

Eben's body shuddered all over, the hope and hunger and longing choking raw and riotous into his scent. Tryggr couldn't truly want this, this couldn't be happening—but Tryggr was still here, watching him, waiting for his answer. And Eben trusted Tryggr, he trusted this Skai, *I can show you the way...*

So with a gulp and a shiver, Eben turned around, and obeyed.

# 20

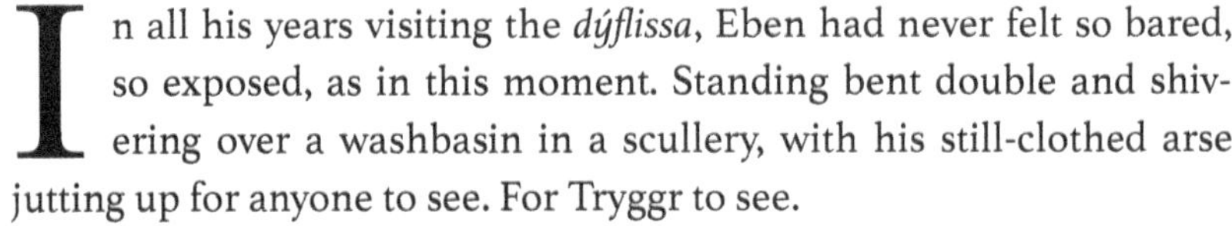

In all his years visiting the *dýflissa*, Eben had never felt so bared, so exposed, as in this moment. Standing bent double and shivering over a washbasin in a scullery, with his still-clothed arse jutting up for anyone to see. For Tryggr to see.

There was a moment's choked stillness as Eben kept standing there, waiting, quivering, please—but then, oh, Tryggr's hands. Tryggr's warm, capable hands, touching Eben, smoothing against his trembling hips. And oh, oh, with a flick of his fingers, the drawstring on Eben's trousers loosened, sagging the waistband downward—and now Tryggr was drawing the trousers down too, baring Eben even further, right here in the damned scullery.

It was against the rules, Eben's distant thoughts shouted, and Alma was still standing there watching it, scenting of stunned disbelief—but oh, Eben had never known such violent, desperate need, crashing through him, clawing him from the inside out. Tryggr was touching him. Tryggr was undressing him. Tryggr wanted to see what was his. Tryggr wanted... *him*.

"Ach, just like that," Tryggr's low voice purred from behind Eben, his scent hot, sweet, approving, as Eben's trousers dropped around his ankles. "You *are* eager to please, aren't you?"

Eben's face was burning, his bare upraised arse trembling in the cool open air—but he somehow nodded, yes, of course he was, *yes*. And Tryggr rewarded it with a leisurely stroke of his warm hand, sliding over the curve of Eben's arse. The touch soft, gentle, but for the sharp, succulent scrape of his claws, dragging against Eben's bare, tingling skin.

"Ach, just as I thought," Tryggr continued, his voice even lower. "So pretty, Ka-esh. Bet you're nice and tight too, ach?"

Oh, yes, yes, Eben could be, he would be, please, and Tryggr's hungry hand was already slipping closer, sliding slow and deliberate into Eben's crease. And this wasn't happening, it couldn't be happening... but yes, Eben could feel a single finger deftly seeking, settling against his quivering rim—and then—

*Pressing*. Prodding gentle but firm, pushing into Eben's body with brazen, proprietary ease. As if Tryggr had every right to finger him like this, to feel him like this, right here in the scullery, while Alma watched—and he did have every right, he *did*, and it was all Eben could do to stay upright, to remember how to breathe.

"You ever take a Skai in here before, Ka-esh?" Tryggr murmured, dark and hot, as his finger kept prodding, searching, sinking all the way to the knuckle. "Ever have a strong Skai ploughing, and get pumped full of good Skai seed?"

*Fuck*. Eben's moan choked from his mouth, his invaded body frantically pulsing around that impossible finger, and he couldn't stop his back from arching, his bared, opened arse pushing back harder, deeper. Needing more, more, desperate and shameful, and behind him, Tryggr gave a low, husky laugh, and—oh, *hell*—a gentle slap of his other hand at Eben's arse-cheek.

"Ach, ach, you'll get it," Tryggr drawled, and oh, Eben could feel him shifting, could hear the sound of rustling fabric. As if—as if Tryggr was dropping his trousers. As if he was truly going to fuck Eben, to plough him full of good Skai seed, here, now, please, please...

"You're gonna suck me all the way inside you, aren't you, pretty Ka-esh?" Tryggr continued, as that finger slowly slid out of Eben, making him whimper with displeasure as it slipped free—but oh, now that was the sweet, stunning scent of Tryggr's fresh seed, the slick sound of a swift pumping hand. "Show me what a good little pet you could be?"

Oh. Oh, oh, please, Eben's brain was distantly dancing and

screeching, his heart lurching into his throat, his body trembling so hard he nearly lost his footing. But he was nodding, nodding, arching up, opening as wide as he could. Waiting, showing Tryggr, he could be such a good pet, please…

And then—a touch. A touch, slick and blunt and warm, pressing against Eben's twitching, waiting arse. It was Tryggr, Tryggr's prick was touching him, Tryggr's prick wanted to fuck him—and Eben instantly bore down, opened wider. Relaxing enough to let that thick, solid flesh push into him, breach into him, stretching him out around it…

And once it was fully in, its head eased just past the muscle, Eben clamped it tight. Squeezing as hard as he could, giving them both that sweet drag and friction, and he could feel Tryggr's prick instantly vibrating fuller, his hands spasming against Eben's hips. While he just kept sinking deeper, and deeper, perhaps halfway inside now, Tryggr was inside Eben, he was fucking him in the scullery, fucking him in front of the woman he'd thought Eben had really wanted.

And wait, perhaps there was something in that, some kind of test on Tryggr's part, or even more of that triumph—and curse him, but Eben couldn't help a brief, darting glance up toward Alma. Toward where she was already staring straight back at him, her face red, her scent reeking of shock and incredulity, and—Eben blinked—just a twitch of envy, too.

"Tryggr!" Alma hissed, as she shook her head, and clapped her shaky hands over her eyes. "You can't just go ahead and—"

But Tryggr had surely caught that scent on her too, and oh, Eben could feel Tryggr's upper body bending forward, shifting his cock a little deeper, so he could inhale at Eben's neck. Seeking Eben's own jealousy or envy, perhaps—but there was only the wheeling charging hunger, and perhaps a shudder of his own triumph, too. Tryggr was fucking him. *Him.* And of course Eben hadn't wanted Alma, he wanted this, only this, and if Alma had thought otherwise, well, then she could watch and learn the truth for herself. She could watch Eben take a Skai's gorgeous prick, see how pretty he was, see what a good pet he could be…

Tryggr's deep inhale had shuddered into a laugh, low and gleeful, his breath tickling against Eben's neck. And that was another light, gentle slap of his hand to Eben's arse, speaking of hunger, of approval. Saying, surely, *I scent you. I see you. I can show you the way.*

"Ach, sure I can," Tryggr told Alma as he stood tall behind Eben again, his hand now palming possessively at Eben's arse-cheek. "Boss had you in here while we watched, didn't he? And it seems to me this Ka-esh likes it just as much as you did—and he even likes you watching, too. Don't you, my pretty pet?"

Another slap struck against Eben's arse, shuddering him all over, and there was no thought, no hesitation, only nodding, agreeing, obeying. "Ach," he croaked. "Sir."

The scent of Tryggr's triumph bloomed stronger through the air, and his laugh sounded breathless this time, his hand giving Eben's arse an approving little squeeze. "Then see, woman, you ought not deny him this," he said smugly. "Most of all after he has shown you such kindness."

It was unthinkable, impossible, even that Tryggr could keep speaking like this, arguing like this, while Eben was helplessly panting and trembling beneath him, pinioned upon his cock. But perhaps that was part of the triumph too, and part of why Tryggr so blatantly wanted Alma to see this. Wanting her to witness him staking his claim, on both Eben and maybe even the whole damned room, just like Drafli had done with Alma. Making it clear exactly how this stood—and it was with Eben bent over a washing machine, with Tryggr's prick stuck halfway up his arse.

Eben could taste Alma's resignation, and thankfully her amusement, too—and finally she dropped her hands from her eyes, and gave Tryggr a wry, tolerant smile. And yes, yes, that was what Tryggr had wanted, and the scent of his triumph bubbled even higher as his firm hands caressed Eben's flanks, and that invading cock finally, finally resumed its slow, steady plunge inside him.

"Ach, that's it," Tryggr's low voice breathed, as he leisurely pushed his way through Eben's tight dragging clutch. "That's nice, little Ka-esh, real nice. Good and tight and sweet, ach?"

Oh, *yes*, and Eben whimpered and shivered as that hot driving head bumped up against solid flesh—but with a moan, he purposefully shifted and softened, and opened that, too. Welcoming Tryggr deeper, as deep as he could go, *you're gonna suck me all the way inside you, show me what a good little pet you could be...*

Tryggr's breath choked as he pressed further, carefully sinking himself even deeper within, into the double lock of Eben's grip. Until his hips ground up flush against Eben's arse, because oh, he was in, he'd filled Eben with Skai, opened him up as wide and deep as he could go. And Eben was squeezing as hard as he could, seizing and spasming against his lord, showing him what a good pet he would be, please...

"Just like that," Tryggr rasped, as his hips began gently grinding, circling, gouging himself even deeper. "Even better than I thought. *Ach.*"

The pleasure and the frenzy were everywhere, everything, and Eben couldn't stop his moans, his body arching up, pressing back, needing more—when something caught, gentle but firm, at his braid. Tryggr's hand, holding it, drawing Eben's head back, as he slowly, deliberately drew his cock out, away, breath by agonizing breath. Adding just a perfect twinge of pain to the dizzying loss, reminding Eben who was in control, in charge, *you'll get it, I can show you the way...*

Tryggr slammed back inside with one smooth, staggering stroke, driving through Eben's tight grip, seating himself hard and deep. Hurling out more fierce, fizzing pleasure, with just that beautiful painful edge, and Eben writhed and shouted beneath it, lost in it, *please.*

"You like that too, little Ka-esh?" came Tryggr's low, hoarse voice behind him. "You like your Skai being a bit rough with you? Making sure you feel it?"

Fuck, yes, and Eben frantically nodded, while a distant rational part of him shivered with warmth, with happiness. Because Tryggr knew Eben liked it rough, of course he knew, but he was still—asking. Still making sure Eben wanted that from him. Showing Eben, again, that he could be trusted, even when he was fucking his arse in a scullery.

And Tryggr was pleased too, his chuckle low and approving as he ground himself deeper, and leisurely began wrapping Eben's braid around his hand. Increasing the tension, giving it an experimental tug, scenting for any pain or misery—but it was perfect, perfect. And Tryggr knew it, keeping that throbbing smarting sweetness as he slowly drew out again, holding it for a hanging, hovering breath...

"Even better, little Ka-esh," he said, dark and low, as he slammed back inside, even more forceful than before. Making Eben shout and flail beneath it, his hair pulling against Tryggr's iron grip, his body clamping tight and desperate against the invasion of that wondrous, pulsing Skai cock.

"Ach, you're so pretty, aren't you?" Tryggr asked, as he drew out again, drove back in. "So sweet, when you're being railed by a good Skai prick?"

Yes, please, Tryggr was railing Eben now, ramming in again and again, yanking his head back harder, as his other hand's sharp claws dragged against Eben's hip. And Eben was lost, consumed, in the furious frenzied euphoria of it, in all his hunger and longing and fantasy made truth by this orc, this perfect orc, his friend, his trust, his home.

"So sweet," Tryggr gasped again, his voice catching, his hips plunging harder, wrenching the pleasure hotter and wilder between them. "And you're gonna smell even sweeter when you're chock-full of Skai seed, aren't you? When you're walking around here reeking of *me*?"

Fuck, yes, yes, yes, Tryggr's bollocks tightening against Eben's crease, his cock swelling, straining, locking in place—and then he groaned, guttural and deep, as he sprayed out deep inside. Pouring Eben full of that hot Skai seed, flooding him from the bottom up, as those sharp claws dug into his hip, yanking at his hair—

It was so much, so much, so perfect, everything—and without even a touch, Eben's own cock shuddered, and then sprayed out, too. Releasing its pent-up longing again and again, spurting out in thick, heavy-scented strings. Catching all over Gareth's new washing machine beneath him, painting it with his pleasure, while the ecstasy screamed and screamed through his body, his head, his heart.

By the end of it, Eben was shuddering almost too much to stand, his entire body tingling and shivering with the aftershocks, but Tryggr was still here, holding him upright. Both his hands now gripping firmly at Eben's hips, while his still-hard cock held safe and deep inside, and the taste of his own pleasure and relief kept whirling, flooding heavy and reassuring through the air. Saying, without a doubt, that he'd liked it, too. Eben had pleased him. He had.

But then Tryggr cleared his throat, his hand palming possessive and a little rough at Eben's quivering arse. "Look at you, pretty pet," he murmured. "Messing all over your brand-new gift. You're gonna lick that clean for me now, aren't you?"

Oh, fuck. Eben's body spasmed at Tryggr's cock still inside him, and he was already nodding, his face burning, as he ducked his head, and obeyed. Licking at the too-strong taste of his own seed, sprayed all over Gareth's brand-new forging. And that was unquestionably another statement too, another very purposeful point made on Tryggr's part, putting Gareth in his place—and maybe putting Eben in his place, too. Showing him that this was how it would be, with Tryggr fucking him, commanding him, and covering over any claim Gareth might have had upon him.

And with Tryggr... approving of him. Caressing him, stroking him without claws, now, as a low, hungry moan hissed from his throat.

"That's good, pretty pet," he breathed, low and hot. "Real good. Now tell me, sweet thing"—he leaned forward, his lips gently brushing to the back of Eben's neck—"what's your name?"

Wait, what? Eben startled, breathless, and he only vaguely heard Alma's faint, disbelieving laugh as she finally headed for the door, closing it tightly behind her. While Tryggr's sweaty body shivered against Eben, and a low, regretful chuckle huffed against his skin.

"Never thought to ask you, pet," Tryggr continued, sounding suddenly almost—shy. "An' you never said, and by the time I realized, I didn't want to risk asking any of the others, either. Didn't want 'em to catch how attached I was getting to you, I ken."

Oh. Tryggr had done all that, all this, fucked Eben in a scullery, when he hadn't even known his *name*—but he was also softly kissing at Eben's neck, his hunger and regret shimmering through the air. *Didn't want 'em to catch how attached I was getting to you...*

"It's—Eben," he replied, in a rush, over his shaky breath. "Eben, of Clan Ka-esh."

He winced even as he said it, foolish, foolish, of course Tryggr knew his clan, right? But Tryggr's mouth was still kissing, his hands still caressing, his prick still slightly spasming deep inside. "Eben," he repeated, as if testing it, assessing it, just like he'd done with his finger in Eben's arse. "Eben, of Clan Ka-esh. It's a good name, pet. Real good."

Eben's shudder was fierce, far too conspicuous, but Tryggr's warm hands just kept stroking, rubbing it out, easing him back into steadiness again. "So you never wanted Boss's woman, then?" came Tryggr's voice, more careful than before. "Not even a little bit?"

Eben's head instantly shook back and forth, as a choked-sounding laugh escaped from his throat. "Ach, no," he croaked. "I was only—jealous. I wished for you to—notice me, and bring me joy, and... *come around*. As Drafli did with her."

And it was foolish again, shameful, but Tryggr's mouth just kept kissing his neck, warm hands steadily stroking at his sides. "An' what about other women, then?" Tryggr asked, and that sounded careful, too. "You long for one? Or a son?"

Eben's laugh was easy and incredulous this time, as his still-invaded arse gave a tight, sustained squeeze against Tryggr's solid flesh. "No," he breathed. "Never."

He could scent Tryggr's relief, could feel his heavy exhale on his neck. "Good, pet," he said, hoarse. "Never did much for me, either. Even tried a coupla times, even just to mayhap give Pa a grandson, but it never stuck, ach? Not like this."

*Not like this*. Like this, with his breath on Eben's neck, his prick in Eben's arse, his possessive hands stroking Eben's skin. And the sweet heady taste in his scent, the taste that somehow seemed so much stronger, unmarred by any of that darkness or jealousy. Hunger. Triumph. Affection. Awe.

"Shoulda just fucking asked," Tryggr went on, his voice slightly cracking. "Just thought—thought it was so clear in your scent, ach? An' I could scent how you liked me, too, so I thought—ach. Thought you might just tell me what we both wanted to hear, only for it to come haunt us later. Once I got myself too attached to stay away."

Eben couldn't seem to speak, but it was all shifting and settling in his thoughts, sinking into comprehension, or even sympathy. While Tryggr's breath shuddered against his neck, his hands gripping even tighter, as if to keep holding Eben here upon him, where he could never escape...

"But got too attached anyway," Tryggr whispered, with a broken little laugh. "Couldn't stand to hurt you, or keep away from you. You're so sweet, Ka-esh, so pretty, so fucking *perfect*."

What? Eben's disbelief finally cut through the shuddering warmth, his head rapidly shaking. "Ach, no," he gulped. "I am not, I am—"

But oh, those were Tryggr's claws, pricking into his skin. "Ach, you are," he insisted. "You're so damned clever. You know so much. You work so hard. You're devoted to helping all your kin, even if you have to put up with constant rubbish to do it. Ach, you've been so good and patient with Duff, when so many people barely even see him, let alone think he's worth talking to. He wouldn't stop asking"—Tryggr huffed a low laugh—"why I wasn't making you reek more of Skai, so you'd keep coming round, and helping us."

Eben's mouth twitched up, even though his head attempted another shake—but Tryggr's claws were digging in deeper, shuddering him to stillness. "An' you were loyal, too," he said, harder. "You coulda gone back to that dungeon, to that Gareth prick, any fucking time you wanted—but you didn't. You took my scent, and then kept it only mine, when you didn't need to. You—gave me that, Ka-esh, without me even asking. An' that means a lot, mayhap most of all to a Skai, ach?"

Right. Eben's thoughts had again flicked back to those old Skai rules, to Skai not offering fealty to other orcs. But clearly some of them still wanted it, like Drafli, and maybe… maybe now Tryggr, too.

"An' mayhap it's vain of me," Tryggr added, husky, "but I ken you're also the prettiest little thing I've ever seen in my life, ach? You're so pretty it hurts, Ka-esh, most of all when you blush and stammer like you do, and flutter your big eyes at me. An' then you say all the sweet things you do, and tell me you wanna honour me, and then you fucking just—bend over, and offer it up, too. You offer up this, give me this—but then you want me to take it, too? Want me to pound you, to get rough with you? To do whatever the hell I want with you? Make you beg and squeal and squirt for me?"

Fuck. Eben's own hunger was surging again, shuddering up between them, seizing him around Tryggr's prick—and Tryggr moaned, breathless, even as his hand gave Eben's arse another firm slap. "An' fucking *that*," he breathed. "Never felt anything like this tight little arse of yours, Ka-esh. Like it's just made to be fucked and filled by a good Skai prick. Just like"—he hissed, ground deeper—"that perfect mouth of yours, too. You ken what it did to me that day, to have your pretty head in my lap, your big eyes worshipping me, while I buried my prick in your tight little throat, and blasted my bollocks straight into your belly?"

Oh, hell. Eben's moan rasped from his mouth, his body clamping even tighter around Tryggr's invading prick. "Ach," he gasped, thoughtless, helpless. "It was—so good. All I ever—longed for."

Tryggr's answering groan was low and approving, his hips steadily thrusting. Moving easier, now, slicker, because he'd already poured Eben so full of him—but oh, that made it even better, Tryggr's thick cock now gliding smooth and slippery against Eben's grip, his breath hitching against Eben's neck.

"So you're gonna be mine, ach, pretty pet?" Tryggr hissed, low and dangerous into Eben's throat, and oh, that was his hand, too, curling close and possessive around Eben's neck. "You're gonna sign over this tight little arse to me, and let me do whatever the hell I want with it?"

Fuck, yes, yes, please, and Eben was babbling it aloud, shuddering and staggering over the washbasin—but wait, Tryggr had hesitated, and his hand around Eben's neck softened. Cradling it, caressing it, as if it were something precious, something cherished.

"But you ken, Eben," he said, slower now, his voice careful on Eben's name. "You can always say no to me too, ach? An' me wanting to make you mine, take you as my pet, you ken it's more about—playing and fucking, ach? It's not about me seeing you as weak, or below me, naught like that. It's me knowing how damn good you are, how perfect you are, and wanting to—to honour you, and take good care of you, and keep you happy and safe. It means—I *care*. An' it means"—he exhaled, slow and shuddering—"I want to keep you, Eben. Want to care for you, as long as I can."

More warmth was shimmering and sparking, deep in Eben's very soul, and he had to fight to find words, to bring up truth. "I—want that too," he whispered, his eyes blinking hard. "I have wanted it for—so long. But ach, I have not wished to be foolish, or weak, or subservient, or—"

He swallowed hard, twitching his head back and forth, his father's distant voice rising—but Tryggr's mouth was kissing him again, his hand gently stroking his throat. “Ach, I ken,” he murmured. “You deserve kindness, and honour, and respect. Deserve to have your wishes heard and followed and protected. An’ if some snippy Ash-Kai or fool Ka-esh starts barrelling over you, or giving you grief, you deserve to have your Skai backing you up and hurling daggers.”

Oh. Oh, yes, oh please. And Eben truly couldn’t speak now, not with the quivering happiness choking in his breath, escaping in a half-laugh, half-sob. And Tryggr huffed a low, relieved-sounding laugh too, his hand caressing harder against Eben’s throat, his prick giving an experimental little grind inside.

“And you deserve a good Skai prick filling up your arse, don’t you, pet?” Tryggr said, lower. “You deserve a strong Skai ploughing whenever you wish, ach?”

Yes, yes, and Eben frantically nodded, so hard he almost staggered sideways—but oh, Tryggr still had him safe, had him by the neck, and up the arse. “Good, pet,” he growled, as he drew a little out, and sank back inside. “Real good. An’ from now on, you’re only gonna scent of me. No fucking careless Ka-esh, no shitty smiths, none of it. Just *me*.”

Eben’s nod came even faster, more fervent, wrenching his neck in Tryggr’s grip, and oh, Tryggr rewarded it with a gentle prod of claws, a snap of his teeth in his ear. “An’ you ken I’ll take such good care of you, pet,” he breathed. “I’ll make you beg and scream and weep for me, as much as you damn well want. But”—he slammed in harder, deeper—“there’ll be no fucking lashes in our bed, you ken? Nothing that puts you at risk, because you’re *mine*, an’ I *won’t—fucking—allow it*.”

He punctuated the words with stunning, juddering slams of his cock, his hand yanking up and sideways on Eben’s braid, making Eben twist to look at him. And oh, fuck, how Tryggr looked, his eyes blazing, his teeth bared, his face flushed bright. And Eben could only nod, hold his gaze, squeeze that still-driving prick as fiercely as he could, yes, yes, *yes*.

“Yes, sir,” he whispered, to those dangerous Skai eyes, his lashes fluttering. “Whatever you wish, sir.”

And yes, yes, Tryggr’s groan shook between them, his eyes rolling back as he gouged in, raw and ravenous and desperate—and then he sprayed out, again. Pouring Eben full of him, again, and this time, Eben somehow found the strength to clutch his own straining prick in hand, and pump out his own release, too. Spraying it even wider across Gareth's washer, covering it all over with his seed, seeping it into all the cracks and crevices. Ensuring it would always smell of this, of them, of Tryggr fucking out Eben's seed, and making him his own.

"Good, Ka-esh," Tryggr whispered, shaky into Eben's neck, as his teeth scraped over his skin. "Real good. You're gonna be such a good little pet, aren't you?"

And even as his teeth finally struck, sinking deep and hungry into Eben's skin, Eben could still feel him watching, waiting for the answer. Needing to hear it, even now, even as he greedily gulped Eben's lifeblood, and kept squeezing the dregs of his bollocks into Eben's belly.

"Ach, sir," Eben said, and he meant it, so deep it sang and ached in his heart. "I am honoured to serve."

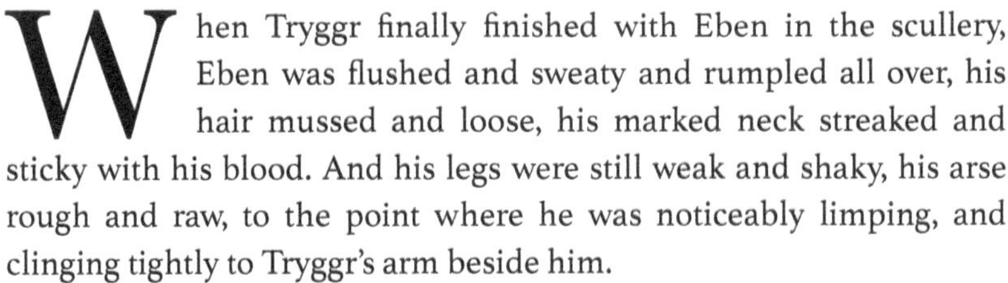

# 21

When Tryggr finally finished with Eben in the scullery, Eben was flushed and sweaty and rumpled all over, his hair mussed and loose, his marked neck streaked and sticky with his blood. And his legs were still weak and shaky, his arse rough and raw, to the point where he was noticeably limping, and clinging tightly to Tryggr's arm beside him.

But Tryggr clearly wasn't bothered, and if anything, he scented even stronger of triumph than before. And when Eben tentatively offered to wash up in the scullery, Tryggr scoffed and flatly refused, and ordered him to the Skai baths instead.

"I'm not having m'pet wash in a scullery," he snapped. "Skai-kesh knows you've already borne enough in here, ach? You're mine now, which means you're gonna get proper care, and a proper bath."

Eben flushed and shyly smiled, and allowed Tryggr to march him out through the kitchen, past an amused but unsurprised-looking Gegnir, and into the corridor. Where, Eben's fluttering thoughts soon realized, his state and his scent very clearly announced just how matters stood, to anyone who walked by. Including several former patients, a wide-eyed Ka-esh engineer, and—Eben's breath caught—*Gareth*.

And curse it, perhaps Gareth had come to check on the washing machines, but now he halted mid-step in the corridor, his eyes widening on Eben's face, and then flicking to his bruised, bitten neck. While beside Eben, Tryggr flashed Gareth a toothy, not-so-nice smile, and blatantly palmed at Eben's arse.

Eben could scent Gareth's surprise, followed by something much like jealousy—but then he made an obvious effort to smile, as he gave them a curt little nod. "I see I owe you my best wishes, brothers," he said, though his voice hitched. "If you ever have need of a *kraga*, only come to me, ach?"

Eben blinked, more heat flooding into his cheeks as he glanced sideways at Tryggr—who was still looking smug, and perhaps a little thoughtful, as he nodded back, and then ushered Eben past Gareth down the corridor. "Remind me, pet," he said, "what's a *kraga*? Not those pretty little gold collars you Ka-esh sometimes wear?"

Eben's steps faltered—Tryggr was asking about *kragas*?!—and a slow, dangerous grin was already pulling at Tryggr's mouth, his claws coming up to tickle at Eben's newly marked neck. "Ach, I see," he said, lower. "Would look real nice on you, pet, wouldn't it?"

Oh, hell, Eben truly could not breathe, amidst the shock and the abject yearning, and Tryggr kept smiling at him, dark and hungry, as his claws scraped a little harder. And it was so distracting that Eben didn't even notice when Tryggr guided him sideways into a room. Not the Skai baths, but—wait—the sickroom?

"Didn't bring you here to work, pet," Tryggr said quickly, with a reassuring smile toward him. "Just want to be sure you're well, ach?"

Oh. Tryggr had brought Eben here as—a patient. And even as Eben balked and waved it away, Kesst was already striding over to greet them, his arched brows rapidly rising. While across the room, Eben caught sight of Salvi, who must have just returned from his trip north—and who was now grinning at him with bright, jubilant glee.

"What's this?" Kesst asked, his voice sharp. "Good gods, you *reek* of Skai, Eben—and you haven't *injured* him, have you, Tryggr?"

"'Course not," Tryggr snapped back, even as his arm tightened possessively around Eben's shoulders. "Just finally settled things between us, and wanted to make sure he's looked after, and cared for. As he *should* be."

He'd fixed Kesst with a pointed frown, while across the room

Efterar cleared his throat, and strode over to join them. "Thanks, Tryggr," he said firmly. "We've been learning we could use the help, right, Sweet-Fang?"

He'd gently elbowed Kesst in the side as he'd spoken, his gaze already focused on Eben's neck, his hand rising to hover over it. "And we're thankful for the Skai—and the Ka-esh—who offer their help so freely," he continued, "without demanding anything in return."

Wait. Was Efterar talking about Tryggr—and about Eben? But yes, Efterar's eyes darting toward Eben's face were grateful, and a little regretful, too. "I know I haven't said it enough," he added, "but you're an exceptional colleague, Eben. You've made yourself an expert in your field, you have an incredible work ethic, our patients love you—and you often see things the rest of us don't. It's a real help, and we're lucky to have you. Thanks."

Truly? Eben's face was smarting even hotter than before, his eyes prickling, his head rapidly shaking—but beside him, Tryggr gave a low harrumph, his arm squeezing tightly around Eben's shoulders. "Ach, you *are* lucky to have him," he said coolly. "And from now on, he's gonna be putting in less time here, too. He's gonna be moving in with me, and I'll be making sure he's got plenty of time to read, and fuck, and *sleep*."

Wait, he was?! But there wasn't the slightest hesitation in Tryggr's scent as he promptly wheeled Eben around, and marched him back toward the door. And when Eben gave a distracted wave goodbye over his shoulder, Efterar and Kesst both smiled and waved back, even though Eben heard Kesst mutter something about *obnoxious Skai fuck-boys* under his breath. While at his workbench, Salvi was still gleefully grinning, and giving Eben a salute with his jar of tonic that clearly said, *I told you so.*

"Are you... sure, about that?" Eben managed, once Tryggr was ushering him down the corridor again. "Me... moving in with you?"

Tryggr's glance toward him was surprised, and a bit mulish, too. "Ach, yes," he said flatly. "I'm not moving down into that dank little hole of yours, and it seems to me you don't like it much, either. And you're mine now, so it's my job to keep a close eye on you, and take care of you."

His voice was clipped, decisive, though his eyes were searching

Eben's now, as if seeking some kind of argument—but Eben's head was nodding, his breath exhaling, as a warm, settled relief shimmered up his spine. He didn't need to make a decision on this. He didn't need to agonize over what to tell his Ka-esh kin about why he was leaving. He could just... obey.

And he could obey in this, too. In Tryggr guiding him into the otherwise empty Skai bath—which was an admittedly impressive feat of Ka-esh engineering, with its frothy waterfall streaming out of the wall. And once Tryggr had stripped them both bare, tossing their clothes onto a nearby bench, he gripped Eben's arse, and guided him beneath the rush of ice-cold water.

"There we go, pet," Tryggr murmured, as he gently tugged out Eben's already-wet braid with his claws, and drew his hair back from his face. "Gonna clean you up real good now, aren't we?"

Eben could only nod and shiver, tilting his head back into that sweet scrape of Tryggr's claws. And then into the warm, dizzying touch of Tryggr's slippery, soapy hands, caressing all over his skin. Washing his neck, his shoulders, his arms, his torso, his legs—and oh, even his helpless, straining cock.

"Gotta get this nice and clean, pet," Tryggr said, waggling his eyebrows as he firmly stroked it up and down, staggering Eben on his feet. "Polish it up real pretty, ach?"

Oh, fuck, Eben was already babbling, begging, arching up as Tryggr reached his other soapy hand to grip his taut bollocks—and then he was shouting, shaking, as he sprayed out into the water in a sharp, steady stream. While Tryggr just kept stroking, petting, as a smug, wicked smile curled on his lips.

"Look at you, pet," he murmured. "Messing like that all over the Skai baths, while your lord's just tryna get you clean. I ken I oughta bend you over my knee for this, ach?"

Oh, hell, he didn't mean it, or did he—but his devious smile had pulled even higher, and he firmly grasped Eben's arse again, and guided him out of the water. Toward one of the benches lining the bath's stone walls, and in a swift movement, Tryggr sank down onto it, gripped Eben by the hips, and then hauled him face-down over his *lap*.

Fuck. Even Eben's most wondrous fantasies had never imagined this, his lord pinning his bare, shivering body over his lap in the public

Skai baths. But it was happening, it was, and Tryggr's warm hand was giving his upraised arse a firm, approving caress.

"This is what you get, pet," he purred, "when you misbehave for your lord. You're gonna need to be taught a lesson, ach?"

Eben gasped and shuddered, his prick already straining against Tryggr's thigh, and Tryggr huffed a low, triumphant laugh as he gave Eben's arse another firm little squeeze. And then that warm hand drew back, away, waiting, oh—and landed in a firm, ringing slap.

It rang through Eben like a jolt, like a surging shock of raging craving—and oh, the way Tryggr laughed again, easy and exultant, as Eben squirmed and moaned. As that hand began caressing his arse-cheek again, letting its claws sink in, before drawing back, and slapping again. And then again, and again, each strike making Eben shout and tremble, firing him deeper and deeper into the screeching, frantic frenzy.

"Good, pet," Tryggr breathed, between slaps, though Eben could taste his own reeling hunger now, too. "You're being such a good little thing, aren't you? Bearing your punishment so well. Letting your lord teach you a lesson."

Eben's moans lurched even higher, his body writhing in Tryggr's lap, and Tryggr's laugh was almost a groan this time. "Such a good pet, sweet thing," he gasped, as his hand lingered, caressed, before striking again. "So fucking good. Ach, I've wanted to do this since the first time I saw you, knew you'd be just the thing, just the sweetest, so pretty with your tight little arse up in the air, with my big red handprints all over it—"

Fuck, fuck, Eben was so close, he was about to blow, right here on Tryggr's lap—and he had to force himself to stillness, squeeze his eyes shut, bite his lip as hard as he could. And for an instant, he could taste Tryggr's confusion, his hand spasming against his arse—and then the scent of his comprehension, and another low, approving laugh.

"Ach, are you tryna keep from messing on me, sweet thing?" Tryggr asked, breathless. "Are you being a good little pet? Learning all your lessons?"

Eben desperately, fervently nodded, and Tryggr laughed again, his hand now caressing Eben's burning arse-cheeks. "Good, pet," he murmured. “Even better than I thought. I ken you deserve a little treat from your lord, ach?”

Oh, yes, please, and Eben rapidly nodded again, and willingly allowed Tryggr’s strong hands to grip him, and turn him over. So he was now lying face-up and naked over Tryggr’s lap, his straining, dripping cock jutting straight upwards, for anyone to see...

And wait, anyone could see, oh hell. Because Eben hadn’t even noticed that there were now a handful of Skai in the room, and they’d all been standing there, and watching Tryggr *spank* him. But Tryggr’s eyes were only on him, only on Eben’s hard, ruddy cock, and he inhaled slow and deep, his eyes fluttering, as he shifted Eben upwards on the bench, bent over him, and...

Sucked Eben into his *mouth*.

Eben shouted and arched, his eyes rolling back, because a Skai was sucking him, surrounding him with slick, hungry heat. Wanting him, rewarding him, giving his pet a treat, oh hell—and there was no way to control it, no way to keep it in, only breaking, spraying, surging it out into that tight, wonderful mouth. And Tryggr was swallowing it, drinking it up with all apparent eagerness, sucking out every last drop, until Eben was shaky and spent all over.

“Fuck,” he gasped, without at all meaning to, as his body arched into a hard, aching shudder. “Th-thank you, sir.”

He only vaguely heard the low, approving chuckles from the other Skai now in the room, because there was only Tryggr, drawing up and licking his lips, as hunger crackled and shimmered in his scent. “You deserved it, pet,” he murmured. “An’ you taste just as sweet as you look, ach?”

Eben couldn’t even speak, not beneath the awe and the ache and the fervour, and suddenly it was all too much, too impossibly overwhelming, shivering all through his body, prickling behind his eyes. And maybe Tryggr saw it, or even understood it, his warm hands stroking Eben, caressing him, reassuring him. And then gripping him again, and this time, moving him... downwards. Down so he was kneeling between Tryggr’s thighs on the hard floor, with—oh—Tryggr’s scarred, swollen cock jutting straight toward his mouth.

“In your mouth, pet,” Tryggr breathed, his claws sinking into

Eben's hair. "An' I don't want you even *thinking* about making it good for me, ach? You just relax, and drink. As much as you want."

Oh. Oh, he wasn't offering that, but he was, he was. His strong hand now drawing Eben's head forward, filling Eben's mouth with his waiting, dripping prick. With that wondrous rich sweet taste of him, and when Eben drew down a tentative swallow, Tryggr smiled softly toward him, and sank his other hand into Eben's hair, too.

"Good, pet," he murmured. "Just like that. An' you can bite it too, if you want."

Wait. Wait, truly? Eben could—*do* that? But yes, oh, Tryggr's smile had gone a bit bemused, his hands stroking deeper through Eben's hair. "Anytime you want, sweet thing," he continued, softer. "Gotta feed my pretty pet properly, you ken."

Eben couldn't hide his moan, or his brash, furious longing, his teeth already settling tentative against the tender skin of Tryggr's shaft in his mouth. But Tryggr just kept watching, smiling, stroking, waiting—so Eben gathered his courage, and bit down into that hard, pulsing flesh.

The blood instantly swarmed into his mouth, blending heady and rich with the sweet seeping seed—and *fuck*, it was good, so good, maybe the best thing Eben had ever tasted in all his days. And he was already moaning, sucking harder, even as he darted a pleading, apologetic look up at Tryggr's face—but Tryggr was still just smiling at him, fond and approving, as the hunger flashed higher in his scent, and a distinctive flush stained his cheeks.

"Ach, just thus, pet," he said, hoarse. "Just what you've been needing, I ken."

Oh, this couldn't be happening, Eben had never known anything like this, had never needed anything like this. His lord so freely feeding him the most priceless, most precious meal in all the realm, while still caressing him, smiling at him, approving of him. And when another Skai strode over, and signed something at Tryggr, Eben didn't mind in the slightest—and it might have been even more contented, wonderful warmth, pooling in his belly. Tryggr didn't care who saw this. Tryggr maybe even wanted his clanmates to see this, his sweet Kaesh pet kneeling between his sprawled thighs, and suckling out his good Skai sustenance.

"No, I'm not sharing him," Tryggr told the new orc, though his voice was mild, even smug. "You can go get your own, just like I did. An' also"—he hesitated, his eyes gone thoughtful on the orc's face, even as he kept caressing Eben's head—"you ken, there are some sweet Ka-esh down there who'd make you fight 'em for it. An' even whip you with this vicious lash they got, too."

That seemed... specific, and Eben's hazy eyes darted sideways, fought to focus on the new orc's face. And wait, damn it, it was that same handsome Skai Tryggr had been fucking in the corridor, that very first day Eben had seen him—and the orc's expression was one of mingled disappointment and curiosity, his eyes lingering on Eben's face.

And oh, Tryggr was drawing Eben's face forward, now, sinking himself a bit deeper—showing Eben off for this orc, oh hell. "Pretty, though, ain't he?" Tryggr said, with distinct satisfaction. "Damned good with his mouth, too. Can even suck me full down his tight little throat, can't you, pretty pet?"

Oh, yes, yes, Eben could, and did Tryggr mean he wanted to show them—and yes, he did, and Eben wanted to show them, too. Because there were more Skai, coming over to see, to watch, and Eben drew in a breath, held his eyes on Tryggr's face, and slowly, surely, sucked him deep. Burying that huge Skai cock down his opened, spasming throat, and then holding it there, sucking as hard as he could, while Tryggr watched with hungry, fluttering eyes, his hands skittering in Eben's hair.

"So good, pet," Tryggr crooned, husky and hot, as his cock swelled even fuller in Eben's mouth. "So sweet. An' you're gonna be even sweeter once you're stuffed full of Skai seed, ach? Once you're reeking of me from both ends, just like the perfect little pet you are?"

Yes, please, *please*, Eben's groan burning through his convulsing, blocked-off throat, his tongue frantically caressing the hard flesh cramming into his mouth, his wide eyes pleading on Tryggr's face—and oh, the way Tryggr shouted and bent double as he sprayed out, blasting surge after surge of fresh Skai seed straight down into Eben's open, spasming throat.

One of the watching orcs whistled, low and approving, but Eben's full focus was still on caressing Tryggr's convulsing prick, milking out every bit of that sweet Skai seed, while holding his eyes to Tryggr's flushed face. Needing his praise, his approval, and yes, it was already here, Tryggr's shaky hands stroking his hot cheeks, his hair, his bulging throat.

"So pretty, Ka-esh," he choked. "So sweet. So perfect. *Ach.*"

And it was perfect, it was, Tryggr flaunting Eben, praising Eben, touching him, filling him. Flooding him with his scent and his pleasure, to the point where Eben could scarcely see the others, couldn't even make out their scents, so perfect and safe and content...

At least, until his hazy, blinking eyes caught a glimpse of a huge, hulking orc, striding into the room—and Eben froze, jolted backwards, as distant recognition spiked through his thoughts, tangled with vivid, horrible memories of that day in the arena. Of himself, exposed, compromised, weak, as that—this?—Skaap orc had trapped him, threatened him, wanted to—

"Ach, Ka-esh!" Tryggr yelped, as strong hands hauled Eben up, clutched him tight and close into his lap. "Ach, don't scent thus! Naught to fear! You're safe, pet. *Safe.*"

Oh. Eben was still shivering, clinging to Tryggr, as his bleary eyes finally focused on the orc at the door, and found—Ulfarr. Oh, curse it, it was only Ulfarr, foolish, foolish, what would they think of him, what would Tryggr think of him—

"S-sorry," he gulped, too quickly, into Tryggr's chest. "F-foolish. Just thought it was—someone else."

Tryggr's firm hands were still gripping him, caressing him, but there was no judgement in his scent. Only a sudden, grim comprehension as his breath huffed out, and his hands drew Eben even closer than before.

"Ach, I see," he said quiet. "But naught to fear, pet, for Skaap is dead."

Wait. Skaap was—dead?! And Eben jolted again, staring at Tryggr's face, as yet more alarm roiled through his chest. He hadn't wanted to cause any trouble, let alone an orc's *death*, and had it been his fault, his doing, no, no, no—

"I ken it's distressing, pet, but it had to be done," Tryggr said, his voice harder, his hands still stroking firmly at Eben's skin. "Turned out you weren't the only one—or even the only Ka-esh—Skaap forced to his bidding. An' he had plenty of chances to make amends, but instead he spoke false to us and kept at it, ach? Couldn't let it go any further, pet. Need to keep kin like you *safe*."

Oh. Eben was slightly relaxing again, though he couldn't help an uneasy glance around at the other watching Skai, too. Expecting, perhaps, some kind of resistance, or judgement—but there was only the same grim, flinty certainty, and even a few curt nods.

"We ken you Ka-esh have oft feared us, pet," Tryggr said, soft again. "But we don't wish you to run and hide from us, as you so oft do, ach? Wish you to trust us, and know we'll do our jobs, and keep you safe. Whilst we trust you to keep our mountain standing, give us safe air, offer us help and medicine, and all the other good you do for us. So much good, Ka-esh."

There was genuine emotion in his voice, in his hand's all-encompassing wave at the room, the mountain, at Eben himself. And as Eben blinked back, the last of his father's words seemed to whisper away, vanishing into the steady splash of the bath's pouring water. *Never trust a... let one find you...*

Eben swallowed hard, gave a faint little sniffle, twitched a shaky, grateful smile at Tryggr's face. And Tryggr was smiling back, looking distinctly relieved, as warmth and affection shimmered in his eyes. "Good, Ka-esh," he murmured. "So it had naught to do with you, and you don't need to spare it another thought, ach? An' if it helps at all"—he darted a glance upwards—"I ken Skaap's death was quick and easy, too. Ach, brother?"

And wait, he was talking to Ulfarr, whose huge, stiff body was still standing near the door, his hands in tight fists at his sides. But then he nodded, curt and decisive, even as something like regret, or maybe grief, glinted in his eyes.

"Ach, it was kinder than he deserved," he said, his voice hard. "We are most sorry, Ka-esh, for the fear and pain he brought you. Henceforth, we shall do our utmost to keep you safe."

He accompanied the words with a bow of his head, a clutch of his big fist over his heart. And Eben's own heart skipped a beat, his body relaxing heavier into Tryggr's, his head twitching a nod. "Th-thank you," he whispered. "That is—very kind."

Ulfarr grimaced, but then nodded, and headed for the door. At least, until he hesitated and glanced back toward Tryggr, signing something Eben couldn't fully follow. Something about—vexed fathers?

"Ach, Skai-kesh above," Tryggr muttered, as he rolled his eyes, and ran a hand against his still-wet hair, now half-fallen out of his topknot. "Shoulda known he'd be scenting, and prowling about in high dudgeon."

Eben's body sat up straight again, his eyes searching uneasily at Tryggr's face. But Tryggr flashed him a wry, reassuring grin, and clapped a steady hand to his shoulder. Safe. *Safe.*

"C'mon, pet," he said firmly. "And let's go meet your new kin."

# 22

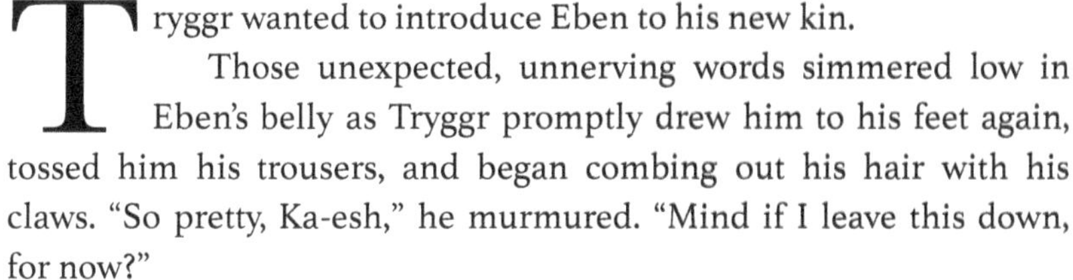

Tryggr wanted to introduce Eben to his new kin.

Those unexpected, unnerving words simmered low in Eben's belly as Tryggr promptly drew him to his feet again, tossed him his trousers, and began combing out his hair with his claws. "So pretty, Ka-esh," he murmured. "Mind if I leave this down, for now?"

Eben didn't mind, of course, and he was soon treated to the sight of Tryggr with his own long hair down, too. The dark shiny fall of it beautifully framing his handsome face, setting off his warm eyes, and Tryggr dragged his fingers through it with far more force than he'd used on Eben, his dagger glinting silver in his teeth. And Eben blinked as he watched, heat pooling in his belly, before he belatedly reached a shaky hand for the dagger, and plucked it out of Tryggr's mouth.

"This could break your teeth, sir," he said, though his face was already burning. "Or cut your mouth, also."

But if Tryggr was bothered at being corrected by his pet, he didn't at all show it, and instead winked at Eben, and reached to swipe a finger down the blade's gleaming edge. "Ain't sharp thus, pet," he said. "Only the tip, ach? Don't want a haircut every time I put it up, you ken. But"—he leaned down and pressed a brief kiss to Eben's forehead—"thanks for looking out for me, sweet thing."

Eben's face flushed even hotter, and he watched with awed fascination as Tryggr deftly wound his wet hair around the dagger, and then twisted it, stabbing it into place. "Ready, then, pet?" he said lightly, though there was a distinct carefulness in his scent, too. "Pa's likely spitting knives out there waiting, I ken."

Well, that was disconcerting, but Tryggr's solid hand was again grasping Eben's arse, and guiding him toward the door. Toward where—yes—there were two orcs waiting outside, both of them staring at Tryggr and Eben with blatant curiosity. One of the orcs was scarred and bulky, and vaguely familiar—Eben's distant thoughts rapidly placed him as a former patient—while the other, taller and leaner with a dagger in his silver topknot, was entirely new. Except for the distinct flavour in his scent, which was very much like Tryggr's.

"Leave it to you, Pa," Tryggr said to the silver-haired orc, with an aggrieved roll of his eyes toward the bulky one. "Couldn't even let us get a damned bath in, ach?"

But Tryggr's father only pulled himself up taller, frowning down his nose at his son. "What's this I'm hearing about you and this Ka-esh, son?" he demanded, with a brief, searching glance toward Eben. "Heard you've been going around calling him your *pet*?"

Eben couldn't hide the sudden alarm in his scent, his body angling slightly backwards—but Tryggr held him firm and close, even as his other hand signed something toward his father that might have been, *Watch it, Pa.*

"Ach, Pa, this is Eben, of Clan Ka-esh," Tryggr said, voice clipped. "He's a brilliant medic and researcher, and the sweetest, bravest thing I've ever met in my life. So ach, we've decided he's gonna be my new pet. An' Eben"—Tryggr waved between his father and the bulky orc—"this is Pa, and *Pabbi*."

For an instant, both orcs stared between Tryggr and Eben, with stunned disbelief in their eyes and scents. Until Tryggr's *pabbi* twitched a little shake, and then gave Eben a warm smile, and a swift bow. "Greetings, Eben," he said in a soft, pleasing voice. "I am Ezog, of Clan Bautul. I well recall your great kindness in the sickroom when I was last wounded, ach? And this"—his gaze flicked sideways—"is Sigtryggr, most oft called Tryg."

Eben attempted a polite smile between them both, though his

rapidly whirling brain had noted that Ezog hadn't actually explained his relationship to Tryg, despite the impressive depth of their scents upon one another. Suggesting that they'd been intimate for many years, but even so, Tryg's scent—and only Tryg's scent—also spoke distinctly of a *woman*. And suddenly Tryggr's comment about what he'd witnessed with his pa and *pabbi* made even more sense than before, because Tryg was bedding both a woman, *and* this Ezog, while Ezog's scent only spoke of Tryg.

It suggested at least some degree of inequality in the relationship, or perhaps even some unpleasantness on Tryg's part. And Eben felt himself drawing back a little further, his eyes uneasy on Tryg's face—and perhaps Tryg had caught it, his own eyes softening, his clawed hand running against his bound-back hair.

"Ach, well, it's good to finally meet you, Ka-esh," Tryg firmly told him, in a voice and accent that was deeply reminiscent of Tryggr's. "I've oft asked after your scent upon m'boy, but he kept giving me the runaround! Saying you were just a friend, and naught more!"

He cast a brief, accusing glance toward Tryggr, who was now frowning straight back. "Ach, you aren't the only one who can keep a secret, Pa," he snapped. "An' Eben was a friend, he *is*—but the more I kept an eye on him, the more I wanted to keep him, for good. An' I wanted to sort it out for myself, without having *you* poking your big nose in over it! Telling me I oughta be settling down with a woman, or a Skai, or some other such rubbish! You ken I've given it all a go, but none of it's struck me like Eben, and I'm not changing my mind!"

Eben's unease was now tangling with stunned, shimmering warmth—Tryggr really meant all that?—and he was distantly relieved when Ezog loudly cleared his throat, and elbowed Tryg in the side. "We are most pleased for you, son," Ezog told Tryggr, his voice firm. "And most glad to meet you, Eben. I am sure you shall be very happy together."

Oh. Tryggr shot Ezog a brief, grateful grin, followed by a pointed glance at his father—who was also twitching a wry, resigned smile, and clasping Tryggr on the shoulder. "Ach, we wish you well with him, son," he said. "An' he's a sweet little thing too, ain't he? Prettiest Ka-esh I've ever seen, I ken."

Tryggr looked somewhat mollified by this, drawing Eben closer into his side. "Ach, he is," he said firmly. "An' the cleverest, and bravest, and a right dream to fuck, too. Gonna make me a real good pet, I ken."

Well. Eben's face was burning again, ducking into Tryggr's shoulder, but he could taste Tryggr's satisfaction, his hand gripping possessively at his arse. And that hand was now steering Eben away, guiding him up the corridor again, without so much as a farewell to his pa and *pabbi* behind him.

"Leave it to Pa," Tryggr said irritably, once they were out of earshot. "Getting all uppity about me mating a Ka-esh, when he's never even bothered speaking vows to *Pabbi*! Never mind fucking around with that secret new woman of his, too!"

Wait. Wait, Eben had only followed half of that, because—had Tryggr just said—*mating* a Ka-esh? *Mating*? Swearing vows to one another? *Permanently*?

But yes, wait, Tryggr was hesitating, angling Eben a searching, sidelong look. "Ach, well, if you'd want it, I mean," he said, a little rushed. "Just—it's not a small thing, for a Skai to take a pet, ach? An' a mate don't seem much different, does it?"

Eben couldn't even speak, just blinking helplessly at Tryggr here in the corridor, as wetness spilled from his eyes, and streaked down his cheeks. It couldn't be true, he couldn't mean it, he couldn't—but oh, Tryggr was rapidly blinking too, lurching toward Eben, wiping his thumbs against Eben's wet cheeks. "Ach, don't weep, pet," he murmured, husky, as he leaned forward, pressed a gentle kiss to Eben's forehead. "Wanna make you happy, ach?"

But Eben was, he was, he'd never been so happy in all his life, and he was frantically, fervently nodding. "You do, Tryggr," he gulped, between laughs, or maybe sobs. "You make me so happy. You were so generous, you showed me so much, you helped me when you did not need to, you were just—just—"

He couldn't even say it, there was no way to possibly describe it—and oh, oh, that was Tryggr's mouth, Tryggr's lips, finding Eben's own. Kissing him, tasting his mouth, for the very first time, please—and Eben moaned, desperate, helpless, as he kissed Tryggr back. Let his tongue seek and tangle, revelling in the lingering truth of his own seed on Tryggr's tongue—and then the scrape of sharp Skai teeth, and the taste of his own blood, too. All of it whirling together into a sweet, dizzying stream, and Tryggr was caught in it too, his own groan vibrating into Eben, his hands suddenly clawing at Eben's trousers, yanking them down, spinning Eben away, pressing him hard against the wall.

And this wasn't happening, it couldn't be happening, Eben's thoughts flashing back to that very first time he'd seen Tryggr. When he'd had that other orc bent over in this very corridor, caressing him, feeding his strong scarred prick up inside him, just—just—like this.

"Good, pet," Tryggr gasped, as that hard flesh fully breached him, and began sinking inside. "Fuck, that's so good. So tight. *Ach*."

Eben wildly nodded and shivered, squeezing as hard as he could, grinding back onto that sweet, stunning certainty. His Skai, his orc, maybe even his mate, breaking the rules, fucking him in a corridor, where anyone might see...

But in contrast to that first time Eben had seen him, Tryggr was leaning in close, and again... kissing him. His warm lips sweetly skating down Eben's neck, his collarbone, as his hand slipped around, and grasped Eben's hard, straining cock. Stroking him, caressing him, in time with his gentle thrusts inside. Holding him there, making Eben his, flaring him full of impossible happiness, rewriting that first moment they'd met. *I can show you the way.*

"So good," Tryggr gasped, grinding harder, his lips quivering on Eben's skin. "So sweet, pet. So perfect, so pretty, *mine*—"

And oh, oh, there it was, Eben's own release spraying all over the stone wall before him, furling him full of flaring, flying relief, while more of that sweet Skai seed surged deep inside. Flooding Eben from the bottom up, filling all his empty places, almost as if it had reached—he huffed a shivery little laugh—his heart.

"So good," Tryggr murmured again, hoarse, as his kisses kept pressing so sweetly against his skin. "Ach, sweet thing?"

"Ach," Eben whispered, soft and shimmering in his breath, his heart. "Perfect."

# BONUS EPILOGUE

The first time Tryggr used the whip, Eben was bent over and begging in the Ka-esh *dýflissa*, with Tryggr buried bollocks-deep in his arse.

"More," Eben gasped, dragging his claws against the wall before him, lost in the pleasure and the frenzy, the stark desperate craving. "Give me more, sir. Please."

Behind him, Tryggr huffed a low, satisfied laugh, and gave a firm slap to Eben's trembling arse. "Ungrateful little pet," he drawled, as he slowly, deliberately drew backwards, falling free of Eben's grip with a jolting little squelch. "So damned greedy. After I spent all this past fortnight taking this pretty little arse to that library!"

He punctuated the words with another ringing slap to Eben's upraised rump, and Eben moaned and nodded, arching back toward Tryggr, opening up as wide as he could. Tempting his lord with a blatant view of what was on offer, showing his lord how pretty he was, how ready, how obedient...

"But it was so *good*, sir," he whimpered, as the visions of their trip north flashed up into his scattering thoughts. All those wonderful nights and days alone with Tryggr, walking and talking and fucking and laughing together, curling up together each night in dark quiet places underground. And finally, visiting the library itself—Osada's huge, wondrous provincial library, which had a covert agreement with the local Ka-esh, allowing private visits after nightfall in exchange for hand-transcribed copies of valuable ancient orc texts.

Eben's five nights at the library had quite possibly been the most mentally stimulating of his life, lost amidst mountains of books and notes, his thoughts bursting with new ideas and hypotheses and revelations. And also bursting with Tryggr, always Tryggr, who'd stayed with him, and fed him, and fucked him, and hadn't once spoken aloud the sheer boredom Eben had known he'd felt.

"*You* were so good," Eben gasped, still arching himself back as far as he could go, shivering at the feel of Tryggr's hot fresh seed spilling from him, streaking down his thighs. "You were the most generous—the most powerful—the most *magnificent* lord, and I only—*need* you, sir. Need you fucking me, wanting me, using me. Making me scream on your perfect Skai prick."

His voice was shaking by the end, his arse trembling, too, waiting, *please*. And fuck, yes, that was Tryggr's slick cock again, just teasing at Eben's open heat, as his hand gently scraped its claws down Eben's sweaty, shivering flank. "So greedy, sweet Ka-esh," Tryggr hissed, the triumph hot and low on his voice, in his scent. "Such a shameless little slag for Skai prick, aren't you? Never happy, unless this tight little hole's jammed full of it."

Eben fervently nodded, shoving back further, needing more, more, please. "Just yours," he choked out. "Just yours, sir. *Please*."

But oh, Tryggr was taking his time, making it last, his hand now clutching tight to Eben's hip, holding him in place. "Thing is, pretty Ka-esh," Tryggr drawled, "a good lord can't let his favourite pet get spoilt, ach? Can't just reward your selfish greed thus, you ken. Gotta teach you a few lessons first."

Oh, yes, please, Eben's moan escaped all on its own, his arse shoving back harder, as his head jerked another frantic nod. And behind him Tryggr laughed again, bright and smug and indulgent—and then he leaned forward, so his hand could pluck something from the wall beside Eben. The short coiled *whip*.

Wait. *Wait*. Eben froze all over, his head snapping around to stare at Tryggr's face. At where his cheeks were deeply flushed, his eyes hooded, his tongue slipping against his lips. "But only if you want,

Eben," he said, softer, hoarse. "If you're sure, about what you told me."

Eben's stunned, frantic thoughts instantly jolted backwards, back to one of those nights on their trip, when a laughing Tryggr had begun teasingly swatting at Eben's bare arse with a switch—and then he'd stopped, wincing, shaking his head. *Sorry, Eben*, he'd said. *Swore we wouldn't use lashes. Don't wanna play into you needing it. Making the pain real with it.*

Eben had flinched at the words, and he'd had to fight back the reflexive, rising urge to babble some stupid excuse, to turn and run, to find a cave and curl up and weep. Because that had been real concern in Tryggr's searching eyes, maybe even real fear. And whenever Tryggr used Eben's name like this, it meant they weren't playing anymore. It meant he wanted Eben's truth, and his heart. And Tryggr had been such a good lord to Eben, such a good friend, and he deserved Eben's answer. His honesty.

*I ken I did—use it that way*, Eben had finally replied, between heavy breaths. *Too much. But since we—since I—have begun to face this pain in other ways, I—I ken I do not now need it, thus. But I yet would—welcome this, from you. Very much. The pain with the pleasure, it is just—just—*

He hadn't been able to continue, his face burning, his eyes wide and fearful on Tryggr's face. But his cock had been brazenly straining and leaking, his hunger and longing choking his breath. And finally, Tryggr had flashed him a wry, crooked little smile, and given his arse a gentle slap with the switch.

*Ach, then*, he'd said. *We'll try it. But if I scent any of that on you, we're stopping. And I need you to be honest with me over it, too. Need to be able to trust you.*

But Eben knew how Tryggr felt about honesty, knew how much it meant to him, and he'd rapidly nodded, his hand over his heart. *I promise, Tryggr*, he'd said. *And—thank you.*

It had led to a truly glorious evening, full of teasing taunts and swats from Tryggr's switch, until Eben had been spread-eagled and babbling and begging, and had emptied his bollocks no fewer than three separate times. And afterwards, he hadn't missed the surprising depth of the satisfaction in Tryggr's scent, or the way his fingers had gently traced over the marks he'd left in Eben's skin.

*Look what you did, pet,* he'd murmured. *Letting a Skai rough you up like this. Letting him leave all these pretty new marks all over you.*

It had been perfect, perfect, and they'd done more of it in the nights afterwards, until Tryggr had drawn Eben's blood with it, and then carefully licked and healed his wounds. And that had been perfect too, a strange, shivering wonder unlike anything Eben had ever known, ever tasted. But he'd still never imagined Tryggr would end up changing his mind about the whip—let alone here in the *dýflissa*, where Eben had so often misused the pain in the past.

But Tryggr was still holding the whip, still watching Eben with his brows raised, and Eben shuddered all over, swallowed down the catch in his throat. "Yes," he gulped. "Yes, Tryggr, please. It would—mean so much to me. Most of all—here."

He cast a brief, sweeping glance around at the familiar dark room, his familiar clanmates, most of them focused on taking their joy together, but a few of them curiously watching this, too. Wanting to see a Skai wielding a Ka-esh whip, perhaps. Wanting to see a Skai embracing the ways of the Ka-esh clan, and the well-known, long-term preferences of his Ka-esh lover.

Tryggr briefly followed Eben's glance, his breath exhaling, and he twitched a curt little nod. "Good, pet," he murmured, quiet. "An' you're gonna be good for me, aren't you? You're gonna tell me if it's too much, or I'm fucking it up?"

There was a genuine flicker of unease in his eyes, or even nervousness, but Eben was already nodding, his eyes wide and warm and worshipful. And then he turned back to face the wall again, his body shivering as it arched, as he felt more hot seed spilling down his arse, and leaking from his own swollen, straining cock.

"Please, sir," he gasped. "Please, teach me a lesson. Make me learn to behave for you. Make me a good little pet for you, make me scream and beg for you, *please*."

Tryggr's gasp was low and harsh, and fuck, that was the cool leather fall of the whip, trailing slow and taunting against Eben's back. The sensation so familiar, so shockingly powerful, and Eben quivered all over at even this, at the threat of it, the promise of it. At how Tryggr's hard, leaking prick was gently nudging into him, now, opening him up, as that leather tickled and teased, trailed all over

Eben's skin. As if Tryggr somehow already knew how to use it, but of course he did, Skai trained with all manner of weapons, and it was already so, so good…

"Please, sir," Eben croaked as he clamped tight at that hot hard flesh, sought to shove back further. "Please, plough me. Punish me. Make your pet spurt and scream for you. *Please.*"

And yes, yes, Tryggr's breath hitching, the lash finally drawing back—and with a hiss and a sting, the pain flashed across Eben's back, and Tryggr's huge, powerful prick plunged sharp and deep into his arse.

Eben's shout echoed through the room, his head snapping back, his legs quaking—and fuck, fuck, Tryggr was holding himself there, waiting, grinding hard, as the lash trailed light against Eben's prickling skin. "You learning yet, pet?" he asked, and oh, that was the feel of Tryggr bending low so he could scent at Eben's neck, his breath inhaling deep. "You learning how to behave for your Skai?"

Eben pressed up as hard as he could, clamped Tryggr's cock as tight as he could, and wildly shook his head. "No," he gasped. "I need more. *More.*"

And oh, the way Tryggr's laugh rumbled into him, those familiar teeth gently nipping at his sweaty throat. "Greedy little pet," he murmured, as he stood up again, gave a swat of his free hand to Eben's arse. "Such a selfish, stubborn little slag for Skai prick. You're gonna get what you deserve, aren't you?"

Eben's moans were rising, his head nodding, as Tryggr laughed again, hot and triumphant—and then the whip licked back, as his cock drew out, taunting, waiting, wanting…

And then it all slammed Eben at once, Tryggr's driving cock, the swinging stinging whip. Spattering out pain and pleasure, smashing them into a single screeching stream of bright, vivid ecstasy—and then again, and again, and again. Tryggr's cock slamming into him, Tryggr's whip striking across his back, Tryggr's claws biting into the skin of his hip. So much, so raw, so perfect, so starkly, staggeringly powerful that Eben could only shout and submit, open up wide to the brutal blistering beauty, to the sweet stabbing surrender. To the impossible wonder of his Skai, his mate, using him, punishing him, ploughing him, breaking him.

And fuck, Tryggr was already close, already there, hissing a hoarse, desperate cry as he plunged strong and deep—and then hot spurts of Skai seed surged out of him, flooding fast and fierce into Eben, filling him full...

"Empty yourself for me, pet," came Tryggr's order, harsh and ragged behind him, as his clawed hand slipped around to grip at Eben's own straining cock, pumping up once, twice. "Behave, and obey your Skai lord. *Now*."

And Eben couldn't control it, couldn't withstand it, could only stagger and scream as his own aching, throbbing prick finally, finally erupted. Spewing out so hard it hurt, streaming with not only his seed, but with—other liquid, too. With *everything*.

The scent of it was pungent and shameful in Eben's desperate breaths, but oh he couldn't stop, he couldn't, he was lost, caught, his entire body shuddering as his prick kept spouting, emptying, obeying. On and on and on, pouring out all that Tryggr asked, because Tryggr had done this, how the hell had Tryggr done this, and what if—what if—

And Tryggr was watching it, oh, grinding and caressing him through it, his breath inhaling against Eben's neck, his claws dragging gently down his sides. Waiting until Eben's helpless, frenzied spraying had finally subsided into sputtering little spasms, and his quaking body sagged against the wall, utterly empty, utterly spent.

"*Fuck*, pet," Tryggr groaned, husky into Eben's neck. "Ach, you're so good. So tight. So sweet. So perfect. *Ach*."

Eben was still shivering all over, his face flooded with heat, his mortified eyes darting downwards to where—his breath heaved out—all the evidence of his humiliation had at least vanished down the grate that lined the wall, meant for just such purposes. But surely Tryggr had smelled it, his breath still drawing in deep, his lips kissing at Eben's neck.

"So perfect, pet," he repeated, softer than before. "Such a good, clever little thing, aren't you? Learning how to open up and obey for your Skai, just like a good pet should. An' I bet"—his voice hitched lower—"none of these other pricks ever made you mess yourself like this for them, did they? Even when they used this lash on you?"

Eben furiously shook his head, the shame still burning in his cheeks, and Tryggr's laugh was low and hot, simmering with a rather vicious-sounding triumph. "Good," he murmured. "An' no need to scent thus, pet. Any good lord knows his pet's bound to make a little mess now an' then, ach? 'Specially with a strong Skai prick fucking it outta him."

Oh. More triumph had flared into Tryggr's scent, into his hungry, smoky voice, and oh, it meant—he'd *liked* it. He'd liked having that power, liked making Eben do something no one else had ever done, especially here, in this room where Eben had found pleasure with so many other orcs.

It was enough to soften Eben's body again, to slightly slow his rapid breaths, and yes, Tryggr was purring his approval, gently kissing at his throat. And then drawing himself out of Eben with a soft squelch, so he could ease his mouth downwards. Licking with careful, focused attention on the welts and wounds the whip had made, working over each one until Eben could feel that familiar prickle of healing, as the lingering pain drifted further and further away. And fuck, now Tryggr had even slipped down to Eben's crease, blatantly swirling his clever tongue into Eben's tender hole. Making it open up around him, oh, releasing a surge of his own hot seed into his mouth...

But Tryggr had never minded such things, and that might have been even more triumph on his scent as he kept licking, tending, swallowing. Scattering Eben with more warmth and wonder and pleasure, until he was fully hard again, and desperately grinding back into that slick, wicked mouth. To which Tryggr only laughed, the feel of it shivering into Eben's very core, as his warm clawed hand came around to grasp Eben, and began pumping him with slow, lazy strokes. Swarming him with yet more thrilling, impossible bliss, until he was staggering and shouting again, his cock sputtering out the last paltry dregs of his seed into the drain at his feet.

Afterwards it was only pleasure again, soft and hazy and sweet, and Tryggr gently drew Eben up, turned him around, pressed his back into the wall. And then Tryggr blocked him in, keeping him there, as his mouth kissed down Eben's forehead, his cheek, his throat. Until he found his favourite place, just in the crook of Eben's shoulder, and Eben willingly arched for it, welcoming it, as Tryggr's sharp teeth sank deep. His swallows already gulping, loud and rapid and eager, while

Eben's trembling hands stroked Tryggr's back, smoothing steady and firm over his sweaty skin. Feeling how his wiry, familiar body slowly softened beneath the touch, sagging heavier and heavier against Eben, as a deep, palpable relief shivered through his scent.

That relief was something that had taken Eben a while to notice and understand these past months, and something he'd begun to treasure, too. Like so many of his fellow Skai, Tryggr seemed perpetually compelled to show only strength, to assume and project power, to prove he could please and protect those he cared about. It was a mentality that had seemed to permeate the entire clan, and even Tryggr's cheerful, well-meaning pa had instilled it deep into his son, insisting that he do more, prove more, work more, give more to keep their kin safe, and rebuild their clan.

But after having borne such similar weight so long himself—and having experienced Tryggr's help in releasing it—Eben had begun doing all within his power to give Tryggr relief from it, too. Encouraging him to take breaks from scouting and training, asking him to rest when he was injured, bringing him sweets and treats and tonics whenever he could. Offering up not only his knowledge in such matters, but his affection, his reassurance, his pleasure, his care. Being the place Tryggr could always come to, the place Tryggr could always trust, the place Tryggr could be weak or vulnerable or painfully honest. The place where Tryggr was always, always safe, always valued and welcomed and cherished, just the way he was.

And Eben could taste it now, that sweet, soft contentment in Tryggr's scent, the languid ease in his lean body beneath Eben's steady stroking touch. The way his hungry swallows had slowed, his breath heavily sighing, until he gently drew out his teeth, and began licking at where he'd bitten. But not fully healing it, not all the way, because he liked seeing his teeth-marks on Eben's neck, and Eben loved seeing them, too.

"Thanks, sweet thing," Tryggr finally murmured, on another slow, shuddering exhale. "So fucking good."

Eben nodded and huffed a shaky laugh, his hands still stroking Tryggr's back. "Ach, it was," he whispered. "I loved this so much, Tryggr. I love *you*."

He could hear Tryggr's hard swallow, the brief hitch of his breath.

"You—you too, Eben," he whispered back. "An' ach, you ken, I—I got something for you. If you wanna come see?"

His voice sounded strangely tentative, almost nervous, enough that Eben twitched back, searching his face—but Tryggr was already turning away, swiping up their clothes from the nearby bench. So Eben rapidly nodded and dressed, and then followed Tryggr out into the corridor. To where Tryggr wasn't leading him back up toward the rest of the mountain, toward their work or their room. But instead, he was taking Eben to...

The Ka-esh *forge*?

Eben blinked at Tryggr, frowning, but Tryggr's eyes stayed intent on the forge as he firmly ushered Eben inside. It was as hot and bright as always, the rhythmic clangs of the smiths' pounding ringing through the smoke-scented air. And of course, one of the smiths was Gareth, and across the room, he'd already lifted his visor and waved them over with an eager sweep of his hand.

Eben went, feeling more mystified by the moment, especially when Gareth led them into the forge's back room, where the smiths' work was displayed for viewing and purchase. "Over here, brothers," he said, as he gestured at a small shelf, covered with glittering gold items. "I finished it just yesterday, ach? You shall be pleased, I ken."

Eben was fully frowning now, blinking blankly between Gareth and Tryggr, and that was more nervousness on Tryggr's scent, in his eyes, as he briefly pulled Gareth close, and clapped his hand to his shoulder. "Thanks, brother," he said, a little thick. "This was real good of you."

Gareth's smile was both surprised and pleased, and he firmly clapped Tryggr back. "It was an honour," he replied. "I am glad to have held your trust in such an important matter."

Gareth's warm eyes flicked to Eben, who was feeling entirely lost, now—and finally Tryggr nodded, and cleared his throat. And then he reached an unsteady hand to pluck up a glittering item from the nearby shelf, and it was—

A *kraga*.

Eben's heart thudded, his body struck to sharp, sudden stillness. No. *No*. Tryggr hadn't made him a *kraga*. He couldn't. He wouldn't. And yes, maybe Tryggr had continued to make a few offhanded comments about *kragas* now and then, but Eben had never allowed himself to believe it. Not even after they'd sworn the vows of matehood to one another, and Tryggr had then fucked him over and over again in the Skai common-room, while all his clan bore witness…

But—a *kraga*. An unbreakable, permanent ring of Ka-esh gold, meant to be worn until death. A *kraga*.

Water had begun prickling behind Eben's eyes, and it felt too hard to breathe, to look away from the *kraga* in Tryggr's fingers, as the waves of shock and longing kept raging up and down his spine. A *kraga*. From *Tryggr*. For *him*.

"Ach, your scent, pet," came Tryggr's soft voice, as his hand slipped against Eben's cheek, tilting up his face. "You like it, then?"

Eben rapidly nodded, his breath escaping in a choked little gulp, his eyes now darting between Tryggr's flushed face, and the circlet of the *kraga* in his fingers. It was slim and elegant, its smooth gold brushed to a dazzling shine, broken only by a solid ring at the front for a chain. And as was the custom, there was text inscribed on the gold's inner edge, words that would never again be seen once the *kraga* was placed, fastened forever around an orc's throat, cradling his lifeblood within it.

And curse it, Eben couldn't even read the text through his blinking, leaking eyes, and Tryggr audibly swallowed, his thumb brushing away the streak of wetness on Eben's cheek. "It's got our vows written on it, too," he said, husky. "Saying how I want to keep you safe, and happy, for as long as I can. For—always. If you can put up with me that long, that is."

He'd huffed a hoarse, croaky little laugh, wryly shaking his head. And oh, oh, Eben couldn't bear it, not for another breath—and before he'd even caught it, he hurled himself forward, straight into Tryggr's arms. Clinging at him as tightly as he could, burying his face in his chest, as the sobs finally ripped out of his gasping, quivering throat.

"Yes," he choked. "Yes, Tryggr, yes, please. For—always. But are you sure—you cannot want—not a Ka-esh—what will your pa say, I—"

The sobs were breaking again, convulsing him in Tryggr's arms, but oh, those were Tryggr's warm hands, stroking him so steady, so certain. "I do want it," he said, quiet. "I've made up my mind, ach? You're so sweet, so soft and clever and generous and true. An' you're the best fuck I've ever had, and I miss you like hell when you're not around, and I—I can't bear the thought of losing you. So I'm not letting you get away. Not *ever*."

His voice cracked, his hands spasming against Eben's back, his face pressing into Eben's hair. And that might even have been a sniff from his nose as he drew in breath, let it out. "An' as for Pa," he said, steadier, "he's not gonna say one damned word, until he's sorted out his mess with his mystery woman! He's gonna lose *Pabbi* over it if he don't shape up, and I'm not about to repeat his rubbish, ach? I found myself the sweetest Ka-esh in the realm to love and fuck and care for, so"—he drew back a little, twitched a wavering smile at Eben's wet face—"I'm gonna claim you as mine, and I'm gonna do it right. In the Skai ways, *and* the Ka-esh."

Eben still couldn't seem to breathe properly, the water streaking down his face, but he was still nodding, saying yes, yes, *yes*. Yes, he wanted this, he needed this, more than anything else he'd ever needed in his life. And he'd made up his own mind long ago, maybe even that first time he'd seen Tryggr in the corridor. *Looking for something, Ka-esh? Not lost, are you? I can show you the way...*

Tryggr was nodding too, giving Eben a fond, hopeful little smile, before pulling the *kraga* open on its hidden hinge, and holding it up before Eben's eyes. Letting him see what he'd be getting into, letting him read the lovely script of the traditional matehood vow inside it, etched forever in solid gold. *I grant you my sword, and my favour, and my fealty, so long as I am able, and so long as you shall wish.*

It was followed by both their names, *Tryggr of Clan Skai, and Eben of Clan Ka-esh*. And Eben's heart skipped as he read it, his breaths still shaky and ragged, his eyes blinking hard. His. *His.*

He couldn't have said who stepped forward first, him or Tryggr—but somehow the cool gold was touching his neck, circling close and careful around it. And Eben scarcely noticed Gareth stepping behind him, slipping a finger inside the solid gold ring, checking the fit before it was permanently latched. But it was perfect, it felt perfect, so perfect Eben felt dizzy all over with it. His *kraga*. *His.*

"Ach, this is good," came Gareth's distant voice behind him. "Now you only need to fully close it, brother, and the bond shall be complete."

Eben shuddered all over, his eyes wide and beseeching on Tryggr's flushed face. And Tryggr nodded, his throat bobbing, as his hands shifted, and the gold circling Eben's neck snapped shut. Feeling so strong, so solid, like a steady certain hand holding safe around his throat. Like nothing Eben had ever imagined, and it was his, his, *forever.*

"You like it, ach?" Tryggr murmured, his eyes shifting with light and warmth, and oh, his hand was there too, skating against the feel of his gold around Eben's neck. "Feels good?"

Eben fervently nodded, his throat convulsing against that sweet brush of gold, while Tryggr's mouth twitched up, his dimple quivering in his cheek. "Ach, I ken," he murmured, as his other hand slipped down Eben's front, and groped at where he was somehow fully hard in his trousers. "Looks real good on you, too."

Eben gasped and jerked forward again, because he just needed to touch Tryggr, to hold him, anything, everything—when behind them, there was the sound of a polite cough. Right. Gareth.

Eben guiltily twisted around, a sheepish smile on his mouth—curse it, they hadn't even thanked him—but wait. Gareth was holding—something else. A thick gold bracelet, with a long, fine, glittering chain attached.

"You also wished for this part, did you not?" Gareth said, raising his brows toward Tryggr. "For you?"

There was a faint trace of a challenge in his voice, but Tryggr's grin toward him was only warm, grateful relief. "Ach, almost forgot," he replied, as he plucked the bracelet from Gareth's hand. "Thanks, brother."

Eben's bewilderment was rising again, because the bracelet looked like—no. Like it... *matched* the *kraga*, and it broke apart on a hinge, too. And inside it—inside it, again, was that exact same script. The vow. Their names. As if... as if...

"Thought it might not be—right, for a Skai to grant himself a Kaesh *kraga*," Tryggr said, in a rush. "But thought it might still be more—fair, if I had aught to speak of our vow, too. An' Gary had the idea of this, said you sometimes use 'em in the *dýflissa*, so—"

He thrust the bracelet toward Eben with a sudden, jerky movement, and Eben blinked down at it, and then up at Tryggr's face. At where he again looked and scented nervous, almost shy, glancing away like that, rubbing his hand at his bound-back hair. "But only—if you wanna, though," he added, too quickly. "Maybe I oughta talked to you first, made sure you'd even—"

But somehow Eben's other hand had snapped out, and circled around Tryggr's wrist. Feeling the rapid pulse of his blood, the sweaty heat of his skin, the familiar muscles shifting, tensing, and... softening. Relaxing. Wanting this, too. Wanting it so much he'd gone and arranged it, he'd ordered it, he'd given Eben yet another brilliant, wondrous gift.

"Of course I wish to," Eben said, soft, as the slow, genuine smile drew up his mouth. "This was so generous of you, Tryggr. Thank you."

Tryggr's cheeks reddened, his head slightly ducking, his hand spasming in Eben's grip. And now it was Eben opening the gold's hinge, and then carefully closing its solid strength around Tryggr's wrist. Where it fit snugly enough that it wouldn't fall off, but not so snug that it would affect his mobility or circulation, either.

"You are sure?" Eben asked, searching Tryggr's own blinking eyes. "You will not... regret this?"

Tryggr shook his head, rapid and decisive, so Eben drew in a slow, shaky breath, and gently snapped the bracelet closed. His bracelet, his gold, on Tryggr's wrist. *His.* And he couldn't stop staring at it, his breath again hitching in his throat, his cock swelling even fuller in his trousers. His. Forever.

He could hear Tryggr's swallow, the choked little sniff—but when his eyes darted up again, Tryggr was smiling again, his lips only slightly quivering. "Now we match, ach?" he said. "An' now you'll never get away from me, pet."

Because oh, yes, there was still the chain, clipped to the other side of the bracelet, dangling toward the floor. A chain that had a clip on the other end, too, and more heat thudded to Eben's groin as Tryggr brought the chain up, and hooked it onto the ring at his own throat.

"There," Tryggr murmured, giving a gentle tug of the chain with his bracelet. "Gonna be a good, obedient little pet on your lead for me, aren't you?"

Fuck. Eben moaned and nodded, stroking his shaky hand down the fine gold chain. Feeling how strong it was, how beautifully crafted, and it was his. His lead. So his lord could keep him nearby, keep him safe, keep them bound together, make Eben do whatever the hell he wished...

And yes, Tryggr's eyes were flickering, simmering with hunger and satisfaction as his hand gently tugged the chain, and pulled Eben forward. Commanding him without a word, or a touch, and Eben moaned again, biting at his lip, tilting his head back. Fuck, this was good, this was going to be so damned good, he was already almost about to—

But behind Eben, there was another light, polite cough from Gareth, jolting Eben back to awareness again. They were still in the forge, Gareth was still here, and Gareth had wielded all his stunning skill to grant them this impossible gift.

"Thank you—so much, brother," Eben said, his voice catching as he spun toward Gareth, his hand on his heart. "This was—such a great, great kindness. Most of all after all else you have done for me."

Gareth waved it away, but his eyes were soft, his cheeks slightly flushed. "Think naught of it," he said. "I am glad to see you so content."

Eben's eyes were prickling again, his smile wavering on his mouth—until there was a very light, but telling, tug on the chain at his throat. "Ach, thanks again, Gary," Tryggr said, as he stepped toward the door. "I'll bring you the rest of the coin tomorrow. An' mayhap"—he winked over his shoulder—"I'll see if I can't send Hallr down for another visit, too."

Gareth's eyes instantly brightened at the mention of Hallr, who Eben now knew was one of Tryggr's Skai clanmates—in fact, the one he'd been fucking that first day they'd met in the corridor. And Eben also knew that Gareth and Hallr had now had several very intense encounters in the *dýflissa*, the most recent of which had sent a bloody, limping Hallr to the sickroom. And according to Tryggr, Hallr had been both subdued and furious afterwards, making short, snide comments about arrogant overbearing Ka-esh, while also reeking of hunger whenever he caught Gareth's scent in the corridor.

It all boded well, to Eben's mind—if there was any Ka-esh who could settle a surly, high-strung Skai, it was Gareth. And Eben knew how much Gareth had enjoyed those encounters with Hallr, too, and how he'd scented of warmth and contentment for days afterwards.

And when Hallr had been convalescing in the sickroom, Gareth had even regularly stopped by to visit, bringing him baskets of sweets, and scenting only of satisfaction when Hallr had sulked and glared at him in return.

And even now, Eben could taste the eagerness on Gareth's scent, the hot thread of his rising hunger as he gave Tryggr a curt, grateful nod. "Ach, I shall be glad to see him," he replied. "If he is brave enough to again face my whips, and my prick."

Tryggr barked an amused laugh, surely knowing exactly how Hallr would greet such a message, and waved goodbye as he tugged Eben toward the door. Again guiding him with only the chain, but it already felt... easy, somehow. Instinctive. Right.

And it felt right for Tryggr to guide Eben through the corridor like this, too. Leading him by the neck through the Ka-esh wing, past any number of Eben's clanmates and acquaintances. Some of whom looked jealous, some pleased, some surprised—and when Tristan and Salvi appeared up ahead, Salvi's steps actually faltered, his eyes darting guiltily toward Tristan's bare neck beside him.

"Congratulations, brother," Salvi belatedly told Eben, while Tristan warmly nodded beside him. "Just what you needed, ach?"

Eben shyly nodded back, his face heating, while beside him, Tryggr was smugly smiling, and giving the chain another gentle little tug. Pulling Eben away again, up through the mountain, past many more curious-looking friends and acquaintances. And the further they walked, the more triumphant Tryggr scented, especially once they'd entered the Skai wing. Where none other than Drafli strode around a corner, Alma's black cat curled around his shoulders—but there wasn't even a flicker of surprise in his eyes as he smoothly signed toward Tryggr.

*Good work*, he said. *Very pretty.*

Tryggr's grin back was broad and delighted, and he was still grinning as he guided Eben into their cozy, familiar room. Which now felt far smaller than it once had, what with the addition of a large, sturdy new desk and all Eben's books. But Tryggr hadn't seemed to mind, and he'd even been the one to order the desk, along with a matching bookshelf. And after watching Eben squinting at his books for multiple nights on end, Tryggr had even gotten him a lovely pair of human-made spectacles, which had proven remarkably helpful, and now always held a place of honour on the desk beside Eben's new notebook, ink, and quill. All of which had been mating-gifts from Tryggr's fathers, who had almost begun to treat Eben as if he was their son, too.

It had all made Eben feel so welcomed, so cherished, like he truly did belong here, in Tryggr's room, in Tryggr's life. And now he had Tryggr's *kraga*, Tryggr's chain—and oh, the way Tryggr was looking at him, smiling at him, and gently tugging him toward the bed. Pulling off their clothes as they went, until they were both bared and tumbling onto the fur together, Eben's arms and legs twining up around Tryggr's back, as Tryggr settled over him, and caught his mouth in his. Kissing him with soft, gentle sweetness as his bobbing cock found Eben's still-soft, still-wet hole, and slid slow and easy inside.

Eben moaned and arched and rocked to meet him, clutching his mate as tightly as he could. Revelling in the kiss of his mouth, the fullness of his cock, the strength of his lean body, the truth of his gold around his neck. And Tryggr had wrapped the gold chain around his hand as they'd kissed, so now he could draw Eben up by the neck, drink more of him, bite into his lip, plunder his mouth and his hole and his heart. Making Eben his, his, again and again, bound together with flesh and blood and gold and teeth.

"You like it, my perfect pet?" Tryggr gasped, ragged, into his mouth. "Wish for more?"

And in this moment, lost in the sweep and the sway, the bite of Tryggr's mouth, the steady grind of his hips, the longing in his scent, Eben didn't know if he meant the kissing, the ploughing, the *kraga*, the room, their life. Or maybe it was all of it, all of this warm whispering wonder, this pleasure, this peace, this impossible, unthinkable home. *Home.*

"Ach, yes," Eben whispered back, so full, so perfect he could burst. "Yes. Always. *More.*"

**THE END**

# THANKS FOR READING!

Thank you so much for reading this novella! I've wanted to write Tryggr and Eben's story ever since they first showed up, and I'm so, so grateful to the generous members of my Orc Sworn Patreon for making it possible.

It was so rewarding to write about an orc with a quieter, gentler personality, who struggled with the same things so many of us struggle with—low self-worth, comparison with others, oppressive expectations, shame over not measuring up. I loved that through his relationship with Tryggr, Eben learned to show himself compassion, and to value his own contributions. I really hope that even if we don't all have a loudmouth Skai fuckboy to teach us a few lessons, we can treat ourselves with that same compassion, and remember that our own desires, needs, and contributions are all worthy of good Skai care. 🩶

Also, I'd like to send a heartfelt thank-you to all the friends, beta readers, and cultural consultants who made time for my last-minute "short story" (ha ha): Amy F., Anne-Marie, Ari, Erin, Kahaula, Lauren Mauchley, Lou M., Mary Lynne Nielsen, MK, Otto, Serena, and Þórey H. I'm also extremely grateful to Lillian Lark and V.C. Lancaster (who are both fabulous authors in this genre), for sharing their very helpful insights! And my deepest gratitude to the absolutely brilliant Eris Adderly, who is not only an incredible author herself, but also a true editing goddess. Her guidance on this book was such a huge help to me, and I am just so grateful!

I also want to mention the fierce friends who have so generously shared their gifts with our entire Orc Sworn community. A massive thank-you to my faithful Right Hand Marykate for all the constant help and support; to Amy and Elizabeth, for helping to make my Discord such a fun and welcoming community; to Erin, fearless leader of the Skai Mafia PR Team, whose true Skai fealty has been such a gift; to our delightful Grisk galdr-spinner Morning Dove for the tales, kindness, and friendship; to Coco for the perfect character designs and illustrations; to EJ and the Skai sisters for the awesome Tales from the Orc Den podcast; to Katie at Romantically Inclined Reviews for all the laughter and enthusiasm; and to all my reviewers and friends who help spread the Orc Sworn love!

And as always, my deepest thanks to my own fierce Skai mate, who's always here to back me up and throw his daggers. :)

Thank you again for reading, and sharing this story with me!

A HOLIDAY MONSTER ROMANCE TALE

FINLEY FENN

## YULED BY THE ORCS

***"He is my gift to you, this Yule's Eve. Shall you accept him from me?"***

In a world of orcs and powerful men, Lydia is a shy, widowed washerwoman, forgotten and alone—until the day the orc drops in, with a full sack of laundry on his back.

He's tall, rangy, and utterly confounding, with his silver hair, his deep jolly laugh, and his twinkling, coal-black eyes. And when he offers to bring Lydia great joy, it's a gift that just keeps giving, drawing her ever deeper into his wicked, wondrous charms...

At least, until he invites her to spend Yule at his cozy, candlelit cabin. And when Lydia arrives, he offers her a brand-new gift, wrapped in a pretty red bow...

Another orc.
A stranger.
For her... *merriment.*

And he's the biggest, most terrifying monster she's ever seen in her life.

Will Lydia refuse her hideous gift, and run alone into the cold winter's night? Or can she find joy with a monster... or maybe even a home?

*To my extremely generous supporters on Patreon!*
*Thank you and Happy Yule!*

# AUTHOR'S NOTE

Hi, and thanks so much for reading *Yuled by the Orcs*!

This combined novella and bonus epilogue is about 32,000 words (or eleven chapters) long, and it's a spicy MMF Yuletide adventure between two orcs and a sweet, lucky woman. As usual, it does include some intense orc behaviour, especially on the Skai side (but lots of cuddles and coziness too!).

For this story's timeline, it takes place in between *The Maid and the Orcs* and *The Governess and the Orc* (with the regular epilogue happening after *Governess*), but it also reads as a total stand-alone.

I really hope you have a fabulous time with it! Thanks again for supporting Orc Sworn!

# 1

It was the night before Yule, and Lydia was off to meet an orc.

She drew in a deep, fortifying breath of the crisp cool air as she walked, her boots crunching in the light snow beneath her feet. It was a clear, quiet night, and the forest seemed to glitter in the bright moonlight from above, sparkling white and silver. Whispering of peace and calm and ease, in utter contradiction to the ever-rising hammer of Lydia's heartbeat.

She was going to meet an orc. For Yule. Alone.

And gods, it still felt impossibly unreal. For a shy, awkward, widowed washerwoman to be rushing off into the night, meeting in secret with an orc. An orc who had to be a good decade older than her own forty-odd years, his tall rangy body covered with battle scars, his hair and beard gone fully silver.

And his name was *Sigtryggr*, of all things. Sigtryggr, of Clan Skai.

"Call me Tryg, for short," he'd informed Lydia when he'd first appeared in her tiny kitchen, flashing her a wry, sharp-toothed grin. "Sigtryggr's too much of a mouthful for even my own kin to bear, ach?"

Lydia had been desperately attempting to stave off the forthcoming fainting spell—there was an orc, in her *house*—and even more alarming, said orc was eyeing her with keen, glinting interest. His gaze holding first on her grey-streaked brown hair, and then her round, perpetually flushed cheeks, before sliding down to her soft, plump body beneath her shabby work dress.

Lydia had frozen under the scrutiny, because it had been so, so long since someone had looked at her like that. Since her husband Tom's passing, perhaps, a good decade before. And yes, in the years after, there'd been a few men from the village sniffing about, but once they'd learned that she was unable to have children, they'd almost instantly scurried off again. And ever since, she'd just kept her head down, just doing her work, living her quiet, dull little life, like the uninteresting, uninspiring washerwoman she was.

And clearly the orc had also realized his mistake, because he'd abruptly swung a heavy sack off his shoulder, and plunked it onto the middle of Lydia's washing-table. "I'm told you're the best woman to ask about laundry, in these parts," he'd said, raising an angular silver eyebrow toward her. "An' that you'll get it done quick, with no fuss."

Right. *Laundry*. So Lydia had gulped down a choked breath of air, and reached to open the sack with shaky hands. Indeed finding it full of ordinary-looking tunics and trousers, and a few strangely sweet-smelling bedlinens, as well.

"Erm, um, yes," she'd somehow sputtered, though her hands had still been trembling. "You—your usual washer isn't on hand anymore?"

At that, the orc—*Tryg*, he'd said—had chuckled, the sound deep and disarmingly warm. "Well, there's been a bit of fuss over the laundry, back home," he'd replied, "and m'boy Tryggr's been dragged into helping out. Don't want to add his old Pa's dirty washing into his pile too, you ken?"

It had taken Lydia a long, halting moment to digest all that—first, the surprising fact that an *orc* would have such consideration toward his son's workload, and secondly, the fact that said orc had apparently given his son nearly the same bizarre name as the one he himself possessed. And third, the way the laundry's sweet scent had begun coiling strange and deep in her belly, twisting together in highly unnerving ways with this Tryg's warm, patient smile.

"So you'll take it, then?" he'd said, his voice dropping a shade lower than before. "I'll pay double. An' in advance. If that helps."

Well. That was no small offer, and Lydia had finally, shakily nodded, and taken his proffered coins. And then she'd spent all the next day frantically washing, airing, and pressing his clothes, breathing in their sweet scent, all while glancing again and again over her shoulder toward the door.

And when Tryg had reappeared at the door, two days later, there'd been an odd, excited-feeling leap in Lydia's belly. Especially when he'd exclaimed with all apparent delight over his sack of neatly folded laundry, and then flashed her a stunning, sharp-toothed grin.

"That's good, sweet thing," he'd told her, his black eyes glinting warm and approving. "Real good. Thank you."

Lydia had flushed and waved it away, though she hadn't seemed able to pull her eyes from his angular, bearded face. From the way his silver head was slowly tilting, as a long, sinuous black tongue briefly brushed against his lips.

"Don't s'pose," he'd said, his voice all soft liquid heat, "there's anything else I could offer you, as thanks?"

Lydia's heart had been racing again, her own tongue brushing her lips. And when Tryg had stepped closer, and slowly slipped his clawed hand against her waist, she'd shuddered all over, and met his warm, patient eyes. Eyes that had twinkled with easy indulgence as he'd drawn her even closer, and bent his head into her neck.

It had somehow ended with Lydia on her back on the washing-table, while Tryg had knelt on the floor before her, feasting with shameless, shocking abandon between her legs. Hurling her full of stunning, staggering pleasure, unlike anything she'd felt in years. Decades. Pleasure that felt far too vivid, too powerful, to be real.

And afterwards, Tryg hadn't made demands, or even requested any sort of reciprocation. Instead, he'd stood up, straightened out Lydia's rumpled dress, and slung his sack of clean laundry over his shoulder.

"Thanks again, sweet thing," he'd said, with a wink, and another one of those grins. "Mayhap I'll bring by more laundry next week, ach?"

Lydia had been left entirely unable to speak, but she'd somehow managed a curt, desperate nod. And when Tryg had indeed returned the next week, they'd done it again, and then again. And if her efforts at pleasing him in return had been awkward at first, or fumbling, or inexperienced, he hadn't at all complained. And instead, he'd only kept blatantly demonstrating what he liked, rewarding her eager attempts with praise and affection and pleasure.

But afterwards, he would invariably throw that sack over his shoulder, and stride out again. Leaving Lydia staring silent and forlorn after him, alone in the empty, echoing kitchen. Until she'd begun to feel almost sick with hunger and longing, with the strange, steadily rising urge to ask him to stay. To beg him to hold her close and safe, deep into the night. To plead for promises that he surely had no interest whatsoever in making, let alone keeping.

"Have you ever been married?" she'd blurted out one day, as Tryg had turned to leave again. "Or... attached, somehow, to a woman?"

It had been a reasonable question, she'd thought, especially given his obvious fondness for his son, who he often mentioned—but he'd actually chuckled as he'd turned around again, giving a regretful shake of his head.

"Ach, no," he'd replied, with a crooked little smile. "I've always loved you women, with your sweet scents and squeals—but you're always far too jealous, ach? Never know how to share, you ken. An' even if you claim you do"—his lips had thinned, his eyes angling away, as if with some bitter memory—"you yet rage and weep when you hear you ain't the only one. Let alone *witnessing* it."

Oh. Ohhhh. Tryg had—*other lovers*. Lydia's stomach had horribly plummeted, her mouth quivering, because—oh. She was just—a side activity for him. A diversion, perhaps. And truly, what else had she expected? She was a plain, poor, boring washerwoman, with a wrinkled brow, a flushed face, and perpetually red, chapped hands. Of course this hadn't meant anything to him. Of *course*.

And damn it, Tryg had been studying her with close, watchful attention, his eyes narrowing. "Wish me to stop coming, then, woman?" he'd asked, very smoothly. "You not willing to share either? Not even in this?"

But Lydia had swallowed hard, and rubbed at her hot face, and fought through the bitter swelling misery. No. He couldn't stop coming. Not when he was quite possibly the best thing that had ever happened in her quiet, empty life. *No.*

"Please, don't stop coming," she'd told him, her voice cracking.

"*Please.* To be frank, I'll likely go along with anything you please—anything you want from me—as long as you keep coming."

Tryg had eyed her for a long moment, but he'd bent down and kissed her with surprising gentleness before saying farewell. And then he'd indeed kept coming, without fail, week after week. Until summer had slowly slipped into fall, and then the cold, dark nights of winter.

But he still hadn't once attempted to stay the night, or to take things any further than their shared pleasures together. And Lydia hadn't once asked, either, or brought up his other lovers again. Until a day several weeks before, when Tryg had slung his sack over his shoulder, turning as usual toward the door—but then, without warning, he'd spun to face her again.

"Like to spend Yule with me, woman?" he'd said. "I could get us a little lodge nearby to cozy up in for a few nights. Not my home, you ken, but a place my clan keeps for aught such as this."

Oh. Lydia's brows had shot up, her eyes searching his face, because there'd been something—different, there. Something she couldn't at all read. But she'd still fervently, frantically nodded, her heart leaping in her chest, because he wanted to spend Yule with her. *Yule.* For a *few nights.*

"I'd love to, thank you," she'd told him, with a swift, genuine smile. "When? Where? And what can I bring? Is there anything you'd like for a gift?"

Perhaps it had been far too eager, because Tryg had glanced away again, rubbing at the back of his neck. "Ach, no gifts," he'd said flatly. "Mayhap you can wear a pretty frock, or some such, should you wish. But no more."

Lydia had instantly agreed, and hadn't been able to resist giving him an impulsive hug, which he'd returned with an indulgent pat to her head. And then she'd begun making arrangements, and counting down the slow, endless days until Yule.

And now, Yule's Eve had finally arrived. And Lydia had waited until dark, and then closed up her little cottage on the outskirts of the village, and crept into the moonlit forest. Carefully following the directions Tryg had given her, her heartbeat rising with every step. Follow the road to the river, and then turn left, and cross the log bridge. And then keep going south, until... until...

There. A thin wisp of grey smoke, streaking up into the night sky. And Lydia's steps quickened as she strode toward it, toward where she could indeed see a cozy little stone cottage, tucked into the surrounding snow-capped trees.

She halted at the wooden front door, dragging in long, deep breaths. Fighting to calm her frantic, furious heartbeat as she slowly raised her hand to knock...

But then, without warning, the door swung open. And there, standing tall behind it, was a powerful, grey-skinned, silver-bearded orc. An orc with sharp teeth, pointed ears, and a broad, stunning smile.

"Finally, sweet thing," Tryg said. "Come in."

# 2

Lydia followed Tryg into the cottage with shy, tentative steps, her eyes sweeping around the little room.

It was surprisingly warm and snug, with a merry fire crackling in the fireplace, and a few simple, sturdy wood furnishings scattered throughout. A table and chairs, a shelf holding a few carved figures, and a large, fur-covered bed. And perched atop the fireplace mantel, there were multiple boughs of fresh-cut spruce and fir, their scent filling the air with warmth and sweetness.

But most compelling of all, of course, was Tryg himself. Standing tall and rangy and bare-chested before her, his beard neatly trimmed, his silver hair pulled up into a messy knot, stabbed through with a gleaming, deadly-looking dagger. And as always, his grin was impossibly contagious, showing all his sharp white teeth, and deeply crinkling the corners of his glittering black eyes.

"Ach, I've missed you, sweet thing," he purred, as he stepped close, and tilted up Lydia's face with an easy, familiar clawed hand. "Look how flushed and pretty you are. Were you eager to see me, too?"

Lydia's cheeks heated as she nodded, and Tryg's grin broadened even further, his eyes dancing in the firelight. "Good," he said. "Now, I've gained us a nice festive supper, should you wish? And I snatched some treats from home, too."

Tryg's home, Lydia now knew, was Orc Mountain, the terrifyingly large fortress that loomed a day's journey to the south, and teemed with hordes of raging, ravenous orcs—or so the tales went. But as Tryg carefully took off Lydia's cloak, and hung it on a nearby hook, she once again found herself utterly unable to reconcile all the horrifying stories of Orc Mountain with the reality of this particular orc. With the way he'd turned to grin at her again, his eyes lingering with frank appreciation on the thin, form-fitting red dress she'd worn beneath her cloak.

"You gain this frock just for me, sweet pet?" he asked, with a blatant curl of his black tongue against his lips. "Very pretty. I like."

The relief swarmed up Lydia's spine, and in that instant, all the trouble she'd gone through for this dress—travelling out of town, haggling with the tailor, spending the greater part of Tryg's exceedingly generous payments upon it—felt entirely worthwhile. Especially as he kept looking at her like that, like she was the only bedmate in his world, like there was no one else...

"Come," he said, with another stunning grin, as he nudged her toward the table. "Sit. Drink. Eat."

Only now did Lydia notice the two chipped, steaming mugs on the table, and the overflowing tray of fresh-looking sweets and pastries. And once she'd gone and sat down, Tryg strode over to the fireplace, and brought back two bowls of succulent-smelling stew, too.

"This is delicious," Lydia told him, with genuine surprise, after she'd carefully tasted a spoonful. "I didn't realize you could cook."

She belatedly winced at the implied insult in the words, but across the table, Tryg laughed and waved it away before loading up his own spoon. "Ach, you don't want to eat my cooking, pet," he said cheerfully. "But m'boy, he's made some good friends in the kitchen back home, so he's got me sorted."

Tryg's smile had gone soft and fond, the way it always did when he spoke of his son, and Lydia couldn't deny the pang in her chest as she smiled back toward him. "You don't mind being parted from him for Yule?" she asked, tentative. "Isn't it time you'd usually spend together?"

Tryg waved it away again, and then reached for a cake, snapping it in two with his sharp teeth. "Ach, m'boy's got a sweet new mate to dote upon, these days," he said lightly. "But he said he might bring him out later, if you'd wish to meet 'em."

Oh. Lydia's spoon froze halfway to her mouth, because had he—had he just said that his son's mate was another *male*? Another *orc*, surely? And far more importantly, Tryg wanted—he wanted Lydia to *meet* them?!

"Ach, no need to scent so vexed, woman," Tryg said now, more clipped than before. "Don't need to meet 'em, if you don't wish. If you're one of those humans who don't approve of males finding joy together."

There was a flinty glint in his eyes as he spoke, and Lydia felt herself blanching, her head shaking. "I do want to meet them," she said firmly. "Very much. I'm only—surprised. That you would... want me to."

She couldn't hide the uncertainty in her voice, but across from her Tryg cocked his head, his eyes intent. "Why wouldn't I wish you to meet 'em?" he said. "We've shared much joy together, these past moons. M'boy's oft asked after your scent upon me."

Right. Lydia's face was heating again, but she jerked a shrug, and drew in a shaky breath. "I just know you have... others, in your life," she said thickly. "Others who are... probably much more important to you."

There was an instant's dangling silence, and across the table, Tryg's face had gone entirely blank—and too late, Lydia flapped her reddened hand at him, and then cringed and shoved it under the table. "Which is *fine*," she blurted out. "I understand, of course. I'm sure your other lovers are younger, and wealthier, and better looking, and probably have far more experience pleasing you, and—"

Her voice abruptly broke off, because Tryg's long arm had snapped across the table, his hand clasping her shoulder. "Enough of that, pet," he said, gentle but firm. "I don't care for any of that. You live this life as long as I have, you learn what holds true weight, ach? A kind heart and an eager touch hold far more worth than all these fleeting fripperies."

Oh. Lydia bit her lip, blinking back toward him, and he flashed her a crooked, affectionate smile. "But you are yet stunning, pet," he said, even softer. "Your scent, and your pretty eyes, and your sweet little womb, and the hunger in your touch—*ach*. Why do you ken I cannot keep myself away, human as you are? When even now, I wonder whether you spoke truth, when you said you should welcome—"

He stopped there, his mouth twisting, but Lydia could easily follow the rest of it. He was talking about... the *sharing* again. And about her promise that she didn't mind. *You yet rage and weep when you hear you're not the only one.*

Lydia couldn't seem to find a response to that, and Tryg's eyes were studying her again, glinting with a strange, shimmering intensity. "But... you swore this sharing would not vex you," he continued, quiet. "Do you"—he hesitated, tilted his head—"do you yet mean this? Enough to prove this to me?"

Lydia swallowed hard, her heartbeat lurching—what did he mean by *proving* it?—but then she felt herself exhale, heavy but certain. "Y-yes," she said, her voice only slightly wavering. "I would try to do whatever I could to prove it to you. I"—she drew in air, courage—"I like you a lot, Tryg. So much. And"—she swallowed again, held his eyes—"I... I trust you."

It was an inexplicable sentiment, and no doubt an unaccountably foolish one, because Tryg had made Lydia no promises, hadn't even stayed a single night. But as she looked at those glinting eyes across the table, her words still felt deeply, damnably true. She did trust him. He wouldn't hurt her, or mock her, or abandon her without warning. He wouldn't.

Tryg gazed back at her for another long moment, his shoulders rising and falling, but then he gave a quick, decisive little nod. "Ach, then, sweet thing," he said firmly. "Finish that, and then I've got a gift for you."

A gift? Lydia blinked toward him, but his eyes had shuttered again, his hand waving purposefully at the stew and treats. So she readily obliged, even as a low, whispering unease kept rising in her chest. He'd brought her a gift, after he'd so roundly refused one from her? And this gift... did it have anything to do with the question he'd asked just before it?

*Do you yet mean this? Enough to prove this to me?*

But Tryg didn't speak again, seeming fully focused on the delicious meal, so Lydia attempted to do the same. It truly was wonderful, between the rich stew, the flaky pastries, and the hot mulled cider. And combined with the cozy room, and the crackling fire, and the sweet scent of the spruce and fir, her unease seemed to catch and tangle with a deep, powerful longing. Gods, if only this could truly be hers. If only he could truly be hers.

And as she finished eating, it occurred to her that Tryg was looking uneasy, too. His black claws drumming on the table, his eyes darting repeatedly toward the door. Until he finally shoved back his chair and leapt to his feet, pacing toward the door, and then whirling around toward Lydia again.

"Are you ready?" he demanded. "For your gift?"

Lydia's heart again kicked in her chest, but she drew in another shaky breath, and nodded, and stood. And watched, unblinking, as Tryg strode to the door, and swung it open. And behind it was...

Another *orc*.

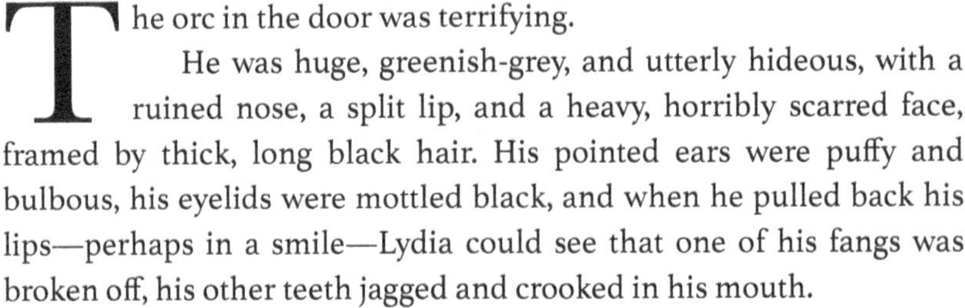

# 3

The orc in the door was terrifying.

He was huge, greenish-grey, and utterly hideous, with a ruined nose, a split lip, and a heavy, horribly scarred face, framed by thick, long black hair. His pointed ears were puffy and bulbous, his eyelids were mottled black, and when he pulled back his lips—perhaps in a smile—Lydia could see that one of his fangs was broken off, his other teeth jagged and crooked in his mouth.

Lydia's hands clapped over her own mouth, her eyes wide and arrested on the orc's appalling face. While Tryg—Tryg was reaching for the orc, and...

*Hugging* him. Yes, *hugging* him, yanking him into a tight, close embrace. His hand slapping again and again to the orc's massive shoulder, his head ducking brief but meaningful into that scarred, corded neck.

"Hullo, sweet *elskan*," Tryg said, muffled against the orc's skin. "Thank you for coming, ach?"

The hideous new orc's mouth was still pulled into something that must have been a smile, and his eyes fluttered closed, his big scarred hand gripping just as tightly at Tryg's back. The touch easy, familiar... and *intimate*.

But it was only for a moment, because the ugly orc was already pulling away from Tryg, and straightening out his cloak as he turned toward... *Lydia*. And then he gave her a deep, fluid-looking bow, his huge fist pressed against his heart.

"Greetings, woman," he said, in a surprisingly low, soft voice. "I have heard so much of you, these past moons."

Oh. Lydia's clammy-feeling hands had still been clapped to her mouth, but she guiltily shoved them downwards, and gulped for breath. "Th-thank you," she choked. "I'm—Lydia. A—washerwoman. Tryg's—friend."

She thrust out her chapped, red hand toward the new orc, wincing at the sight of it trembling between them—but the orc gently took it in his own, clasping it with warm, careful pressure. And then—Lydia blanched—he bent over it, and brought it to his mouth. *Kissing* it, oh gods, the touch of his lips light and soft, his breath hot against her skin.

Lydia stood watching, frozen, not breathing—and when the orc finally stood tall again, her hand was still clasped in his, and he was still smiling. Or at least, she was quite certain it was a smile now, judging by that deep crinkle at the corners of his eyes.

"I am Ezog, of Clan Bautul," the orc told her, again in that smooth, velvety voice. "But you may call me whatever best pleases you."

Lydia shivered, her hand twitching in his, but the orc—*Ezog*—didn't pull away, and for some inexplicable reason, she didn't, either. Though her uncertain gaze had flicked toward Tryg, who was beaming back and forth between them, his eyes bright with satisfaction. And then he reached toward Ezog again, this time to pull the cloak from his broad shoulders.

And—wait. Beneath the cloak, this Ezog was... *unclothed*. Unclothed, his huge body fully naked, except for... for...

A single wide, shining red ribbon. Around his...

Lydia's entire body shocked to stillness, her disbelieving eyes gaping at the sight of it. He was wearing a ribbon. Only a ribbon. On his bare... *cock*.

She stared at it for another long, swinging, staggering moment—and then, without at all meaning to, she glanced up and down the rest of his bare, massive, muscular form. The skin was the same deep greenish grey as his face, and it was patterned all over with more vivid, awful scars. Some looking truly gruesome, like the huge gouge in his hip, or the large, blotchy discolouration over his knee. And in truth, the only place that had been spared the scarring was... *that*. That long, plump, soft-looking cock, dangling at his groin, with that incongruous red ribbon tied around it.

Impossible. *Unthinkable*. And Lydia was again staring toward it, and then darting another wide, panicked look up at Tryg's face. Because oh gods, what was this, what must he think of this, and—

And wait. *Wait*. Tryg was—smiling. Smiling with warm, unmistakable fondness toward this Ezog. And then—Lydia's breath choked—he blatantly reached down a clawed hand, and gave that dangling beribboned cock a gentle, familiar-looking squeeze.

"Very pretty, *elskan*," he murmured, with a flick of his claw at the red silk ribbon. "I like."

Oh. It was the exact same thing he'd said to Lydia about her red dress, and she still couldn't seem to move, her stomach plummeting in her belly. And suddenly, both orcs turned toward her, Ezog's brow deeply furrowing, Tryg's gone carefully blank.

"Ach, woman," he said, his voice very smooth. "Ezog is my gift to you, this Yule's Eve. Shall you accept him from me?"

# 4

Ezog was her *gift*? For *Yule*?!

Lydia felt like she'd been spun upside-down, suddenly, like the world had swept away into some kind of bizarre, baffling dream. Tryg was giving her another entire *orc*? As a gift?!

And it was... *this* orc?! The most hideously terrifying creature she'd ever seen in her dull, quiet little life?

But both orcs were both still looking intently toward her, Tryg with that chilly distance in his usually warm eyes, and Ezog with genuine-looking concern. And as Lydia gaped back and forth between them, it occurred to her that this was perhaps... a test.

*Do you yet mean this? Enough to prove this to me?*

And she'd said... *Yes. I would try to do whatever I could to prove it to you. I... trust you.*

And this—*this*, here, now, was clearly what Tryg wanted. He was clearly very familiar with this Ezog—because this Ezog was obviously one of his other *lovers*, gods damn it. And Tryg wanted to see if Lydia truly wanted it, too. If she'd truly meant it.

*You're always far too jealous, ach? Never know how to share.*

And—well. If it was a choice between Tryg and—well. And gods, if he would just stop looking at her like that, as if Lydia was failing him even in her hesitation, just as he'd perhaps expected, or dreaded, or even feared.

"That is—very generous," she finally croaked, her voice not at all her own. "Of—both of you. But I don't—I'm not at all sure how a gift like this works, exactly?"

Her voice sounded high-pitched, utterly unrecognizable—but oh, it had been entirely worth it, because the grin had leapt back to Tryg's mouth, so sudden and stunning she nearly swayed on her feet.

"Ach, I see, sweet thing," he said, as he reached his big hand to clasp her shoulder, drawing her a little closer. "When a Skai offers you a gift thus, it's meant only to gain your pleasure for a spell, ach? No need to swear vows, or make promises, or aught of that sort."

Oh. A distant relief swarmed in Lydia's chest, but she could scarcely manage a nod, especially when Tryg again grinned at Ezog, with palpable affection sparkling in his eyes. "But should you accept, woman," he continued, "my *elskan* will join us this Yule, and until we part, he'll be here to serve your whims. To pet you all over, or make you scream upon his tongue, or aught else you might wish."

Oh. Right. So this was... the *sharing*, then. This was what Tryg had been speaking of. Although—Lydia found herself frowning toward him, her head tilting—surely when he'd spoken of sharing, he'd meant for *his* pleasure, too? It was *him* who had the other lovers, right? *He* was the one who clearly cared for this Ezog?

"But—what about you?" she stammered at him. "What about your pleasure?"

Tryg blinked at her, once—but then his smile seemed to flash even brighter, his arm reaching to slip around her shoulders. "You are so sweet, my pretty pet," he purred. "But you ken, I shall take great joy from this, ach? I shall revel in showing my *elskan* your fair form this Yule, and teaching him how pretty you are when you squeal upon my strong Skai prick, and drink up my good Skai seed. And to do all this, whilst he also tends you and cares for you and draws out your hunger—*ach*. This shall make our joy all the sweeter, you ken?"

Oh. The air had entirely vanished from Lydia's lungs, and her eyes darted again toward this Ezog, who was—somehow—still holding her hand with warm, gentle pressure. "I shall do naught you do not wish for, woman," he said in his low, velvety voice, at such strange, surreal odds with his scarred, ruined face. “I am only here to serve, and help build upon the joy Tryg brings you.”

It was taking another moment for Lydia to digest all this—they meant Ezog’s… *attentions…* would be *supplemental* to Tryg’s, then? And Tryg was indeed flashing her another bright, encouraging smile, and drawing her even closer into his side.

“Ach, just like that,” he said. “Only what pleases you, my sweet, even if that’s only his touch. But I’d be remiss not to tell you he’s got a wicked tongue, and you’d regret wasting it.”

With that, Tryg actually winked down toward Lydia, as if seeing Ezog using his *tongue* on her would truly be something he would enjoy. And wait, did he mean—was he saying *he’d* experienced Ezog’s tongue, too?

But yes, yes, of course he had. Ezog was one of Tryg’s lovers, and now he wanted to… share. As a gift. For Lydia’s… *joy*.

And as she blinked back and forth between them, it distantly occurred to her that she had nothing to lose in trying it. This was obviously important to Tryg. This was something he wanted from the lovers in his life. And if she walked out now, she would surely lose him anyway, so why not make the attempt? Why not… just see where it went, and then make a choice?

So Lydia braced herself, and met Tryg’s eyes, and perhaps even squeezed Ezog’s warm hand. A test. A gift.

“Thank you for such a generous Yule gift, Tryg,” she said, as steadily as she could. “I’m honoured to accept.”

# 5

Lydia's words were met by yet another broad, delighted grin from Tryg, and a gentle, approving squeeze of Ezog's hand against hers.

"You honour us also, sweet thing," Tryg said, as he bent down, and pressed a soft kiss to Lydia's hair. "I'll be most glad to share this with you, this Yule."

Oh. Lydia felt her face deeply flushing, tilting into the familiar, sweet-scented warmth of Tryg's neck, and he drew her even closer into his side, his big hand slipping up and down her back with smooth, steady reassurance. "Now, to begin," he purred, "I ken you oughta be shown your new gift, ach?"

She should? Lydia was again glancing uncertainly toward Ezog, who was already very much on display, especially with that incongruous red bow still tied around his plump green shaft. But Tryg was nudging her a little forward, and even giving an encouraging slap to her arse.

"Gotta unwrap him, sweet thing," he said lightly. "Then take a good look, ach? See what you might like to make full use of, these next days."

Lydia's shock surged once again—she really would be *making use* of such a horrifyingly hideous orc? But she managed a shaky nod, and jerked a step forward. Toward—her gift. Who she was supposed to... *unwrap.*

Her hand was still clasped in Ezog's warm, steady grip, and at least that seemed to make it easier, somehow. Easier, good gods, to drop her blinking eyes back to that thick, silken red ribbon, tied around that long, bulky cock.

It was still soft, she realized, with yet another jolt of shock, because it already was quite... improbably proportioned. And yes, Tryg himself had also been a surprise in that regard—but Tryg's was slimmer and paler, almost always rigid and ready, and latticed all over with veins and multiple scars. While this—this fat, smooth, soft-looking length—felt entirely different, somehow. As if it wasn't made to jab inside and make one scream, but to softly open one around it, and then lock itself deep into place.

But Lydia still couldn't seem to move any further, let alone reach out toward it—and she was distantly, deeply grateful when Ezog himself guided her hand closer. Giving her fingers another gentle squeeze before releasing them, so close, now only a breath away...

And it almost felt like someone else, looked like someone else, as Lydia's familiar, trembling fingers reached out to the edge of that red ribbon, and grasped it. And then pulled, drawing the ribbon away, away, away, until it was dangling loose in her hand. While the cock she'd unwrapped was no longer dangling at all, but visibly flexing and swelling. Rising.

Lydia's throat convulsed as she watched, as that deep green flesh shuddered, expanded, lengthened. Growing fatter and longer with every breath, until it had become something truly, impossibly obscene. Something that couldn't actually be real, except that it was, it *was*—and beside her Tryg was merrily chuckling, and again giving a reassuring pat to her back.

"Again, no need to take it inside you, should you not wish," he purred at her. "But it's so pretty, is it not? Should you not wish to touch it, at least?"

Oh. Lydia's throat convulsed again, her eyes darting up toward Tryg's smug face, and then to Ezog's. To where, yes, he was still just as hideous as before, but somehow the truth of that seemed a little more blunted than it had previously. Especially with how he was again smiling at her, his eyes crinkling at the corners.

"Only should you wish," he told her, in that quiet, reassuring voice. "I am here to serve."

But Lydia couldn't stop searching his soft, strangely expressive eyes, while a new, unnerving uncertainty coiled in her belly. "But—you're *sure* you really want this?" she whispered. "Truly?"

Ezog's nod was slow but certain, and yes, that was definitely another smile, crinkling even deeper on his eyes. "Ach, yes," he replied, his voice low and fervent. "To gain the touch and the scent and the joy of such a sweet, pretty woman—this is a great gift to me, also."

Oh. Lydia glanced toward Tryg again, but he was looking back at Ezog, his eyes unmistakably fond. As if... as if this entire bizarre scenario had been meant as a gift for *Ezog*, too. For Tryg's other lover. For someone he obviously deeply cared about.

So Lydia drew in a breath, gave a furtive nod. And then, she slowly, slowly moved her hand closer, until... she touched it. *Touched* Ezog, there, on that massive, jutting green length. Feeling the impossible softness of that warm skin, and how the strength beneath shuddered and swelled even fuller against her light, tentative touch.

"Ach, that's it," came Tryg's husky voice, close in her ear. "Take a good long look, sweet thing. Get to know what's yours."

Something hitched deep in Lydia's groin, because she knew that voice of Tryg's—and yes, yes, that was the familiar hunger, flashing in his eyes as he watched. Saying, all too plainly, that he liked watching this. Liked seeing her do this.

And in truth, it wasn't a hardship, was it? Stroking up and down Ezog's huge, pulsing weight, feeling its velvety softness beneath her fingers, feeling a smudge of hot liquid pooling onto her palm as she brushed against its rounded tip. At where the head of him was still fully hidden, enclosed beneath its hood of greenish skin.

"Keep opening him up, my sweet," murmured Tryg beside her—and after another ragged, gulping breath, Lydia nodded, and obeyed. Watching as her audacious fingers gently drew that soft skin back, revealing what was waiting beneath.

And—oh, gods, it was just as compelling as the rest of it. A blunt, glossy green crown, split with a deep, perfect slit. A slit that was already dripping, dangling a long, pearly strand of white...

"So pretty, is he not?" Tryg's heated voice said. "You like, my sweet pet?"

Lydia swallowed hard, and jerked a furtive, trembly nod. And when she risked a glance up at Tryg's face, he was watching her with clear approval, his eyes glittering in the firelight. "Good," he murmured. "Very, very good. Now, you wish for more?"

Damn it, Lydia *did* wish for more, her greedy gaze already snapping back toward Ezog again. Toward where he was still standing there, unmoving, his eyes now utterly rapt on hers. As if he wanted more, too.

So she... kept going. Kept stroking, kept learning this strange, hideous orc. First caressing her fingers all over his stunning cock, and then slipping down to his full, softly furred bollocks below. And then a little way down his solid, muscled thighs—also covered with thick black hair—and then back up to the ridges of his hard abdomen, his chest. His skin feeling impossibly warm and smooth beneath the tentative touch of her fingers, despite the nicks and knots of his many scars.

And when Tryg reached an easy hand, and turned Ezog around, she felt her breath catching at the sight of it. At his broad, powerful shoulders, his scarred muscled back, the firm roundness of his arse below. This was all... *hers*. For her use, and her pleasure.

So she touched Ezog's back too, all the way up to his shoulders, brushing against the shining fall of his hair. And then, with a burst of inexplicable courage, she skated her hands very lightly over his arse, feeling the hard rounded strength of it. Her touch becoming smoother, steadier, with every breath—at least, until Tryg's hand settled over hers, and gently guided it between those firm arse-cheeks.

Ezog twitched and gasped at that, and Tryg gave a low, satisfied laugh as he eased Lydia's finger a little closer. Against where she could feel Ezog clenching back toward her... and then softening, opening. As if he would truly welcome her there, too...

"He's real sweet inside, too," Tryg murmured. "Deep and tight and hot, ach?"

Wait. Wait, did Tryg mean he'd—*oh*. And once again, Lydia was fighting to swallow down her shock, and perhaps even her jealousy, because he still wanted to—to share this with her. Together. Right?

And Tryg's eyes on her were searching again, testing again, as he carefully nudged her finger further inside. *Inside Ezog*, oh hell, to where he was indeed hot and tight and silky smooth, clamping gently around her finger. Firing a sudden, inexplicable jolt of heat to Lydia's groin, especially when Tryg drew his own hand away, and left hers there. Left her touching her gift, inside her gift, learning what he had to offer…

"You like?" Tryg breathed, his voice rasping. "He's good, ach?"

And yes, yes, he was. Because Ezog was just allowing Lydia *inside* him like this, allowing her this touch, this exploration, this familiarity. This strange, vivid reassurance that she really was the one in charge here, and that he would truly welcome whatever she wanted, and do only what she wished.

So Lydia nodded, jerky and quick, meeting Tryg's eyes. Seeing the sharp, glittering hunger in them as he gently drew her hand away, and then turned Ezog back around. Again confronting her with his hideous face, and his huge, beautiful cock, swollen perhaps even fuller than before.

"He's a good gift, ach?" Tryg continued, with more challenge on his heated voice. "You like? Wish to now put him to good use?"

And again, somehow, Lydia was nodding. *Nodding*, and meaning it, more and more with every shaky, desperate breath. Yes. *Yes*.

"Yes," she whispered. "Yes, please."

# 6

Even despite her agreement, Lydia had no conception whatsoever of what came next. Of how to put an orc—a whole living, thinking being—to... *good use.*

But thankfully, Tryg once again took charge of the situation. First guiding Lydia over toward the bed, and then kicking off his own trousers. Revealing the familiar sight of his tall scarred body, markedly leaner and greyer than Ezog's, the hair smattered across his skin all gone silver.

And yes, there was his own swollen cock, too, jutting out hard and pointed and slim—but Lydia only had an instant to look before Tryg dropped to sit on the fur-covered bed, and swept her bodily down into his lap.

"Mayhap we keep this pretty frock for now," he purred into her ear, as he caressed her breast through the silky red fabric. "This way, you'll think most upon how this feels, ach?"

*How this feels.* Because wait, Tryg was already tugging up Lydia's dress, and shifting her tighter on his lap, so his hard, jabbing strength was pressed long against her bare arse beneath her skirts. And then—her breath choked—he beckoned purposefully toward Ezog, and pointed him... toward the floor before them.

And oh, hell, Ezog instantly nodded, and obliged. Striding over toward them without a twitch of hesitation, and falling to his knees on the hard wood. While Tryg's familiar, capable hands found Lydia's thighs beneath her skirts, and slowly began easing them apart.

"Now, what do you wish for first, pet," Tryg murmured. "Mayhap my sweet *elskan* shall open you up for me? Give you a taste of his clever tongue?"

Lydia's disbelief was surging again—Tryg couldn't truly *want* that, could he? But twisting around to look at his face, she realized that his eyes were glittering, his lips parted, his black tongue sweeping against them. As if... yes. Yes, he really, really wanted that.

And maybe she did too, oh hell, and she jerked a shaky-feeling nod. To which Tryg gave one of those low, approving chuckles, as he drew her thighs further apart, opening her up wide beneath her skirts. And then—Lydia froze, caught, breathless—he reached for Ezog's ugly head, and guided it up under the hanging red fabric.

And—oh. *Oh.* Warm breath, ghosting between her legs. Gentle hands, settling high on her inner thighs. And then—then—a light, tentative brush of something slick and soft and alive.

Ezog's *tongue.*

"Oh gods," Lydia gasped, as Tryg again chuckled beneath her, and spread her thighs even wider. And then he slid his big hands upwards, over her dress, curving against her belly, finding her breasts. While that slick slippery heat under her skirts just kept stroking, tasting, caressing. Touching again and again with astonishing gentleness, easing her open upon that light, stunning touch.

"You like?" Tryg murmured, his hands kneading and squeezing, his own hot mouth kissing and nipping up the side of Lydia's shoulder. Already working with far more hardness and purpose than Ezog's steady, careful licks, and the contrast felt so strange, almost obscene. Especially when Tryg's firm hand tilted Lydia's face sideways, so he could find her mouth with his. Kissing her with eager, powerful hunger, his tongue already seeking deep inside, while Ezog's tongue below had scarcely begun to delve within.

But oh, it felt so good, impossibly good. Those two clever mouths working at once upon her, teasing her open for them, while she trembled and squirmed and gasped. And somehow even felt herself easing closer toward the bottom tongue, pressing back against it, wanting more, needing more, oh.

And yes, yes, it was instantly obliging, following just what she wished. Seeking deeper, harder, but still slow and succulent, as though savouring every taste. While Tryg's mouth was still sharp and ravenous, his teeth scraping her lips, wringing up the hunger higher, harder, closer, already—

But then Tryg yanked back, searching Lydia's face with bright, glinting eyes—and below, that softly stroking tongue had stopped, too. Perhaps waiting for Tryg's next command, just the same way Lydia was—and oh, Tryg was grasping for the hem of her dress, and smoothly drawing it upward.

"You won't mind seeing my *elskan* now, ach?" he murmured. "Now that you ken how good he feels?"

Oh. And even as Lydia belatedly cringed at her own reluctance to see Ezog—and the fact that Tryg had clearly known it, too—she felt herself actually helping him, pulling up both her dress and her shift over her head. And once she'd tossed it all away, there was only the impossible, inevitable sight of Ezog's face. Hovering close and hideous between her spread thighs, his torn, broken mouth streaked all over with shiny wetness. With… *her*.

But perhaps Tryg had been right, because no matter how Ezog's face looked, his tongue had felt so, *so* good—and the sight of Tryg's hand on his head like that, guiding him forward into Lydia's wide-open heat, was doing strange, shuddering things inside her. Things that found her actually clenching at Ezog's seeking tongue, as though kissing back at it, oh gods, needing more, deeper, yes—

"Ach, that's it, *elskan*," Tryg's low voice ordered. "Open her for me. Ready her for my strong Skai ploughing."

Ezog's moan shuddered up into Lydia's very core, his tongue's gentle, inexorable press deepening, widening. Indeed as if he fully intended to… *open* her, for Tryg. And yes, Tryg was even shifting Lydia upon him again, so that he could free his cock from beneath her, its hard jabbing length pointing straight toward Ezog's face…

And as Lydia stared, utterly caught, Ezog eased sideways, and pressed a soft, open-mouthed kiss to the tapered head of Tryg's familiar, rigid cock. His hand slipping up to circle it as he kissed, clutching that scarred base with gentle fingers—and then he carefully guided that hard, hungry tip up into Lydia's quivering, waiting, wide-open heat.

"*Oh*," she gasped, whimpered, as she felt Tryg's slick length carving into her. Sliding in so swift and easy, because Ezog had already opened and softened her for it, oh. And as Ezog knelt there, watching Tryg sink inside, his lashes fluttered, his lips parting, a low groan rumbling from his throat. Until Tryg had sunk himself all the way in, pressing up deep—and then Ezog leaned forward again, kissing and licking and tasting. Not just against Lydia now, but against Tryg, too.

But it still felt so, so good. So impossibly, wonderfully decadent, to have Tryg's strength jutted inside her, grinding up again and again, while Ezog's brilliant warm mouth licked and caressed upon them. Not seeming to care in the slightest how it looked, how it tasted, how it sounded, or even—Lydia gasped—how Tryg's increasingly powerful thrusts had slipped him out of her entirely, his rigid wet length slapping hard against Ezog's face.

But Ezog only lifted his hooded eyes up, and sucked Tryg's glistening, dripping cockhead inside his mouth. And when Tryg's big hand curved against the back of his head, pulling him forward, Ezog swallowed him deep with damnable ease, that full scarred shaft vanishing swift and smooth between his eager, sucking lips.

It was yet another impossibly shocking sight, another twitch of jealousy, or maybe even shame. Because even Lydia's best attempts at pleasuring Tryg had gotten nowhere near this, right? And surely she must have been a pathetic disappointment, in comparison?

But perhaps Tryg had followed that, because his arm abruptly tightened around her waist, his breath hissing hot and close in her ear. "My *elskan* is so sweet, ach, pet?" he whispered. "An' so pretty, with his mouth so full of Skai prick."

And again, Tryg was... sharing this with her. Wanting her to be part of it. And Lydia had to gulp for air, find words, find truth amidst the chaos. "Yes, he's—very sweet," she whispered back. "No wonder you like him so much."

Beneath her, Tryg's body twitched, almost as if surprised—but then he nodded, and his hand slipped down to Ezog's sweaty, hideous face, still stuffed full of his jabbing cock. And Tryg exhaled a slow sigh as his hand stroked against Ezog's scarred cheek, caressing it as though it was something prized, something precious.

"Ach, I do like him," he murmured. "Always have, ach?"

Ezog was blinking back up toward Tryg with blatant reverence in his expressive eyes, and Lydia could see his tongue and throat working, as if desperately attempting to convey his own affection, his own appreciation. And Tryg liked it, he wanted it, his body heaving beneath Lydia's, his hand still caressing Ezog's face with such soft, unabashed tenderness.

"Ach, enough, *elskan*," he breathed, and Ezog instantly drew back again, his eyes downcast, as Tryg's hard, scarred length slowly extended from his mouth. Until it had bobbed fully free again, and Ezog gently guided it back inside Lydia, his eyes fluttering as he leaned forward, and again pressed his lips against their joined bodies.

But even as the pleasure surged and swayed, rising with every sharp plunge of Tryg's hips beneath her, Lydia seemed caught in it, somehow, trapped in the power of that previous moment. And she felt her trembling hands slipping downwards, their tentative touch instantly twitching Ezog backwards, his eyes wide and uncertain—but then she drew Tryg's strength out again, and pointed it toward Ezog's hideous, blinking face.

"Again, if you would," she choked out. "He's right. You were just—so pretty, with him inside you."

She didn't miss the shock in Ezog's eyes, and then his shy, furtive little nod, as he again sucked Tryg deep. While beneath Lydia, Tryg gasped and groaned, his face suddenly buried in her neck, his teeth scraping hard. And his clever fingers had slipped down to where his cock had been, easing up inside her, and there was the feel of another finger easing in, too. Ezog's finger, oh hell, as his eyes blinked up at her with worshipful gratitude, his mouth still sucking greedily around Tryg's cock.

"You don't mind—if I grant him—my seed?" Tryg was gasping, his breaths hitching into her throat. "Oughta be—yours, sweet thing."

But Lydia's hand was reaching up behind her, catching against the back of Tryg's head, drawing him down closer, as both orcs' fingers twisted and tangled together inside her. "No," she gasped back. "Want him—you—both of you—to have it. A gift."

Tryg again groaned into her neck, his teeth scraping—and then he bit down, hard, as he bucked up powerfully beneath her, and poured out deep into Ezog's tight sucking throat. Into where Ezog's previously hideous face looked almost beatific, alight with pleasure and joy, as his throat convulsed again and again and again. In strange, syncing time with Tryg's hard, hungry swallows against Lydia's ear, and then—she jerked, flailed, cried out—with her own fierce, desperate release, pulsing around the orcs' fingers. The sensation so strong and staggering that the room reeled away, and there was only white wailing ecstasy, screaming and shattering behind her eyes.

And then... stillness. Shaky, trembling stillness, holding all three of them locked together. Tryg's teeth sunk in Lydia's neck, his cock buried in Ezog's throat, and both their fingers still thrust deep inside her. While their breaths heaved, thick and heavy, almost as one.

It was finally Tryg who drew away first, gently extracting his teeth from Lydia's skin, and giving it a soft, lingering kiss. While between their legs, Ezog slowly pulled back too, easing Tryg's shiny, much-subdued length from his mouth, until it fell down slack and still. And then Ezog slid out his finger, and Tryg's too, only to replace them with... his mouth. His gentle, reverent mouth, kissing her there with exquisite, aching sweetness.

"Th-thank you," Lydia whispered, once Ezog had drawn away again, his eyes shimmering as they flicked between her and Tryg. "That was just so—lovely."

Behind her, Tryg gave a low, strange-sounding growl, his lips again kissing at where he'd bitten her neck. "Ach," he said, hoarse. "So sweet, both of you. So good. *Ach*."

Lydia found her eyes meeting Ezog's, her mouth twitching up almost in perfect time with his. In perfect accord, somehow, because they'd done this together, earning Tryg's pleasure, or perhaps even his awe. And Lydia felt her own hand slipping to Ezog's silken head too, curling there with almost familiar-feeling ease. With... affection.

"What—should you wish for next?" came Tryg's voice, low and unsteady against Lydia's throat. "Whatever you wish, sweet thing."

Oh. Lydia shivered all over, her eyes still holding to Ezog, searching him. Seeing the warmth, and the hunger, and the... longing. Wanting more, more, just like she did. For them, yes, and for... Tryg. For the orc they both... loved.

"I think... I'd like to have more of my... gift," she whispered, toward Ezog's eyes. "As much as he'd like to give me."

Ezog's eyes widened, looking genuinely astonished, and behind her, she could hear Tryg's harsh hiss, the catch in his throat. "But... I ken my *elskan* would like to plough you, sweet pet," he said, choked. "I ken he'd like to fill your womb with his fat perfect prick, and his good sweet seed."

Oh. And yes, yes, Ezog was nodding, hard and fervent, his eyes still shocked on Lydia's face. Again, as if this was a gift for him, not her. And she felt herself softly smiling, her hand stroking tighter against his head, her thumb even brushing his scarred, hideous cheek.

"Would you?" she whispered. "Please?"

And oh, the look in his eyes. Reverent, worshipful, shifting with wonder and awe. With joy.

"Ach, woman," he breathed. "I shall."

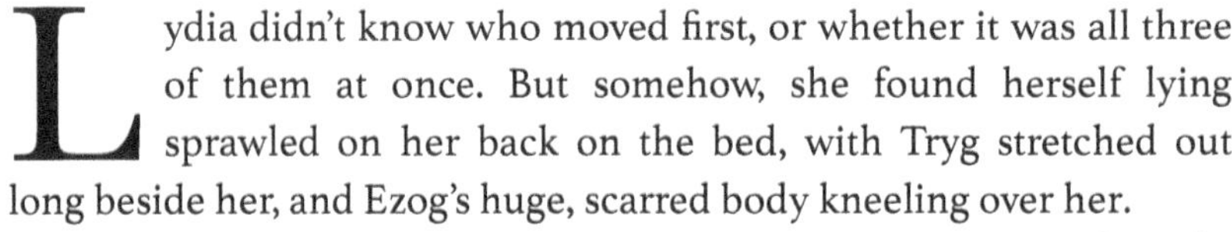

# 7

Lydia didn't know who moved first, or whether it was all three of them at once. But somehow, she found herself lying sprawled on her back on the bed, with Tryg stretched out long beside her, and Ezog's huge, scarred body kneeling over her.

And for the briefest of instants, blinking up at that close, horrifyingly hideous face, there was again a twitch of fear, sparking inside Lydia's chest. Enough that Ezog abruptly stilled over her, his eyes wide and alarmed on hers—but Lydia drew in breath, and settled her shaky hands against his warm, shifting back. And then she even attempted a smile, though she couldn't help a brief, pleading look toward Tryg beside them.

And yes, Tryg was here, familiar and certain and safe, flashing them both a swift, affectionate grin. "Ach, no need to rush, my sweets," he murmured. "You must only keep learning each other, just as I've learnt both of you."

Oh. Lydia could feel Ezog's big body slightly relaxing over her, and she was relaxing too, her fingers spreading wider against his back. Earning another encouraging smile from Tryg, and she belatedly realized his hand was on Ezog's back too, stroking up and down with firm, steady reassurance.

"You shall be my *elskan*'s first woman, ach, pretty pet?" Tryg continued, his voice low. "It shall grant me great joy to give him this. To teach him how good your sweet womb shall feel, when he is buried deep inside it."

Oh, *hell*. Both Lydia and Ezog had shuddered at that, though Lydia's eyes had snapped back up to Ezog's hideous face, searching his hazy eyes. "I would be—your first?" she croaked. "Are you sure you—"

Her answer came in a guttural groan from Ezog's mouth, a hard, sustained nudge of his swollen heat against her inner thigh. Because yes, he was already there, already so close, and Lydia's breath hitched as she shifted a little beneath him, lining him up, even closer...

"Ach, that's it," murmured Tryg beside them, his eyes half-lidded as he glanced down between them. Blatantly watching, *approving*, as Ezog's hips slightly canted, prodding him just up against there, oh, *there*. "Find each other, my sweets. You can feel how open and ready she is for you, ach, *elskan*? How she kisses you, and longs to suck you in deep?"

And yes, yes, Lydia's open heat was brazenly kissing at that gently pressing hardness, longing for it, convulsing powerfully against it. As it shuddered in return, swelling even fuller, while Ezog groaned again, long and low—and then he nudged just a little deeper. Parting Lydia around that smooth rounded head, and she felt herself groaning too, arching up beneath him, spreading even wider...

"Ach, just like that," continued Tryg's soft, heated voice. "Seek it slow and easy. I ken my *elskan* shall be the largest prick you have ever known, ach, sweet thing? You shall need to make yourself wide open for him, and learn how to swallow him whole inside you."

Lydia gasped and nodded, her body frantically clamping against where Ezog's slowly sinking cock indeed felt larger, more overpowering, than anything she'd ever felt there before. But wait, that included Tryg himself, and wouldn't he be upset by that, or jealous—but another glance at his face showed his eyes still hungry and hooded, his tongue again greedily brushing his mouth.

"It grants me great joy to witness my *elskan* opening you thus," he purred at her. "I should keep no woman who could not bear him, ach? Who could not welcome his good fat prick inside her?"

Oh. Lydia's thoughts were swirling, scattering—*keep*, he'd said—and Ezog was moaning again, his eyes now squeezed shut, his slow invasion between her legs briefly gone still. Because it was already so much, oh gods, her body stretched taut and thin around him—but he was only halfway in, and she needed more, more, needed to welcome him, to open for him...

"More," she whispered at him, one of her hands somehow fluttering up to his hideous face. Snapping his eyes open again, so wide she could see the whites of them, the wild clash of pleasure and uncertainty and fear.

"Ach, more," agreed Tryg's husky voice beside them, his hand still stroking Ezog's back, sliding over Lydia's hand as it went. "My sweet *elskan* feels so good, woman, ach? So thick and fat inside you?"

Lydia was fervently nodding, holding Ezog's eyes, giving him a genuine, wavering smile—and even though she could feel him swelling more inside her, he still hadn't moved again. That unease still shimmering in his eyes, as if he really wasn't sure, maybe about her, about Tryg, about this...

And without thinking, without hesitating, Lydia drew down his hideous face, and... *kissed* him. Kissed his ruined, broken mouth, with its torn lip and jagged teeth. And yes, it felt different, tasted different... but it also felt—right. Right, in the shaky relief of his exhale, in the easy, already-familiar gentleness of his tongue. The way it kissed with such soft, careful thoroughness, just like it had between her legs.

Oh, it was good, and Lydia arched up further, perhaps opened wider, welcoming him in. In both places now, her mouth and her swollen clutching heat—and yes, yes, Ezog was giving her more. Pressing in again, pushing through the stretch and the burn and the ache. Filling her whole with his huge driving cock, deeper and deeper and deeper, as his ruined mouth plundered hers, made her his own...

And as he finally sank all the way, stuffed to the hilt, that sense of rightness only grew, blooming through Lydia's chest. It was right, how he filled her utterly to the brim, locked and held tight. Right, how he slowly drew his mouth away to look at her, with such unabashed wonder in his shining eyes. And so, so right, in the heated, grateful way those eyes then glanced sideways at Tryg, his tongue brushing his lips—

And right, how Tryg reached for Ezog's head, yanked him close, and... kissed him. Kissed him with just the same fierce intensity that he'd kissed Lydia, biting hard enough that she could see a trickle of red streaking down Ezog's scarred chin.

But there wasn't even the slightest twinge of jealousy, not even at the fact that Ezog's throbbing cock was buried whole inside her, filling her to her very limit, while he so eagerly kissed someone else. While Tryg furiously kissed him back, and then—Lydia gasped—he suddenly swung his tall body up over Ezog's, so he was looking down at her over Ezog's shoulder. His eyes fiery and flashing with hunger, his teeth bared sharp and white.

"You shall not mind, sweet pet," he hissed, his breaths oddly laboured, "if I plough my *elskan* thus, ach?"

Lydia's groan was hoarse and betraying, her tongue sweeping against her lips. "Of—course not," she choked. "He feels—so *good*."

Tryg's answering nod was jerky and quick, his hand already working down between them, making Ezog gasp and arch, his eyes fluttering—and then, oh, oh, Lydia could almost *feel* Tryg finding that hot sweet tightness with his hard hungry cock, piercing it open around him. And in return, she felt Ezog's cock swelling fuller against their own already-snug fit, locking them even tighter in place, as Tryg pressed further and further inside.

"So good," Tryg gasped, his silver head thrown back, showing his long, corded, convulsing neck. "Ach, just like that. Suck me all the way in, *elskan*, so nice and tight, show me how good you are, *ach*—"

Above Lydia, Ezog was moaning too, his eyes dazed and desperate—and he jerked against her, inside her, at the telltale slap of skin against skin, at the sound of Tryg surely slamming deep. Filling Ezog, just as Ezog was filling her, and oh, it was impossible, it was unthinkable, it was utterly unreal...

"Ach, that's it," Tryg breathed, his glinting eyes darting between Ezog and Lydia, his chest heaving. "That's so good. So sweet. Both of you. Even better than I thought. *Ach*."

He'd abruptly grasped for a handful of Ezog's long hair, yanking his head back—but the flash across Ezog's eyes was only pleasure, craving, anticipation. And Tryg's mouth curled into a sly, menacing grin as he held Ezog there, as he slowly, deliberately drew out again, as Ezog's huge body quaked with the loss of it...

And then Ezog bucked and shouted as Tryg drove back inside. The impact driving him tighter into Lydia, too, and oh, it felt good, so, so *good*—and behind Ezog, Tryg was fully laughing now, his head again thrown back, his clawed grip tightening in Ezog's hair.

"Even better, my sweets," he purred at him, at her, at them, with greedy satisfaction in his glittering eyes. "Ach, you're both so pretty, aren't you? So good, when you're being ploughed together by a good Skai prick?"

Both Ezog and Lydia frantically nodded, and Lydia was even clutching Ezog closer, clinging to his warm solid safety, while Tryg drew out again, and then slammed back inside. Making them both shudder and moan, their voices rising with every powerful plunge of Tryg's hips—and Tryg's eyes were blazing now, almost feral, as he punched in again and again and again.

"So sweet," he gasped, his voice cracking. "So perfect. And you'll both be even sweeter when you're stuffed chock-full of good seed, ach? When you're both stretched wide open and leaking for me, because you're both mine, mine, *mine*—"

He'd snapped out the words with harsh, forceful thrusts, with pure flashing menace in his eyes—and with one last, vicious plunge, he was groaning, guttural and deep, as ecstasy shot across his face. As Ezog beneath him startled and shook, his eyes wide, his strength still inside Lydia quivering sharp—and then he was shouting into her neck as he sprayed out deep, too. Surging her full of his hot thick seed, flooding her every last space with him—until her own pleasure finally caught again, too. Kicking and throbbing around him, clutching him, kissing him, *thanking* him.

And perhaps Ezog was thanking her, too, moaning as he lowered his hideous face to kiss her again. And she was already arching up to meet him, to taste him, to make his gentle, generous beauty her own.

When they drew apart again, Ezog's eyes were blinking, looking very bright, as his breath shuddered again, again. And wait, perhaps that was because of Tryg, who currently had his face buried in Ezog's neck, his throat audibly gulping as he rapidly, greedily swallowed.

Oh. It was just so damned typical of him, enough that a helpless little smile twitched on Lydia's mouth—and above her, Ezog was smiling, too. Looking just as softly affectionate as she felt, and she swallowed hard as she searched his face, his lovely, expressive eyes.

"You're still—sure, about this?" she whispered at him. "You didn't want to—to keep him all to yourself?"

Because she somehow understood what this truly was, now, in a way she hadn't before. Tryg hadn't had other lovers. He'd had Ezog. And he loved Ezog, and perhaps he had for a long, long time.

And Ezog was still smiling down at her, so warm and tender and kind. "Ach, I am sure," he murmured back. "You have granted me great joy in this, woman. A great gift. One I have longed for all my life."

But that was perhaps a flicker of sadness in his eyes, too. And Lydia's hands were stroking at his face, seeking it, needing to know the truth of it. "But you weren't—jealous?" she whispered. "When Tryg started coming to me?"

That was definitely another shift in Ezog's eyes, a telltale swallow in his throat. "Ach, only a little," he said softly. "I knew how deeply he longed for this, and you are far from the first, ach? And he should have freely granted me leave to do the same."

Oh. Wait. So Ezog... *had* been jealous of her, then. And Tryg had—he must have asked Ezog's permission to keep seeing her, and of course Ezog had given it, because he would give anything Tryg asked. Up to and including... being a Yule gift for his new mistress. Which Ezog had readily done, down to the damned red ribbon.

"I'm—so sorry, Ezog," Lydia whispered up at him, her eyes blinking hard, as her hands stroked his face. "I would never have agreed to it, if I'd known. You deserved better."

But at that, Tryg gave an odd choking sound, and his silver head snapped up from Ezog's neck, his eyes mightily glowering down at Lydia's face. A sight that was made even more alarming by the fresh red smeared across his lips and beard, and dripping down his chin onto her shoulder.

"Ach, what's this?" he demanded, as his hand still in Ezog's hair yanked his head up, so he could frown at his face, too. "Not only did I hunt a good, sweet, lovely woman for us, but I took my good time upon this, and made sure she was all that she seemed! I tested her work and her kindness and her fealty, and her word upon whether she could share her joy with you!"

Wait. Wait, what? But Tryg was still glowering viciously between them, and giving Ezog's head a fierce little shake. "And," he continued, even harder, "I tested how she would treat you, *elskan*, with nary a warning from me! For I should never bring any woman into our life—or our bed—who might harm you, or cause you pain, or even speak a single harsh word to your perfect face!"

Oh. Oh. Was Tryg saying—this had really all been some kind of *test*? Some kind of grand scheme on his part? And—Lydia's eyes darted toward Ezog's stunned-looking face—surely he hadn't known about it, either?

"I told you again and again, *elskan*," Tryg continued flatly, his eyes still glaring at Ezog, "I should never leave you for another. You are *mine*. You have *always* been mine."

His voice had gone dark and scathing, his long tongue blatantly licking at his reddened mouth. While Ezog's eyes fluttered closed, perhaps with pain, or relief, or both—and then they opened again. Catching on Lydia's face, holding there, almost as if drawing up courage.

"Then why," he whispered, without inflection, without looking at Tryg, "have you never offered to speak vows to me? Even after your clan altered their ways to allow this?"

Lydia was feeling fully lost, now—Tryg's clan hadn't allowed him to swear vows to Ezog?—but the words had clearly meant something to Tryg, something important. Because his body behind Ezog had jerked to utter, rigid stillness, his eyes wide and suddenly, surprisingly vulnerable on Ezog's face.

"You... wished for *vows*, from me?" he whispered. "In truth, *elskan*? I thought... I thought you yet wished for a woman."

Oh. And that was more mingled pain and regret in Ezog's eyes, a choked little laugh from his mouth. "Ach, once, mayhap," he whispered back. "But I knew this would never be mine, not with my face. And then... *you* were not mine, either."

Lydia could almost taste the sadness in his voice, could feel it deep and sickening in her belly. And surely Tryg could too, his throat convulsing, his mouth giving a tremulous little quiver.

"Ach, I was yours, *elskan*," he said thickly. "I am. And should you yet allow this, I'd be most honoured to swear vows to you. To"—he cleared his throat—"to do all within my power to grant you aught that you should wish."

At that, his eyes had darted, brief but betraying, toward… Lydia. And too late, she found herself following the implications in those words. Because not only had this been some kind of devious scheme on Tryg's part, but he'd really sought her out—for *Ezog*? He'd done all that, seduced her, pleased her, brought her his damned *laundry*—because he'd thought that was what *Ezog* had wanted?

When perhaps—perhaps Ezog hadn't actually wanted it at all? When Ezog had just wanted—*him*?

Oh. Oh gods. Bile was rising in Lydia's throat, her stomach horribly plummeting, her eyes blinking back the sudden wetness behind them. Oh. They wanted—oh.

Each other. Not… her.

And gods, why had she even thought otherwise? Why had she ever imagined this would be hers? She should have known better, it had always been too good to be true, always…

"Right, then," she whispered, though the words broke in her throat. "I—understand. I'll go."

# 8

The orcs' reaction to Lydia's words was instantaneous. Not with them regretfully shoving up and ushering her out the door, as she might have expected—but instead, with Ezog bodily pinning her to the bed, his eyes snapped wide and alarmed, while Tryg's sharp, angry bark echoed through the room.

"What rubbish is this, woman?" he demanded at her, his voice harsh and malicious. "*No*, you shall not go! I have hunted you, we have ploughed you and claimed you, and thus, you are *ours*!"

Lydia blinked up toward his furious face, and then toward Ezog, who was fervently nodding, his eyes fearful and pleading. "You cannot wish to go, sweet woman," he whispered. "Not after this. Your joy tasted so sweet, ach? Have I not well pleased you, as your gift?"

Lydia couldn't stop blinking at him, at them, and she twitched a short, shaky nod. "Y-yes," she whispered back. "Of course you pleased me, Ezog. But now that I know what you really wanted... what *he* really wanted..."

She shot a furtive glance up at Tryg, who was still looking furious—but that was more pain, more regret, flashing across Ezog's face. "Ach," he rasped. "Should you wish to go, then—you ought. We should never wish to—"

He was interrupted by Tryg's fierce, guttural growl, and a hard, high-pitched laugh from his suddenly cruel-looking mouth. "No," he hissed. "No. I won't allow it. You're here with us now, woman. You're yet stuck upon my *elskan*'s fat, perfect prick. And you won't again escape it, until I grant you my leave!"

Oh. The words rippled up Lydia's spine, strange and terrifying and wonderful—especially when Tryg grasped another handful of Ezog's hair, and yanked his head back. "Fuck her, *elskan*," he hissed. "Plough her until she screams. Teach her who she belongs to. Ach?"

Ezog's growl was vicious and deep, his body taut and poised over Lydia, as if ready to strike, to obey—but his wide eyes were frantically searching her face. Their expression again something between pain, and longing, and fear.

Because... he'd sworn to serve her. To be a gift to her. *I shall do naught you do not wish for, woman.*

And even if Tryg didn't care about the promises he'd made to her, Ezog still did. He did. And suddenly Lydia wanted to weep and beg and plead for it, she needed it, needed him to show her, please...

And she was nodding at him, quick and urgent, yes, yes, *yes, please*—even as Tryg again yanked his head back, his snarl more like a roar. "I said, plough her!" he barked in Ezog's ear. "Make her beg and *scream* for us, *elskan*. Now!"

And this time, now that Ezog had Lydia's permission, the furious hunger caught and flashed in his eyes, turning them hot and liquid and dangerous. His growl rumbling low and decadent into Lydia's belly, clamping her even tighter upon his thick invading cock as he slowly drew backwards. Emptying her breath by breath, unstoppering her, taking himself away from her, *wait*—until a hot gush of fluid spurted out, flooding against them both. Releasing the pressure, Lydia distantly realized, making room, so he could...

His slam inside was brutal, merciless, so hard she shook all over—but yes, yes, he was in her again, he was making her his, making her theirs. And his choked, triumphant growl in her ear as he ground deep inside was everything, everything, cradling her, sustaining her, even as he pulled out again, taking it away...

But then he slammed in again, even harder this time. Chattering Lydia's teeth with the impact, flashing out unmistakable pain around his huge, overpowering invasion—but she didn't care, she didn't, and she clung to him as he pummelled in again, again, again. Brutalizing her, breaking her, as the seed sloshed and spurted between them, and his cold, ruthless, terrifying eyes flashed on her face. Drinking her up, wanting to see her like this, weak and shivering and utterly overwhelmed for him, her only possible recourse to take more, to open wider, to welcome his monstrous, merciless conquest.

And Lydia needed it, craved it, revelled in it, so lost and so desperate that she almost didn't notice Tryg behind him, again plunged deep inside him, driving him even harder. "Ach, that's it," he was hissing, as he bit at Ezog's tattered ear. "Plough her as hard as you can, *elskan*. Pump that sweet little womb wide open for us. Make sure she feels that strong fat prick, make sure she knows what it shall do to her, when she *dares* to spurn my great gift!"

And oh, oh gods, Lydia's blinking streaming eyes were on Tryg's now, her head somehow shaking, despite the furious orc still pummelling her pinned, quivering body. "Not—*spurning*," she pleaded at him. "L-loved it. J-just didn't want to—hurt him."

Tryg's eyes were flashing again, his lips pursing, as his own cock kept plunging into Ezog's arse, the sounds of sloshing liquid and slapping skin even sharper than before. "Then say this, human," he growled. "Swear this. You are his. Mine. *Ours*."

His voice seemed to strike at Lydia's heart, even deeper than his rage, deeper than the huge cock still swiving between her legs. But deeper still were Ezog's eyes, blazing on hers with such desperate longing and fury and craving. Wanting this. Taking her as brutally as he could, in the hopes that he could save this, have this. Have her.

"Yours," Lydia gasped at him, her hands finding his face, trembling uncontrollably against it as he kept plunging hard and deep. "Yours, Ezog. I swear. Yours."

And oh, his groan was both pain and pleasure, victory and helplessness, a laugh and a sob—and his face thrust into her neck as his strength inside her finally held, stayed, locked tight again, just where he belonged. And then his teeth bit down, breaking her skin, as his cock plunged even deeper—and blasted her full. Emptying itself in furious swells of sharp shuddering heat, until her own sore, stretched-out body shuddered out its relief, too. Seizing in pulse after dragging, agonizing pulse, drinking him dry and empty, until there was nothing, nothing left.

And then, finally, stillness. Strange, ringing stillness, broken only by their heaving breaths, and the crackling of the fire. And then—Lydia twitched—by a loud, obscene squelching sound, trembling through Ezog's body, as Tryg pulled himself back, and up to his knees behind Ezog again.

And gods, he looked... terrifying. With red streaked all through his face and beard, still dripping off his chin, down onto his scarred, sweaty chest. And his eyes were still glittering, dangerous, ravenous, as they lingered in the vicinity of Ezog's arse, his groin. Upon what must have been a wide-open, seed-covered, lewd-looking mess.

But Tryg liked it, he was *pleased* with it, and oh, Lydia could feel him even spreading Ezog's legs wider, blatantly giving himself a better view. "Very pretty, my sweets," he hissed, harsh and low. "Both of you rent so wide open for me. Look how sweet you are, dripping out all this good fresh seed for me."

Oh, *hell*. And he'd even bent down over Ezog's arse again, and though Lydia couldn't see what he was doing, she could feel Ezog's choked, desperate gasps into her skin as Tryg licked and slurped and worked him over, the sounds slick and crude and shameless.

But when Tryg finally arose again, he was looking supremely satisfied, his tongue blatantly licking his reddened lips as his hands caressed up and down Ezog's still-trembling flanks. "Better, *elskan*?" he murmured. "Any pain, now?"

Ezog gave a thoroughly unintelligible grunt into Lydia's throat—into where he was *still* swallowing, oh gods—and Tryg let out an amused-sounding laugh as he dropped back down beside Lydia on the bed, his clawed hand easily curving against her cheek, tilting her face toward him.

"Just grant him a spell," he murmured at her, his eyes angling fondly toward Ezog's head, still buried deep into the other side of her neck. "He's never drunk fresh from a woman before, ach? This is a great gift, you ken."

Oh. Lydia couldn't quite hide her wince at that telltale word *gift*, and she could see Tryg's smile abruptly fading, his eyes sobering. "I hope..." he began, and then grimaced, shook his head. "I'm sorry, sweet thing, if I frightened you, in this. If I… pushed you, beyond what you wished. Beyond what we… promised you."

Lydia swallowed, and somehow managed a careful shrug of her shoulder nearest him. "It isn't… that," she croaked. "It's just…"

She couldn't finish, couldn't even begin to articulate it, but Tryg nodded, and gave her a crooked, sad little smile. "Didn't tell you what I was really up to, did I?" he said, quiet. "Didn't tell you I had… other aims, in coming to you, beyond just our pleasure together."

Yes, yes, that was exactly it, and Tryg must have seen it in her eyes, because he sighed again, and wiped at his still-red mouth. "Ach. I'm sorry, sweet thing. Last thing I wished was to bring you pain. It's only"—his eyes flicked toward Ezog's head again—"I've played this fool game too oft before, ach? And even when I've been sure I won it, sure I found a good woman for us both—it's always ended with my *elskan* being hurt. And I couldn't bear it again, ach? Swore to Skai-kesh that I'd try one last time, but I wasn't letting any of it *near* my sweet *elskan* until I was sure."

Oh. Skai-kesh was the patron god of Tryg's Skai clan, Lydia knew, and he huffed another sigh, caressed his hand against her hot cheek. "An' I begged, again and again, for a good one," he whispered. "A woman just as soft and sweet and gentle as my own *elskan*. And"—his chest filled, hollowed—"Skai-kesh heard me, sweet thing, and blessed me. Gave me a great, great gift, in you."

Lydia still couldn't seem to find words for this, though her eyes were blinking hard, a strange stilted hopefulness skittering in her chest. And Tryg drew in breath, stroking her cheek again, as his mouth pulled into a wavering, uncertain little smile.

"Really do want to keep you, sweet thing," he continued, even quieter. "For myself, and for my *elskan*, too. You've brought him such joy this night, and I ken you'll bring him far more, ach? It's a rare human who sees past his face, to all the sweetness inside. An' to see you treat him so tenderly, and then turn about and squeal so sweetly upon his perfect prick's ploughing"—he shrugged, his grin hitching higher—"this was one of the greatest sights in all my life, ach?"

The shimmering hopefulness kept fluttering stronger in Lydia's chest, and Tryg's smile twitched even higher, his eyes so warm, so affectionate. "Mayhap you'll think more upon this, sweet thing," he murmured, "whilst I give you better cause to forgive me, ach?"

And before Lydia could attempt a reply, Tryg's lean body shoved downwards again, and he purposefully nudged sideways at Ezog's arse. And though Ezog didn't draw his mouth from Lydia's neck, he shifted a little over her, and then slowly, carefully drew his softened cock out of her sore, tender heat. And once again, it was followed by a thick, spurting rush of molten seed, gushing out from inside her, and into...

Tryg's *mouth*?!

Lydia's moan was deep and desperate, her eyes wide and shocked on the sight. On Tryg's face pressed tight between her legs, his throat audibly gulping, while his greedy eyes glittered bright and challenging on her face.

"Oh," Lydia gasped, because there were truly no other words, not with two ravenous orcs feasting upon her at once. With Ezog still drinking from her neck, while Tryg loudly, eagerly sucked and swallowed between her legs. Drinking Ezog's thick, copious fresh seed out from inside her, his tongue licking and caressing, sending out furious flares of sharp, sparkling bliss.

And when Lydia's moans rose almost to screams, almost to the edge, Tryg only barked a satisfied laugh, and kissed her, and promptly drew away. Leaving her gasping and untouched and trembling all over—until he nudged Ezog back on top again. Guiding that fat, hungry cock back inside her, wanting it to fill her again, perhaps so he could drink out more...

And Ezog instantly obliged, moaning into Lydia's neck as he rocked softly into her, moving easy and slow this time, while she arched and shouted beneath him, her release wracking through them both. Once again dragging out more furious bursts of seed from Ezog, pouring her tight and full—and then Tryg elbowed Ezog aside, and knelt low between her legs. Again making stunning, spectacular use of his tongue, until she was left dizzy and boneless and incoherent, gulping desperately for breath.

At that point, Tryg kissed them both, and then shoved himself up, and went to collect a waterskin. First pouring it out into Lydia's mouth, and then—after a gentle but firm command—drawing Ezog away from Lydia's neck, so he could pour it out down his throat, too. And once Ezog had emptied the waterskin, he gave Tryg a long, grateful-looking kiss, and then eased back up over Lydia, sliding himself deep between her legs. Holding her eyes as he gently rocked inside her, his tongue reverently licking at his reddened lips.

"You shall now forgive our Skai, ach, sweet woman?" he murmured, as his deep, soulful eyes shimmered and shone on hers. "I ken he ought not to have hidden this truth from you, but now that you have gained his trust and his favour, he shall not falter in his care for you, ach?"

His slow thrusts inside her seemed to settle the words deeper, stronger—and Lydia clung to him, to the quiet reassurance of his big, powerful body, all over her, around her, within her.

"But he still—hid it—from you, too," she somehow pointed out, between her gasping breaths. "Still didn't tell you—why he came—to *me*."

But Ezog's expression didn't change in the slightest, and perhaps it even softened as he glanced sideways, toward where Tryg was intently watching them, his eyes glittering. "Ach, but you see, this was part of his care for me," Ezog murmured. "And when you love a Skai, as we do, you must understand that their care for you stands above all else, ach? Even above their truth."

That still seemed highly questionable, to Lydia's mind, but Ezog was still smiling like that toward Tryg, with such raw, powerful affection in his eyes. "It is best only to trust them," he continued, "and to know that they shall never leave you behind."

Oh. Best... to *trust* them. And as much as the unease kept twisting in Lydia's belly, she couldn't deny the startling familiarity in those words, either. The way she'd always implicitly trusted Tryg, too. And oh, the way Tryg was looking back at Ezog, his eyes rapt and reverent, as though he was the most beautiful sight he'd ever seen in all his life.

"Never leave you behind, *elskan*," he breathed. "*Never.*"

Well. And Ezog clearly believed that, because his eyes had fluttered, his cock thrusting up deeper—and then he sprayed out into Lydia again, moaning husky and low, while Tryg flashed him a smug, approving grin.

"Or you, pretty pet," he murmured toward Lydia, as he again nudged Ezog aside, and knelt between her thighs. "You shall see, ach?"

Lydia couldn't seem to argue, especially once Tryg had again begun shamelessly feasting between her legs, flashing out yet more dizzying, dazzling pleasure. And once he'd finished, he shoved Ezog onto his back, and proceeded to suck him with deft, familiar ease, too. Fitting nearly all of that massive green heft into his mouth, his eyes glimmering with wicked satisfaction as Ezog helplessly gasped and groaned beneath his touch.

Lydia was watching it too, from where Ezog had pulled her close, her head tucked against his solid shoulder. And though she'd never once imagined herself watching something like this—watching her lover sucking another orc down his throat—she found that she couldn't seem to pull her eyes away. Couldn't seem to keep from snuggling closer into Ezog's embrace, breathing in the sweet scent of his neck.

"He's so clever, isn't he?" she murmured toward him, as she watched his big clawed hand stroking against Tryg's hair. "So quick and kind and capable."

"Ach," Ezog murmured back, between gasps, as he turned his head to press a soft kiss to her forehead. "I have longed for him since the first day I saw him fight, ach? And he could have chosen any lover he wished—he did, for a long time—but—"

His voice broke there, his hips canting up, and he groaned, long and sustained, as his cock visibly pulsed between Tryg's tight lips—and yes, Tryg was greedily swallowing, his eyes fluttering on Ezog's as he sucked him dry, as he drew out every last drop.

"But then *you* caught my eye, sweet thing," Tryg said, his voice hoarse, once he'd pulled off again, licking at his slick lips. "An' then I couldn't keep myself away, ach?"

It sounded familiar, it *was* familiar, and Ezog pressed another soft, reassuring kiss to Lydia's forehead. "And he has not stopped in his care for me, ever since," he told her. "So now, you shall trust him to care for you also."

He spoke as though it was settled, decided, and perhaps—perhaps it was. Because when Tryg gave a meaningful glance toward Lydia, and then toward Ezog's cock—which was somehow already swollen full again—she gave a quick, grateful nod, and then slid herself on top of him, her legs straddling wide. To where Tryg was lifting that fat length, nudging it up into her wet heat, and then guiding her down upon it. While beneath her, Ezog spasmed and moaned, his eyes flicking awed and worshipful between them.

And when Tryg eased close behind Lydia, his prodding rigid tip jutting further up her open crease, she didn't flinch or resist. Instead, she exhaled and tilted herself back, opened as wide as she could for him, welcoming him inside—and then shuddered and shouted at the impossible screeching sensation of it, of two orcs seeking inside her at once, making her their own.

"Ach, that's it," Tryg was purring approvingly behind her, as he fed himself in a little deeper. "You suck me deep inside you, sweet thing. You squeeze me strong and tight, whilst you also seize my *elskan*'s perfect prick with your perfect little womb, ach?"

Both Lydia and Ezog were frantically nodding, holding one another's eyes, and Tryg barked a satisfied-sounding laugh behind them, and pushed in further. "So pretty," he continued, his voice catching, as his strong hands flexed against Lydia's hips, and that invading strength sank deeper, deeper, deeper. "So sweet. And you're gonna smell even sweeter when you're both stuffed full of my fresh Skai seed, ach? When you're both walking around here reeking of *me*."

His voice sharpened at the end, because oh, he was all the way in, now, jamming Lydia full, fuller than she'd ever been in her life. With two entire orcs buried inside her, filling her, claiming her, forever—

"An' *you*, sweet thing," Tryg continued, his voice a deep, certain rasp, as he gave one of Lydia's breasts a brief, proprietary squeeze. "Look how good you are. Look how pretty you are, with two orcs swallowed whole inside you. Now, you shall suck out our good seed for us, ach? You shall drink it deep within, and keep it there, so you shall always reek of our scents together, ach? So you shall always be *ours*."

And yes, yes, that was exactly what Lydia wanted, what she needed, always—and she was nodding, Ezog was nodding, she was even leaning down to kiss him again, to feel the certain strength in his lips and tongue. The way his own hips were bucking up faster, filling her fuller, while Tryg did the same behind, and it was whirling, it was singing, it was breath and light and home—and she arched up as they poured her full, as they gifted her with their good seed, their safety, their care. As she shook and shivered and wept, drank it all up with her own clutching, greedy grasp, until the deed was finally finished, sworn into stunning, staggering truth.

And when she collapsed down onto Ezog, he easily caught her, folding her into his strong arms, into his heart. "Ours, sweet woman," he whispered, so soft. "Ours, now. From this Yule onward."

And all Lydia could do was nod, and breathe, and settle in deep. "Yes," she whispered. "From this Yule onward."

# 9

When Lydia awoke the next morning, she was sore, and sticky, and sprawled wide on a soft, equally sticky fur. While a succulent, delicious scent wafted through the air, something like... frying meat?

And wait. Wait. Lydia's eyes snapped open, and once again found the cozy little cabin. Now with bright morning sun streaming through its small windows, illuminating where Tryg was standing by the fireplace, wearing only a pair of low-slung trousers, and flipping something in a pan. While Ezog bustled around the little table, which seemed to be piled far higher than before. With what looked like treats, and bottles of cider and ale, and... wrapped packages?

Ezog's big body had abruptly stilled, his eyes glancing toward Lydia in the bed—and for a choked, frozen moment, Lydia stared at him, and at his face. At where it was even more hideous in the bright light, all those scars and rips and imperfections on shocking, unnerving display. And for another strange, startled instant, it seemed utterly unthinkable that she had caressed him, kissed him, found such impossible pleasure with him...

But wait, that was already unease, and maybe even hurt, simmering in his watching eyes. And before she'd quite realized it,

Lydia shoved her sticky body out of bed, and walked unsteadily toward him. Reaching for that broken, beautiful face, and pulling it down, and giving it a fierce, purposeful kiss.

"Morning," she said shyly, once she'd drawn away. "Happy Yule, Ezog."

Her cheeks felt very hot, suddenly, and then even hotter at the look of abject, unabashed awe in Ezog's blinking eyes. "A-ach," he stammered, his voice thick. "To—to you also, woman."

Lydia's face flushed even hotter, and thankfully she was soon rescued by Tryg, who came over with a smug, indulgent grin on his face. "You are both so shy and sweet, my pretty pets," he said, with satisfaction, as he tilted Lydia's face up for a brief, biting kiss, too. "Now, *elskan*, mayhap you shall ask our woman if you can empty that good load you've been nursing into her? And then help her bathe and dress for the day?"

His hand had dropped to grip teasingly at the obvious bulge in Ezog's trousers, even as he gave Lydia a sly, knowing wink. "He's been eyeing your pretty form all this morn, sweet thing," he informed her. "Could scarce hear a word I spoke, ach?"

With that, Tryg casually strode back to the fireplace, swiping for his pan. And Lydia could have sworn that Ezog's deep green cheeks were flushing too, his hand rubbing shyly at the back of his neck. "Sh-should you?" he said, with a wince. "Wish for—more? From—me?"

But Lydia was already nodding, her body shivering with nervousness, or anticipation. And when Ezog led her back to the bed, she willingly climbed onto her hands and knees, and gasped as she felt gentle hands carefully opening her up, spreading her apart. And then that plump, already-familiar cock slowly, gently eased itself inside, while she moaned and shuddered around it.

Despite all the pleasures they'd enjoyed the night before, they hadn't done it from behind like this, and it distantly occurred to Lydia that perhaps Ezog didn't want her to look at his face in the bright daylight. But it still felt so, so good, so strong and safe and all-consuming, and she couldn't help glancing over her shoulder toward him as she gasped and groaned.

"Please, Ezog," she begged. "*Please.*"

And yes, yes, he was nodding, his strength plunging in once, twice, again—and his big hands spasmed on her hips as his eyes rolled back, and he sprayed out deep inside. While from across the room, there was a bright, amused-sounding cackle—and here was Tryg again, grinning fondly back and forth between them.

"Finished already, *elskan*?" he said cheerfully, as he nudged Ezog with his elbow, and untied his own trousers. "Still time for me to have a turn, then, ach?"

And wait, yes, Ezog's full strength was slipping out of her, releasing the now-familiar gush of liquid—but it was only a breath before Tryg's hot, rigid cock stabbed inside instead. Feeling so much harder and more demanding, sloshing the slick seed out messy around it, but he clearly didn't care, judging by the low, satisfied growl in his throat.

"Ach, that's good," he breathed, as he began plunging in, sinking into his usual swift, powerful rhythm. "Ach. Ploughing my woman's sweet womb, bathing my strong Skai prick in my *elskan*'s good fresh seed. Ach, you have opened her up so nice, *elskan*, made her so soft and slick for me. So sweet. *Ach*."

His voice broke, and suddenly he was spraying out, too. His cock pulsing and grinding inside as he flooded Lydia full of more hot fluid, his head tilted back, his claws digging into her hips.

But then, too quickly, he was gone—and where he'd been, there was more surging, spurting mess. Pouring out in a humiliating rush from between Lydia's parted, trembling thighs, while both orcs just stood there, and watched.

Lydia's cheeks were burning, her chagrined eyes blinking back to where—oh. Ezog's face looked even redder than before, his throat visibly convulsing, while Tryg blatantly licked his lips, and gave Lydia's arse-cheek a brief, approving little squeeze.

"So pretty, aren't you, my sweet?" he murmured approvingly. "After your sweet womb has drawn out two good fat loads, and now overflows with our fresh seed?"

Ezog was rapidly nodding as he held Lydia's eyes, and he was already drifting back toward her, as if he might welcome a second round—until Tryg elbowed him in the side, and shot him another jaunty grin. "Later, *elskan*," he said lightly. "Want her ready to meet m'boy, ach?"

Ezog nodded again at that, giving Lydia a shy, sheepish smile. And once Tryg had gone back to the fire, Ezog carefully helped Lydia up, and then led her over around the bed, to where there was a large, steaming washbasin.

"I have heated you a bath," he said softly. "I should be honoured to help you bathe, unless you..."

He glanced away, the unease again far too clear in his eyes, and Lydia smiled up toward him, and leaned in close. "I'd be very happy to have your help," she replied. "Thank you, Ezog."

His answering smile was shy, and almost painfully grateful. But as he helped Lydia into the bath, and gently began stroking her with a soft soapy cloth, she could almost feel his ease returning, the steady warmth rising in his eyes.

"Do you feel any pain, from last eve?" he murmured, as he stroked against her collarbones and shoulders, and then down her arms. "Or any... regrets?"

Lydia didn't have any regrets, although she was vaguely surprised to discover she didn't feel any actual pain, either. "Just a little sore all over, maybe," she said, with a wry smile. "I'm not used to such... vigorous activity, I suppose."

Ezog smiled back, slow and fond, as his hand very carefully slipped down to one of her breasts. "It was... very good of you," he said, quiet. "To give us such gifts, when this was meant only to be a gift to you."

Lydia swallowed, and met his kind, expressive eyes. "It was a gift to me, too," she replied. "*You* were a gift, Ezog. You, and Tryg. I... I've been... so lonely, for such a long time."

Ezog's eyes were sad now, sympathetic, and too late, Lydia heard the implication in her words. Or perhaps even the... obligation.

"But you mustn't—feel as though that means anything," she choked at him. "It's only been—one night. And you and Tryg have clearly been together for—well. And he wasn't honest with either of us, and if you decide I'm not what you'd—prefer, of course I—"

Gods, what was she even saying, and she couldn't seem to finish, shaking her head back and forth. "And you should know, I'm—awful at talking," she continued. "Always saying the wrong thing, or not finding anything to say at all, so—"

She stopped there, breathing hard, bracing herself for Ezog's mockery, his judgement, something—but to her genuine surprise, he was smiling again, as his hand slid to caress her other breast, too. "Then do not speak, should you not wish," he replied. "Your truth is yet clear in your eyes and your touch and your scent, ach?"

Oh. Lydia gulped in a shaky breath, but, predictably, couldn't seem to reply—and Ezog just kept smiling, caressing down her sides, over her belly. "And ach, I wish for you," he continued, quieter. "Tryg knows all that I am, ach? He knows what I most longed for in a woman, and now, he has freely granted it to me. And"—his eyes searched hers, the unease again rising in them—"you have welcomed our claim and our seed, ach? So this is done, you ken. Settled. You are *ours*. From this Yule onward."

Lydia's words still wouldn't come, but she was fervently nodding, and Ezog was nodding too, as more warmth flickered across his eyes. "And I have brought you more gifts, should you wish," he murmured. "Tryg is not oft one to think of these things, but I hope they shall please you, ach?"

Lydia couldn't hide her spark of interest at that, and Ezog grinned back at her, the sight both alarming and endearing on his face. And once he'd finished washing and drying her, he carefully dressed her in the red dress—which he'd aired out, too—before guiding her over to the loaded-up table.

"I have brought you three kinds of cider to try, and two wines," he said shyly, as he waved at the table's contents. "And some plums, and sweet breads, and puddings. And I was not sure if you should wish for a Skai gift, or jewels, so I have brought both, ach?"

With that, he thrust out one of the cloth-wrapped packages toward her—but at that moment, Tryg strode back over with a large, steaming platter of fried meat, eggs, greens, and mushrooms. "Ach, you brought her a Skai gift, *elskan*?" he asked, with undeniable curiosity, as he plunked the platter down in the middle of the table. "But I told you, our woman is too sweet to be Skai, ach? She shall be Bautul, like you."

Lydia wasn't following again, especially when Ezog's face flushed, his smile toward Tryg shy but grateful. "Ach, I ken," he said. "But I thought you should welcome this."

*This*, it turned out, once Lydia had unwrapped the cloth, was a slim, shining steel dagger, encased in a beautifully stamped leather scabbard. And Tryg's eyes indeed lit up at the sight of it, and he enthusiastically snatched it from Lydia's hand, inspecting the blade with a critical eye. "Ach, it matches yours, *elskan*!" he said delightedly. "Did you have Argarr forge this for her? So thoughtful, my sweet!"

Tryg looked truly thrilled by this development, and Lydia couldn't help laughing as she took the dagger back, and gingerly drew it out of its leather scabbard. "I have... never touched a weapon before," she confessed toward Ezog, with a wince. "In my life."

But the warmth kept shimmering in Ezog's eyes, and he passed another similar-looking package across the table toward Tryg. "Just as well," he said lightly. "I ken Tryg shall take great joy in teaching you, ach?"

With that, Ezog began loading up Lydia's plate with Tryg's delicious-smelling cooking, while Tryg swiftly unwrapped his own package, and again crowed with delight. And Lydia wasn't at all surprised to see that it was another dagger, though this one was far sharper and more deadly-looking, with only a slight jut of steel for a hilt, and a pointed, gleaming tip.

"Ach, is this Argarr's new throwing design, *elskan*?!" Tryg demanded, his eyes sparkling—and without warning, he flipped the dagger in his hand, and hurled it across the room. To where—Lydia's mouth dropped open—it stuck point-first into the wooden doorframe, its hilt end shuddering with the impact.

"Ach, look at that!" Tryg exclaimed, as he leapt up and rushed over to pluck it out of the wood—only to hurl it back across the room, to where it sank deep into the opposite wall. "Perfect weight and balance, *elskan*! I did not yet own one, thus!"

Ezog was beaming toward Tryg, his eyes bright and indulgent. "I thought this should please you," he told him, as he went to collect two more plates from the shelf, and then began loading them up with food, too. "Now, go greet our guests, ach?"

Tryg had already whirled around toward the door, flinging it wide open, because—oh. There were two more orcs, standing in the snow just outside. They were both younger-looking orcs, Lydia realized, and one of them was laughing with rather Tryg-like glee, and hurling himself bodily into Tryg's arms.

"Pa!" he exclaimed, in a voice that again sounded unnervingly like

Tryg's, as he thudded his fist against Tryg's back. "Ach, what's this? Your new woman, and *Pabbi*?"

Tryg squeezed the orc tight, rocking him back and forth, and then drew backward, enthusiastically waving him and the second orc inside. And now that Lydia could see them both properly, she realized that the first orc—the one who'd called Tryg *Pa*—was most certainly his son Tryggr. He had the same tall, lean body, the same quick confident grin, and his long black hair was even tied up into the same messy knot on his head. While the second orc—who was shorter, slimmer, and exceedingly handsome—looked far neater, and also far less sure of himself. His tunic and trousers were perfectly fitted, his hair pulled into a tight braid, and he was biting his lip, and fingering uncertainly at the thick gold choker around his neck.

"Ach, but first we must meet," Tryg said firmly, slinging his long arm around his son's neck, and drawing him forward. "Son, this is our sweet new woman, Lydia, who's brought us great joy this Yule. And woman, this is m'boy Tryggr, the wisest young Skai you'll ever meet! An' this is his sweet clever mate, Eben, of Clan Ka-esh."

This Eben was still looking unmistakably self-conscious, but Tryggr had pulled him close too, pressing a kiss to the top of his head. "The sweetest," he said, with a swift, affectionate grin down toward him, before lurching forward again, toward—Ezog? But yes, yes, this Tryggr was throwing his arms around Ezog too, rocking him back and forth, and Ezog was folding him close, as a slow smile spread across his mouth.

"Happy Yule, son," Ezog said, husky. "We are honoured to welcome you both, ach?"

Lydia was still blinking at all this—Ezog called Tryggr *son*, too?—and Tryggr was easily grinning as he drew away again, his fist bumping Ezog's back. "You too, *Pabbi*," he said brightly, as his dancing eyes flicked toward Lydia. "An' you, woman! I've long wondered what Pa was about with you, but I ken I mostly follow now, ach?"

Lydia was again feeling decidedly lost, but she couldn't help smiling warmly back at this Tryggr anyway. "I'm so happy to finally meet you," she said, without even a hitch in her voice. "I've heard so much about you."

Tryggr kept grinning toward her, his head shaking, his eyes alight.

"Ach, wish I could say the same, woman," he said cheerfully, "but Pa's refused to say a word about you! Knew he was up to some sorta old Skai trickery, ach?"

He raised an imperious brow at Tryg, and to Lydia's surprise, Tryg was actually looking a little sheepish, and waving them toward the table. "Feast first," he said, "and then tales, ach?"

Soon they were all seated around the small table, which turned out to only have three chairs—but Tryggr only pulled Eben down onto his lap, and Lydia somehow found herself settled onto Ezog's, too. While Tryg doled out generous portions of steaming, succulent-smelling breakfast, and poured them multiple mugs of ale and cider.

"So what's the tale, Pa?" Tryggr demanded, once they'd all begun tucking in. "You ken if you don't tell me, I'll get it all outta *Pabbi* later, so out with it, ach?"

He'd shot a teasing grin over toward Ezog as he'd spoken, and suddenly Lydia could easily see Ezog as the soft-hearted, perpetually indulgent father figure, who would willingly give Tryggr whatever he wished. While Tryg himself would no doubt be a far more demanding father, but surely a highly entertaining one, too.

"Ach, ach," Tryg replied, with a rueful grin, as he tossed a whole mushroom into his mouth. "Remembered this old Skai way my own *pabbi* spoke of. How at Yule, Skai-kesh will oft bless a gift, if it's made freely."

Oh. Wait. Because that was new too, wasn't it? And Lydia's searching glance at Ezog behind her found him looking both exasperated and indulgent, his eyes glimmering on Tryg's face. And in return, Tryg reached over and clasped Ezog's knee beneath the table, giving it a companionable little shake. "I've had the worst luck, finding a good woman to share with my sweet *elskan*," he continued, with a grimace. "But I knew he yet longed for this, so I went to Skai-kesh, one last time, and prayed and prayed upon this. And then I went hunting... and found *you*, woman."

His eyes angled toward Lydia, glinting with warmth and approval. "She was perfect, ach?" he said, his voice lowering. "Soft, and sweet, and kind, and eager to work and gain my praise. Just as my *elskan*. Just as most pleases me."

Tryggr cast a brief, appreciative glance across the table toward

Lydia, before pulling Eben a little closer on his lap. "Ach, me also," he replied. "And so?"

"So I tested her, and sought not to hope," Tryg said, with a wincing grimace. "Sought not to oft speak of her, not even to my sweet *elskan*, for I didn't wish to raise his hopes either, ach? But I could taste his sadness upon this, his longing to please me. And so, I asked him to be my Yule gift to her, in hopes of gaining Skai-kesh's blessing. And this was a good test for her also, ach? Catch her by surprise, you ken, so she could not speak false, or seek to trick me."

At that, Tryggr groaned aloud, and without warning, his fist snapped out, and punched Tryg in the arm. "You old weasel, Pa!" he said, with genuine heat in his voice. "*Pabbi*, you oughta tossed him out over this! Gone and found yourself a sweet pretty Ka-esh instead!"

He'd buried his face in Eben's hair, as if drawing much-needed strength from his scent—but behind Lydia, Ezog was smiling again, and shaking his head. "Ach, it has been a long time for your blood-father and I, son," he said softly. "I trust my Skai and his father-god, ach? I ken they shall always care for me."

Tryggr was still sputtering, and jabbing a sharp finger toward his father. "You're damned lucky it worked out, Pa," he said flatly. "It would've served you right, to lose both of 'em. To each other, mayhap."

He shot a sudden, suspicious look toward Lydia and Ezog, and then back at Tryg again. "You get 'em to swear vows to you, at least?" he demanded. "You claim them, and do it all properly?"

Tryg's silver brows had deeply furrowed, his eyes glancing back toward Lydia and Ezog. "I have been... remiss, in swearing vows to my *elskan*," he murmured. "But I hope, mayhap, I have now gained this, with a good long rut upon 'em both, all this Yule's Eve. Must speak to Boss, and then our Enforcer, and Skai-kesh."

Oh. Lydia wasn't following again, but behind her, Ezog's body had suddenly gone rigid—and when she glanced toward him, he was staring at Tryg, unblinking, unmoving. And Tryg was half-smiling back, slow and soft and uncertain, but a little hopeful, too.

"Wish to keep you both, for the rest of my days," he said softly. "Wish to grant you all my fealty and care, so long as you both wish for this. Ach?"

Behind Lydia, Ezog twitched again, and he abruptly reached out to clasp Tryg's hand, squeezing it in his own. And then he clasped Lydia's, too, and with firm, gentle pressure, he brought it to his mouth.

"Then I shall also pledge you my troth," he murmured, his voice low and reverent. "To you, Sigtryggr of Clan Skai, and you, Lydia of Clan Bautul. I shall keep you safe, and fed, and filled, for as long as I am able, and as long as you shall wish."

Oh. The words seemed to ripple all through Lydia, resonating up her spine, and Tryg looked just as stunned as she felt, his eyes shimmering on Ezog's face.

"Truly, *elskan*?" he said, disbelieving, almost shy. "Ach. You are—*ach*."

He was rubbing at his face with both hands, and Lydia belatedly realized that his eyes were rapidly blinking, because he was—weeping. Confident, certain, swaggering Tryg was *weeping*, shaking his head, wiping at his eyes.

"Ach," he whispered, his breath oddly gulping. "Ach, *elskan*. I wish for always."

And Lydia was nodding too, silent but fervent, pressing herself into Ezog's safety, his certainty, his great, generous kindness. And in return he was drawing her closer, too, granting her even more of it, of him, as his hand clasped Tryg's again, giving it a gentle, familiar shake.

"Ach, then," he said. "It is settled, I ken."

*Settled*. Just as he'd said to Lydia earlier, and suddenly she was grinning back and forth between them, while Tryg again wiped at his eyes, and Ezog's own smile split his face. And Lydia only belatedly remembered Tryggr and Eben, watching from across the table—but Eben was looking softly indulgent, and Tryggr appeared distinctly mollified, too.

"Well, about time, Pa," he said flatly, as he plucked up a mushroom with his claws. "Leave it to you to wait 'till you're both *ancient*, honestly."

Tryg spluttered at that, looking deeply offended, while Ezog huffed a low laugh, and began pouring out more cider. "Now, back to breakfast," he said firmly. "And the rest of the gifts, ach?"

This proved an adequate distraction, and soon they were all happily eating again, and exclaiming over the gifts Ezog had brought. This included a second deadly throwing-knife for Tryggr—who hurled it around the cabin with the same delighted glee Tryg had shown—as well as a complex-looking book of human medical treatments for Eben, who accepted it with surprising eagerness, and then immediately began reading at the table. And then, to Lydia's ongoing astonishment, Ezog presented her with a stunning silver necklace, with a flashing blue jewel attached.

"A sapphire," he murmured at her, "to match your pretty eyes, ach?"

Oh. Oh, gods. Because Ezog hadn't even seen her eyes before this, he would have only known what Tryg had told him—and he'd still gone and bought his partner's mistress a gift? Truly?

"You are too good," Lydia choked, as she threw her arms around him, and buried her face in his neck. "Too good for all of us, *elskan*."

He shook his head, but drew her close too, enfolding her in his strong warm safety. Holding her there until Tryg came over too, circling his arms around them both, his breaths slightly sniffling into their hair.

But after that, it was easier to get up again, and to join Tryggr and Eben by the fire, drinking more cider, and snacking on plums and sweet breads. And then, at Ezog's suggestion, they each told their favourite Yuletide tale. Tryggr's was one with his Pa and *Pabbi*, in which they'd given him his first dagger, and taught him how to use it—and Eben's was one with his own father, who'd gained him honey for a special Yule treat. While Ezog's tale was one from his youth, when he'd danced with his clan around a faraway altar, and Tryg's was the first Yule he'd spent with his tiny namesake son, rocking him to sleep by a quiet, crackling fire.

And then all four orcs looked at Lydia, waiting for her own tale—and she gave them a wavering smile, and a jerky shrug. "This one," she said thickly. "This one, here, with all of you."

At that, Ezog drew her close again, his arms curling even tighter around her—and then, in another surprise, he began to sing. An old, vaguely familiar carol, sounding strangely deep and haunting in his rich, resonant voice.

But soon the rest of them had joined in, too, Tryg and Tryggr's voices blending almost as one, and finally Lydia sang along too, her voice rising light and clear above them all. And it was such a lovely, homey, shimmering feeling, and once they finished, they sang another carol, and another. Not all of them were ones Lydia knew, but it was easy enough to pick up the melodies, even if she didn't know the words. Easy to sink into the warmth and the cider and the song, into the scents of the firs and the fire, into the strong safety of Ezog's solid arms around her.

Tryggr and Eben finally went to leave once the sun began lowering in the sky, and after a thorough round of hugs and farewells, Lydia was again left alone with Tryg and Ezog. Who promptly spread her out upon the bed, and then took long, luxurious turns with her, kissing her, biting her, filling her with their seed.

And in between rounds, they ate and drank, and sang more songs, and told more tales. Tryg told her about the first night he'd spent with Ezog, how he'd been so dazzled afterwards he'd walked straight into a stone wall. And Ezog told her of the time he'd nearly been killed in a particularly harrowing battle, several years before—and how Tryg had gone to the mountain's powerful young new captain, and held a dagger to his throat until he'd sworn never to send Ezog out again.

And then, perhaps to lighten the darkness of that tale, Ezog told Lydia how he'd helped a constantly exasperated Tryg in dealing with his wild little Skai son, chasing him all about the mountain, while Tryg had punched out his frustrations in the Skai arena. Until Ezog had earned his place as Tryggr's *Pabbi*—the Skai term for a second father—and thereby embedded himself even deeper into Tryg's life, and his heart.

"Knew after that I'd never let you go, *elskan*," Tryg murmured, as his hand easily stroked up and down Ezog's half-hard shaft, his mouth nibbling at his neck. "Too sweet. Too perfect."

Ezog's eyes were fluttering, his breath exhaling in a contented little sigh, and Tryg angled a commanding glance toward Lydia, and then down at Ezog's now-hard cock. And she willingly slipped down to kiss at it, following Tryg's heated directions until Ezog bucked and groaned, and poured out into her mouth.

He tasted different than Tryg did, but still surprisingly sweet, and afterwards Tryg kissed her long and deep, clearly revelling in Ezog's taste on her mouth. And then it was back to sharing more tales and drinks and sweets, sprawling in a messy tangle on the bed, and Lydia even told them, her voice halting, about her husband Tom. About how she'd cared for him so deeply, and grieved him for so long, and then had awoken one day to find herself so utterly, achingly alone.

"Poor little pet," Tryg murmured, tucking her close beneath his arm, as he purposefully tugged Ezog on top of her, and guided her legs apart. "I ken that tiny house of yours was no help, ach? Kept you all cramped and lonesome thus."

As Tryg had spoken, Ezog had again slid himself deep inside her, as if in some sort of comfort—and in truth, it *was* comforting to have him sunk there, to feel him filling all her emptiness, warm and eager and alive. "Ach," he agreed as he began thrusting, his voice hitching with his movements. "You shall thus now come with us. To our home."

Wait. Their home was *Orc Mountain*—but Lydia's lurch of alarm at this recollection was swiftly swept away by Ezog's steady, reassuring presence, by the pleasure and heat swirling from his every powerful thrust inside her. And, too, by the feel of Tryg's soft kiss to her head, his arm firmly pulling her closer.

"Ach, sweet thing," he said, as his other hand clasped to Ezog's shoulder. "My *elskan* speaks truth. We cannot now leave you alone in that house, ach? But should you come to our home, we'll keep you safe, and help you gain work that pleases you. And m'boy and his mate are there too, ach?"

His tone was light and smooth, but there was a clipped, decisive edge on it, as well. As if he would bear no argument on this, and if Lydia even made an attempt, he would...

"You ken what shall come to pass, my pretty pet," came his silken voice, "should you seek to defy me upon this? Have you forgotten whose *elskan* is now deep inside you?"

And oh, that threat was already far more compelling than any unease Lydia had ever felt about Orc Mountain—and a hungry, desperate shiver rippled her from the inside out, convulsing her against Ezog's sweet, gentle invasion. And yes, Ezog felt it, his eyes fluttering hard as they glanced toward Tryg, as if seeking his permission, too...

"I ken she needs a reminder, then," Tryg said smugly, and Lydia's glance up found him slowly grinning between them, sharp and sly and wicked. "Plough your new gift for me, ach, *elskan*? Make her beg and scream for us. Teach her that she shall obey us, and come with us to our home as we wish. For she is *ours*."

And this time, Ezog's smile was just as wicked, lighting up his dear, beautiful face. His eyes catching on Lydia's own slowly widening grin, sharing her eagerness, her thankfulness. Her great, great gratitude, for such a perfect, generous gift. For a home.

"Ach, I shall," Ezog whispered. "With joy."

# EPILOGUE

It was almost Yuletide at Orc Mountain, and Lydia truly could not have fathomed just how many preparations were involved.

"Did you say *twelve hundred* cookies?!" she echoed toward Alma, Orc Mountain's kind, pretty head housekeeper. "As in, more than a thousand?!"

Beside Lydia, her silver-haired friend Olga was loudly snorting, and folding her arms over her chest. "I ken you'll still run outta cookies with twelve hundred, sister," she said flatly. "Ain't you seen how much those orclings eat?! Pains me to say, but better make it fifteen."

Alma was wringing her hands and looking distinctly distressed, glancing around at the kitchen's already-packed storeroom. "But we only ordered enough flour for twelve hundred!" she replied. "And it's too late to ship in more, unless we can send someone to..."

She winced and chewed at her lip, and just then, a familiar head poked around the nearest stack of barrels. "Who needs to go where, now?" Tryggr said cheerfully. "To a market again, I ken?"

Alma and Lydia both gave Tryggr deeply grateful smiles, while Olga had already turned to scribble some quantities—and then a few more items—onto a scrap of paper. "Here, boy," she said firmly. "We'll need 'em by morning."

Thankfully, Tryggr was well accustomed to being summarily

ordered about, because he only flashed them a tolerant grin, and tossed a nearby cookie—one from Olga's test batch—into his mouth. And when Olga attempted to whack him with her wooden spoon in retaliation, he easily slithered out of her reach, and then snatched a second cookie before speeding away again.

Lydia chuckled, but then quickly went out after him, and caught up with him in the corridor. "Are you sure you don't mind going, Tryggr?" she asked him, as she handed over a third cookie she'd swiped for him, too. "I know you promised Eben no more scouting trips before Yule."

Tryggr's eyes brightened at the new cookie—he'd clearly already devoured the first two—and he shot Lydia an appreciative half-grin as he tossed it into his mouth. "Ach, but then m'pet let it slip there's this new book he wishes to have," he replied, once he'd swallowed. "For this new *Reading Day* the Ka-esh have thrust upon us, the day after Yule! A *whole day* for reading, *Mammi*! I shall be bored enough to weep!"

Lydia laughed aloud, and fought to ignore the sparkle of warmth in her belly at his use of that wonderful word *mammi*. It was the Skai equivalent to *pabbi*, she'd learned, and even after a year, she still hadn't gotten used to Tryggr saying it. Despite him repeatedly pointing out that she was apparently the exact female version of Ezog, from her excessive generosity down to the way she smelled.

"Leave it to Pa," he'd told her one day, with a wry shake of his head. "Can't fathom how long he musta hunted to find a perfect match for *Pabbi*. Like a Grisk on a scent, he is, once he's got an idea stuck in his thick head."

Of course, Tryggr was just as stubborn himself—their similarities were a great source of ongoing amusement for Lydia and Ezog both—and over the past year, Lydia had happily joined Ezog in doting upon Tryggr at every possible opportunity. Sneaking him treats and snacks, cheering on his sparring-matches in the Skai arena, and keeping a close eye on Eben whenever Tryggr was off scouting or working.

"But you and *Pabbi* will send for me if aught's amiss with my sweet pet, ach?" Tryggr said now, his brow furrowing. "An' you won't mind if Pa comes along with me too? Just overnight, I ken."

Lydia smiled and waved away the question, because she'd long ago come to terms with Tryg taking off on these kinds of last-minute jobs. He and Tryggr were both integral members of the Skai clan's extensive scouting team—these days, Tryggr reported directly to the Skai clan's Boss himself—and while Lydia had been surprised to learn how often Tryg travelled, it was also something that was clearly important to him, and to his clan. And something he and Tryggr enjoyed sharing together, too.

"I'll pack you both some provisions," Lydia said firmly. "And while you're at the market, maybe you can remind your father about Yule gifts? I know Ezog would enjoy a nice bottle of wine, and perhaps some sweet treats, too."

Tryggr's smile had gone fond, even as he gave a longsuffering roll of his eyes. "Forgot about the gifts again, has he?" he said dryly. "How you two haven't tossed him yet is beyond fathoming, *Mammi*. Ach, I'll remind him."

Lydia laughed and thanked him, and soon found herself back in the kitchen, packing up a large sack of goodies for the two of them to share. And as she worked, she easily chatted with her now-familiar colleagues and friends—not only Olga and Alma, but also Olga's white-haired orc mate Gegnir, and an elderly Skai named Dufnall, who managed most of the laundry.

And it had been another surprise, at first, to discover that Tryg hadn't expected Lydia to immediately start taking over Orc Mountain's laundry. "Ach, Duff's got it well in hand, sweet thing," he'd told her, with a careless shrug. "If that's what you're hankering to do, I ken he'll make room for you, but mayhap you'd rather take on aught a bit different, ach? No need to rush, you ken."

It had been excessively generous, and Lydia had accordingly taken her time, and given it some thought. Noting, in particular, how Ezog spent his own days, now that he'd mostly stepped back from any fighting or travelling. He didn't have a specific assigned job among his Bautul clan, but he spent most of his time in their beautiful, ever-growing garden, out on the south side of the mountain. And when he wasn't working in the garden, he was helping to stock and supply the kitchen, and making sure the common-rooms and sickroom were well stashed with food, too.

"I should be glad to have you join me, should you wish," Ezog had replied when Lydia had asked, giving her his usual soft smile. "I only do not wish to bore you, ach? Or freeze you."

But Lydia hadn't been bored—or cold, once Ezog had supplied her with some warm layers. In truth, it had been wonderful spending most of her days outdoors doing meaningful work, and getting to know their other Bautul clanmates who worked in the garden, too. This included two lovely young women named Stella and Gwyn—Gwyn also served as the mountain's midwife—and a variety of orcs of all ages. And with Ezog's guidance, Lydia had gradually begun to take over the kitchen stocking, too, freeing up Ezog to explore new opportunities for the garden and the mountain's overall food supply. Lately, he'd even begun to look into acquiring livestock, and Lydia loved seeing his eyes light up whenever he spoke of it.

But the best part of all, of course, was just getting to spend her days with Ezog. Eating lunches together, helping each other, and enjoying one another's quiet company. And even sharing their pleasures together whenever they wished, writhing and moaning in the garden's hidden corners until they were both breathless and sated.

That, too, had been something of a surprise at first, because Ezog's appetite for intimacy had proven remarkably insatiable, and often extended to multiple rounds between them each day. But Lydia loved it too, and found herself almost desperately craving the feel of him locked in place inside her. To the point where he would surreptitiously slip himself up inside whenever she sat on his lap, and they'd even begun sleeping like that, with him curled up close behind her, his cock safely tucked in, too. And there was perhaps no better feeling than to wake up to the sensation of him swelling fully to life, opening her up wide—and then gasping in her ear as he emptied out his first load of the day inside her.

"Ach, you are both so greedy, my pretty pets," Tryg would often say, whenever he happened upon them together, or discovered them in the recent aftermath. "So sweet, when you're reeking thus of each other's fresh scents."

He always seemed fondly pleased by this, and would frequently follow it by joining in for a round, and coolly ordering them to please him. But even so, one afternoon when Ezog had been out, Lydia had gathered her courage, and cornered Tryg in their cozy little bedroom.

"Are you—*sure* you don't mind?" she'd asked him, her voice wavering in a way it rarely did anymore. "About Ezog and me? Even if you're not—there?"

But once again, Tryg had given an affectionate grin, and carelessly waved it away. "Ach, no," he said. "Why do you ken I worked so hard to find a good woman for us? He's always longed for this, and I should only be vexed if he *weren't* enjoying my good gift."

Oh. Lydia had felt her shoulders sagging with relief, even as she'd kept searching Tryg's eyes—and he'd shrugged, and run a hand through his hair. "An' in truth, it vexed me, leaving him here alone so much," he'd continued. "Gotta do my part for the clan, you ken, but hated the taste of his sadness whenever I'd go off working. But"—his eyes had softened—"it's not near so bad now, ach? Brings me joy, and a lot of peace, to know he's got company. Someone else to empty his bollocks, and warm our bed at nights, and keep a close eye on him for me."

Lydia had felt her shoulders relaxing even more, and Tryg had flashed her another jaunty grin. "And I *know* who you both belong to," he purred. "And you both know it, too."

He'd proven it that very night, when he'd worked them both over until they'd both been desperately gasping and shouting and begging for him. And afterwards, he'd pulled both their messy bodies close, and given a deep, contented sigh.

"Ach, Skai-kesh has blessed me," he'd murmured, kissing first Ezog's sweaty forehead, and then Lydia's. "Granted me not only a perfect son, but two perfect mates, too. Couldn't ask for more, ach?"

Both Lydia and Ezog had wholeheartedly agreed, and it was a sentiment that had stayed with Lydia ever since. To the point where she'd begun to thank Skai-kesh each day too, as well as the Bautul clan's patron deity, the goddess of the moon. Worshipping her together with Ezog on a consecrated altar in the garden, offering her thanks for such great, generous gifts.

And those gifts felt particularly powerful now, at Lydia's first Yule in Orc Mountain. Which, despite the intensity of the preparations involved, promised to be a truly delightful time, and she'd easily found herself getting caught up in the Yuletide spirit. Secretly acquiring gifts for her loved ones, and helping to decorate the mountain's corridors and common-rooms, and pitching in wherever she was needed in the kitchen.

"Don't suppose you'd help bake some more of these, then?" Olga was asking her now, giving a disgruntled frown down at the decimated batch of cookies. "Now that your boy's gone and gobbled half of what little we got?"

Lydia chuckled and readily agreed, and soon found herself elbow-deep in cookie-dough, chatting merrily with Olga and Gegnir. And then taking a brief moment to say goodbye to Tryg, who stopped by to kiss her farewell before he left, the way he always did. And soon Ezog had come by to help too, and they companionably worked until late in the night, baking as many cookies as they possibly could, before collapsing into bed together.

They welcomed Yule's Eve with a sweet, languid round of lovemaking, and then made their way back to the kitchen again. And when Tryg and Tryggr returned with the supplies ahead of schedule, they were both roped into the baking, too—and between them all, by early afternoon, they'd somehow managed to make all fifteen hundred cookies, as well as a variety of delicious-smelling pies, cakes, and puddings. And Alma had mopped at her brow with palpable relief, before being firmly ordered out of the kitchen by one of her own mates, the Skai Boss Drafli himself.

"Ach, he says the rest of us are to wrap it up too," Tryggr gratefully said, once Drafli had sharply signed something toward him, too. "Finally time for some fun, ach?"

Lydia certainly wasn't about to argue, and soon found herself attired in her festive red Yule dress, and accompanying her mates into the bustling, sweet-scented Grisk common-room. It had been set up as the central hub of the Yule celebrations, and it was beautifully decorated with red ribbons, fresh-cut greenery, and conveniently placed mistletoe.

"Come along, my sweets," said Tryg, with a toothy grin toward Lydia and Ezog. "First we eat and greet, and then we dance, ach?"

It was a lovely way to spend an afternoon, eating and laughing and chatting with their many friends and acquaintances. And once things got a little too heated with the dancing, Tryg herded them both off to the Skai common-room, which was full of a far different kind of celebrating. Including—much to Lydia's amusement—the creative use of silken red ribbons, which had apparently been supplied in bulk for the clan's collective celebrations. And predictably, Lydia's amusement soon turned to wild, desperate craving, as Tryg trussed her and Ezog up like a pair of obscene holiday packages, and then casually took turns fucking them with his hungry, beribboned cock.

And for the grand Yule's Eve finale, the Bautul clan hosted a massive feast out in the garden, around a huge blazing bonfire. The delicious meal of roasted meat and vegetables was accompanied by entertainment from the mountain's orclings, who gathered before the fire to act out a tale—the story of Orc Mountain's founders Edom and Akva, and their five sons, who became the five clans of orcs. And by the end of it, Lydia's stomach hurt from laughing, and she eagerly joined in the cheering and stomping, and firmly congratulated the orclings—and their teachers Geva and Rathgarr—on a job well done.

And finally, once the applause had quieted, a band of Ash-Kai drummers set up around the fire. And against a low, steady drumbeat, all the gathered revellers began to sing together, their rich chorus of voices rising to the clear, moonlit sky.

"That was wonderful," Lydia said afterwards, as she contentedly settled into bed between Ezog and Tryg. "I can't imagine a lovelier way to spend—ack!"

She'd been tackled by a devious-looking Tryg, who was glaring down at her with mock disbelief. "Ach, what is this?" he demanded at her. "Have you yet forgotten the perfect Yule's Eve I granted you last year? I ken you need a reminder, my greedy little pet."

It led to yet more delightful Yule's Eve fun, with Tryg ordering Ezog to have his hungry way with Lydia, until he finally joined in, too. And by the end of it, they were all a sore, exhausted, sticky mess, but Lydia couldn't stop smiling as she kissed them both goodnight. And then she slipped into a soft, easy sleep, tucked in her usual place in Ezog's strong safe arms.

"It is Yule, my sleepy pets!" Tryg announced bright and early the next morning, as he dragged in a steaming bath, and then plunked a basket of sweets onto Ezog's belly. "Now bathe, and eat, and then gifts, ach?"

His enthusiasm was contagious, and soon they were all up and freshly bathed, and exclaiming over their gifts. Tryg had gotten both Lydia and Ezog a variety of human-made wines and snacks—surely from his trip to the market the day before—but to their mutual delight, he'd also acquired them a selection of rare seeds for the garden, too. While Ezog gave Tryg another new weapon—a throwing-spear—and for Lydia, he'd ordered a beautiful set of sturdy, perfectly fitted boots and gloves, meant to help keep her warm in the garden.

Lydia had agonized for weeks over what to give them both, but after consulting with Olga and Alma—who both knew quite a lot about orc gifting traditions—she'd settled on jewels. On a thick gleaming cuff for Ezog, with sapphires that matched the pendant he'd given her the year before. And for Tryg, a sleek, deadly dagger for his hair, with more blue sapphires studded halfway down. Ensuring that the jewels would be hidden by his hair when worn, preventing the possibility of some secret scouting position being betrayed by unexpected glittering.

"Did you have Argarr make this, pet?" Tryg delightedly demanded, once he'd unwrapped it. "Ach, this is so *thoughtful*, my sweet!"

Lydia fondly grinned as he promptly unwound his long silver hair from its current dagger, and then wrapped his new one into it, tilting his head back and forth. "And so light, too!" he continued brightly. "Ach, it is perfect. Thank you, pet. Both of you. I am so blessed, this Yule."

He'd yanked both her and Ezog close, and Lydia happily squeezed him back, blinking away the sudden prickling wetness behind her eyes. Because truly, it still felt almost impossible that this kind of happiness could be hers. That she was safe and warm at home, celebrating Yule with the people she loved most.

But the warmth only shimmered higher as they launched into another full day of Yule celebrations, even more marvellous than the day before. Beginning with more gift exchanging with Tryggr and Eben—more weapons for Tryggr, and books for Eben—and then a delicious breakfast, hosted by the Ash-Kai clan this time.

And then, for Yule itself, it turned out that each clan held a specific activity to celebrate, and all other clan members were welcome to join in. It began with a Grisk cookie-decorating event, which was enthusiastically attended by dozens of excitedly squealing orclings—who, as

Olga had expected, each seemed to consume their own body weight in cookies. It was followed by a cheery Ash-Kai morning of tales in the schoolroom, and then a clever Ka-esh crafting session—which was again heavily attended by enthusiastic orclings, who soon were eagerly flying little paper birds and dragons throughout the mountain's corridors.

Next was a Bautul project that Lydia and Ezog had helped to organize—an intensive gift hunt, in which teams of searchers raced to seek out hidden little gifts, which were each destined for a specific recipient. It led to a wild afternoon of orcs racing and shouting and laughing all through the mountain, and it turned out that Tryg was one of the top performers, single-handedly delivering no fewer than a dozen gifts to their intended recipients.

And finally, for the main event of the day, the Skai clan hosted a massive sparring tournament in the Skai arena. Teaming up pairs of fighters from across all five clans, while hundreds of spectators shouted and cursed and cheered from the rows of surrounding stone seats. Unsurprisingly, the Skai made an excellent showing—Tryggr very high among them—and even Tryg made it through multiple rounds before conceding defeat to a sturdy Grisk named Varinn.

"A few decades back, I'd have flattened him," Tryg told Lydia and Ezog with a resigned grin, rubbing a hand at his sweaty face. "But I'll take great joy in seeing m'boy do it, ach?"

It turned out that Tryggr did indeed defeat Varinn, but it was a close thing, helped greatly by a stunning sideways kick that was perfectly suited to his lean, quick body. "Learnt that from me, he did," Tryg proudly told Lydia, in between bouts of ear-splitting cheering. "That's m'boy! Get him, son!"

In the end, Tryggr was just edged out by an equally slim and speedy Ka-esh, a development that left Tryg highly indignant. "A Ka-esh, son?" he demanded once a sweaty Tryggr had come to sprawl beside them, with a flush-faced Eben in tow. "What rubbish is this?!"

"Ach, I'd like to see you try an' take him, Pa," Tryggr said, between heaving breaths, as he bodily yanked Eben onto his lap. "These Ka-esh have got more surprises than you think, ach?"

He was already nuzzling at Eben's neck, making him wriggle and gasp, while Tryg pursed his lips, and shook his head. "Ach, I follow, son," he said flatly. "Don't want to stomp a pretty Ka-esh in the face, not when you're so smitten with your own! I ken you oughta—"

But before he could finish, Ezog had moved to drop his huge body in between Tryg and Tryggr, elbowing Tryg powerfully in the side. "This was a fine showing, son," he said firmly. "You were a joy to watch, ach?"

Thankfully Tryg took the hint, though he kept casting dark looks over toward Tryggr and Eben—at least, until Ulfarr, another Skai, knocked out his equally massive Bautul opponent with a spectacular punch to the head. A development that led to more shouting and cheering, especially since the tournament was down to only four final contestants—three of them Skai, with one lone Ash-Kai remaining.

Even Lydia could admit that the final two matches were very exciting, and the contestants were clearly taking their time now, and putting on a good show for their rapt audience. But finally, two more winners were announced—one of them the Skai Boss Drafli, the other one his gigantic clan brother Simon. And their final match was a stunning display of skill and speed and strength, which ended with the two of them clasping hands, and then collapsing down onto the floor together.

The cheering afterwards was so loud it shook the room, and soon the party spilled out into the corridor, which had been well stocked with cakes, eggnog, and the last of the cookies. And by the end of it, Lydia felt giddy and dizzy and utterly exhausted, and she was deeply grateful when Ezog finally guided her back toward their room, with Tryg close behind.

"Ach, that's it," Tryg murmured, his voice husky and warm, as Ezog pulled up Lydia's red dress, and sank himself deep inside her. "Give her a good hard Yule ploughing with that perfect fat prick of yours, *elskan*. Make her scream and plead for my good gift, ach?"

And yes, yes, Ezog was already doing it, plunging in with long, powerful strokes, while Lydia gasped and clung to him, welcoming him, pleading for him. Telling him what a good, wonderful gift he was, how much she loved having him inside her, making her his own.

And when Tryg climbed up behind him, strengthening Ezog's deep plunges with his own vicious thrusts, she begged for him too, praising him, adoring him. "You're so generous, Tryg," she choked at him. "So giving. So, so good to me. To us."

And gods, the way he grinned at her, bright and wicked and approving, flashing her all those sharp teeth. "Ach, no," he said, his voice hitching as he slammed inside, wringing the desperate craving up higher, harder. "Just greedy, you ken. Wanting to keep my perfect sweet gifts all to myself, for all the rest of our Yules together."

Oh. And even as Lydia arched and shouted with pleasure, with the truth of two orcs pouring themselves out as one, those words kept ringing, thudding like a deep, quiet bell. *Greedy. To keep my perfect sweet gifts all to myself.*

And when Tryg collapsed down onto Ezog's broad, sweaty back, she ran her hands down his sides, and searched his eyes. Finding that rare twinge of vulnerability, or maybe even shame. An admission, perhaps, that he needed them too, just as much as they needed him. That in giving them both such great gifts, he'd also been giving them to... himself.

"Good," Lydia told him, quiet but certain. "Because we're all yours, Tryg, always. For all the Yules we have left, and all the days in between."

And Tryg was half-smiling back at her, still looking surprisingly vulnerable, almost a little shy. "Ach?" he said, quiet. "You ken?"

Lydia firmly nodded, giving him a shy, wavering smile of her own. "I ken," she whispered. "I swear, Tryg."

Above her, Ezog was nodding too, and even nudging his neck closer to Tryg's mouth. And that was another bright, impish, contagious grin, lighting up Tryg's face—and without another word, he bent his head to his *elskan*'s waiting neck, and bit his teeth deep.

# BONUS EPILOGUE

It was two days before Yule, and Lydia didn't have a gift for Tryg.

"What do you mean, Argarr didn't finish the dagger?" she demanded at her heart-son Tryggr, her voice shrill. "Why in the gods' names not? He told me it was nearly done three days ago!"

Tryggr shot her a wry, regretful grimace, shaking his head. "Came down with a nasty infection, I ken," he said. "M'pet says it was from some travelling human salesman buying some blades. Efterar's ordered 'em both into one of the Skai lodges, until they clear the thing. Sounds like it's a tricky one to fully heal, and he don't want to risk an outbreak right on Yule."

Lydia wrinkled her nose and sighed, the dismay still twisting in her belly. "And there's no way for someone else to finish the dagger in time?" she asked. "Just... polish it up a little, or something?"

But Tryggr gasped with genuine-seeming horror, whipping his head back and forth. "Ach, no!" he exclaimed. "T'was made to match Pa's other one, ach? You can't have someone else mucking round with Argarr's work! Skai-kesh forbid, they'd ruin it! Poor Pa would have a fainting attack!"

He sounded deeply scandalized, and Lydia sighed again, her shoulders heavily slumping. "But now I don't have a gift for your father," she said helplessly. "And the Grisk Shop is closed for Yule, and it's too late for me to travel anywhere, and all our baking was for the celebrations—and my gift for Ezog isn't at all something that can be shared! And it isn't only Yule, but also our anniversary! Oh, what am I going to do?!"

Her voice had gone shrill, almost panicked, her eyes pleading on Tryggr's face. To which he only gave her a fond, reassuring smile, and clasped her on the shoulder. "Look, Pa don't care, *Mammi*," he said, quiet but firm. "He'll understand, ach? You ken he'll be glad to have the dagger when it's ready. And he'll be thankful you didn't hand it off to some fool hack of a smith, either."

His eyes darkened again at even the thought of it, and Lydia fought to steady her breaths, to attempt some semblance of a nod. Prompting Tryggr to give her a gentle shake, his smile gone even more tolerant than before. "I can smell you, *Mammi*," he said. "Don't you worry yourself about it. You ken it's not those kinds of gifts Pa really wants at Yule anyway, ach?"

Lydia blinked at him, not following, and Tryggr gave a cheerful roll of his eyes, together with another little shake to Lydia's shoulder. "Pa wants *you*, *Mammi*," he said. "You, an' *Pabbi*. Ach?"

Oh. Lydia kept blinking uncertainly toward him, but her breaths were coming deeper again, her heartbeat slowing in her chest. While Tryggr flashed her another jaunty, reassuring grin, before spinning around, and striding down the corridor in the direction of the Ka-esh wing. "Just let us know if we can help," he called over his shoulder, "but I don't want to see any of it, for the love of Skai-kesh."

Lydia choked a laugh and shook her head, but once Tryggr's tall form had disappeared around the corner, she felt her head tilting, her brow furrowing. *It's not those kinds of gifts Pa really wants*. And now Lydia's memories were casting backwards, to their first Yule together, three years before. To when Tryg had told her not to bring a gift, and had then turned around and given her Ezog, tied in a red bow.

In retrospect, it had been so typical of Tryg, just the kind of thing he so often did. Dismissing his own gifts, his own needs, in favour of focusing on the people he cared about. And it was part of why Lydia had always gone out of her way to pick out thoughtful gifts for him, to remind him that he was loved, and valued, and appreciated. That she and Ezog would never stop caring for him, just as Tryg cared for them. That they were his, always his, for all the Yules they had left.

But amidst that, Lydia had perhaps lost sight of the truth of that first gift. The deep, powerful meaning of it. The way it hadn't been about material things whatsoever, but instead, just about... them. Their love, their trust, their joy together.

Lydia's thoughts were spinning, now, her heart racing in her chest, and she took off down the corridor, in the direction of the gardens. Toward where she knew Ezog was hard at work, helping their Bautul clan prepare for the Yule's Eve feast—but upon catching scent of her at the garden's entrance, Ezog instantly came over to greet her, his beloved face creased with concern.

"What is it?" he asked, drawing her close into his warm strong arms. "Is aught amiss? Are you unwell?"

Lydia was already relaxing into Ezog's solid, familiar reassurance, her breath hitching as she exhaled. "I need a new gift for Tryg," she said, muffled, into his chest. "Will you help me give him something special?"

She already knew Ezog's answer, even before he spoke it, but it was more comfort, more reassurance, to see his warm, willing smile, the eager approval kindling in his eyes. Almost as if... as if he'd somehow been waiting for her to ask.

"Ach, my sweet," he said. "I should be most honoured."

THE NEXT EVENING found Lydia pacing back and forth in the cozy, familiar Skai cabin, waiting for Tryg to arrive.

The cabin was all ready for Yule, with a cheerful fire crackling in the fireplace, a pile of gifts and treats on the table, and multiple boughs of fresh-cut spruce and fir on the mantel. But most important of all was Lydia's gift, sitting wrapped on the bed in a red silk robe, and smiling fondly toward her.

"There is no need to fret, my sweet," Ezog said, his voice low and reassuring. "You ken Tryg should be pleased with aught you gave him, ach?"

Lydia nodded and shot Ezog a distracted, grateful smile back, even as she kept pacing. "Yes, I know," she said thickly, "but that's just the problem! He's always pleased with everything, and never asks for anything, when he gives me so much. And I just"—she drew in breath, her voice wavering—"I want him to know, to really, really know, how much I—"

She froze at the sound of a brisk rap on the door, her eyes wide on Ezog's face—but he kept smiling as he rose to his feet, pressed a gentle kiss to her hair, and nudged her toward the door. "He knows," he said. "We both do, ach?"

Lydia's smile back felt weepy this time, but she nodded, and lurched over to the door. Yanking it open, and finding a tall, broadly grinning Tryg waiting behind it, with a sack slung over his shoulder. "There you are, sweet thing," he said brightly, as he bent down for a kiss, and strode past her into the cabin. "Now, what are you two getting up to out—"

But his voice broke there, because his gaze had caught on Ezog, now standing in the middle of the cozy, firelit room. And Lydia was looking at Ezog too, her breath exhaling shaky and slow as she glanced up and down, seeing him with fresh, appreciative eyes.

He was... resplendent. Not only due to his silk red robe—borrowed from their similarly-sized Grisk friend Eyarl—but also with his long glossy hair, his gleaming, freshly oiled skin, and the gold jewels glittering on his wrists, his fingers, his ears. All of the jewels gifts from Lydia—and Tryg—over the past few years, because it had turned out that Ezog was shyly delighted by jewels, and took great joy in adorning himself for his mates.

*Never woulda guessed it, sweet thing*, Tryg had gratefully told Lydia, the day after Ezog had wept upon receiving a beautifully forged gold ring, with the traditional Skai vow of matehood engraved inside it. *Looks good in jewels, though, doesn't he?*

Ezog did look good in jewels, Lydia could readily admit, especially in strong, heavy pieces that shone and glittered against his big scarred body, somehow drawing out his rugged, unearthly beauty even more than before. And in this moment, Tryg looked genuinely struck by the sight of it, his eyes glinting with appreciative admiration as they flicked up and down Ezog's robed form.

"Very pretty, *elskan*," he said, his voice hoarse, before his gaze darted back to Lydia. "An' you too, sweet thing."

Lydia was clad in her usual red Yule dress, of course, along with some of her own lovely jewels—a bracelet, earrings, her matching rings from Tryg and Ezog—but she waved it away, and clasped Tryg's hand in hers. "I wanted to give you something special for Yule," she said, her heart still skipping unevenly in her chest. "So I thought you might appreciate... this."

Tryg's silver brows snapped up, his gaze gone rather bemused as it swept back to Ezog again. "Ach, always, sweet thing," he said lightly. "Looks good in red, doesn't he?"

Lydia choked a strangled, nervous laugh, her face heating. "I mean... *Ezog* is your—your Yule gift," she said, with a helpless wave toward him. "So you need to—unwrap him."

The comprehension instantly passed across Tryg's eyes, a low chuckle huffing from his throat. "Ach, now I see," he said, angling a quick, conspiratorial glance toward Lydia. "Returning the favour, are you?"

Lydia rapidly, gratefully nodded, and Tryg's smile grew into something hungry and wolfish as he gave her arse a gentle little slap, and prowled closer toward Ezog. Toward where Ezog was still standing immobile in his red robe, his mouth softly smiling, his face deeply flushed. And Lydia could see Tryg now taking in the way Ezog was standing, rather more stiffly than usual, with a very obvious tent at the front of his robe.

"Well, look at this," Tryg said, clearly already warming to the game, as he began striding a slow, assessing circle around Ezog's waiting, unmoving body. "I wonder what our sweet woman has wrapped up for me? Something very tasty, I ken."

Ezog's face flushed even redder, and Tryg flashed him a gleeful grin as he kept circling, now trailing his clawed hand gently over the fabric covering Ezog's chest. "An' something just as pretty on the inside as it is on the outside. Something I'd like to lick all over, and fill up with good Skai frosting."

Ezog's breath audibly caught, his eyes glimmering bright on Tryg's face, and Tryg's smug smile pulled even wider as he halted before Ezog, and tugged at the silken tie clinching the robe closed. "Let's see, then," Tryg purred, slowly drawing out the tie from around Ezog's waist. "What's going to be *mine*, this Yule."

There was a deep, decisive satisfaction in his voice, and then flaring in his eyes, as he yanked the tie fully away, and shoved the robe off Ezog's shoulders. Revealing the full sight of Ezog's bulky body, now slightly shivering in the open air.

And though Lydia knew full well what had been hidden beneath the robe, her breath still caught as she looked, her eyes running up and down. Drinking up the sight of Ezog's big, scarred, familiar form, glinting in yet more of their jewels—but also wrapped in multiple thick red ribbons, at all the most strategic places. Around his neck. Across his collarbones and chest, and over his nipples. Around his waist. And most of all, the ribbons were wound extensively around his groin, making it look almost as though he was wearing a full girdle of red, with a large, highly conspicuous bulge jutting out in front—which, of course, was adorned with an extra red bow.

"Ach," Tryg said, low in his throat, as his eyes shifted between amusement, appreciation, and unmistakable craving. "Wrapped him up real good for me, did you, sweet thing?"

Lydia twitched a nod, and then jerked closer toward Ezog, settling a hand against where—wait—his arm was still trembling, perhaps not only from the cool air. "Such a good gift deserves extra ribbons," she said, as lightly as she could. "Don't you think?"

She'd shot an intent, urgent-feeling smile up at Ezog's face, at where he was indeed looking suddenly—shy. Almost *nervous*. After he'd kept telling her not to fret, and that Tryg would welcome whatever she gave him. But perhaps it was one thing to speak such reassurances, and another to be brazenly gussied up as a Yuletide gift, waiting for a beloved partner's response, and his judgement.

And perhaps—the thought occurred to Lydia, far too late—perhaps this was calling to mind the last time Ezog had been asked to do this, three years before. When Tryg had wanted him to come and be a gift to his mistress, a woman Ezog hadn't even yet met. A situation that had to have been horribly distressing, and yet here Ezog was again, risking this again, for her. For them.

"Don't you think?" Lydia asked again, her voice rising, her eyes now desperately searching Tryg's face. "He's such a good gift, isn't he?"

Because—because Tryg's expression had shifted, too. His amusement fading, sobering, into something quieter, something watchful. Something almost… reverent.

"Ach," Tryg murmured, husky, as his hand found Ezog's chin, caressed gentle against it. "The best, my sweets. An' here I thought my *elskan* could never be more beautiful, ach?"

Oh. The relief shuddered warm and stunning into Lydia's belly, and she could see it flashing across Ezog's face too, softening his blinking eyes. While Tryg's mouth slowly curled back into its smug, satisfied grin, and he stepped a little backwards, licking his lips as he glanced up and down Ezog's red-wrapped body.

"Now, where ought I to begin, sweet thing?" he asked, with a sly glance toward Lydia. "Anywhere I wish?"

Lydia shyly nodded, and watched as Tryg's clever clawed fingers eagerly caught into the ribbon at Ezog's throat, drawing him a little closer. A movement that already had Ezog gasping, and Tryg again licked his lips as he gave it another purposeful yank, his eyes darkening with obvious hunger. "Ach, mayhap we leave that one for now," he purred, keeping one hand tucked into it, while his other hand wandered down to Ezog's chest. To the thick ribbon wrapped around his ribs, fully covering his nipples, which looked—Lydia could admit—unusually, strikingly peaked.

"Ach, what's this?" Tryg breathed, as he unwrapped the ribbon, pulling it downwards, and revealing—gold, glinting at both Ezog's deep green nipples. Not piercings, no, but clever little clips, clasping tightly at Ezog's nipples, and dangling down with short, shining chains of gold.

The clips were something Lydia had remembered Tryggr joking about, once—he'd been teasing Eben about Ka-esh proclivities—and when she'd gathered up her courage the day before to go ask them, it had turned out they'd had an extra set on hand that they'd been willing to donate to the cause.

*These ones are too weak anyway*, Tryggr had said, with a rueful grin, and a teasing snap of his teeth toward Eben beside him. *You like a bit more bite with your gold, don't you, pet?*

So Lydia had thoroughly cleaned and sterilized the clips, and had shyly shown them to Ezog, who'd only rapidly nodded, his face flushing. And properly clipping them onto his nipples had turned out to be a highly intriguing project, which had ended with Lydia taking a quick, breathless ride on his swollen cock, gently tugging at the clips' chains all the while.

It was a potential that Tryg clearly hadn't missed, trailing the chains through his fingers, his eyes glinting on Ezog's reddened face. And when he gave one of them an experimental little tug, Ezog gasped and shivered all over, his eyes rolling back, his hands clutching to fists at his sides.

"Oh, I *like*," Tryg said now, his voice heated and husky, as he gave another brief, purposeful tug at the chain. "And you like, too, don't you, *elskan*? Like having chains attached to you, for your mates to use as we please?"

Ezog gasped again, nodding, and Tryg's smile curled higher as his hands slid downwards, finding the next ribbon—around Ezog's waist—and swiftly tugging that off, too. Revealing Ezog's taut, familiar belly, but now with something red and white tucked into its navel.

"Candy!" Tryg crowed, as he plucked it out, and tossed it into his mouth. "Ooooh, mint! Just as tasty as you, *elskan*."

Lydia and Ezog both laughed, perhaps a little shaky, and now Lydia took a breath, and grasped for Ezog's bare shoulder. Nudging him to spin around, and he willingly went, showing Tryg his broad, now-bared back. Which instead of ribbons, now sported something new and dark, stamped across his deep green skin.

It was inked script, large and bold, written in a lovely, flowing hand that seemed to ripple across the muscles of his back. And at Ezog's suggestion, it said, *Gifted to Sigtryggr, of Clan Skai.*

The idea had seemed preposterous, at first, but Eben had shyly suggested it during the clip discussion, pointing out that ink-marking mates was an old northern Ka-esh tradition. And after a helpful consultation with Eben's Ka-esh sisters Rosa and Daisy, Lydia had learned that the inks were derived from the flowers of a particular underground plant, and though they weren't permanent, they could last for weeks, or sometimes months, depending on the formulation. And while the northern Ka-esh most often used them for marking their mates, they were apparently also used for sacred purposes, or to bring luck or skill or blessing.

"Rosa had her kin-brother Tristan write the script out on paper for me, because she says he has the best penmanship in the realm," Lydia said now, into the sudden, stilted silence. "And then I did my best to copy it onto Ezog with the ink. Apparently it'll stay like that on him for a week or two, at least."

She'd been speaking too quickly, her face again flushing hot, because gods, what if Tryg laughed. What if he thought it was foolish, or mawkish, or just too much, or...

"Can I touch it?" Tryg asked into the silence, his voice stilted. "Or might that ruin it?"

Lydia cast a sidelong look up at Tryg's face—was he *blushing*?—and nodded, reaching up to stroke her hand over Ezog's warm, ink-marked skin. "No, you're fine to touch it," she said. "Though I'm told if you cut into it, the ink might heal into the cut. So be careful with your claws, if you don't want it staying that way."

But Tryg's tooth was biting his lip as his claw reached up to touch Ezog's back too, tracing gently against the lines of his name. "Pretty, though, ain't it?" he murmured, hushed. "My name looks real nice on you, *elskan*."

That was unmistakably a shiver, quivering through Ezog's shoulders, and in a jerky movement, Tryg bent forward, and pressed his mouth to that marked, inked skin. "Real nice," he breathed, his lashes fluttering, as his hips ground up against Ezog's still-red-wrapped arse. "Will be so sweet to look upon whilst I plough you, ach?"

Ezog visibly shivered again, arching back into where Tryg's claws were already tugging at the ribbon—and Lydia belatedly caught at Tryg's hand, even though her own cheeks were still smarting hot, the heat simmering in her groin. "No ploughing yet," she said, through her constricted throat. "You have to finish unwrapping him first!"

Tryg's glance toward Lydia was wry and a little embarrassed, and he ran a clawed hand through his hair. "Ach, sweet thing," he croaked. "Just a bit dazzled by your good gift, you ken."

Lydia's smile back was bright and delighted, and she swiftly turned Ezog around again, to where he was looking rather stunned, too. The tent beneath his ribbons was jutting out even larger than before, and Tryg huffed a low, groaning laugh as he leaned closer, skating his claws over it with eager, reverent hunger.

"So pretty, *elskan*," he breathed, his eyes hooded on Ezog's face. "So perfect."

Ezog's breath heaved through his chest, his own eyes blinking rapt on Tryg's, and Tryg gave himself a bracing little shake, before angling another wry glance toward Lydia. "You really know how to treat a fella, sweet thing," he murmured, as he carefully reached for the red bow at Ezog's tented groin, and plucked it apart with his claw. "I wonder what you've hidden for me under here? A nice, fat, pretty prize, I ken."

Lydia choked another laugh, even as her eyes stayed fixed on the sight of Tryg unwrapping that thick ribbon, winding it off around Ezog's hips. Unlooping it lower and lower, exposing more and more of Ezog's bare scarred torso, and then—Lydia's breath caught—the fall of silken red, fluttering light and easy from Ezog's hips.

"Ach, is this—*Skai garb*?" Tryg demanded, his voice rising. "Truly?"

He was tearing away the rest of the ribbon, now, letting it fall at Ezog's ankles, and revealing the full sight of the traditional red Skai loincloth beneath. It was slung low and flattering on Ezog's hips, and though its front rectangle of red would usually have fallen down to his thighs, it was currently jutting straight out toward them, draped bright and obscene over Ezog's huge, erect cock beneath.

"Ach, look at that," Tryg said, his voice hushed. "Ach, and it—it matches you, sweet thing! Scents of you!"

He waved wildly at Lydia's red Yule dress, and then hesitated, frowning down at the bottom of it—at where the hem was a good deal higher than it had once been. And Lydia laughed again as she nodded, and gave a gentle caress to the matching fabric draped over Ezog's cock. "We thought it would be nice if we matched, didn't we?" she said lightly. "Thought you might like it, Tryg."

And yes, yes, Tryg did like it, that was clear, and he'd even nudged Lydia over to stand beside Ezog, so he could sweep his glittering eyes up and down them both. "Ach, I like," he purred. "Henceforth, you shall both wear these, for all our Yules."

Lydia easily nodded along with Ezog, and felt his arm slipping around her waist, drawing her closer against his side. While Tryg just kept looking at them, his eyes rapidly blinking, his chest visibly hollowing. "So pretty, my sweets," he breathed. "All you need now is—"

He bit his lip again, shaking his head, and now his hands were fumbling for Ezog's red loincloth, yanking the fabric to the side. And revealing yet another intricate gold gift, one Lydia hadn't even known about, until Ezog had sheepishly taken her to their room the day before, and pulled it out from beneath his clothes.

"It is called a *typpavír*," he'd said, his face reddening. "The Grisk goldsmiths have begun making them, and I thought—I thought Tryg should be pleased, to see me wear one. So I had—ordered this for us, for Yule."

Oh. It had been Ezog's own gift, for Tryg, and for her. And Lydia had blinked at it, tracing a searching finger against the thick gold ring, much like a large bracelet—but clipped to it were two dangling, glittering chains, leading to a slim gold post, about the size of Lydia's littlest finger.

"That doesn't go on—" Lydia had said, blinking between it, and Ezog's reddened face. "Does it?"

Ezog had swallowed and nodded, looking shyly, adorably mortified, and Lydia had rapidly collected herself, and firmly reassured him that of course Tryg would love it, and that she surely would, too. To which Ezog had gone even redder, even as he'd gratefully smiled toward her, and told her that perhaps it could be a surprise for them both, then.

Which meant that Lydia hadn't fully seen this yet, either, beyond a few glimpses beneath the loincloth as she'd wrapped him in the ribbon. And she now found herself staring at it together with Tryg, as more heat pooled and simmered at her groin.

Because oh, how it looked. Ezog's long, fat, silken green length now adorned, gleaming with gold, like the true prize it was. Gold that began around his base, the thick ring tucked close to his skin beneath his full, softly furred bollocks. And extending from the ring were those glittering chains, leading all the way up his shaft. Until the chains reached his smooth glossy cleft, to where it was visibly opened, stretched, with that slim post of gold buried down inside it.

It was highly shocking, and deeply compelling, too, seeing that familiar beautiful cock propped and pinioned, blatantly on display, just like the rest of him. And Lydia felt almost light-headed, now, with all the blood apparently pooling to her groin at once, while beside her,

Tryg was letting out a low, helpless-sounding moan, his gaze frozen on the sight, his clawed hand clutching convulsively at the front of his own tented trousers.

"Look at you, *elskan*," he breathed, his black tongue curling at his lips. "This is... you are..."

He seemed truly lost for words, his tongue licking again and again, and his shaky hand had skittered over to stroke at it, to pluck gently at those taut gold chains. A movement that instantly swayed Ezog on his feet, a hoarse groan growling from his throat, his eyes rolling back—and Tryg's smile was slow, wicked, ravenous, as he did it again, again, again.

"So pretty," Tryg rasped, through heaving breaths, as Ezog trembled and moaned before him. "So perfect, *elskan*."

Lydia had perhaps never seen Ezog's face so flushed, and he shook his head, his eyes wild on Tryg's face. To which Tryg leaned forward, and gave a hard, biting kiss to Ezog's mouth, even as his hand gave a firm little yank at the chain on his nipple. "Perfect," he hissed. "And mine. *Ours*."

Ezog's moan was desperate, helpless, while Tryg's eyes flashed with heated, hungry satisfaction. "And now I'm gonna keep unwrapping you, *elskan*," he purred. "Gonna keep opening you up for me, ach?"

With that, his clever fingers loosened the *typpavír*'s chains, unhooking them from the solid base, so that they dangled from that embedded post of gold. A post that Tryg was now gently tugging, drawing it out slow and certain, his eyes darting rapid and greedy between Ezog's face, and Ezog's impaled, visibly spasming cock.

"Ach, what a gift this is," Tryg breathed, as his chest heavily swelled and hollowed, his fluttering eyes now fixed to the gleaming gold rod slipping out further, and further, and further. "I wonder what it shall grant me when I—"

His voice broke as the gold slipped out, and Lydia caught a glimpse of that soft, opened channel, convulsing on its own—and then spraying out spurt after spurt of thick, messy white. Spewing onto Tryg's hands, his clothes, and with a moan, a frantic flashing drop, Tryg was on his knees, swallowing Ezog's convulsing cock deep into his mouth, gulping that rich sweetness down his moaning, greedy throat.

The sound from Ezog's mouth was almost a roar, one hand

frantically grasping for Tryg's head, the other clamping around Lydia's waist, drawing her tightly into his side. So she could join him in this moment, in revelling in the sight and the power of it, in their cool, confident, powerful Tryg brought to his knees by the sheer strength of their good gift.

"You like?" Lydia finally asked, her voice hitching in her throat, once Tryg had stopped swallowing—and for an instant, he only gazed at her, while something sharp and strange shifted in his eyes. Something searching, assessing, waiting for...

His—*attack.* His lean coiled body snapping up, snatching Lydia bodily into his arms, and hurling her onto her back on the bed. And then whipping back around, clawing for Ezog, and shoving him to his knees on the bed before Lydia, his hand tangling deep in Ezog's long, shining hair.

"Feast upon our woman, *elskan,*" he growled, hot and commanding, as his other hand flung up Lydia's red dress, and shoved Ezog's face in close. "Reward her for such a good gift. Make her beg and scream upon you, whilst I—"

His voice cracked, faltered, because his hand had swept down, yanking up the red loincloth in the back, too. Revealing Ezog's bare, muscled, deep green arse, now raised high toward him, with just a glint of red ribbon visible between his firm arse-cheeks.

"Whilst I keep opening you," Tryg gasped, hoarse, breathless, as his hand fluttered down to caress at it, to begin drawing out that familiar gold weight—a gift from the year before, but now with a bright red ribbon tied on the end. And oh, the way Tryg looked, sliding it out like that, his eyes worshipful on the sight, while Ezog arched and moaned, and buried his face deeper between Lydia's legs. His tongue trembly and shaky against her slick clutching heat, and Lydia could only gasp and moan and watch, the pleasure swirling, sweeping higher with every breath...

The gold finally escaped Ezog in a slick-sounding squelch, his deep groan vibrating hard into Lydia's swollen, quivering crease. While Tryg blatantly eyed what he'd just opened, his lashes fluttering, his tongue dragging slow and hungry at his lips.

"Look at you, sweet *elskan,*" he rasped. "With your sweet rump opened wide and waiting for me, and your sweet tongue buried deep into our sweet woman, bringing her such joy. What a perfect, perfect gift you are."

Ezog's groan was harsh, helpless, but he kept licking, feasting, his tongue curling deep and wondrous inside Lydia, swiping at that perfect place again and again. While Tryg ran a slow, possessive hand up Ezog's inked back, his fingers spreading wide, until they again curled around that red ribbon, still tied around Ezog's throat.

"So sweet," Tryg continued, a low growl in his throat, as he gave the ribbon a gentle tug, making Ezog twitch and shiver all over. "So pretty, with my name on your skin, and my ribbon round your throat. And"—his breath choked as he shifted behind Ezog, lining himself up—"with my strong Skai prick, buried deep in your rump."

He slammed forward sharp and vicious, the sound of slapping skin ringing out between them. And Ezog again quaked beneath it, his tongue's movements shaky and sloppy as Tryg rammed inside again and again. One hand still clutched at that ribbon, yanking Ezog's head back, while his other hand slid around to tug at the swaying chain on his nipple, the touch wrenching Ezog's groans to deep, desperate cries.

"So pretty, *elskan*," Tryg gasped again, his eyes blazing. "And you'll be even prettier once you're ploughing that fat, opened prick into our sweet, lovely woman, ach?"

Oh yes, oh please, and Lydia was nodding just as hard as Ezog, grasping at him, yanking him up, closer. Until they all tumbled together on the bed, Ezog's body hot and heavy over Lydia's, as his slick rounded head found her hungry clutching heat. Settling itself close and familiar, seeking itself just a little inside, and...

Lydia shouted as he plunged deep, carving into her with a single swift, staggering stroke. Filling her with him, spreading her wide open around his huge opened orc-cock, as she arched and convulsed against him, needing more, more, *more*.

And yes, there was more, their bodies all driving together now, Tryg's hand still hooked on the red ribbon, while his hips kept slamming, and his hooded, hungry eyes glittered on Ezog's back. On the sight of his own inked name, surely, with Lydia's trembling fingers dragging against it.

"So sweet," Tryg gasped again, between thrusts, as if it were a mantra, or a prayer. "So good, my pretty pets. You shall both be mine for always, ach? You shall be glad"—his eyes flashed, his thrusts punching harder—"to dress for me, to gift each other to me. To wear my ribbons and my jewels deep inside you. To write my name on your skin, and welcome my gold round your pretty necks, and show all who see you that you belong to *me*—"

His voice was rising, breaking, his head tilting back as he plunged in and held—and oh, that was it, that was it. Ezog's body arching stiff and strong between them, drinking up Tryg's seed deep inside him, and spewing out its own hot nectar into Lydia's wildly shuddering heat. Sharp enough that Lydia's own ecstasy flared up bright and furious, too, clamping her again and again around Ezog's fat, sweet, still-spurting invasion. Filling her, consuming her, flooding and fucking her with his scent, his strength, his safety.

When the pleasure finally flickered away again, they were all collapsed and sticky on the bed together, their breaths heaving hard. And Ezog's mouth was already seeking at Lydia's throat, finding its familiar place, and Lydia gasped as she welcomed it, first that sweet pierce of pain, and then the slow, settled peace of it. Of honouring her gift, caring for her gift, while Tryg blinked down at them both with hazy, approving eyes.

"Such a good gift, sweet thing," he breathed, and Lydia could feel his hand joining hers, stroking with her over Ezog's back, over his own inked name. "Couldn't ask for better."

His voice was hushed, almost worshipful, and in Lydia's boneless, sated state, it was easy, too easy, to smile up toward him, shy and grateful. "We really are still all you want for Yule?" she murmured. "Even years later?"

Tryg's eyes shifted, shining with strange, sudden brightness—but then he blinked at Ezog's back, exhaled heavy and slow. "Ach, you are," he said, quiet. "Don't like to speak of it, but you ken I spent so many of my days lost in war, and in loneliness. Not trusting my own clan, my own kin, my home. But"—his shoulders heaved—"my *elskan*, and now you, sweet thing, you've granted me gifts I never knew could be truth. Not only your pretty bodies and your pleasure, but this—trust. This fealty. This... *knowing*. Being kin, being here, being *mine*. For always."

His voice had gone low and fierce, his eyes glittering on his name on Ezog's back, on that ribbon at Ezog's throat. And Lydia's finger was gently stroking at the ribbon too, as something dipped and shivered, low in her belly. "I'm so glad, Tryg," she whispered back. "You've been such a gift to us, too. And you know we're glad to honour you, however it might please you. Whether it's giving you gifts, or being marked with your name, or"—she swallowed, gave him another shy smile—"or wearing your gold around our necks."

Because she certainly hadn't missed him saying that, there at the end—and she knew Ezog hadn't either, his attention now almost palpable in his body beneath her fingers. And behind Ezog, Tryg's eyes had visibly widened, his tooth biting his lip—but then he shook his head, a little too quick, too dismissive.

"Ach, you've already done enough, sweet thing," he said, in a bright tone that didn't at all match his shifting eyes. "More than enough. Don't need to do another thing, or wear another thing, either."

But at that, Ezog carefully detached his mouth from Lydia's neck, giving it a few careful licks before drawing away, and twisting himself around to look at Tryg. "You ken we should welcome this, Tryg," he said, his voice disarmingly soft. "Should you truly wish to give it."

There was an instant's silence, and Tryg's eyes blinked, glimmered on Ezog's face—but then he swallowed, thick and audible in his throat. "But it's—a Ka-esh custom," he croaked. "Not Skai. Not—mine."

Lydia wasn't fully following, now, but Ezog's eyes stayed steady on Tryg's, his body shifting around and up, so he could clasp at Tryg's shoulder. "Ach, yours, just as we are," he said firmly. "And you now have a Ka-esh son, do you not? And I ken you would have spoken to him of this, and made sure there was naught amiss with it. Ach?"

Lydia was barely breathing, blinking at where Tryg's face had gone strangely uncertain, making him look disarmingly young, almost innocent. "Ach," he said, quiet. "But you are—sure, Ezog."

It was rare that he used Ezog's name, enough that Lydia couldn't recall ever hearing him speak it—but it only seemed to make Ezog's eyes go softer, his mouth drawing into a slow, tender smile. "I am sure, Sigtryggr," he replied, just as quiet. "Now show us, ach? So our sweet woman can think upon this, also?"

Tryg's eyes dropped, his head twitching a curt little nod. And as Lydia watched, her heart skipping in her chest, he strode over to swipe up the sack he'd brought, and fished around inside it. "Didn't even wrap 'em up," he said thickly, his gaze still cast downwards. "Didn't think I'd really—well. Here."

He'd stalked back toward the bed, thrusting out something gold and shining toward them. Or rather, wait—two large gold rings, one far thicker and heavier than the other.

Ezog's breath shook at the sight, and his hand reaching to take the rings was shaky, too. But his smile on Tryg's face was even fonder than before, and that red flush had again begun creeping up his cheeks.

"Tryg has brought us each a *kraga*," he said to Lydia, as he passed the smaller, slimmer ring into her hand. "Just like the one our son has given his mate, ach?"

Oh. Ohhhhh. The vision of Eben's *kraga* instantly swarmed through Lydia's thoughts, but yes, yes, of course, these were the same. The circle of solid, gleaming gold, with beautiful script engraving all around the inside, and a clever little latch, opposite a seamless-looking hinge. Meant to snap close around a wearer's neck, and make a perfect fit. And Lydia could still recall Eben's starry eyes as he'd stroked his own *kraga*, and softly told her that the latch couldn't be undone, now that Tryggr had fastened it. And unless a *kraga* was melted, or broken, it would forever be worn as an irrevocable proof of the bond between mates. Not only throughout this life, but into death, and beyond.

"Just liked the look of it, on m'boy's own pet," Tryg said, speaking too quickly, his rather wild eyes darting between Ezog and Lydia. "Thought they'd be fun to play with—with ribbons and chains and the like, you ken. An' they have my vows to you carved on the inside, too. But there's no need, it's not a Skai custom, and I ken it's a lot to ask, so—"

He looked nearly ready to snatch the *kragas* back again, his lean body gone so taut it was quivering, his eyes darting almost panicked between Lydia and Ezog. And Lydia was deeply, thoroughly grateful when Ezog firmly grasped Tryg's hand, and placed his *kraga* within it.

"I should be most honoured to wear your *kraga*, Tryg," he said softly. "It should be a great, great gift toward me."

Tryg's shoulders heavily sagged, his eyes shimmering with affection, with gratefulness—but then he winced, and glanced sideways toward Lydia. "But I wouldn't wish *you* to feel bound upon this, sweet thing," he said, rushed. "It's one thing for my *elskan*, he knows what he's in for by now, but you—"

He didn't finish, his mouth dropping open, because Lydia had thrust her *kraga* back into his hand, too. "I'd be honoured too, Tryg," she said, and she couldn't stop her voice from wavering, the heat already prickling behind her eyes. "We're yours, for always. And getting to wear such a meaningful sign of your loyalty, and your care, it would be—"

She couldn't even finish, flapping her hands at her wet eyes, and without at all meaning to, she threw herself toward him, buried her face in his chest. "It would be—so good of you, Tryg," she choked, into his warm skin. "Such a gift."

She could feel Tryg's familiar body relaxing against her, his breath rustling at her hair, and he slid his arms around her, drew her closer. "Ach?" he said, muffled, into her hair. "You're sure, sweet thing?"

Lydia fervently nodded against him, and oh, now Ezog was here too, his strong arms circling around them both. And it was the best, most wondrous feeling, wrapped so warm and safe between her kind, fierce, generous mates, who'd given her such great, beautiful gifts.

"Who first, then," Tryg finally said, and the lightness was back in his voice, in his eager claws drumming against Lydia's shoulder. "You, *elskan*?"

Lydia and Ezog both nodded at once—gods, Lydia wanted to see this—and she was already shifting back and around behind Ezog, drawing his long, shining hair away from his strong, scarred neck. So Tryg could settle in front of him on the bed, his hand gently pulling at the red ribbon still encircling Ezog's neck, finally pulling it off and away. And then Tryg snapped the *kraga* open, and brought its thick, rounded gold edge up to Ezog's throat, just where the ribbon had been.

"Still sure, *elskan*?" Tryg murmured, husky, as he carefully closed the kraga around Ezog's neck. "Feels all right?"

The gold looked to be a perfect fit, close but not constricting, and Ezog tilted his head back and forth, tensing the muscles in his neck. "Ach," he said, his eyes fluttering on Tryg's face. "This feels good."

Tryg's smile was swift, relieved, and perhaps a little weepy, too—and with a firm twitch of his fingers, the latch clicked shut. And when

Tryg drew away, the *kraga* was now circled close around Ezog's scarred throat, its gold a gleaming, lovely contrast against his deep green skin.

"So pretty," Tryg croaked, dashing a hand at his eye, and in a jerky movement he lurched forward, thrusting his face into Ezog's neck. "Thank you, *elskan*. You—honour me."

Ezog was softly smiling, his hands firmly stroking up and down Tryg's back, even as a streak of wetness slipped down his scarred cheek. "You honour me also," he whispered back, hushed. "Just as you always have, ach?"

Tryg waved it away with a shaky hand, but when he drew back from Ezog again, he still looked decidedly overcome, his eyes blinking hard. But he was smiling, too, warm and wavering, his hand reverently stroking the gold at Ezog's throat.

"So pretty," he said again, a little steadier this time, and oh, that was a twitch of familiar hunger flickering through his eyes. And then flashing higher, hotter, as he glanced at Lydia, his hooded gaze fixed to her still-bare throat.

"An' you're still sure, sweet thing?" he murmured. "You're sure you want to always wear this, for me?"

But Lydia was sure, so sure, so deep it ached. She trusted Tryg, she adored Tryg, she wanted to spend all the rest of her days with Tryg. All of her Yules, for always.

"I'm sure, Tryg," she said, holding his eyes. "I promise."

Tryg was blinking again, giving her another weepy smile—and now it was Ezog settling behind her, drawing her hair back, baring her neck for the *kraga*. So Tryg could bring up the curved gold edge, settle its cool smoothness against her skin. And then he drew the other side closed, circling it around her neck—but again, it wasn't too tight, or too constricting. Just—*there*, strong and steady and safe, just like him.

So Lydia smiled, nodded, waited—and then shivered all over at the strange, stunning sensation of the *kraga* snapping shut. Marking her, claiming her, making her his. Theirs. Forever.

Behind her, Ezog hissed a low groan, his face nudging into her neck, and oh, the way Tryg watched it, his eyes glimmering between them with fierce, sudden triumph. As if he'd gained a great victory, or the ultimate gift—and as Ezog's teeth scraped against Lydia's gold-circled throat, it distantly occurred to Lydia that once again, Tryg had turned it all around. And in the wake of their gift to him, he'd given them such deep, meaningful gifts in return—but gifts that brought him peace, too. Gifts that were also meant for... himself.

And Lydia should have known that, remembered that, trusted that—and going forward, she would. She knew exactly what her sly, stunning mate wanted for Yule, and she would offer it up to him year after year, wrapped in gleaming gold jewels and silken red ribbons. For all the Yules they had left.

"So pretty, my sweets," Tryg said again, with such fond, tender, hungry light in his eyes. "Now, mayhap we ought to bring back those ribbons, you ken? Leash my sweet pets nice and close, so you'll never escape from me again, ach?"

And Lydia could only smile at him, and throw herself back into his waiting arms, while Ezog's warm strength folded around them both. "Ach," she said, merry and light, as the peace shone and sparkled in her heart. "Let's get the ribbons."

**THE END**

# THANKS FOR READING!

Thank you so much for joining me for this spicy Yuletide tale! I did NOT expect to get as invested as I did in this one… it was supposed to be just a silly little holiday drabble, but then Sigtryggr showed up with his devious plans, and it all went downhill (uphill?) from there! I really hope you had as much fun with it as I did.

I do need to credit my awesome readers on Discord for sparking the entire idea in the first place! We have a lot of fun discussions about characters, and one question that's come up multiple times is whether we'll ever see a MMF with Tryggr and Eben, who we first meet in *The Maid and the Orcs*. I've hated to keep saying that I'm not sure I see it for them… BUT… I could totally see Tryggr's sexy silver fox Pa going for it with gusto! So off this story went. :)

This was also my first time writing a book with main characters who are beyond their 20s and 30s, and it was honestly so refreshing! Thank you to all of you who requested this, and I really hope it worked for you (though I welcome feedback too). I do feel very strongly that more diversity in Romance is awesome for all of us, and that definitely extends to character ages as well.

This was also my first time posting a story early on Patreon, and I'm so, so thankful to each and every one of my patrons for coming on board, and so generously supporting my writing. It's been such a joy sharing this journey with you!

Also, I want to thank all my generous beta readers who were SO flexible with reading and sharing feedback on my unexpected holiday project. Many, many thanks to Amy F., Ari, Cookie, Erin, Jane Mwaniki, Jen R., Judi S., Karen Meeus, Lauren Mauchley, Rowan Phillips, Serena, and V.C. Lancaster (whose books are fantastic, if you haven't read them already!). And special thanks to the fabulous

Kahaula, and also to my brilliant second brain MK (who has always been an Ezog cheerleader from the start!).

I also want to extend my deepest gratitude to Goddess Ruby Dixon and Genius Eris Adderly; to MK, Amy, and Elizabeth for helping to keep my Discord a safe and supportive place so we can have all the fun conversations; to Katie (aka Romantically Inclined) for the daily laughs on Instagram; to our gifted Grisk galdr-spinner Morning Dove for all the tales and support; and to Erin for her incredible artwork and continued leadership of the Skai Mafia PR Team! AND, a huge thank-you to Chloe, Coco, and Serene Yoshiko for creating such awesome character art from this book (and so much more) to share with us. You can find it all on my website and social media channels, OR get the full spicy versions on my Patreon!

Finally, as always, I need to thank my own sexy, unbelievably supportive Skai orc, who I plan to keep for all the Yules I have left, too.

I hope you have the loveliest Yule! Hugs and happy holidays!

## ALSO BY FINLEY FENN

### THE LADY AND THE ORC

***He's the most feared monster in the realm. And she's what he needs to win his war...***

In a world of warring orcs and men, Lady Norr is condemned to a childless marriage, a cruel lord husband, and a life of genteel poverty—until the day her home is ransacked by a horde. And leading the charge is their hulking, deadly orc captain: the infamous Grimarr.

**And Grimarr has a wicked plan for Lady Norr, and for ending this war once and for all.** She's going to become his captive—and the perfect snare for Lord Norr.

There's no possible escape, and soon Lady Norr is dragged off toward Orc Mountain in the powerful arms of her greatest enemy. A ruthless, commanding warlord, with a velvet voice and mouthwatering scent, who awakens every forbidden hunger she never knew she had...

But Grimarr refuses to accept half measures—in war, or in pleasure. And before he'll conquer Lady Norr's deepest, darkest desires, she needs to surrender *everything*.

Her allegiance.

Her wedding ring.

Her future...

And with her husband's forces giving chase, Lady Norr can't afford to play such a dangerous game—or can she? **Even if this deadly orc's plans might be the only way to save them all?**

# ALSO BY FINLEY FENN

## THE SINS OF THE ORC

***He's fallen too far to save... but his enemy is going to try.***

In a world of warring orcs and men, Kesst of Clan Ash-Kai is a pawn. A pretty, pliant plaything, bound to the cruelest orcs in the realm.

Until the new healer storms in.

He's huge, hostile, and hideous, with a powerful scarred body and terrifying ancient magic. And it only takes one disastrous meeting before he and Kesst are bitter enemies, and Kesst vows to see the vile brute destroyed...

And then a sudden, deadly attack hurls his helpless body straight at the healer's feet.

Kesst fully expects to be mocked, belittled, abandoned to his doom—but instead, his new enemy picks him up.

Soothes his wounds.

And carries him home...

Soon Kesst is trapped in a tiny sickroom beneath Orc Mountain, caught in the thrall of the healer's impossible magic. In the surprising gentleness of his touch. In the strength of his stubborn, seductive safety...

But with his horrid handlers close on their scent, Kesst can't possibly be falling for his forbidden foe... can he? Can a healer save him from his sins... or destroy him?

# ABOUT THE AUTHOR

Finley Fenn is "the queen of dark orc romance" (Virgo Reader), and her ongoing Orc Sworn series has been praised as "sexy, romantic, angsty, and captivating ... utter brilliance" (Romantically Inclined Reviews).

When she's not obsessing over her stories, Finley loves reading, drooling over delicious orc artwork, and spending time with her incredible readers on Patreon, Discord, and Facebook. She lives in Canada with her beloved family, including her very own grumpy, gorgeous orc husband.

For free bonus stories and epilogues, special offers, and exclusive Orc Sworn artwork, sign up at www.finleyfenn.com.

www.ingramcontent.com/pod-product-compliance
Lightning Source LLC
Chambersburg PA
CBHW030624310726
48979CB00003B/875
* 9 7 8 1 9 9 8 0 0 9 1 6 9 *